PRAISE

FOR THE ORPHAN'S DAUGHTER

"Jan Cherubin writes with tenderness and force and humor. Her spellbinding debut novel, *The Orphan's Daughter*, swept me away."

—E. Jean Carroll, author of *What Do We Need Men For? A Modest Proposal*

"Jan Cherubin's touch is both assured and nuanced; her story is full of vivid details and wry observations. *The Orphan's Daughter* is a novel that will stay with you long after you've finished reading it."

—Daphne Merkin, author of *This Close to Happy* and *22 Minutes of Unconditional Love*

"*The Orphan's Daughter* is beautifully specific, evocative, and emotionally charged."

—Lynne Sharon Schwartz, author of *Disturbances in the Field* and *Truthtelling*

"*The Orphan's Daughter* is both sharp and moving, which isn't easy to pull off. The narrator, Joanna Aronson, is convincingly troubled and likable. And her father is a flat-out great character, not like anyone I've read about before but immediately recognizable and plausibly individual."

—David Gates, author of *A Hand Reached Down to Guide Me* and *Jernigan*

MORE
FROM THE SAGER GROUP

Seven Men: Memories of an Unconventional Love Life

Lifeboat No. 8: An Untold Tale of Love, Loss, and Surviving the Titanic

The Stories We Tell: Classic True Tales by America's Greatest Women Journalists

New Stories We Tell: True Tales by America's Next Generation of Great Women Journalists

Newswomen: Twenty-Five Years of Front-Page Journalism

Janet's World: The Inside Story of Washington Post Pulitzer Fabulist Janet Cooke

High Tolerance: A Novel of Sex, Race, Celebrity, Murder . . . and Marijuana

For more information, please see
www.TheSagerGroup.net.

A NOVEL

THE ORPHAN'S DAUGHTER

JAN CHERUBIN

This is a work of fiction. Many of the details, places, characters, and events were inspired by real life. None of it really happened; none of the people really exist. Any resemblance to actual persons or events is entirely coincidental.

The Orphan's Daughter

Cover Designed by Siori Kitajima, SF AppWorks LLC

Cataloging-in-Publication data for this book is available from the Library of Congress
ISBNs:
Paperback
978-1-950154-15-9
eBook
978-1-950154-16-6

Published by The Sager Group LLC
www.TheSagerGroup.net

THE ORPHAN'S DAUGHTER

A NOVEL

JAN CHERUBIN

THE SAGER GROUP

Artifex Te Adiuva

The Hebrew National Orphan Home,
1919-1958.

CONTENTS

Chapter 1...1

Chapter 2 9

Chapter 3 13

Chapter 4...21

Chapter 5 27

Chapter 6 33

Chapter 7 39

Chapter 8 53

Chapter 9...61

Chapter 10 77

Chapter 11...81

Chapter 12 93

Chapter 13...101

Chapter 14 111

Chapter 15...119

Chapter 16 123

Chapter 17...131

Chapter 18 135

Chapter 19 141

Chapter 20..145

Chapter 21 147

Chapter 22 153

Chapter 23 157

Chapter 24 161

Chapter 25 179

Chapter 26 189

Chapter 27 195

Chapter 28 197

Chapter 29 203

Chapter 30 209

Chapter 31 211

Chapter 32 219

Chapter 33 227

Chapter 34 231

Chapter 35 233

Chapter 36 237

Chapter 37 241

Chapter 38 247

Chapter 39 257

Chapter 40 259

Chapter 41 269

Chapter 42 279

Chapter 43 287

Chapter 44 301

Chapter 45 307

Chapter 46 313

Chapter 47 321

Chapter 48 333

Chapter 49 343

Chapter 50 353

Chapter 51 361

Chapter 52 365

Chapter 53 371

Chapter 54 385

Chapter 55 391

Acknowledgements 395

About The Author... 397

About The Publisher...399

CHAPTER 1

I broke into the house I grew up in to steal back my childhood. It was easy. The dog chomped on a greasy bone while I took what I came for. Eventually my stepmother noticed a manuscript missing, figured out where the hell the dog got that lamb bone, and swore out a warrant for my arrest.

Relatives were spilling onto Aunt Shirley's front porch, plates piled with bagels and lox like any Jewish family back from the cemetery, when sirens came wailing and two black-and-whites screeched to a halt at the curb. At first I didn't catch on. I was talking to Liz Stone. I was always relieved to see Liz—we'd been friends since we were eight—and I wondered out loud who the cops were after. Liz said, "you," and we both laughed. Red lights lit my grandmother's face, then cast it in shadow, then lit it red again. Uncle Harry's mouth fell open and his cigar dropped out.

The cops couldn't possibly want me. I was a white girl in Baltimore. I used to wave when the police drove by, like most suburban children in the sixties. I was no longer a kid, but I was barely out of my twenties and I still saw myself as obedient, dutiful, adoring—in short, a daughter. It was true that I was finally coming out of the shell I hadn't even known I was in. And I did trespass and enter the house. But c'mon—two, then three police cars?

The service at the cemetery before the brunch had gone along as planned, for the most part. Friends and family gathered on a beautiful fall day for the unveiling of the headstone on my father's grave. The unveiling ceremony was supposed to end a period of mourning, but while the designated amount of time had passed—the funeral was in February and it was now October—it still came as a shock when my sister Susan and I peeled the gauze cover off the stone and saw our father's name etched in granite. Clyde Aronson, dead at 69. Every step I took into the future without him was a blow. I thought the old rabbis must have been onto something with their ritual, though, because that day in the cemetery I felt something new along with loss. I felt a sense of my own worth. I felt it when we chanted prayers in Hebrew under the trees in their autumn beauty, and I felt it when my father's schoolteacher buddy Shep Levine recited Yeats. There were tears, and there was laughter of course, and then a line of cars leaving the cemetery gates full of my famished relatives hurrying to the brunch.

Aunt Vivian trotted across Aunt Shirley's porch and threw her arms around me. "Oh, Joanna, I loved your father so much. He was my favorite brother. Don't tell the other two." She squeezed so hard my glasses dug into the side of my nose, but for once I didn't want her to let go. "Where's Brenda?" she asked, before releasing me. "I didn't see her at the cemetery."

"I don't know," I said.

"No one knows," said my mother.

Brenda was my father's second wife, my stepmother, and it was Brenda who arranged for the unveiling with help from my mother's family. My parents stayed friends after their divorce, and since Brenda Aronson (née McLean) was naturally unfamiliar with the Jewish ritual, my mother's sister, Aunt Shirley, volunteered to make the food and Aunt Shirley's husband, Uncle Lou, a member of the temple's burial society, met with Brenda to plan the ceremony. Brenda was in charge, though. She was the one who picked the stone and set the date for October 25th, 1987. Why wouldn't she come, then? Yes, we were fighting over the will, and I took the manuscript and some other things from the house, but I thought she had calmed down about that already.

Brenda was pleasant and harmless, Uncle Lou said, and I would have said the same thing, once. She was always a little odd, but in ways that could be attributed to shyness, or just the awkward nature of the stepmother relationship. I used to feel grudging sympathy for her. She had to know my parents were still in love with each other. When Susan and I were growing up, our parents spoke often about their epic love affair, drawing a tight circle around them even as they were trading insults and hurling dishes. So I knew how it felt to be left out. But then my father got sick, and Brenda and I took care of him together. You learned a lot about a person under those circumstances. I stopped feeling sorry for poor Brenda and started to think of her as the bad part of my father. The damaged part he excised and finally put outside of himself.

My glasses were crooked after Aunt Vivian's embrace, one lens resting higher than the other, so I took them off and applied cautious pressure to the red plastic temples, then put them back on. I had a small face, dark hair, big features. I turned to my mother and pushed the glasses up on my nose. "That's better," she said. We were close now, my mother and I. Once Susan and I grew into adults, my mother wanted our friendship.

"Here, sit down, Joanna," my mother said, scraping her chair over the concrete and making a space for me next to the pink porch railing.

"So what's the story?" Aunt Vivian said. "Why isn't she here?"

"I told you, it's a big mystery," my mother said. Then she put her mouth around a forkful of apple cake topped with vanilla ice cream. Brenda's absence gave my mother an appetite. My mother swallowed and licked her lips.

I could hear my father. "Ice cream used to taste better," he was saying. Even before he died, he was always talking to me in my head. I could see us sitting at the kitchen table on Cedar Drive eating Neapolitan supermarket ice cream out of smooth ceramic bowls.

"You think everything you used to get in New York was better," I said.

"No. That's not it," my father said. He took a spoonful and swirled the ice cream in his mouth. "In the old days, when I was little, it was creamier."

I tried to imagine him little, a small boy on the steps of a vast brick asylum I had seen in a photograph. "What about Breyers?"

"Nah. No-oo. I'm talking creamy."

"Häagen Daz?" I said.

"Nah," my father said. "I'm talking about ice cream they made fresh in the back of a candy store. Forget it, kiddo. Doesn't exist anymore."

I wanted to know how my father got ice cream from a candy store when he had grown up in an institution. But he was no longer around to ask. He used to talk about how great the orphanage was—they rode horses, he had hundreds of friends—but even a child could tell he was hiding something. I excused myself and went inside to find Liz. The house was filled with people. Unveilings were typically small affairs, but my father had the kind of big personality that was sorely missed, and he drew a crowd. Whether you loved him or hated him, his death left a hole in the world. He'd been a high school English teacher, and I recognized two of his former students at the buffet table talking to Shep Levine and another teacher. My father's old girlfriend Darleen and her husband were there, and most of my father's family from New York, as well as my mother's entire family, including her brother Nat who hadn't spoken to my father in years. My sister Susan's husband Larry was there, and my boyfriend Fred who had flown in from L.A. Everyone was there but Brenda.

Laughter rang out from the kitchen over the groan of the oven door. I found Liz in the dining room cornered by my father's brothers. "It's Joanna's fault," Uncle Alvin was saying, his voice like wet gravel. "Brenda's upset. That's why she isn't here."

"Joanna's fault?" said Liz. She caught my eye and I came over.

"My fault?" I said. "Listen, I only took what belonged to me."

"Not what she says," said Uncle Harry. He had the same gravel voice as Uncle Alvin. My father had the voice, too. All three brothers spoke like they were gargling with rocks.

When my father was seven and Uncle Harry was five, they were the ones sent away and put in the orphanage. Now Uncle Harry was unsure of how to show his loyalty to his big brother—by standing with Brenda, or with my mother and me. He chewed solemnly on a piece of bagel, cheeks full, meaty lower lip in a pout. He had a tough guy's baby face—a face frozen at five years old.

"C'mon. Let's go outside and have a smoke," said Uncle Alvin. "You got those Cuban cigars with you?"

"Fred," said Uncle Harry, "c'mon out to the porch with us and try a nice cigar from Havana. Hand-rolled."

Fred looked at me.

"Go ahead," I said. "Smoke their cigars. They're mad at me, not you."

Almost everyone was outside, either on the front porch or in the backyard. The day was warm with a dazzling blue sky. The screen door clapped shut behind Fred. A few of us stayed inside, Aunt Vivian huddled by the coffee urn with Cousin Mitzi. "Joanna, what was that poem the teacher recited?" Mitzi said. She came toward Liz and me with a plastic cup full of coffee snapped into one of those brown plastic holders.

"'The Wild Swans At Coole,'" I said. "'The trees are in their autumn beauty, the woodland paths are dry.' My father liked Yeats."

"What does it mean?" Mitzi asked.

I thought about it. I stared out the window at my mother on the porch laughing at something my uncles were saying, and I tried to think of a short answer. There was a flurry of activity outside. The sound of a car door slamming, Fred rushing down the steps to the street, and my mother jumping up from her chair, hurrying inside.

Aunt Vivian grabbed my mother's arm when she came in. "Evie, we were just asking about that poem at the cemetery."

My mother nodded, trance-like. "Joanna," she whispered hoarsely. All of the color had drained out of her face. Even her lips were pale.

"What's the matter, Ma?"

Her eyes widened. "There's a cop outside," she said.

"What's a cop doing here?" I said.

"Don't be stupid," she said.

Sirens, merely background noise seconds ago, wailed louder, then cut off on a whoop. Brakes screeched. Another car door croaked open. Susan brushed past us and into the den where her husband was watching a football game with Shep.

I still didn't get it. It had to be a joke. "Looking for me?" I said.

Red lights danced on Aunt Shirley's walls. My mother's hand tightened on my wrist. She yanked me away from the window. I'd never seen her like this. She spoke through gritted teeth: "Why else would the police be here?"

"What do you mean?" I said.

"Who else would they be coming for?"

My heart started banging on the offbeat. Brenda sent the cops after me. I couldn't believe it. I thought I was invulnerable, protected not just by privilege, but specifically the new feeling of self-worth I'd never had before. Susan always felt it, like a sixth sense. But for me, that kind of entitlement was a novelty. I was not wanted. My father *had* to have a boy, and I had been his last shot. Only at the end of his life, he discovered a girl was just as good. He could talk to me, about more than ice cream. We could share the life of the mind. He could do that with a daughter, how shocking it was to learn. In those last dying months, with icicles dripping from the overhang and a blanket of snow out the window behind our easy chairs, he reached for my hand and held it. "Would you like me to leave you my books and papers?" he asked. It turned out I was his rightful heir all along.

Liz skidded into the foyer and pressed her face to the screen door. "Fred's yelling something about a warrant. He wants to see the warrant. Way to go, Fred," Liz said.

"Your boyfriend's all riled up," said Mitzi.

I heard clanking, scraping. Handcuffs, dress shoes clomping on concrete. I didn't have much time. I had to make a move. Shep bolted out of the den and grabbed me in a bear hug. The light had gone out of his eyes. He turned my body toward the kitchen.

"Out the back door?" I said.

"Exactly," said Shep. "Through the kitchen into the back-yard, climb on top of the retaining wall, then up the hill and onto the neighbor's property." He released me and gave me a push. "Walk fast, but don't run. Cut between the houses to the other side. Go. Go. Hurry."

CHAPTER 2

When I was little, I used to watch my father reading and smoking at his spot on the end of the sofa. He'd clear his throat and tap the ash off his cigarette into the ashtray on the coffee table without looking away from his book. I'd stand there and stare at him. I was trying to bore through his skull to see inside his head. Using all my powers of imagination, I entered his mind and wandered around in the darkness until the trees parted and I came upon a little orphan boy peering at me from behind an iron fence. My father reached out and tapped the ash off his cigarette into the ashtray. He looked up. "What do you want, you stupid kid? Get out of here."

He died in winter. I got annoyed with Brenda at the shiva. It really bothered me when she leaned over the funeral candle in the tall blue jar with the Star of David and lit her cigarette off the flame.

We sat shiva only one night, and then I flew back to the West Coast with Fred. He was a screenwriter and had a deadline. Leaving right away was a mistake. I should have stayed and helped Brenda clean out the house, but I couldn't bear another minute with her. So I fled with Fred to our rented bungalow in Venice, California, where the light was clear and hard as glass. I walked along the sand and let the ocean lap at my ankles. White stucco everywhere. I missed the seasons. "Are you kidding?" Fred said. "You really want to go back to the cold?"

"I can't remember anything without seasons," I said. I couldn't place myself—was I wearing a winter coat, were the dogwoods in bloom, was it one of those hot summer nights? Fred shrugged. He was happy living in a desert. I watered the lemon tree. The light was as clear as glass, but I was still in a fog. I felt numb and cut off. I had nowhere to go, nothing to do. I'd had a job as a copy editor at a little newspaper, but I quit to take care of my father. It was a crappy job anyway. The editor-in-chief hired me as a favor to Fred. I'd find something better.

But first, I'd have to turn around and go back East again and sort through the homemade birthday cards, mine to my father and his to me: *How come you're twenty-five, and I'm still alive? When you are fifty, will I still be nifty?* He was supposed to be a writer, that was his promise, unfulfilled, and I felt sure that besides birthday rhymes there had to be a manuscript hidden somewhere. I was excited at the prospect of what I might find, but I stalled because of an irrational obsessive fear that the amount of stuff in the house was literally infinite. I was convinced if I started sorting through things I would never finish. It was a sorcerer's apprentice job—the boxes would fill up as soon as I emptied them, while Brenda stood over me clicking her tongue, disgusted by my sentimentality.

He was a saver like me. The Eisenhower jacket from his army uniform still hung in the front hall closet. A felt hat lay above it on the top shelf and whenever I saw the hat, I thought how strange that men in the nineteen-fifties and even the early sixties regularly wore fedoras. No man left the house without his hat, as I remembered it. My father palmed his, thumb fitting into the right dent, fingers into the left dent, a ship's prow above the black band. He placed it on his head and went out into the world. I watched with solemn eyes, aware I could not go out into the world like him, since I was a girl and could not wear that sort of hat.

To be fair, sometimes he took Susan and me with him, usually to the Forest Park Branch of the Enoch Pratt Free Library. The library, for us, was like church must have been for other people. The smell was heady—paper, ink, wood, and glue. I sat in the children's section on a low mahogany bench worn down like a sucked candy. "You borrowed that book last week," Susan said.

"So what?" I said. "I like it."

My father disappeared into the stacks, a flash of crew cut and black glasses.

"Put it back!" Susan said.

"No!"

He reappeared studying a book gray with type and no pictures. The book was so thick if it were a sandwich I wouldn't be able to put my mouth around it. "Children," he said in his mock schoolmarm voice. "Quiet. You're in a library." He smiled to himself.

Outside, I climbed a mountain of broken pavement in front of the Forest Park Branch and stood on the precipice. In Baltimore, people said payment for pavement. We said balling for boiling. If you were Jewish, ants were called pussy ants. Your mother killed the pussy ants on the payment with a *chynik* of balling water. We got into the car and drove away from downtown, over the railroad tracks toward the suburbs, until we came to our street of ranch houses cut out of a swath in the woods. Our new block was as bland and bright as only the future can be.

"Did you get anything for your wife?" my mother said, waiting at the kitchen door.

"*Doctor Zhivago*," my father said. "Should be good, my darling."

CHAPTER 3

In early June I finally got up the courage to face Brenda and I flew to Baltimore, rented a car, and drove to Cedar Drive. The weather was brutally hot and humid, and to top it off, cicadas were falling out of the sky. Red-eyed insects the size of dinner rolls rained down on the neighborhood like one of the plagues in the story of Passover. If I hadn't known it was the return of the seventeen-year locust, right on schedule in the spring of 1987, I might have believed the scourge of prehistoric bugs was an omen warning me to stay away from the house.

I drove on heedless, down the hill past the elementary school to the stop sign, then left onto Cedar Drive. When I was a kid, my father liked to ride the bike to his friend Leon's house around the corner to smoke and talk, and I would ride with him, straddling the blue bicycle's back rack. Pedaling along at a leisurely pace, my father told me how great our block was. Baltimore was a second-rate town, New York was it, but our particular street in Baltimore was paradise. "It's like a post-card," he said, gazing up at the treetops. He took one hand off the handlebars, wobbling the bike, and swept the panorama. "Look at it! If you didn't know where it was, you would come here for a vacation."

He was always reinventing the world so we were at its center, and that made him irresistible. I bought everything he said. I believed Cedar Drive was the best place on earth and my father was the smartest man in the world. He tacked up a sign in the den advertising an Alfred Kazin book in block letters: NEW YORK JEW. That's who he thought he was. He was a schoolteacher in Maryland, but to his family, friends, and students, he was as gutsy as Norman Mailer or Philip Roth. As smart as Albert Einstein. He even had Einstein's bushy hair and mustache.

I drove the rental car around the curve in our street past identical shingled shoeboxes, one after another with their carports, white gravel roofs, and redbrick trim, and I started getting excited. It was probably a depressing sight to most people—such small houses and all the same—but I shared my father's rosy view and noticed the generous lawns and mature trees left standing in the backyards by a developer who had some sense of decency, saving the street from complete suburban tackiness. Also, the houses across the street from ours were built on a creek with red clay banks and willow trees, and the low ranch houses seemed sunk into the ground like mud houses on a riverbank, towered over by hundred-foot pin oaks.

I turned into the driveway and parked behind Brenda's Mazda. There was nothing to be afraid of, I told myself. The worst had already happened, my father had already died, and Brenda had to be glad I was coming to help, although I didn't know how we were going to clean out all that stuff in a weekend. I wondered if the old suitcase with the yellow Bakelite handle was still buried in the back of the den closet. Maybe I'd find a clue of some kind. In spite of my father's big personality, he was maddeningly difficult to know, and I needed clues, there had to be clues. When I tamped down my terror at the enormity of the task, I started to feel genuine excitement. I'd get to the bottom of all those papers, and then I would be granted access to what I had been barred from. The things he shared with his students and not with me—his writing, his thoughts.

Brenda was in the carport laughing, watching me get out of the car clawing at my clothes like a B-movie actress in a horror film. "You're scared of the cicadas," she said.

"I'm not really," I said and (rather fearlessly, I thought) plucked off an armor-backed insect clinging to my hair like a barrette. The dog barked behind the side gate. He was pacing frantically, his tail swishing the mesh part of the fence.

"Hoffman!" I called. He put his paws on the fence rail and I went over and hugged his shaggy neck. He wasn't named after Dustin Hoffman as my sister sometimes said, but for a friend of my father's from the Home. Brenda held the screen door open impatiently, so I let Hoffman lick my face and then I went in. As soon as I crossed the threshold, I was sorry I had come alone. This was the kitchen where my father's vegetable soup used to simmer on the stove, where my mother made pancakes on Sunday mornings, where Susan and I stamped snow off our boots in winter and in summer stood dripping in our bathing suits. And where, once we were grown, my father greeted us when we came home, his arms open, a cigarette in his hand, and where (and everywhere) he would never greet us again.

The house was alive with him. His carpentry, his paintings, his garden. He loved our little place. He had wanted land, and he got land, a fraction of an acre. Thanks to the G.I. Bill, he was able to own a house. He was a realist who knew in order to survive he had to be a fabulist. He pretended he had a vast estate. He pretended money didn't matter. He planted trees and flowers. He grew vegetables like he did on the orphanage farm gang. They had twenty acres at the H, he said. The H was short for the Home.

"Some estate that was," my mother would say. They'd laugh.

He'd put his hand inside a burlap bag from the nursery. "Horse manure," he said, pulling out a clump. He held it under my nose. "Smell that. I love it. Cleanest shit there is." He liked to say shit in front of Susan and me, it made my mother laugh. They were communists. Now they were landowners. They didn't believe in God.

"C'mon, step lively. Help me out here."

I drew a gun out of my Lone Ranger double holster and pointed it at him. "Stick 'em up," I said.

"Very funny," he said. "Put that away." He handed over a trowel. "You know what happened to us in the orphanage when we didn't step lively?"

"The belt?" Susan said. She sat in a lawn chair swinging her feet in Mary Janes, her dress spread around her like petals. My father went over and touched Susan's golden hair. He was holding a cigarette, which made the gesture especially tender, the delicate care he had to take. He bent and kissed her head.

"Not the belt," said my mother. "The cane."

"Tell the other one to put a shirt on," my father said.

"She refuses," said my mother. "She wants to be like you."

He pretended he didn't mind not having a son. He had surrogate sons instead, his students at Baltimore City College High School. Like the orphanage, City was all boys. Hundreds of boys, plenty to choose from. His favorites were the ones who worked on the *Collegian* newspaper. He was the faculty adviser. He pretended, but he couldn't pull it off. He wanted a real son like the boy he once was, the boy who had lost his father. I would have been happy if he got his wish. I saw right away boys were the main people. At the toy store, I asked for cap guns and race cars, not to please my father, but as the logical choice. Who didn't like the pop sound and burnt smell of gunpowder? Or a miniature car that moved by itself? I roamed the neighborhood bare-chested, my holster slung over my shorts. "Go ahead, walk around like that," my sister said. "You have nothing to hide."

My mother lounged in a black strapless bathing suit like a Modigliani by our inflated baby pool and dreamed of Greenwich Village. She hadn't wanted kids and waited impatiently for us to mature into adults alongside the scrawny saplings my father planted, roped to two-by-fours. We were a job for which my mother felt overqualified merely by being an adult, and we didn't interest her much. She drank coffee and smoked Chesterfields with the other mothers in the neighborhood, pushed her carpet sweeper dreamily, or at times with enthusiasm while she listened to "Oklahoma!" on the hi-fi, and drove the sloping '49 Chevy she named Betsy to the Food Fair with us standing up in the back. She talked to us because she had no one else. There were things she couldn't tell the women in the neighborhood. Her life used to have meaning. She said during the war (how she missed the war years!) she was in the leadership at the local Communist Party headquarters. We weren't supposed to tell anyone. It was important work, she said, it was exciting, they were fighting fascism. She was going to change the world by making sure poor people got more money. It was a secret. Something stopped her, though. Something happened, and she never did change the world.

Sometimes we'd get into the Chevy and she would drive us backward into her history, past the Forest Park Branch of the Enoch Pratt Free Library, and the old row house where we lived when I was born, and farther downtown until Liberty Heights became Pennsylvania Avenue. Black girls in pink curlers sat on the marble steps. My mother turned right and stopped in front of 1837 North Avenue. "This is where I lived when your father walked into my life," she said. "Your grandma took in boarders." The third-floor windows on the row house were broken. The first-floor windows were covered with plywood. It looked as if no girl ever lay on her bed reading poetry there, not a white girl or a black girl. My mother started the car and drove east a few blocks to the Young Communist League at No. 1019. It was just a house with a stone foundation and a sagging porch.

At bedtime she brought down the storybook from the shelf, but we begged her to tell us a true story instead, about hearing Paul Robeson sing in person, and how she cried when Franklin Roosevelt died. She told about the iceman and candy stores and streetcars for a nickel, and playing in Druid Hill Park, a place as mysterious as its name. My mother felt sorry for us growing up in the suburbs with no parks and nothing to walk to.

Didn't she know we had the creek? At least I did. Susan was an inside child. I spent the summer with Tom from next door, squatting on flat rocks in the white water, poking under stones with sticks. We caught minnows, crayfish, and eels, and came running up the red clay bank to burst between the houses onto the hot asphalt when we heard the dinga-linga-ling of the Good Humor truck. How could my mother not know what it meant to me, the silver handle like a crank popping open that back freezer door?

My father never read to us or told stories at bedtime. "I didn't have a father to read to me," he said. So we didn't get one. He told his stories around the kitchen table at suppertime instead and made it seem like regular conversation. "Every one of us at the Home had a number," he said. "We had to line up for clean underwear. My number was 271."

I was bewildered. It was impossible. I didn't believe him. My father couldn't be 271. He was number one, numero uno.

"'Line up!' the supervisor said, and he threw us our clean underwear, and you better be in the right order or you'd get the wrong pair."

"The Colonel made sure you were in the right order," my mother said.

"Yeah, the Colonel," my father said. He held a cigarette between his fingers and flicked the filter end with his thumb. Susan and I had a word for it. Pep your cigarette, we'd say irritably, when we noticed the ash getting long. "Forget about the Colonel," my father said. "You wanna know something?"

"Yeah, I wanna know something," Susan said.

"I'll tell you something. We didn't have it so bad. We had twenty acres to play on. Friends, did we have friends! And horses. My favorite was Playboy."

"Was his shit clean?" I asked.

"You bet," my father said. "Playboy's shit was the cleanest of all the clean shit there is. Every other Sunday my mother came to visit."

"Uncle Archie pushed Walnettos through the fence," my mother said.

"But there were kids who didn't have anybody come," said my father. "Sundays were sad for them." He leaned forward and pepped his cigarette again. "There was this one kid, Shmuel Hefter, shy kid. He'd pack his suitcase every Sunday because you know, these single parents were always telling their sons one day they'll get enough money or a bigger apartment and bring them home. His little Yiddishe mama, she says to him: 'Shmuel. . . .' What are you laughing about?" my father said. "This is sad."

"It's the name, Daddy. Shmuel," Susan said. We doubled over giggling.

"Actually," my father said, "we called him Shmecky. That was his nickname."

"Shmecky! That's even worse." We laughed and laughed.

"Anyway, the mama says to him before she puts him in, 'soon as I get enough money, I'll take you home.' So every Sunday the poor kid packs his suitcase and sits out on the steps. All day he sits there and no one comes. Cries himself to sleep every Sunday night for years. Then one Sunday, lo and behold, Shmecky's mother comes to get him. We can't believe it. Off they go, Shmecky walking down Tuckahoe Road with his suitcase, holding onto his mother's hand."

"That's a nice story," Susan said.

"It's not over yet, kid."

"Aw Clyde, don't tell them the rest. They're too little," my mother said.

"Tell us! Tell us!"

"Forget it," said my father. "Who wants to go for a ride?"

It was summer and through the open windows dishes clacked and silverware clinked in kitchens up and down the block as mothers cleaned up from dinner. Screen doors slammed and children ran into the street calling to each other.

"C'mon, Jo," he said. "Finish your dessert. Anybody else? You wanna go for a ride? Susan? Evie?"

"Maybe later," Susan said.

"I've got this mess to clean up," my mother said.

My father took hold of the handlebars on Susan's blue bicycle leaning against the rose trellis. He kicked up the kickstand, and got on. I straddled the back rack and we coasted down the driveway. The summer sky was radiant and the evening sun cast a golden glow over the lawns and sidewalks. The bike bumped into the gutter with a clatter and glided onto the smooth asphalt of Cedar Drive. I held onto my metal seat with both hands.

"We have a great block," my father said as he pedaled along. He waved at some neighbors on the sidewalk. "Hi ya, Lefty," he said to one of the men as we rode past.

"It's Lucky," I said.

"Oh yeah," my father said. "Lucky." We rode around the bend where we could see willow trees leaning over the creek between the houses. My father gazed up at the taller treetops. "Look at it. It's like a postcard," he said.

"I think so, too," I said. I let go of the seat and put my arms around him and pressed my cheek against his back.

CHAPTER 4

I was lost in thought sitting across the table from Brenda when a cicada smacked against the dining-room window and fell onto the outside sill. Its lacy wings buzzed frantically.

"Guess what?" Brenda said. She was unusually perky and girlish. She speared a chunk of chicken and diced celery with her fork. My father would have complained that chicken salad was not a proper meal for someone coming all the way from California, but I thought the cold supper was perfect in the blistering heat.

"I can't guess. What?"

"I've been dating." She popped the forkful of chicken into her mouth and chewed close-lipped and smiling.

"That's nice."

"James," she said. "Not Jim, and never Jimmy. I met him at the singles group where I met your dad."

"OK. James." I didn't know what else to say. I couldn't very well take the moral high ground about her dating so soon after her husband died. Certainly not on my father's behalf. In the first place, there was a twenty-five-year age difference between my father and Brenda, which already made him suspect. And in the second place, he'd played by his own rules so why couldn't she? When Brenda moved in, he was still seeing Darleen, his favorite, on the sly. Not much moral ground there. I didn't want to hear about Brenda's dating life, though.

"Can I let Hoffman in?" I said.

"Go ahead."

I went out and unlatched the side gate. Hoffman jumped up. He was a big shaggy mutt no one bothered to train. I plucked a locust off his back and threw it in the grass. He followed me into the house and I gave him a treat from the box on top of the fridge.

"So what do you think?" Brenda said, when I sat down again.

"What do I think of what?"

"Of James." She waggled her eyebrows like Groucho Marx.

"I don't know."

She lit a cigarette. "Don't feed Hoffman from the table," she said.

"Sorry."

"He's rich, you know. James is." Brenda tossed her head back and blew out a cone of smoke. She must have wanted to freak me out with her new boyfriend—prove she was a rebel, not the boring bookkeeper I easily ignored in the past. She finally showed some personality during my father's illness, but what she thought was cool was just cold. "He's really got you under his thumb," she'd said a few times as I hurried to refill a humidifier or fetch my father a cup of tea. Maybe she was right, he had me under his thumb. But he was dying. If he wanted a cup of tea, I would bring him tea.

Now she was goading me again, telling tales as if we were in the same class in junior high. I watched her carefully. I wondered if she had heard that my mother recently got a surprise check in the mail. I didn't think Brenda knew yet. She would have made a big stink about it if she had heard. Eventually, she would find out. For the time being, my mother was keeping the news to herself. She told only Susan and me, and Uncle Harry, who at that particular moment was tight with my mother. Then Uncle Harry flipped to the other side, although he swore he hadn't talked to Brenda. He did talk to me, though. He called and started yelling: "You made a promise to your father! Don't you dare break it!"

Uncle Harry had a point. I made a promise to my father, and so did Susan. Brenda inherited the house plus money from my father's insurance policy and a savings account, but she expected more. Specifically, the money from a credit-union account my parents opened when Susan was born. As soon as my father got sick, Brenda demanded he change the beneficiary on that account from Eve Aronson née Braverman (my mother) to Brenda Aronson née McLean. It wasn't right to leave money to an ex-wife, Brenda argued, and eventually my father agreed.

During one of my sister's visits in the winter, he called us to his bedside. He said everything he had would be split between Brenda and the two of us except for the house. That went to Brenda alone. He asked us to promise no matter what, in addition to the house, Brenda would get a full fifty percent of his estate. Susan and I would divide the other half between us. We promised. He had only been married to Brenda four years, and it was our childhood house. But we were terrified at the thought of his death and would have agreed to anything he asked.

In the end, though, he never completed the forms required to change beneficiaries, and my mother's name stayed on the credit-union account. Now Uncle Harry wanted me to persuade my mother to return the $20,000 check to the estate. The money would then be divided according to my father's instructions. "It was my brother's dying wish," Harry said.

Could I break the promise I made to my father? We'd gotten so close during his illness. Always on his terms, though. We still weren't able to talk about a lot of things. I never confronted him about the past. Not really. I didn't stand up to him. I never thought about what I might need or deserve from him—or how early on, I was left to fend for myself.

"What about the promise he made?" I said to Uncle Harry.

"What the hell are you talking about?" Uncle Harry said. "What promise?"

"The promise to protect me," I said, my voice catching on the last two words.

"Yeah, so?"

"So he broke it."

I asked my mother why she hadn't taken her share of the money years ago when she and my father split up. He'd bought her out of the house, so why didn't they divide up the cash too? "It was a mistake, obviously," she said. "But at the time, I wanted to leave on good terms. I didn't want to fight with him. I didn't take it because . . ." She paused. "Because, honestly, Joanna . . ." Her spoon scraped the bottom of her coffee cup, an idle stir. "I never dreamed he would get married again." He was a philanderer. She thought he wanted his freedom.

Once in a while, "just for fun" my mother would say, she fished a random letter from the war out of an old cardboard box. She'd read aloud from the onionskin writing paper, laughing here and there at a private joke, and then her voice would trail off, and I'd realize she was reading to herself, and I'd have to remind her that I was there, that I wanted to hear, too.

> Somewhere in England
> 23 Nov 1944
>
> Dearest Evie,
>
>   This terrible parting must come to an end. Then we'll love each other always, won't we darling Evie? We'll never let anything come between us, because if the biggest catastrophe that has ever befallen mankind could not come between us what else could?
>
> Yours forever,
> Clyde

"You know your father was supposed to be a writer," my mother said wistfully.

He never said this himself. He said he was happy teaching English and satisfied with his life. Only occasionally, glimmers of regret flickered through the bluster of his bootstrap optimism—two times that I could think of in particular. Once when I was twelve and I dragged out the brown suitcase with the yellow handle I found buried in the back of my closet. I didn't remember thinking I was doing anything wrong by opening the suitcase. I must have figured if it was stored in my room, even if the room had once been my father's den, then the suitcase couldn't have been top secret or off limits. That wasn't quite fair, though—he gave up his den reluctantly when Susan couldn't tolerate sharing a room with me anymore, I was too messy, and the deal was that he'd still keep some of his things in there. At first I was afraid to sleep alone in the room lined with his bookcases, but I got used to it, even got to like it, and soon the titles glowing on spines in the dark were infiltrating my dreams. *The Magic Mountain, Freud and Marx, The Adventures of Augie March.* I remembered slipping out of bed one night when I was around eleven and turning on the light to read a few incomprehensible pages of a book called *Death and Sensuality* by Georges Bataille, and then pulling out the dictionary to look up sensuality. No matter how many times I read the definition I couldn't understand what it had to do with death. I was on my knees looking for something else, probably my Tric-Trac racing set that got shoved way back in the closet, when I first found the suitcase. I dragged it out. The button locks clicked decisively when I slid them with my thumbs, the latches sprung open and the lid popped up. Inside on top of some old manila envelopes lay a thick, crumbling black photo album. I opened the cover. It was titled "Ye Olde Picture Booke" inscribed in white ink so the lettering would show up on the black page, and then the date, June 23, 1934. I did the math. My father was seventeen that year and about to leave the orphanage. I started reading the descriptive paragraphs he'd written below the photographs, and right away I felt I knew the boy who looked out at me with a steady gaze from the steps of the Home, the boy who had written in white: "Off we go in joyful glee, a score of sinful orphans we." The discovery was thrilling and I felt shy because of it, but I went in search of my father anyway. I wanted to look at Ye Olde Picture Booke with him, and maybe I could meld the little orphan behind the iron fence with the older boy in the photographs, and then with the man who lived in my house and was supposed to belong to me. I wandered around holding the black album open in my hands like it was the Book of Kells until I found him sitting on the edge of the bed putting on his shoes. "Daddy," I said dreamily, still hypnotized by my journey into the past, "you should write a book."

A shadow passed over his features. "Write your own book," he said. He stared at the floor between his knees. Neither of us moved, but I felt as if a door had been shut in my face. I backed out of the small space between the bed and the dresser, turned and carried away the album, leaving behind a trail of crumbling black confetti.

The only other time I witnessed a glint of ambition, I was just a little older and I stayed hidden in the hallway. He was huddled at the dining-room table with one of his students, Peter Grafton. They weren't poring over Peter's poetry as they often did. My father was sharing his own writing. He was showing fifteen-year-old Peter a manuscript and explaining how he put it together using diaries, letters, issues of the orphanage newspaper called the *Oracle*, and captions and rhymes from Ye Olde Picture Booke. That was the last I saw or heard of the manuscript. Occasionally over the years, I revisited the photograph album, but I knew enough to keep it to myself. With me, he shared only birthday rhymes. *When you are fifty will I still be nifty?*

CHAPTER 5

"I'm not hungry for dessert," I said. "Maybe we should just start. I'll get the ladder."

"Not so fast," Brenda said. "Have some pie." She was stalling, but why, when I was there to help her with a big chore? We weren't in competition for his things. She'd told me a few times she had no interest in any of it. I thought she'd put me to work right away.

"All right. I'll have a small piece." I wasn't great at mind games. I was usually stupidly guileless. But Brenda was playing at something, and so I'd have to be cunning, too. I'd pretend to get along with her for the weekend, until I collected my stuff, and then I would leave and never look back—just like Susan, who had little interest in the past. I'd be free to live my life then. I'd get out from under his thumb, and out from under Brenda's, too. I'd stand up to the dark part of him. I'd break my fucking promise. I would not make sure Brenda got the house plus fifty percent of his estate.

I cleared the table and she brought in the dessert. The chocolate-cream pie had freezer burn, but I lied and praised it. I'd pretend to listen to Brenda go on about James, smile and compliment her dinner, admire her earrings. I decided I wasn't going to let it bother me in the slightest that she hadn't turned on the air conditioner even though it was still over ninety degrees outside. I'd survive—I had shorts on and a light, loose tank top—and besides, I liked having the windows open, the cicadas blindly banging into the screen. The tropical atmosphere reminded me of the days when Cedar Drive was new and neighbors came outside after dinner to escape the heat. No one even owned an air conditioner then. Susan and I would dart from house to house with the other kids catching lightning bugs while the adults brought chairs onto the front lawn and had coffee there, or on the square of concrete my mother and father jokingly referred to as the East Terrace.

We could hear the roar of bathwater filling a tub through a neighbor's window, a screen door banging, and the voices of children younger than we were being put to bed. And then it was quiet, nothing but the chirp of crickets and the reflective murmur of our parents' muted conversation echoing off the creek bank in the velvet night. We were like prairie settlers in those early suburban days, our wagons drawn together until morning when we woke and saw that it was light everywhere, newborn, tender as grass.

"What are you after anyway?" said Brenda between bites of pie. "Most of what your father has is junk."

"I don't know, his papers, gardening journals," I said. I kept my tone flat, not wanting to arouse her contempt. Brenda was the least nostalgic person I could think of. She made Susan look like Proust. "Sure, come back and go through the house and take what you want," Brenda had said. "But you better do it already, because I'd just as soon haul that junk down to the curb for the garbage man."

"There could be a manuscript hidden somewhere," I said.

"What about the letters?" she said. "Are you planning on taking those?"

"Oh right. I can't forget the letters. My mother would kill me."

"Your mother? What's she got to do with it?"

"They're her letters." I wasn't sure what Brenda was up to.

"Evie's?" said Brenda.

"Yes. Evie's. The letters he wrote her during the war."

"Not those," said Brenda, with a dismissive laugh. "I'm interested in the letters from Caitlyn Callaghan." Brenda leaned back in her chair, pleased. "Ah, so you don't know about Caitlyn, do you?"

"I know about Caitlyn. You know I do. I'm just not interested in her letters." I stabbed at my pie.

"There are a lot of things you don't know," Brenda said.

"That's why I want to go through the stuff," I said. "He wanted me to. He said he wanted to leave me his books and papers. But I know about Caitlyn." I put my fork down ready to push my chair away from the table, when Brenda leaned in confidentially.

"Just ask me, dear," she said. "Your father told me everything."

I should have been enticed by the offer. But Brenda's comments about people were unreliable. Even after four years of pillow talk with her husband, I didn't think she'd have anything of value to say. I was probably wrong, she probably knew things, but I didn't see it. I thought he should have married Darleen. She was easier to get along with than Brenda. I would have felt weird being two years older than my stepmother—Darleen was only eighteen when she walked barefooted into his community-college class. But Darleen won me over when she said she saw my father in me, that I made her laugh because of it—something about the way I spoke, not with a masculine gravel voice, of course, but the phrasing we used and how we both blinked when we were thinking, and how our long arms were all elbows when we talked with our hands.

When I was little, I got upset when anyone said my father and I were alike. It felt false. They had to be making fun of me. "Look at her, a chip off the old block," my father would say. Then he and my mother laughed because everyone knew a girl couldn't be a chip. I was a fraud. They called me a chip because of trivial things. We both liked soup and sucking marrow out of bones. The examples were silly. Over the years, a few similarities surfaced that couldn't be snickered at and I started to hope there was something to it, that it wasn't all a joke, because I very much wanted to be like my father. Both of us liked watching the sky, noting cloud formations and constellations. That wasn't a joke. We were both good at drawing and fixing gadgets. The things that annoyed him were the same things that annoyed me, such as people asking if you liked the movie when you were still walking slowly backward away from the screen with the credits rolling. We both loved trees and when the seasons changed, for both of us it was as if the leaves were growing out of our bodies in spring and dying on our limbs in autumn.

But his disappointment in me overshadowed everything else. He looked at girls and saw sex. He saw weakness. He started to teach me to play chess, to set paving stones in the ground, to lay out a newspaper like the *Collegian* boys did, but with me he stopped halfway, he never followed through. I was left knowing how much I didn't know. Boys are smarter, he said.

"He's mad at his mother," said my mother.

"Look around," he said. "There are no great women chefs. No great women chess players, no great women composers."

Why say that to his daughters? Could he be in competition with his own children? We were girls in a man's world. He was God. He couldn't be insecure.

"He's mad at his mother," my mother said.

"So you're going through all that crap tonight?" said Brenda.

"Tonight and tomorrow. If I don't finish, I'll load the boxes into the car and sort through them when I get home." By home, I meant my mother's apartment. I tried to sound unconcerned, but I still felt anxious about the job. I cleared the table and half-heartedly offered to do the dishes. Brenda said she'd clean up, so I went out to the carport to get the ladder from the utility room. I'd start with the attic, really just a crawl space above the hallway. I had a portfolio of my drawings from high school stored up there. I held the screen door open with my hip and tipped the ladder under the doorframe. I was hoping

Brenda would keep her back to me at the sink so I could slip by without comment, but it was impossible to bring the ladder into the house without rattling the door. I was careful not to bang the walls, though, walls that were now Brenda's.

She came after me, drying her hands on her apron. "You're not setting that thing up now," Brenda said. "Get that ladder out of here."

"But a lot of my stuff's in the attic."

"It's late," Brenda said. "You should have gotten here sooner."

"You asked me to come for dinner."

"I'm going to bed, and I don't want you touching anything without me."

"Hold the door open then." I held the ladder horizontal, backed out again and left the ladder leaning against the carport trellis. I came inside. I'd go up into the attic in the morning. Brenda left sheets and a blanket on the sofa and I made up my bed, although I had no intention of going to sleep at eight-thirty. I figured I would read until she turned off her light and then I'd quietly start working in the den. I'd forgotten to bring a book, but I noticed my copy of *Time and Again* by Jack Finney on a shelf. I had finished the novel over the winter, but I wanted to go back to the passage when he first time travels to 1880s New York. My mind started to wander and the pages fluttered and the book dropped onto the carpet. I ignored it, staring into space, running my hand over the round top of the little three-legged table next to the sofa. The table legs were carved to look like elephant trunks, with little ivory tusks glued on. It was an anniversary present, hand-carried from India, my mother never failed to mention, by Eddie Zakian, a poet they knew when they lived in the Village.

"You want that table?"

I looked up. Brenda was watching me trace my finger over the ivory Taj Mahal. "Yes, I've always wanted this," I said. "My parents' friend brought it back from Delhi."

"I'm sorry to burst your bubble, Joanna," Brenda said. "But your parents' friend brought them a cheap piece of tourist junk."

My mouth dropped open. I was startled by the hostility, and also the truth of her remark. No one I knew growing up had anything like the Indian table with the elephant-trunk legs in their living room. Now that Brenda called it cheap tourist junk, though, I easily pictured stacks of them at Pier One. I drew my hand away from the tabletop. Elephants were destroyed for the ivory inlay. I'd be better off denying any connection to the tainted piece of furniture. But I was loyal to the past. "It's not junk," I said.

CHAPTER 6

We had years of family happiness. We really did, the years I was in elementary school. My mother was no longer stuck at home with me. She had a job as a secretary at Beautiful Kitchens with a paycheck and she was happier out in the world, even if it wasn't fighting the good fight. Hardly, she would say. My father convinced her to bleach her black beatnik hair blonde, and she dressed in fake Chanel suits, wore a glamorous French knot, and brought home presents the salesmen gave her. Susan and I went two doors down to the neighbors after school until my father and mother came home, threw down their keys and coats, briefcase and purse, and together started preparing the chicken or hamburger or (wonderfully transgressive to them) unkosher pork chops defrosting in a puddle on the draining board. "From each according to his abilities," my mother said, quoting Karl Marx while holding aloft a pot by its aluminum handle. And then, as she spooned a pile of Birds Eye peas onto my plate, "to each according to his needs."

My father was a performance artist before his time, putting on an act for his students at City, trying to scandalize with radical views or unpopular views, and later when things loosened up in the late sixties, lacing everything with profanity and sexual reference. He was a provocateur, in the service of learning. If you were for the Vietnam War, he'd challenge you, but if you were against the war, he'd challenge you, too. He hated phonies, the pious, and the pompous. He was disgusted by weakness, by inaction. He could be mean if you were too earnest or shy. He was earnest himself, though, and strict but not close-minded. He had a temper. Some kids were afraid of him. The smart kids weren't, he said. He got agitated not being able to smoke in the classroom, although he got away with smoking in the *Collegian* newspaper office. In class, he ate peanuts instead, something he could do with his hands, dropping shells on the floor. His jacket pockets bulged, filled from the bushel bag in the trunk of his car, a present from the newspaper staff. "The will, the will. Yes, let's stay and hear the will," he said and cracked open a shell one-handed with the snap of his thumb. "You boy, front row! What's the importance of Caesar's will?" His thunderous voice was like boulders tumbling down a mountain. I sat in the back of the classroom with Susan. My father had taken us to work with him because school was canceled that day in Baltimore County for some reason, but school was open in Baltimore City.

It figured City College High School was all boys, because boys got the best of everything. If I went to City I would flunk out. You had to memorize eighteen rules of grammar. There was no way I could go. They had an indoor swimming pool and the boys swam naked. This was supposed to build character. At the time, I didn't know what character was, only that girls couldn't have it. Susan and I were hurried past the pool entrance. I thought if I went through that door, I would know everything.

On Fridays, my father brought teachers home to have dinner with us, bachelors they were called then. John Heinz was always there, the bald drama teacher from West Virginia who spoke with a British accent. Without hair, he seemed cleaner than ordinary people. He wore white Jack Purcell sneakers with his summer suits and had no family waiting at home, my father said. So we'd give him a home-cooked meal. When Shep Levine came, he usually brought a girlfriend. Shep was husky and tall, with dimples that made a long groove in each cheek when he smiled. He was always laughing and joking around. Students were invited, mostly *Collegian* staff. They ate with us at the table where hours before they had laid out and pasted up the weekly newspaper. Shep brought his guitar. "This is for you, Evie," he said, dimples showing. It was impossible not to smile when Shep smiled. Then he sang "Union Maid." Some students blushed so much in front of my mother they had to leave the room. My father watched with confused happiness.

Peter Grafton was there even on weeks with no paper to lay out. He was a genius, my father said. We had to fetch him in the car from his parents' apartment building where he'd be leaning against the wall waiting for us in a raincoat with a paperback. One time he was reading E. M. Forster's *A Passage to India*. That night Peter admired the little table from Delhi. "When you leave this house, Joanna," he said, "you must take this table with you." I gazed at him with solemn eyes. "Why would I leave this house?" I said. He laughed.

With the others gone and only Peter left, I lay in bed as he and my father recited "The Waste Land" into the reel-to-reel tape recorder on top of the hi-fi cabinet in the living room. My father's voice overpowered Peter's and traveled toward me through the hallway in the dark. *And when we were children, staying at the arch-duke's, my cousin's, he took me out on a sled, and I was frightened. He said, Marie, Marie, hold on tight. And down we went.* Why did they say this with such seriousness, when it was only about children on a sled? I felt a strange excitement and had the urge to climb out of bed and join them. But I wasn't sure where I belonged. Certainly not in the material world of dresses and errands my mother and sister lived in.

My father didn't know what to make of me. Maybe I'd never get married. He worried about it. He told everyone to stop calling me Jo. Only Joanna. When I was in fourth grade, he insisted I quit clarinet lessons. He said clarinet was a boy's instrument. Piano was better for girls. I had been looking forward to playing the clarinet in the elementary school band, but I didn't say anything out of fear I wasn't good enough at the clarinet to play up on the stage. My parents went into debt buying the goddamn piano.

"Yes it is," said Brenda. "That table's a cheap piece of tourist junk."

I glared at her. Finally she sashayed down the hall to get ready for bed. She and my father had separate bedrooms, across the hall from each other. As far as I knew, the arrangement hadn't had anything to do with the state of their sex life, but only that my father "needed his space." I told Brenda when I first arranged the visit that I didn't want to sleep in my father's room because it would haunt me so soon after his death and Brenda accepted the explanation, as I knew she would. In truth, I wasn't nearly as timid as she believed, and I wouldn't have been afraid to sleep in his bed, or felt it was morbid or incestuous. I didn't want to sleep in his room only because I didn't want to be stuck in the back of the house near her. I spread the sheet and blanket on the sofa, and sat and waited, propping my feet on the little Indian table, half expecting the cheap piece of junk to collapse. I waited while the water ran in the bathroom sink and the toilet flushed and the bathroom door opened and her bedroom door clicked shut, and then, when a little more time had passed, I went down the hall and stood outside Brenda's door and listened for her slow, rhythmic breathing. When I was sure she was asleep and not faking it, I tiptoed into the den to search for the suitcase with the yellow handle.

The den no longer had a bed or a couch, but only a rolling cart with Brenda's sewing machine on top and a desk the length of one wall that my father built when I was little. I remembered him using the picnic table in the carport for a sawhorse, the woody smell of particleboard, the careful way he glued on the Formica veneer, then fitted drawers together, and wired lights. The built-in desk was one of several feats of craftsmanship that survived him. Catty-corner to that was the closet. I rolled open the sliding door, kneeled on the floor and crawled into the dark end, jacket hems brushing my forehead, and soon I was backing out grinning like a wolf. The suitcase! Its latches clicked without much resistance. They flipped up and the lid popped open. I sighed with deep satisfaction. There was the black orphanage photo album, Ye Olde Picture Booke, just as I remembered, on top of two manila envelopes, the inter-office kind, each with a red paper button and a red string latch. The linoleum floor in the den was hard on my knees and I had a lot to look at, so I closed the lid under one arm and brought the full suitcase into the living room and put it down on the sofa. June 23, 1934. I turned the page and studied a snapshot of my teenaged father bare-chested on a horse: *Bestride my steed Playboy about to set forth upon a journey.* He wrote the captions in a biblical style with a nostalgic tone that was sometimes edged with irony, the grim institution lurking as backdrop. *Thither in winter we stored us sleds, in summer we loaded knapsacks.* In my favorite picture, a group of orphans is splashing around at a swimming hole. Under this one he wrote: *Aye verily, a Garden of Eden.* This place where, I later learned, they beat the children with their fists.

When I was twelve, the pictures and captions were so tantalizing I stayed glued to the Picture Booke and paid no attention to the manila envelopes. Now I unwound the red string on the paper button of the first one and lifted the flap. It was all bureaucratic correspondence, so I put that envelope aside and unwound the red string on the second one and there it was. The manuscript he showed Peter.

Tuckahoe it said at the top, typed on our old Royal typewriter with the sticky "e" that landed slightly higher than the other letters. My pulse quickened as I flipped through the pages. It looked like a novel. But I noticed he hadn't changed names. Uncle Harry was Harry. My mother appeared and she was still Evie. Her family was still the Bravermans. I put the suitcase on the floor under the coffee table so I could stretch out. I couldn't wait to read about the orphanage, and maybe, somewhere, something about me. I propped up the pillows and slipped between the covers.

CHAPTER 7

Tuckahoe

One Saturday in the spring of 1924, my father took me downtown to see the building where he worked. Why I will never know. Rarely was I alone with my father, but for this trip it was just the two of us. I was in the second grade and the oldest of four. Papa said he wasn't interested in babies; they couldn't have a decent conversation. The outing, as well as that comment, held a lot of promise for me. I felt anointed.

Times were good in the Bronx in those days, if you could speak English without an accent, and sometimes even if you couldn't—the tabloids were calling it the Roaring Twenties. In fact, my mother and father were doing fine, better than the rest of the family. My mother was expecting a fifth child, my littlest sister, as it turned out, and my father had a nice job in an office at the Metropolitan Life Insurance Company down on Madison Square where we were headed. At 153rd Street the elevated train went underground, plunging us into darkness, and I let go of the pole we were holding onto and grabbed my father around his legs. He laughed at me, but kept his hand on my shoulder the rest of the way. As soon as we came up from the subway, I spotted the Metropolitan Life tower with the clock on it high in the sky. It was the second tallest building in the whole world at the time, the tallest being Woolworth's. I asked my father to slow down while I cleaned my spectacles with my shirttail. I'd just gotten the eyeglasses and I liked seeing everything clearly. We crossed the street and stood on a corner by the park and shared a hot dog, and then he hoisted me in his arms and pointed up at the clock tower. "That's where I work," he said. I knew that already. I asked why we didn't go inside. I wanted to see the giant gearwheels behind the clock face. He didn't answer.

Summer came and in July of the same year, 1924, we went on another outing. Papa took all of us this time—me, Harry, Vivian, and Alvin—but I didn't complain since we were going for sundaes at Jahn's Ice Cream Parlor way down on Alexander Avenue. My mother stayed home, feet up, resting with the baby in her belly. I couldn't wait to dig into the gooey chocolate and whipped cream with the cherry on top, but for some reason, after one bite, I felt nauseous. Papa said it was thanks to the man at the next table smoking a cheap cigar. I went to the john and threw up, then rinsed my mouth at the sink. I felt a little better, and when I got back to the table, I ate a few more bites of the sundae. I could tell that made my father happy. He leaned back in his chair and watched the four of us eat while he smoked a cigarette with a private smile on his face.

"You feel better, Clyde?" my father said.

I nodded and swirled a spoonful of ice cream in my mouth. Afterward, my father put us on the streetcar headed for home with me in charge. "You tots listen to Clyde," he said. "I have to take care of some business." He jumped off when the car started to move. I watched him through the window, walking west. Later, people said he disappeared into thin air.

"Let your father's family suffer," my mother said. "I'd like to see those no-goodniks keep a clean house with four kids underfoot."

I wasn't sure what my mother meant, but I listened with keen interest in case she speculated as to my father's whereabouts. I nodded sympathetically, standing on a stool filling the soup kettle with water, using all my strength to lift the pot onto the stove for her. Her big belly was in the way. She could hardly reach to turn on the gas. What did she mean, let your father's family suffer? I couldn't figure out what my mother was talking about half the time. Nevertheless, I was her confidant. Seven years old, and she told me everything.

"You're intelligent, Clyde. You understand things. So you'll go live with your *bubbe*, your papa's mother, Grandma Aronson. Maybe she'll tell you where your father is. She has room for you and Harry over there on Gerard Avenue. Whereas my mother has a full house with poor Sadie not married and Slow Uncle Archie still at home."

"But Grandma Aronson has Uncle Bert, Moe, and Estelle," I said.

"How am I supposed to feed all of you, when your father leaves me with nothing? Your Grandma Aronson tells me I should go to work after the baby comes, get a job. A regular genius, that one. And who takes care of you kids?"

Our relatives on both sides were poor, except my mother's brother Rich Uncle Seymour, and he was on the road with his carnival. Everyone else squeezed into cold-water flats in the South Bronx, some of the aunts sleeping on couches, and uncles three to a bed, head to foot. No one volunteered to take us in, so Mama picked somebody.

"I don't want to live with Grandma Aronson," I said. I could just see myself sleeping with Uncle Moe's feet in my face. "Make Vivian go."

"You can't always get what you want," my mother said, and this burned me up because I hated being told what I already knew.

Harry and I dressed in our best clothes like we were going to shul, which we did only rarely. I wore knickerbockers, but Harry was five years old and still in short pants. "Someone should take a picture," my mother said, hurrying us downstairs. Even with her belly, we could hardly keep up. There wasn't much time. The lady across the hall could spare only an hour to watch Vivian and Alvin. My mother's high heels scraped the sidewalk, scrape-tap, scrape-tap over to the Grand Concourse, aptly named, as it was a wide boulevard with a grassy median and automobiles and carriages clattering in both directions, and then two more blocks to Gerard Avenue, which was so hot the asphalt stuck to our shoes. "Sixth floor," said Mama. "628. Ring the bell."

"You want us to go up there alone?" I said. Everyone expected too much of me. I pictured my father in his crisp collar, waistcoat, and jacket, unaffected by the summer heat, hopping gamely off the streetcar.

"She's not a monster," my mother said. "Grandma Aronson just isn't as fond of me as she is of you and Harry. Here." She handed over the beige suitcase with the brown trim and the yellow Bakelite handle. Papa had told me how Bakelite was invented in 1909 by a couple of mad scientists in Yonkers, which was in the countryside, my father said, up in Westchester, north of the Bronx. The scientists mixed the potion in a laboratory over their garage at Snug House (their house was so important it had a name), and you could pour the liquid Bakelite into a mold in any shape or color you wanted. Now those mad scientists were millionaires. My father loved that story and always ended it by singing: *If I was a millionaire, kids/ If I was a millionaire/ There wouldn't be nothin' too good in the world/ For me and my pals to share.*

Harry and I got out of the elevator on the sixth floor and walked down the wide hallway tiled with tiny white hexagons, and I put the suitcase on the doormat in front of 628 and rang the bell. There was no answer. I pressed the buzzer again and waited. It was quiet except for the sound of water running somewhere, and a muffled voice.

"Aw, nuts," said Harry. He knocked my arm out of the way, stood on his tiptoes and jabbed at the bell with his thumb. Buzz buzz buzz! I let him get away with it. Finally footsteps, and the door opened a crack.

My grandmother poked her head out. "I don't know where he is," she said. "That's the truth, the *emis.*"

I got a whiff of her apron—a perfume of fried onions and Dove soap, as familiar as my pillow—I was her little boychik—and yet she kept the door cracked the way she did for junkmen selling pots and pans.

"Hello, Grandma," I said.

"What's this?" she said. "What's this—with the suitcase?"

"Hi Grandma," said Harry.

"Oh, no!" she said. "No, no. I'm an old woman. Go home. *Gay avec.*" She pulled her head back inside and slammed the door.

I looked at Harry and he looked at me, and we ran like hell. Just as we reached the stairs, Grandma Aronson flung open her door and called after us: "Tell your mother I'll see her Friday night for poker!"

But she wouldn't see my mother Friday night because the very next day my mother told me to run down to Shulevitz's candy store to the public telephone, and hurry! The taxi took Mama to the lying-in hospital. We stayed with Grandma Aronson for one week (and one week only) while my mother was confined. Uncle Moe kept his feet out of my face and let me count out the poker chips. Mama named the baby Gertrude.

Weeks passed. People in the neighborhood got used to the new baby and bored with the topic of my father's disappearance. My mother registered with the National Desertion Bureau, a Jewish agency for abandoned immigrant women, and to my great shame, she ran my father's picture in the *Jewish Daily Forward's* "Gallery of Missing Husbands," a weekly feature, and that was that. Neighbors stopped bringing over strange-smelling casseroles, and relatives avoided us.

My mother surprised both grandmas and went out and found herself a job. The manager at Kohl's department store hired her to stand behind a counter and sell cosmetics for $11 a week. Grandma Cohen (Mama's mother) said a woman had to be good-looking to get this job. I thought my mother was pretty, even with the space she had between her two front teeth, but

I worried other people might think the gap looked cheap. They might think, why didn't this woman get her teeth fixed? The little gap thrilled me, though. My mother would smile, or just part her lips, and there would be about her, immediately, an air of mischief. The space was a sign my mother was open. I could run into her arms whenever I wanted and she would enfold me.

Unfortunately, the Kohl's paycheck wasn't big enough to feed all of us, and there was still the problem of where she would put us while she was selling lipstick. My mother was like the old woman who lived in a shoe.

So my mother, Harry, and I set off on another journey, this time far into the countryside by subway and bus to Getty Square in Yonkers. I pleaded with Mama to let us visit Snug House where the Bakelite scientists lived, but she said there wasn't time. Yonkers was an odd place, I thought, made of tenements and brownstones as if a piece of the Bronx had been sliced off and plopped down in the middle of nowhere. If I were to build a town starting from scratch there would be spacious houses and buildings on a green surrounded by trees the way it was in England. I knew about this from reading. No time, Mama said, no lollygagging, and we hopped onto a trolley to Nepperhan. This was a village more to my liking. But again, there wasn't time to explore, for we were to embark on the final leg of the journey by foot. All three of us were tired and dawdling when my mother's hat blew off and pin-wheeled down the dirt road. She went after it and a farm truck swerved just in time, clattering away in a cloud of dust.

"Got it!" she called, plucking the hat in mid-spin along a stand of goldenrod.

I cheered and that's when I noticed Harry was gone.

"You're gonna get yourself killed!" Mama shrieked. Harry was kneeling in the middle of the road collecting apples that had fallen off the truck. He crossed back to us grinning with fruit dropping from his elbows. My mother didn't even yell at him for running into the road like a stupid idiot. I scowled. Harry was brave all right, but he was reckless. He used poor judgment. He was irresponsible. I was hungry, though, so I kept my trap shut.

My mother put the suitcase down in a clearing. The yellow Bakelite handle fell on its hinges with a clack and she sat on it.

"Here, Brother," said Harry, handing me an apple. That's what Harry called me. Never Clyde or anything else. Only when he said brother, it came out "brudder," which was part-baby talk and part-Yiddish.

We ate the apples greedily, juice running down our chins, my mother dabbing at her mouth with a handkerchief while Harry and I used our shirtsleeves. We threw our cores in the grass.

"OK, enough sitting," said my mother, although she was the only one sitting. "Let's get there already."

We began again. The road grew darker with woods on either side of us. After a while, we came to a mailbox at the end of a lane leading to a house visible through a break in the trees. Smoke puffed from the chimney. I thought I saw a figure move behind a window. I had the strange idea it was my father. He had the same waistcoat and collar on, standing behind a boy I'd never seen before. Even from that distance, I could swear I saw him leaning over and cutting the boy's roast beef. "Look! Look, it's Papa!" I said. Mama said I was *meshuggenah* and I should stop *hocking* her *a chynik*. Harry lingered in front of the mailbox and cranked up the red tin flag. "I don't want to go to a new school," he said.

I pounded the flag back down. "Don't touch that," I said. "It's a sign for the postman."

"I don't care," said Harry. "I don't want to go to a new school. I want to go to my old school."

"You don't have an old school," I said. "You've never been to school. You can't even read."

"Yes, I can so read," said Harry. He took off his cap and wiped his sweaty forehead with the back of a chubby hand.

"No, you can't," I said.

My mother had gone on ahead and now she came back to get us, to hurry us along.

Harry put his cap back on firmly. "I want to go to Brudder's school," he said. "Whatever school Brudder's going to, that's where I wanna go."

"Perfect," said my mother. "Because Clyde is going to the new school."

"How much longer?" I said.

"Another mile," said my mother. "Maybe less."

We walked along the road.

"What time do we come home?" said Harry.

"You don't come home, boychik," my mother said. "I told you. You sleep there. It's a boarding school."

"I don't want to sleep there," Harry said. "I want to sleep at home with you." Tears spilled out of his eyes.

My heart started beating faster. "Stop crying, Harry," I said. "Be a man."

"I don't wanna be a man," said Harry. He stamped his foot.

I didn't know why, maybe it was the way Harry said it, or the sight of his knobby knees in those short pants, but I burst out laughing. Soon my mother was giggling, and then laughing full- out. She touched a gloved knuckle to the corner of her eye.

Harry turned red; he hated being made fun of. But then he started up, too, and the three of us stood on the side of the road bent over in fits of laughter.

After a while, we regained our composure and continued past a gasoline station, a meadow full of wildflowers, and a brick warehouse, another sliced-off hunk of the Bronx deposited in a tangle of brambles, and then the road rose up a hill so high it seemed to drop off a cliff.

"Race you," said Harry.

Harry may have been a daredevil, but I was fast. I made it to the top first. "You gotta see this. Quick," I called. I ran back and took the suitcase from my mother and helped her up to the precipice. The three of us gazed out upon a valley under a domed sky. Fluffy clouds floated in an expanse of blue. To the east, the Bronx River Parkway snaked along, mirroring the movement of the river beside it, until both the river and the road reached the point at which the sky met the earth.

"The horizon," my mother said.

A few Model T Fords crawled along the white roadway. To the west, meadows and forests unspoiled by progress stretched lazily toward low hills. I had the urge to break free, to run down into the valley and go on alone. I put the suitcase on the ground and stretched my arms out like wings. I wanted to fly, I wanted to soar above everyone but I felt guilty for wanting it because I was excited about leaving home and going to the new school, and I was ashamed of harboring such a peculiar feeling. Truthfully, I was tired of the responsibility at home. I loved the baby, but no matter how much I played with Gertie she wanted more. I worried about Mama. I felt that I alone was aware, unlike my brothers and sisters, of every penny my mother spent, and the price of milk and bread and meat, and when the rent was due and how my mother had to deny herself pretty things, and she loved pretty things. I hated the whispering Mrs. Shulevitz was unable to suppress when I wandered into the candy store, *oy fatherless*, and even worse, the pity on the faces of my cousins, especially Fat Ellis and Mitzi, who regarded me with exaggerated concern.

Sometimes in the afternoons when the others were napping, I lay on the bed and read the comic strips in the newspaper, Gasoline Alley and Krazy Kat, and if Harry wasn't snoring so loud I couldn't think, I read real books like *The Swiss Family Robinson* and *Tom Brown's School Days*, *Treasure Island* and *Gulliver's Travels*. The books were difficult; I was only seven. But when the story was good I stuck with it, and I was able to get away from trouble and enter other worlds. Both my grandmothers said I shouldn't read so much, no wonder I had to wear glasses at such a young age. And eventually I did get tired. Then I'd put down the book and lay my glasses on top, and put my hands behind my head and stare at the ceiling. I'd think back to that hot, hazy Saturday in July and imagine convincing my father not to take us out for ice cream, but instead to stay home with me, and work on the model aeroplane we had started, and later walk over to the park as we had planned, for swimming lessons. I wanted to travel back in time and make everything right. But I could only do it in my mind. When I thought of my father actually coming home now, it felt wrong. There would be no way to be normal again, and since I couldn't go backward and change anything, I wanted to go away somewhere and start fresh in a place where no one knew me. There would be no pity from Mrs. Shulevitz or my cousins or anyone, an island somewhere, some place where I could eat the fruit off the trees, like Fritz in *The Swiss Family Robinson*, and there might be other people my age, maybe even a girl my age. When my mother told me the new school was in the countryside and I would live there, it was a boarding school like the ones for rich English boys, like Tom Brown at Rugby School, I had the oddest reaction. My mother pleaded with me to forgive her for sending me away, and I felt so terribly sad, I did, because I couldn't possibly lose my mother; not her, too. But then, how to explain the excitement, the thrill I got imagining the future, what was that? So I hid the feeling. I'd wait until everyone was asleep, and then, just as I could go back to the past in my mind, I would travel into the future. My mind would leave my body and walk ahead of me like a scout, laying out in moving pictures what was to come. I didn't want to part with my mother, though. Maybe I could take her with me. When my father left and she said "Clyde, you're the man of the house now," I felt pride, but also a weight on my shoulders. It was the weight of the cast iron pots on the stove, and the heavy black stove itself, the weight of Alvin climbing on my back, and Gertie in my arms, and Vivian and Harry pulling on my shirttails, and now the burden was lifting. I was floating like a glider over the fields and meadows of Westchester and the winding dirt lane on the way to the village of Tuckahoe and the new school.

The three of us walked down into the valley together. I struggled with the suitcase, which was suddenly heavy. I was getting hungry again, and my clothes were hot.

"What the heck is that?" said Harry.

My mother slowed and stopped. An enormous red brick building rose out of the treetops.

"That's it," I said.

"Yeah. That must be it," said my mother.

We came to a swanky tree-lined driveway curving around to a marble portico with marble steps and pillars on either side of double glass doors. My mother hesitated.

"Mama?" I said.

"It's so big," she said.

The massive building was U-shaped with the bottom of the U facing the road and two wings extending back for a city block. I looked up and held onto my cap to take it all in. Above the portico, bronze letters a foot high stretched across the marble lintel spelling out the name of the institution.

"Mama!" I said sharply.

"What is it?" my mother said.

"The sign," I hissed. My heart banged against my ribs. I couldn't believe what I was seeing. My mother lowered her eyes.

"What does the sign say?" said Harry.

My hands balled into fists and I swung at the air, but my arms only twisted around my body helplessly like a tetherball twists around a pole.

"Brudder! What does it say? Read me the sign," Harry demanded.

I unclenched my fists and let my fingers go limp. "Hebrew National Orphan Home," I said. "Satisfied, stupid?"

"Like the salami?" said Harry.

"Yeah," I said. "Just like the salami."

All the excitement I felt, it was all a lie. A boarding school for rich kids. Ha. What a dope I was. I swallowed the saliva pooling in my mouth. Gradually, my heart slowed to its normal rhythm, an achingly dull rhythm pumping me full of sorrow.

"It's a school," my mother said. "I swear to you. Inside that *groys* building, believe it or not, there's a New York City school, P.S. 403, Bronx Annex," she said. "It has its own shul too, and a gymnasium and a marching band." she said. "Swings and a playground. Horses! Horses, Clyde," she said, and forced a smile.

I blinked at the little gap between her teeth. I would have to use logic on her. "Orphans don't have mothers," I said. "We don't belong here."

"It's only until I make enough money," she said. "Then I'll bring you back to the Bronx."

"Why should I believe you?" I said.

My mother squeezed her eyes shut and pressed her lips together. I took a few steps backward. I'd run away. That's what I'd do after all. I turned and started walking toward Tuckahoe Road. I crossed the gravel driveway onto the sloping lawn and kept moving farther and farther away. It was easy. Nothing mattered anymore. When I looked back, my mother was kneeling in the driveway with Harry's face buried in her jacket. She was covering his head with kisses. I panicked. She's kneeling on gravel, I thought. What an idiot! Her stockings. They'll rip. They'll snag and run and she'll bend her knee and the rip will get bigger, and she can't afford another pair of stockings. Not right now. She'll have to mend them and she's terrible at mending. I'd seen the result—lumpy caterpillars crawling up her legs. "Mama, stand up!" I yelled. But she wasn't paying attention and stayed crouched, she and Harry dwarfed by the gigantic building. "Your stockings!" I shouted. But she didn't hear. I hurried back across the lawn, stumbled over the curb, and came up the driveway. I pried Harry's fingers out of the crook of my mother's arm, grabbed his wrist and pulled him away from her. She stood up brushing gravel from her skirt.

"C'mon, Harry," I said. "Be a man."

Harry slipped his hand into mine and I led him toward the portico. Boys who had been hanging out on the porch scrambled inside to spread the word about the new inmates approaching.

CHAPTER 8

On Cedar Drive, I woke in my sweaty tank top and shorts, legs tangled in the sheets on the sofa, still walking down Tuckahoe Road in my mind with my grandmother who was holding the very suitcase with the yellow handle that I had stowed under the coffee table. Brenda was banging around in the kitchen clanging pots, probably gloating at being awake earlier than I was. I had stayed up late reading, but hadn't gotten very far because I kept stopping to study the orphanage photos in the black album and to blow my nose from crying. I'd finish it all when I got home. Now I was impatient to get working on the den and the attic. First, though, I wanted to put the suitcase in the trunk of the car. I fumbled for my glasses, and reached under the coffee table, but the suitcase was gone, with the manuscript and Picture Booke inside.

"Where's the stuff I was looking at? Where's the suitcase?"

Brenda had her back to me at the stove frying eggs. "I put it away," she said.

"I wasn't finished with it."

"You can look at it later." She turned around. "Want some breakfast?"

"No thanks." I tugged on my tank top to smooth the wrinkles. Brenda was wearing shorts and a tank top, too, and her skin glowed under a sheen of sweat. She usually dressed conservatively—slacks instead of jeans, suits for work. But it was another blistering day. I wasn't used to seeing this much of her exposed and I noticed she was a bigger woman than I had thought. Not that she was fat or tall—her body was medium in every way—but she was solid. There was strength in her thighs, in her plumped arms and freckled shoulders. A peculiar worry flitted through my mind. I thought if I had to move her the way you move a piece of furniture, she wouldn't budge.

I turned away and slipped quietly down the hall to the back of the house. I definitely shouldn't be doing this alone, I thought. "I can't leave my kids," my sister had said when I asked. "Besides, I don't want any of that junk." And then my mother, in her unnervingly reasonable therapist's voice: "It would be inappropriate for *me* to go through the boxes, since your father left the house to Brenda." Thanks, Ma. Thanks, Susan. I went straight to the den to search the closet—no suitcase—and then I tried my father's bedroom. Not there either, but as I left his room I slid a gilt-framed picture off its nail. In the photograph, my chubby-cheeked father at about age three is standing on the steps of a brownstone in a sailor suit, his little hands balled into fists—not defensively as far as I could tell, but eagerly. This was the only photograph of him taken before my grandfather deserted the family, and I was glad that someone had seen fit to capture an image of my father undamaged. I peeked into Brenda's room hesitantly, but there was no need to even cross the threshold. The suitcase was right by the door! I brought it into the living room along with the picture, and shoved the boxy frame into my daypack, shoved my feet into my Keds and fished my car keys out of the small zipper compartment in the pack. The sooner I locked these things in my car the better. I slung the pack over my shoulder, and reached for the Indian table. I hadn't remembered it being so light. I always imagined my parents' Armenian poet friend in a crowd of colorful saris awkwardly lugging a piece of furniture, but the wood was almost weightless, so I lofted the table one-handed, gripped the suitcase by its Bakelite handle with my other hand, and headed out so fast I almost crashed into the obstacle blocking my path. It was Brenda, sturdy as a credenza, barring the door.

Brenda didn't raise me of course—she was only twelve years older than I was—but I called her my stepmother because I thought the word captured the fake attachment, and later, the menace in the relationship. Brenda was my stepmother but I hardly knew her. She came from a Catholic family, one of six kids. Her father died when she was young. She worked in the accounting office at Hutzler's department store. She and her mother didn't get along. I hadn't wanted to know more. I hadn't wanted her to exist. Even grown children wished their divorced parents would get back together, some did anyway, and considering my loyalty to the past, it was natural that I was one of those who wished it. My father complained about Brenda off and on, giving hope to the fantasy of my parents' reconciliation. He said living with Brenda was difficult. She suffered from depression and spent whole weekends in bed; she had no friends. He liked being needed, though. He liked people dependent on him. Not Susan or me. Never us. We got kicked out of the nest, such as it was, unceremoniously. But in his romantic relationships, he liked being in control of his women, that's why he picked them so young. (He plucked my mother when she was sixteen.)

Married life wasn't easy for my father, but it wasn't easy for Brenda, either. He was tyrannical, although also kind-hearted. About two years into their marriage, my father told Uncle Harry about the days and days Brenda spent with her head under the covers. Uncle Harry counseled my father to get the locks changed while Brenda was at work, pack her clothes and leave her bags in the driveway. Of course, my father didn't, couldn't. Uncle Harry would have. He'd been married and divorced eight times. My father couldn't leave no matter what (my mother was the one who left) and Uncle Harry couldn't stay. So Brenda and my father struggled along, and after four years as husband and wife, he woke up one October morning transformed into something monstrous—not exactly Kafka's giant cockroach, but something huge and troubling possessed him— a giant throbbing headache of unknown etiology. It was a hideous metamorphosis. The throbbing was excruciating and relentless. He underwent all kinds of tests and x-rays, tried all kinds of painkillers, but nothing helped, nobody knew what was wrong with him, and Brenda decided he was faking.

My father liked to put on an act, for sure, especially for his students, but he wasn't a faker. A provocateur, yes. But always himself. I knew he wasn't faking. And yet, I was the least likely candidate to enter the scene and right things. I had a job in far-away California, I was known for being personally irresponsible (sloppy, absentminded, burdened by unopened bills and unsent thank-you notes) and to top it off, he and I were awkward with each other. Whenever I got close, he pushed me away. I knew certain things about him. Not from his childhood, but from my own. He didn't like that. Things that happened when I was a teenager. I could tell he thought I was judging him—either harshly or too well. If he caught me staring at him, he got mad. Whenever he called California, he wouldn't even say hello. I'd pick up the phone and I'd hear, "Yeah?"

"Yeah?" I'd say.

Silence. Then he'd say something like: "I made this great soup. You want the recipe?"

"Yeah."

He'd give me the recipe and we'd hang up.

We'd had a good time the last time I visited, in September, just before he got the headache. We drove to Annapolis with Hoffman. He was happy I liked his dog. I thought the visit might be a turning point. But more likely, the next time I saw him, he'd just push me away again. He'd say something dismissive. No one could get too close. Not Harry, not Shep Levine, who occupied his own happy center of the universe. Maybe my mother, once. Maybe our friend Johnny Dolan, once. But Johnny was dead and gone.

When I heard my father's headache wasn't going away, I called Baltimore and Brenda answered. She said he was better. "No,

I'm not!" he shouted in the background. "Don't believe her."
He grabbed the phone.

"Yeah?" he said.

"You sound bad," I said. "I'll come home if you want."

"Yes, Joanna. Please. Come home."

I was stunned he wanted me, even after that nice day in
September with his dog. I was thirty and I still got on his
nerves. What are you standing there for? Go to bed. Don't you
know how to peel a potato? Is that the only book you've read
in the last six months? Don't you know how to beat an egg?
You want air in there, stupid. Lift it, lift it, faster. Haven't you
ever swept a floor? Leverage! You make a fulcrum with your
thumb and forefinger.

There was more. Deep down, he didn't trust me. We had
Lake George between us, miles of cold black water. The first
stop on a camping trip when I was fourteen. We hadn't spoken
about Lake George since that summer sixteen years ago.

No. He couldn't possibly want me. Susan was the better
choice. She wasn't afraid of him. She was good at taking
charge, cheerfully bossy. Susan never stood there and stared at
him like a weirdo. She offered her casual affection, and lived a
few hours away with Larry and their kids in New Jersey. But of
course, Susan had those little girls to take care of, and besides,
she said she didn't want to step on Brenda's toes. "Brenda's
the wife," Susan said, and my mother agreed. "Let Brenda deal
with him." When we first heard about the headache, all three
of us chuckled meanly about how we were lucky Brenda was
there to play nurse, letting us off the hook. But something
wasn't right. It struck me how alone he was. So I went back
to Baltimore in early December to see my father for what I
thought would be a week.

"You better be prepared," my mother said on the way to Cedar
Drive from the airport. She glanced at me, then back at the
road, the worried glance of the initiated to the innocent.

Hoffman barked from the side yard, but there was none of the usual fanfare at my arrival, no act, no put-on Yiddish accent: "Mine daughter, all the vay from California she comes, to see her poor daddy." None of that shit. He sat at the dining-room table holding his head as if it were a delicate piece of china. "Close that door. I don't feel good," he said. "You heard?"

I put down my bag and came around the table to give him a hug. He shooed me away with his cigarette. "You heard? I don't feel so good." He was camped out surrounded by an ashtray heaped with butts, matches from the Golden Dragon Chinese restaurant, a crumpled package of Benson & Hedges, a copy of *An Illustrated History of the English Garden*, and a plate of odd, assorted food: a slice of rare roast-beef wrapped around a glob of cream cheese with a crescent bite torn out; a soft-boiled egg, the puddled yolk glistening; and a mound of apple sauce plowed into furrows with the tines of his fork. Brenda sat across the table staring at his plate. She turned to me as if I had broken her reverie. "Oh, hello there."

My mother kept her coat on, her purse hanging from her shoulder and a clump of keys in her hand the way she always did whenever she came over to Cedar Drive. Except when she and her boyfriend Marty Geller were invited for dinner.

"Are you going or staying?" I asked.

My father perked up. He kept his head in his hands and moved his eyes until he settled on my mother. "Well?"

"I'll stay for a little while," my mother said.

"Then put your purse down," I said. "Put your keys down." She kept jangling her mass of jailer's keys, some of which actually locked people up at the state mental hospital where she was a social worker, a midlife career. "You're making me nervous," I said. I didn't want her to leave.

My father jumped up, tapping into a hidden energy reserve, as anxious to keep my mother there as I was. "I'm losing weight, Evie, whaddaya think?" He unbuckled his belt and held his jeans out from his waist. I'll let you know when I get down to 127."

My mother laughed as if this were some hilarious joke. My father managed a small laugh, too. "That's how much Clyde weighed when I met him in 1942," she told Brenda.

"That's the *emis*," said my father. "She got so mad when her sister introduced us and I mispronounced her name. 'Not Evy! My name isn't short for Evelyn. It's Ee-vie with a long "e."

"Evie is the diminutive of Eve!" my father and mother said in unison.

"She was so cute," my father said, "in bobby sox and saddle shoes, sixteen years old."

"He was so skinny he had to hammer extra holes in his belt," my mother said.

"That was before I enlisted in the army and got three squares a day." He started to buckle the belt he was wearing now. "I'd never seen so much food. First day of chow I go up to the sergeant and I say, 'Who am I supposed to share this with?' I thought they made a mistake."

"They fed you in the orphanage, though," I said.

"They fed us. But I still went to bed hungry." My father shot me an angry look.

CHAPTER 9

Tuckahoe

The social worker at the Hebrew National Orphan Home told my mother to go. "No!" we cried. "Mama, don't leave us! Please don't leave us!" But Miss Claire Beaufort said the sooner you get out of here, Mrs. Aronson, the better, so Mama turned around and walked out. "Mama, come back!"

Miss Beaufort had a flapper hairdo and looked fun, like someone who would be nice to children. "You boys belong in Company E," she said, a peculiar smile flickering at the corners of her mouth. Her jazzy style was a hoax.

Just then the office door swung open, prodded by a cane, and in walked a tall man wearing a uniform from the Great War.

"Follow the Colonel upstairs. He'll show you where to unpack," Miss Beaufort said. The smile flickered.

"Are we in the army?" said Harry.

"No talking, boy," said the Colonel, pointing the cane at my little brother. The man lowered his stick after a few seconds and leaned on it. I was eye level with his jodhpurs, right where they bloomed at his hips. Fear sloshed in my guts, but I put on a brave act for Harry.

"Just watch the other boys, do what they do," Miss Beaufort said brightly.

"Forward march!" The Colonel straightened his pith helmet and led us out of the office and into the hallway. Shrapnel, I thought, must be the reason for the cane. "Hup, two, three, four." I thought he was joking the way Slow Uncle Archie joked when we played war. The Colonel raised the cane and held it like a baton. "Close your mouth, boy. Step lively."

Along the darkened corridor, the odor of boiling tar and oily beef tallow. My nostrils flared and a tear rolled down my cheek. A couple of bull-necked fellows crossed our path and dashed up a flight of steps. I stared after them. Even with fear in my belly, I was spellbound by examples of what I might grow into. Not here, though. I wasn't going to grow up here. "Face front!" the Colonel snapped. He seemed upset by the older boys walking around on their own, and waited until they were gone before we climbed to the third floor, knees high. Halfway up the creaking staircase, the Colonel made us go ahead of him, and he made a quick motion with the cane, like a golf putt. I watched the rubber tip catch Harry on the seat of his pants and lift him up, then bring him down onto the step again. I gasped and the cane's rubber tip nudged into the seam of my own trousers, poked into my backside. I was deeply offended. I swiped the seat of my pants but couldn't get rid of the odd feeling. Harry was quietly crying. I wanted to kick the Colonel in the shins. I wanted to bite him. In the office, my mother had said if we were good, she'd bring us home on Visiting Day if she could save enough money by then. And so I was good and I did not kick or bite the Colonel.

At the entrance to Company E, fresh fear spilled into my heart when I saw the whiteness. Everything like a hospital. White walls, white window frames, white blankets, white-iron beds in rows. The Colonel put two older inmates in charge of us, monitors they were called.

"No talking number 271, that's you, boy," said Shorty Lapidus, not short, but lanky with pimples. I didn't like a kid calling me boy. Beiderman, built like a weight lifter, hit me in the stomach with a package. It was all happening so fast. I tore open the brown paper. Sheets, underwear, and pajamas, each item embroidered with 271. There was no way back.

"Look out, 87." Shorty sent a package sailing toward Harry. It hit him right in the smacker and fell on the floor. "Pick it up, moron," Shorty Lapidus said.

People kept shouting at us. Beiderman demonstrated how to make a bed with hospital corners. "Taut! Taut!" he screamed, although we were standing right next to him. More shouts rang out, but these were the good kind—the joyful shouts of children running through the doorway laughing, shoving, cussing—and this scared the shit out of me the most. All kids around my age, seven, eight, nine, with a few as young as Harry. I didn't know what expression to put on my face. They called to each other. Blocky, Cheesie, Skelly, Hirsh. The walls of my throat swelled. I blinked and swallowed.

Harry rushed up the aisle. "Brudder, my bed can bounce a nickel!"

"Good going," I said.

"Listen up. Somebody's gotta go downstairs and get Shmecky," said Beiderman. "You, Hoffman, and take the rookie with you. Not 87. The taller one," he said. I followed Hoffman down the hall toward a back staircase. He was thin like me, and he wore glasses same as me, and he didn't seem weak or shy like other children with glasses, just as I wasn't in normal circumstances. I listened to the sound of our footsteps along the quiet corridor away from the rowdy dorm, and then our weight creaking the wooden stairs and I felt an unexpected rush of feeling for this boy, Hoffman. I asked his given name: Jesse. He didn't ask mine and without a word took a flying leap landing neatly on the plank floor. Show off.

"This here's the kitchen," he said. "One of them. We got two. One for milk, one for meat."

I tried to see into the high-ceilinged room but billows of steam obscured the view. "A whole kitchen for milk?" I said. We each wiped the fog off our glasses with our shirttails.

"Gotta. We're Orthodox," Jesse said. "All the Homeboys, 381 of us. That means you, too."

"We are? I am?" My throat closed again, this time for being included.

"Calm down, kid," Jesse Hoffman said. "We don't hafta grow *payes* or wear fur hats."

"What do we hafta do?"

"You'll see. C'mon, we gotta go get Shmecky," he said. I followed Jesse into the wood-paneled lobby decorated with portraits of old men, and in the center of the foyer, a dark gleaming staircase. "Genuine mahogany," Jesse noted. "And that there's Justice Aaron J. Levy. Says so on the pitcher frame. New York Supreme Court. He's our patron."

I didn't ask what a patron was, only followed behind Jesse who stopped to look out the double glass doors onto the portico. A little boy was sitting outside on the steps. He had a suitcase by his feet.

"What's he doing out there?" I said.

"That's Shmuel Hefter. Shmecky. His mother was supposed to take him home, but it looks like she ain't coming. C'mon Shmecky," he said, opening the door. "You better go back to the dormitory and unpack."

When do we eat, I wanted to know, and why aren't we allowed to talk except at certain times and how was I to know when I was allowed to talk if there was no logic as to why? I thought I could ask Jesse Hoffman, but after getting Shmecky, he made a point of ignoring me. I didn't want to make friends anyway. I didn't want their orphan stink on me. I vowed to keep myself apart. Aside from something to eat, I wanted only one thing: my mother.

Harry and I were separated most of the time, as our beds were at either end of the dormitory. We were issued caps and told to stand in line according to size, in my case behind a boy named Albert Shack. Shorty Lapidus said I'd stand behind Al Shack the rest of my life unless one of us had a growth spurt, and I spoke up and said, "no, not the rest of my life, just a week because my mother's coming to get me and my brother on Visiting Day," to which everyone laughed uproariously. This sent the Colonel into a rage. Eyes bulging, he charged down the line and whacked each one of us on the legs with his cane. "Now march to supper," the Colonel said.

I soothed myself with thoughts of chicken falling off the bone, hot pastrami on rye, brisket with gravy, fresh Kaiser rolls. We marched along the kitchen corridor toward a dishwater smell and even that had me licking my lips like a dog. I followed Al Shack greedily into what I assumed was the dining room, but instead we landed on wooden benches facing a podium behind which a man with a long white beard muttered and swayed. My heart sank. How many hours had it been since we'd eaten the apples by the side of the road? The rabbi droned on in Hebrew. Hunger gnawed at me and the droning and the gnawing merged until I felt I had swallowed the rabbi and he was gnawing on my stomach from the inside. A smack to the back of my head pitched me forward. "Sit up, boy."

"Don't move a muscle-ussel until the Colonel gives the signal-ignal." Instructions echoed from a megaphone in the dining room and still no food. "No talking-awking! If you breathe a word during supper-upper, you will all get demerits-errits!"

"Aw go to hell Piggy Rosenthal, you fat fuck." A curse out of nowhere directed at Supervisor Arthur Rosenthal and randomly ignored. The Colonel sliced the air with his cane—the signal. Three hundred and eighty-one chairs scraped the floor in unison. Still no food and more *bruchas*—prayers, lots of prayers. Finally a bowl passed around our table of eight, but in such a way that it reached me last. One lousy wrinkled kreplach left in a watery puddle. I gulped it down and glanced across the table at Jesse Hoffman's plate of dumplings and vegetables. He looked away. Next to him, Stanley Hirsh popped carrots into his mouth like a machine.

"What are you lookin' at, ya mope?" said Stanley.

I shook my head just slightly to indicate I wasn't looking at anything.

Lights out, privacy at last under the stiff covers, belly empty and aching. I closed my eyes and saw my mother walking along a ridge, silhouetted against the night sky. She was carrying the suitcase. I knew that was wrong. The suitcase was right under the bed.

"Brudder, wake up."

"Harry, what are you doing? Go back to sleep. We'll get in trouble."

"Brudder."

"What's the matter?"

"I shat my pants."

Only a dim nightlight in the washroom. "Take off your pajama bottoms and hurry up before somebody comes." I saw his little pecker and I wanted to cry.

"Now what?" said Harry.

"Go into the stall and really wipe yourself. Get up in there."

He cleaned his ass with paper while I scrubbed the soiled pajamas with tallow soap in one of the sinks in the long row, shit crumbs falling on the dingy floor. I did like Mama did, rubbed one part of the cloth against another, then rinsed.

"These better dry by the morning," I said, holding up the dripping mess. "Here. Hang 'em over your bed frame."

Harry sniffed the bundle. "Smells pretty good now," he said.

"Oh yeah, delicious," I said. We laughed so hard we had to hold each other up, and all without making a sound.

Back in bed that first night, I was denied even the comfort of sleep. I bobbed alone on a dark sea, the hours passing like slow ships that never stopped to pick me up. When I get out of here, I thought, I'll find my father wherever he is and I'll kill him. No I won't, I thought. I'll run to him. Lights pulsed

in the corners of my eyes and flames licked the bed frame.
The Colonel came creeping past with a lantern, his shadow
stretching across the ceiling. I threw the covers over my head
in terror. When I peeked out to see what was happening, no
one was there. The only light came from the moon glowing as
round as a face through a high window. Tears slid out of my
eyes and wet the collar of my pajamas.

"UP! UP! Everybody up. Up and at 'em!"

Bang! Clank! Clank! The Colonel whacked his cane against
the radiator. Morning at the Hebrew National Orphan Home.
Watch the other boys, do what they do. Jump out of the covers,
stand at the foot of your bed shivering.

"Rise and shine!" Beiderman called. "Up and greet the day."

Clink-clank, clink-clank. The Colonel in full uniform
banging his cane on the railings of each white-iron footboard
that lacked a boy standing in front of it. He was like a kid dragging a stick along a picket fence, except he was furious. "Get
up! Get up!" he snarled. His eyes bulged like boiled raisins. The
deep sleepers roused and each shot to the foot of his bed.

"Colonel, sir, all accounted for but 246," said Shorty Lapidus.
"The brat won't budge."

The Colonel threw his cane at the lump in the covers. "UP!
UP! UP!" the Colonel screamed. The cane bounced. A wave of
fear swept over me and shuddered up and down the row of
inmates.

"UP! Do you hear me?" The Colonel swooped in and overturned the mattress, tossing the boy onto the floor between
the beds—a space that was precisely eighteen inches wide
according to Company E regulations.

After breakfast, where I got more or less the same amount
of oatmeal as the other boys at the table, we swept the dormitory passing the broom from one bed to the next.

"Leverage! Use leverage," screamed Beiderman.

What was leverage?

"Numbskull!" shouted Shorty Lapidus. "Make a fulcrum out of your thumb and forefinger and slide it through."

Chick Scheiner, a boy with a red crew-cut and freckles, showed me how. I swept under the bed and created a dust pile just like the other boys' dust piles. Chick smiled—he even had freckles on his lips. I didn't smile back. No orphan stink on me.

"OK, pass it on," said Shorty.

The broom went to Skelly Schwartz and then Manny Bergman and down the line. I felt a sense of pride and accomplishment, which I resented.

The others played baseball after school. I stood in the weeds looking back across the field at the brick asylum looming over the grounds. I dreamed of Sunday. What if something happened, something beyond my mother's control, and she couldn't come? How would I get the message? There was no candy store with a telephone. Harry and I would have to wait on the steps with Shmecky until darkness settled on the playground, and one by one, the yellow lights came on in the building.

"Brudder. Wake up."

"What is it now?"

"I'm hungry," Harry said.

"I am, too. Try not to think about it."

"Can I sleep with you, Brudder?"

"We're not allowed."

"I'm scared."

I leaned on an elbow and scanned the dormitory. There were others doubling up. "Awright, c'mon." Harry climbed in, and soon he was snoring softly. His little body radiated welcome heat. I lay awake for a while longer. The week was a corridor, I thought. All we had to do was walk to the end and Harry and I would reach Sunday. It was easy. No thinking necessary. They told us to march and we marched, pray and we prayed, piss and we pissed. Hup two three four, up the stairs to P.S. 403, the grammar school right inside the big building just as my mother had said. No talking, knees high, march to school, march to Hebrew class, march to shul, march to supper, and gradually the days of the week would fall away. I wrapped an arm around Harry, snuggled against his warm back, and fell asleep.

On Sunday morning, Visiting Day, the scene was mayhem. I couldn't believe it. The guys were acting like a bunch of girls getting ready for a dance. They shined their shoes, put on their best clothes, slicked down their hair if it wasn't already shaved off. Harry and I watched carefully and did what they did, like Miss Beaufort said. We made ourselves look as lovable as possible. When we were done, we stormed the main portico along with the other inmates vying for a seat on the steps and hanging off the balustrades. A fight broke out, but quickly dissolved. All eyes were on Tuckahoe Road. You would have thought President Coolidge's motorcade was due, or the Yankees for a ticker-tape parade. I kept my eyes wide open, but I still couldn't pinpoint when the first vague blurs took shape. They appeared out of the mist, figures from our dreams, apparitions in worn-out coats streaming through the pedestrian gate. Some walked up the terraced lawn and some chose the curving driveway. Deserted women, widowers, bachelor uncles, and grandmothers clutching paper sacks of fruit and halvah.

"There she is!" I said.

Harry started jumping up and down.

"Naw. It's not her," I said, my voice hollow. Harry punched me in the arm. I watched the others on the portico find their people and peel off. I didn't own a wristwatch but we'd come onto the steps at one o'clock and I estimated fifteen minutes had passed. Then twenty. Then half past. The crowd on the steps thinned. Shmecky kicked his suitcase and hummed to himself. I had planned to bring our suitcase down, too, so

Harry and I could leave immediately, not even have to go back into the building, but then I thought better of it. The suitcase was all packed, though. There was room to sit now, but I didn't want to. I leaned against one of the marble columns. I hadn't seen Jesse Hoffman all day. It annoyed me how I was always wondering where Jesse was. He didn't give a crap where I was. I watched Harry play a game with Chick Scheiner's little brother Pinchus that involved bumping up and down the steps on their backsides. Then Chick and Pinky walked off with a man in a felt hat who must have been their father. I wondered if my own father knew where I was. Did he know about Visiting Day?

There were five of us left on the steps. They let us walk around on Sundays like normal kids so I went back inside past the portrait of Justice Levy and down to the office to get a look at the clock. It was nearly two. I lingered in the lobby by the glass doors. Harry bumped down the steps past Shmecky and a few others, heads hanging under the weight of their disappointment. Then I noticed a woman walking up the driveway in short quick strides just the way my mother walked, scrape-tap, scrape-tap, with her hat cocked just the way my mother wore her hat, only my mother didn't own a gray cloche hat with a blue band. Harry ran toward the woman anyway and she was running toward him and my heart went wild. I pushed open the door and rushed down the steps and followed Harry into my mother's arms.

"You smell like cream soda," I said. It was sickening. The hat, too. I hated it. She laughed and kissed me on both cheeks, and my forehead, and one ear.

"It's Kohl's vanilla scent," she said. "Forty percent off. Cream soda. You're so funny, Clyde. For the hat, too, they give the employee discount."

If she had the money to buy a hat and vanilla perfume, even with the discount, maybe she had made enough money to bring us home. I started to feel better, but I knew enough to wait for the right moment to ask about it. We spread our blanket between two tall trees. My mother apologized for our small picnic and not bringing Vivian, Alvin, and Gertrude to make a big happy party, but I was glad she came alone. She promised to bring the others next time, and I thought I wouldn't mind seeing Gertie since she was so little I expected she changed from day to day and then I thought, wait a minute. Next time? I stood on the edge of the blanket squinting at my mother, stunned by her presence, as if I had conjured her, and meanwhile trying to understand the words "next time."

"Miss Beaufort's mean," said Harry.

"Miss Beaufort? What does she do?" said my mother.

"Nuttin'," said Harry. "Only she's not nice like you, Mama."

My mother's face lit up with the compliment. Her eyes brightened and she smiled a mischievous gap-toothed smile and I fell onto my knees and put my arms around her neck. She grabbed Harry and pulled him down, too, and we were a laughing pile of arms and legs. "Next time" was probably just a slip of the tongue. After a while, she sat up. Her hat had fallen off and she put it back on. She asked me if it looked all right. I said it did. She glanced at the building. "Are you getting enough to eat?" she asked. Harry shook his head no. "Here, take." She pulled two sandwiches from the brown bag.

"We already had lunch in the dining room," I said, though we never got enough to eat.

"Gimme," said Harry. "I'm hungry."

She took a banana from the bag, and a honey cake baked into a pleated wrapper.

"Does this salami have meat in it?" Harry said.

My mother laughed.

"It's not funny," Harry said. "You put butter on the bread! Louis the Long Beard might see!"

"He's the *mashgiach*," I said. "He blesses chickens kosher and waits for us to break the rules. We have two kitchens, one for meat and one for milk."

"*Oy vey*," said my mother. "Don't tell anybody. But you want *treyf* today, you can have *treyf*." A Dr. Brown's Cel-Rey Tonic appeared out of her purse, along with a bottle opener. "Listen, Clyde, before I forget. Slow Uncle Archie wants to visit but he works Sundays, a night watchman."

"If he's a night watchman then he can come in the daytime," said Harry.

"Yeah, he's called a night watchman," my mother said. "But it means whenever nobody's there, daytime too, then your Uncle Archie protects the place."

"Does he have a gun?" said Harry.

"No, he doesn't have a gun," my mother said.

"Then how does he keep the robbers away?"

"I don't know, boychik. He runs and gets a policeman. Listen to me. I'm trying to tell you, Uncle Archie wants to come and visit on a weekday. Like a Monday or Tuesday. But he's not allowed. So he wants to know when you go outside to play?"

The rule was strictly enforced. No visitors except Sundays. I told my mother the longest we had to play outside was between regular school and Hebrew school from three to four o'clock. She said we should watch and maybe we would see Slow Uncle Archie.

"Well, listen my little boychiks," my mother said, "Miss Beaufort tells me I should visit every two weeks instead of every week. Less upsetting, she says. So I'll do what the social worker tells me."

I pulled away. "You mean you're not taking us home?"

"I can't. Not yet. Soon, though," she said.

I wanted to hit her but I let her hold me, and I kept my face pressed to the warm crescent of cream-soda skin above her collar. I should have known. She wouldn't have gone to the trouble of putting us here only to take us back in a week. No wonder the fellows laughed so hard the Colonel beat our legs. I knuckled away the wet streaks on my face and hardened my heart.

When I had finished the salami sandwich, a buttery slice of honey cake, and half a banana, I peeled the bark off a stick, and made a sword. I was a swashbuckler wandering among blankets and benches littered with destitute and neglected children. Jesse Hoffman said if we weren't full-fledged orphans, then that's what we were—destitute, neglected, or both. Jesse knew all there was to know about the H. We weren't exactly friends, but like every know-it-all, Hoffman enjoyed dispensing information when he was in the mood. He said the HNOH was started in 1912 by a Romanian Jewish secret society called the Bessarabian Verband. Back then it was down on the Lower Eastside in a tenement on St. Mark's Place. When the tenement got too crowded, the Verband went looking for a place in the country with fresh air, and found the future Home building squatting in a field on Tuckahoe Road up in Yonkers. It had been the German Oddfellows Home, a place for German orphans and also German old folks.

Jesse Hoffman knew everything, including when there would be meat for supper or just potatoes, which of the supervisors were decent and which would beat you for no good reason, and when Colonel Anderson would make us drop our drawers and strike our bare asses with his cane or when he'd do it over our breeches. Some porters and kitchen staff were drifters, Jesse said, just passing through. Some were hobos tired of riding the rails, ex-convicts willing to work for room and board. He said Colonel Anderson hadn't injured his leg in the war, but his head.

"The cane's for his head?" I said.

"Shell shock," said Jesse.

I glanced back at my mother and Harry still sitting on the blanket breaking off pieces of honey cake. I swiped at a bee with my sword. The same murmuring came from every bench and blanket dotting the terraced lawn. *Do they give you enough to eat?* The same whispered imploring questions. *Are you warm enough? Do you sleep all right?* And then it was five o'clock, and the relatives got up and walked out the way they had come in, vanished out the gates in their shabby coats, my mother, too, and there was no more of her soft talk or caresses.

Was it so bad? Yes and no. You get used to anything. Beatings, marching, the aching loneliness, no one to care for you day after day, no mama to tuck you in at night, no kisses, starved for love. There were sweet bits, though. Friends, of course, never in short supply, some who would lay down their lives for you, no shit. That was big. I learned to appreciate smaller things, too. The warmth of the sun after a freezing dawn, stolen apples, stolen eggs, a piece of meat mistakenly left on a platter, candy when we could get it. How we worshipped candy. Slobbered over it, slurped it down, were sick from it. Orphan smack, we had to have it, drowned our sorrows in Mars bars and Goo Goo Clusters, Walnettos and Chuckles and Neccos, an occasional Charlotte Russe handed out by the Ladies Auxiliaries of White Plains or Bronxville. We got benefits, for sure, things a poor kid couldn't get living with relatives. Every Wednesday night in the old gym we saw movies, for instance. Of course we froze our asses off sitting on the concrete floor with the cold seeping into our bones, but it was worth it unless we got stuck behind one of the columns holding up the sagging ceiling and blocking the title cards. This was before talkies. We saw "The Hunchback of Notre Dame" with Lon Chaney, "Sherlock Holmes" with John Barrymore, "The Prisoner of Zenda" with Ramon Navarro, all kinds of stuff. In summer, we reveled in the woods and splashed in the B. A. creek or lolled on its banks. The initials B. A. stood for bare ass, because who the hell had a bathing suit? We built our creek pond in an idyllic spot just beyond the Home property on the grounds of the Grassy Sprain Golf Club. The club groundskeepers were always tearing down the dam, and we were always building it back up, restoring our Bare Ass Swimming Hole, or as we called it, the Bare Ass Hole. Of course, the supervisors beat us when we were caught trespassing but it was worth it. Frankly, they were terrified of us having free time and so we were urged to participate in every legitimate activity, go out for every sport. Eventually, I stopped resisting. I joined the archery club, the aero club, and later, the radio club, the *Oracle* newspaper staff, the photography club. I learned to paint in the art room. I was a drummer in the band. I grew vegetables on the farm gang, collected eggs, cared for the horses—Playboy, Joe, Sally the mare.

Sometimes seniors from the dramatics club came downstairs to Company E at bedtime and retold the plot of a movie, or read to us. I wanted to do that when I got older, tell stories to the younger kids. I thought I'd be back with my mother in the Bronx by then, but I'd visit and read to the little kids for charity. Not long after I arrived, a senior named Artie Klein started reading *David Copperfield* to Company E. We were at the part where David Copperfield's cruel stepfather sends Davey away to boarding school. Chick held the flashlight over Artie's shoulder and Artie read: "The rest of the half-year is a jumble in my recollection of the daily strife and struggle of our lives; of the waning summer and the changing season; of the frosty mornings when we were rung out of bed, and the cold, cold smell of the dark nights when we were rung into bed again; of the evening schoolroom dimly lighted and indifferently warmed, and the morning schoolroom which was nothing but a great shivering-machine; of the alternation of boiled beef with roast beef, and boiled mutton with roast mutton; of clods of bread-and-butter, of canings, rulerings, hair-cuttings, rainy Sundays, and a dirty atmosphere of ink, surrounding all."

The room stayed hushed for moments after Artie closed the book and put out the flashlight.

"Who wrote that?" a little voice called out in the dark. It was Shmecky.

"Charles Dickens," said Artie.

"Is he in Company A or B?"

"Neither."

"C or D?"

"Dickens never lived at the H," said Artie.

"Then how did he know so much about it?" said Shmecky.

The older boys howled with laughter.

"Quiet!" somebody yelled from the end of the row. "I'm trying to get some shut-eye."

I kept *David Copperfield* in my head as I marched through the tar-smelling corridors of the old brick building. I had a mother and so did Davey. Davey's mother was forced to send him away, like my mother was forced to send me away. But he loved her all the same.

CHAPTER 10

"Got it," I said. "They fed you at the orphanage, but not enough. So you went hungry anyway."

"Don't be a wise guy," my father said. I hadn't meant to be. For a few minutes he'd been animated, like his old self. But I sensed his headache coming back, a shadow lengthening across his face. He buckled his belt on the last hole. "So Evie, I'll let you know when I get down to 127 again."

My mother murmured a laugh and tilted her chin down, her signature look of affection, then left Cedar Drive clasping her clump of jailer's keys, and my father's burst of energy fizzled completely. He slunk back to the table. "I can't read," he said. He looked me plainly in the eye. He had his glasses off, lying next to his plate—the weight on his nose and temples was intolerable. I'd hardly ever seen his eyes not through a lens. He blinked. They were sad eyes. All those years, I thought, it might have been only a pair of glasses that kept me from knowing him. "I can't eat, I can't do the crossword. It hurts." He held his head between his hands, a cigarette poking out between his fingers like a unicorn horn.

"How can you bear to see him like this?" I said.

"I'm used to it," said Brenda.

I made my bed on the sofa and lay with my arms folded behind my head. I'd try to be helpful and not get in Brenda's way. I'd do the dishes, run errands, walk the dog. I'd be there, camped out on the sofa. For a week at least, Brenda could go to work without worrying that he was going to fall asleep with a cigarette and burn the house down. But that was it. I wasn't signing up for anything more. I had no experience with doctors or sickness, and I didn't want any. I was young. I hadn't taken care of anyone before. Why would I have? The thought was gruesome and horrifying. Needles and bedpans. Let Brenda do it, or my sister. Susan took care of her kids. It was the same thing, sort of. She was organized and he favored her, so let her pay him back. He'd always been deaf to my needs, shutting me down enough times that I stopped asking for anything. We were supposed to feel lucky for having a father at all. It was already better than he got. We were supposed to be grateful. Our father was there, even more than the other fathers on our block, the salesmen and Westinghouse technicians. A teacher was home by four o'clock. He was there, bigger than life, meeting the day-camp bus in gardening clothes—cut-offs, no shirt, a gondolier's hat—waving with a cigarette in his hand. Singing to embarrass us. I saw him every day. I was grateful. He didn't see me, though.

Hoffman's tag jingled as he shifted his weight on Brenda's bed. A car door slammed across the creek on Dalton Drive, and then it was quiet. I was sound asleep when a sharp cry pierced the night. I shot up and bolted out of the covers and rushed to his room.

"My TV!! Where's my TV? She took my TV! Why? Why?"

Brenda was sitting on the edge of the bed in a pool of orange light tenderly rubbing Lanacane on his right temple where he felt the most pain. I was about to tiptoe away, thinking I had dreamed the cries, when my father noticed me standing in the doorway. He struggled to a sitting position.

"Joanna," he said. "Where'd she put my TV?"

"She's right here," I said. "Ask her."

"The damn thing was in my way," Brenda said. "Try giving Dilaudid injections with all that junk on the bed. It did nothing for him, the Dilaudid. Which, by the way, Dr. Cromwell says is impossible."

"But you're not giving injections anymore. Can't he have his TV back?" All he got now was Tylenol with codeine in tablets that he couldn't swallow.

Brenda screwed the top onto the Lanacane tube. "You try dealing with him," she said, and went across the hall to her room. Uncle Harry had sent the little TV. Uncle Harry who hadn't been speaking to my father for a couple of years because of some slight, real or imagined. But then Harry heard about the headache and forgot about the slight and started calling and sending expensive presents—a juicer, a short-wave radio kit, the TV. My father loved that TV. He couldn't see the big one in the living room clearly from his reclining chair without his glasses and his glasses hurt his head. But the one Uncle Harry sent was so small my father could have the TV in bed with him. He'd pull it close to his face, careful not to yank the plug out of the wall, and Harry's gift became his connection to the world.

After a lengthy search with no help from Brenda, I found the TV on a chair in the corner. She had hidden it under a pile of clothes. "My TV from Harry," he said. "From my brudder." I plugged it in and put it down on the rumpled sheet. He wrapped his arm around it.

CHAPTER 11

Was Uncle Harry's scheme so outlandish—changing the locks on the doors? Brenda had a family. They'd take her in, get her help. Maybe throwing her out was just common sense, because obviously she was nuts. I was ready to do it, but then I'd change my mind. I'd find Brenda holding my father's hand cooing "honey" and "sweetie," and I'd picture my plane ticket to LA tucked in an envelope and I'd think she's not so bad. He needs her, I need her.

And so I took my sister's advice, tried not to step on Brenda's toes, and there were moments when my stepmother and I got along. The first morning, for example, she demonstrated how to make farina the way he liked it, and we laughed together about his ridiculous demands. After she left for work, I followed her recipe and placed the steaming bowl in front of him at the table. He chopped at the hot cereal with a spoon as if I'd given him a bowl of rocks. "This is no good!" he said angrily. "Cook it one-and-a-half minutes. Not two minutes! Don't stand there like an idiot. Do it over." The whole day he bullied me. I ruined his tea (didn't boil the water long enough) and answered the phone wrong. "No! No!" he shouted. "How is anyone supposed to know who Joanna is? You don't live here anymore!" That one really stung.

When Brenda came home from work, we commiserated about his tantrums, and allied by our common enemy, we agreeably cooked dinner together—leftover brisket she doctored, potatoes I sliced paper-thin and roasted, a recipe from Nora Ephron's *Heartburn*—but that turned out to be one of the few days Brenda and I got along. My father sat with us at dinner, although he could barely even sample the gravy. My mother stopped by afterward for coffee—to check on me more than him—and I appreciated her presence, as we all did.

Even Brenda. She peppered my mother with questions—where did you get those shoes, Evie? I love your hair, who does it?" And when my mother got up, ready to flee to her apartment downtown, Brenda remarked about how my mother must have hated living on Cedar Drive, she was always in such a hurry to leave. This stopped my mother. She felt misunderstood. She put her leather bag down on the buffet. My father, Brenda, and I were still at the table, and we watched hopefully as my mother dropped her keys on top of the bag. I heard the familiar snap of her ankle as she shifted her weight. She folded her arms defensively. "No, I didn't hate it here," she said. "I made the best of it. It was just that, you know, I never thought I would end up in the suburbs. I thought we'd live in New York."

My father gave her a small smile of encouragement, nodding for her to go on, and I wondered, as I often did, why my parents weren't together when clearly they belonged together.

"Well, we did live in New York for a few years after the war," my mother said, warming to the topic.

"So? What happened?" Brenda said.

"We ran out of money, that's what. So we came back to Baltimore, to my family. The plan was to live in Baltimore for a year or two until Clyde got his writing career going. Of course, then he started teaching English at City and he liked the high school job so much he wanted to stay. And he never did write like he said he would."

I glanced at my father to see if he was annoyed by her reference to his thwarted ambition, but he was rapt as a child listening to a bedtime story.

"New York was romantic," my mother said, "but I had my own reasons for coming back to Baltimore. I had connections here in the leadership." My mother's eyes were shining with the memory. "I thought if I stayed local, I could work my way up in the organization, whereas I'd be a nobody in New York."

"What organization?" said Brenda.

My mother lowered her voice to a whisper. "The Maryland chapter of the CPUSA. You know, the Communist Party," she said, and then went back to her normal voice. "But my brilliant career never materialized. The McCarthy hearings happened instead." My mother pulled out a chair and settled into the seat lost in thought.

"Clyde told me you were a communist but I never took it seriously," said Brenda.

"I think Clyde was more scared than I was," my mother said.

My father shrugged. He took a drag off his cigarette and flicked a chunk of ash into the ashtray.

"Clyde thought we could blend in by moving to the suburbs and having kids—we'd live the American Dream, he said, and slip under the radar. At the time, we had a nice apartment on Liberty Heights in Baltimore City and I said, fine, I'll get pregnant. But no way we're moving to the suburbs. I'd die of boredom. Downtown Baltimore was lively then. Shops nearby we could walk to. Row houses, streetcars, candy stores."

"I guess you let Clyde call the shots," said Brenda. "Seeing as you ended up in the suburbs in this house."

"No. It wasn't Clyde," my mother said. "Something else happened that changed my mind."

"They made her an offer she couldn't refuse," my father said. He and I smiled at each other. He must have been feeling better. "Tell her, Evie," he said. "Tell Brenda the story."

"Really? It's a long megillah."

"We're not going anywhere," said Brenda with a laugh.

"It used to be a big secret," my mother said. "This happened in '53. So what is it now, '86? Thirty years ago. Jesus, I should be able to talk about it at this point. That apartment on Liberty Heights was on the second floor of a row house, and I remember coming downstairs onto the front porch with the baby on my hip—it was Susan, not you Joanna. Susan was six months old. You weren't born yet. My plan was to take the baby for a walk, but one of the baby-carriage wheels was caught between the white slats or posts or whatever they're called in the wood porch railing. The carriage wouldn't budge, so I looked around to see if Daddy was on his way back from the library, but nobody was out on the street. It was a lovely October day, bright orange leaves on those big trees."

"Those are gone now," my father said. "Dutch elm disease."

"I noticed a strange car parked on the block, a few doors down. One of those tanks we used to drive," my mother said. "And I'm thinking, why the hell isn't Clyde around when I need him? But that wasn't really fair. Clyde was around a lot. That day, though, he was off for some kind of grading period, right Clyde? Wasn't that it? And instead of hanging out with me at breakfast, he walked to the library. The Forest Park Branch was a few blocks away. I was wearing those black Capri pants I loved and a white blouse with big black buttons, crouched down holding the baby in one arm, yanking on the carriage wheel when a sound startles me and I jump to attention and almost drop Susan. Three men are standing at the bottom of the porch stairs in suits and hats and shiny black shoes. I was glad I was alone. Mrs. Mankewitz who lived in the downstairs apartment was away visiting her daughter in Richmond. I didn't need the neighbors watching."

"You must have been scared all by yourself," Brenda said.

"I was mainly worried about the neighbors. That they would know what the men wanted, as I did."

"You knew?" said Brenda.

"Why else would the Feds show up at my door in 1953? 'We'd like to ask you a few questions, Mrs. Aronson.' The stocky guy in the middle was the only one who talked.

"C'mon, Evie, you had to be scared," Brenda said.

"Sure I was scared. I held Susan tight and I kept thinking, I'm a good person, I'm a good person. My baby is certainly innocent. My husband is innocent. And then I remembered— Clyde signed the oath.

I'm standing on the porch in front of these G-men shouting in my head: 'Shit! Shit! Don't come home, Clyde. Stay at the library! Don't show your face!' Because you see, that year, for the first time, the State of Maryland asked public schoolteachers to sign a loyalty oath. And of course Clyde signed. He had to in order to keep his job, and besides, he wanted to because Clyde was the most patriotic person I knew. Still is."

My father smiled.

"You were one patriotic, John Philip Sousa humming, red-blooded American communist, right, Clyde? That last part, though, that was the tricky part. That was where he'd get into trouble, because although not a so-called card-carrying member of the Party like me, he was a fellow traveler, a May Day marcher, a writer of letters to the editor, an attender of meetings. You know how he *kvells* all the time, 'greatest country in the world.' He did back then too, even during the McCarthy years. Yeah, Brenda. Your husband's full of contradictions. Like any thinking person." My mother lowered her chin and gave my father an admiring look.

"Sure I was scared. I didn't know exactly what they had on me, or Clyde, or how they would use it. I remember the adrenalin crackling in my chest, though. It felt like an electric current or something, you know what I mean?"

"Not really," said Brenda.

"I was thinking about the Rosenbergs," my mother said. "It had just happened. Having Susan with me gave me courage. 'Look at this child,' I wanted to say to the Feds. 'My baby is American as apple pie.'"

"That's right, 100 percent American," my father said.

"So then the agent says, 'You do understand, Mrs. Aronson—the Federal Bureau of Investigation has jurisdiction over matters pertaining to the internal security of the United States.' And I nodded yes, and finally he asks the question I've been waiting for.

"'Are you or have you ever been. . . .'

"I interrupted him and said 'Yes, I was a member. Many years ago.' That's what I had decided to do—tell the truth right away but point out that it was ancient history. I didn't think I had much to lose coming clean. I had no job to be fired from. I was nobody. But then he keeps it up, he says, 'See, the trouble is, Mrs. Aronson . . . It says right here you're still receiving the *Daily Worker*, a newspaper well-known to disseminate communist propaganda.'

"I told him he was wrong, I hadn't gotten the paper since 1946. Which was a lie, and I hated lying, but it was a small one. Imagine these creeps telling me what I can and cannot read? Then the bastard says, 'You're a pretty young woman. What on earth are you doing associating with an organization intent on destroying our way of life?'

"I can't say which part of that question made me madder. 'I'm not sure what my looks have to do with it,' I said. My anger must have given me courage, too.

"The FBI man smirked. 'Yet you admit, freely, to taking orders from the Soviet Union?'

"'That's ridiculous. I was in high school,' I said. 'I joined for social reasons.'

"'Social reasons?' he says.

"'They threw parties and picnics . . .' God, it pissed me off having to trivialize the good work I'd done. Yes, I enjoyed the social part. But that wasn't the reason I joined. I had ideals. I wanted a better world, decent wages for the working class.

"'So who attended these parties and picnics, at, let's see, 1019 North Avenue, or the colored Elk's Lodge, 1528 Madison Avenue?'

"'I don't remember names,' I said, and that was a lie I enjoyed. I hated lying about the *Daily Worker* and I hated saying I joined for the damn picnics. But lying to save someone else's ass? Boy, that felt good. So he says, 'You don't remember names?

Is that so? Let me ask you something, Mrs. Aronson. What was a nice girl like you doing over at the colored Elk's Lodge?'

"Can you believe the gall? 'There were lots of nice people over there,' I said. I wasn't going to let him intimidate me.

"'Nice people like George Goldsmith?' he says. 'Or can't you remember him either?'

"Jesus Christ. Right there on the porch while I'm holding my baby, he wants me to ruin a man's life? George had four kids by then and a job at Social Security he couldn't afford to lose. He played the piano at 1019, you know, our clubhouse, and did the books. I wouldn't have betrayed George under any circumstances, but thankfully I didn't have to worry about it, because I hadn't signed anything, so I couldn't perjure myself. I couldn't be blacklisted or blackmailed. But, of course, my husband could be all of those things, and I had lost track of time. Clyde would be home any second, walking up the street into a trap! I came down off my high horse and I looked over the heads of those G-men and searched the sidewalk for Clyde. You know the loyalty oath, don't you Brenda? You were alive then."

"I was ten years old," Brenda said.

"*I do not advocate the overthrow of the government by force and violence.* This was what the teachers had to sign. *I have never been a member of any organization that advocates the overthrow of the government by force and violence . . .* Clyde had everything to lose, and he would lose it, too, because if there's one thing Clyde does not do, it's snitch on his buddies."

"Those hypocrites!" I said. "A loyalty oath promising you'll rat out your friends. It should be called A Rat's Oath."

"Good one," said my father.

"The point is," Brenda said, "you're loyal to your country, and no one else."

"I like Joanna's joke, though," my father said.

"Let me finish my story," my mother said. "So, I was still up on the porch with a pretty good view. I'd be able to see Clyde coming home from the library from more than a block away.

'No. Not George Goldsmith,' I said. 'I never saw George at the Elk's Lodge,' I told the FBI men. I remember switching Susan from one hip to the other. She was getting heavy.

"'But you know Goldsmith?' he said.

"'Yes.'

"'Through your political activities?' he said.

"'No.'

"'Then how did you meet George Goldsmith?'

"'I don't remember,' I said. 'This is a small community—this corner of Baltimore. Everybody knows everybody.'

"'Huh. Everybody knows everybody. But no one remembers anyone's name?'

"'It's been a long time,' I said. 'So, no. I don't remember anyone's name or how I met George Goldsmith.'

"I sized up the three agents. Cold, smug, and bored. They could not begin to understand how alive I was during the war, how urgent and meaningful my life was thanks to the CP. How engaged I was with the world. I missed those days. I still miss those days. That was my youth. And then he starts with this anti-Semitic insinuation. 'This small community, this corner you speak of . . .' he says, 'you're talking about the northwest corner of Baltimore, isn't that right?'

"'I guess that's what I mean,' I said.

"'You mean the Jewish section?'

"'Yes,' I said. 'The Jewish section. That's where I live. I'm Jewish. That's not against the law, I hope.'

"'There's no need to get testy, ma'am,' he said.

"'It's just—what did we win the war for?' I said. I was dangerously prolonging the interview. I needed them gone—Clyde would be back any second."

"So why get into it with them?" Brenda said. "That seems sort of stupid, if you don't mind my saying."

"It wasn't stupid. Not really. I had a point to make. You see, Brenda, in a very meaningful way I wanted them there, because they had come to interview me. They hadn't come for Clyde. I was the important one for once. I was the one in a leadership position at the Young Communist League. I was the one who worked to get FDR re-elected. Yes, Clyde was off fighting the war, but goddamnit, I represented our YCL chapter at the CIO convention in Philadelphia. This was my moment. I was proud of the work I'd done. So yeah, Brenda, I got into it. 'If I have to be worried about being Jewish and having Jewish friends,' I said to that asshole, 'then what did we win the war for?'

"'We won the war to triumph over fascism, ma'am,' he says, utterly without irony.

"I just shook my head at the obtuseness. But he isn't finished. He asks if I've been to any political meetings lately and he's waiting for an answer. 'Ma'am?' he says. Always so courteous with the ma'ams. Meanwhile, I've got my eye on Calloway Street when a brown fedora pops up, bobbing above the privet hedge. The stride is unmistakable. It's Clyde. You know—head jutting forward, always looking for action. Slow down, I'm begging him. He's almost at the corner.

"'Mrs. Aronson? Do you still attend political meetings? May Day parades?'

"Clyde's about to turn left onto Liberty Heights. If he gets to the house, he'll be questioned, and investigated. A teacher poisoning young minds. I couldn't afford to play a game of wits any longer, I had to start playing dumb, and I knew how to do that, too. Every woman does. Right, Brenda? So I quickly change tactics. I get buttery sweet. 'Oh no, I wouldn't go to political meetings anymore,' I say, arching my back, sticking my chest out. I was amazed how quickly the men responded to that, shifting in their suits. 'I'm a mother now, after all,' I cooed. Just like the mother you burned in the electric chair, I'm thinking. Of course, I was nothing like Ethel Rosenberg – she was brave, or foolish, or both, and refused to play dumb.

"The FBI man gives me this condescending smile. 'I can see you have much more important things on your mind now,' he says, with a nod to Susan.

"I was probably visible on the porch from far down the street, but I wasn't sure if Clyde saw me. I doubted he'd be able to see the men. I watched him pause at the corner. 'Is that all?' I said. I was finished now and begging the men silently: Go. Leave.

"Clyde turns the corner, but instead of left, he goes right on Liberty Heights and walks away from me and my interrogators. I let out a breath. He has books under one arm and something white in his other hand—an envelope. He turned right not because he saw the men, but because, as luck would have it, he had to mail a letter at the mailbox on the next corner.

"'That's all,' the stocky one says. 'Thank you. We appreciate your time, Mrs. Aronson.'

"He tips his hat and turns to leave with the other two just as Clyde pulls on the blue handle. The mailbox door creaks open and clanks shut. Clyde starts down the block toward us.

"'Wait,' I say. 'There's one other thing.'"

"You stopped them from leaving?" Brenda said. "You wanted Clyde to get in trouble?"

"No, of course not. I had an idea. I decided to throw a diversion in their path. I don't how I got the nerve, but let's say I had a moment of brilliance. You see, if you signed the oath and you were seen at a meeting or a rally, something that small, they could indict you for perjury. If they questioned Clyde, he would be asked to betray his friends, name names, or lose his job—at the very least. That was the choice. It was such a great job. City was public, you know that, but it was as good as any prep school—such bright boys. And the faculty was terrific, so many parties. There I go again with the parties. What can I say? We had fun. It wasn't my clubhouse, no, it definitely wasn't 1019, these were Clyde's colleagues, not mine. But when Tom Mulligan played guitar and Shep Levine played the banjo, what songs do you think they sang? Union songs, of course. *There once was a union maid/she never was afraid/of goons and ginks and company finks.* . . . We all sang, a little drunk. *Oh you can't scare me, I'm stickin' to the union.* We were full of life and hope for the future, the chance to bridge the gap between rich and poor, to make a difference in young people's lives, not indoctrinate them, but open their minds. It might have seemed corny to outsiders, even naïve, but how else would progress come without that kind of innocence? Guilty of innocence, that's what we were. Very few teachers were members of the Party like me, but many shared my ideals. They supported labor, civil rights, women's rights, socialized medicine. I had the naïve urge to talk sense into the FBI men at my door. I'd rejected the Party line by then, but why throw the baby out with the bath water? In Europe, democracies put the good aspects of communism to use. In America, even socialism's a dirty word.

"I said none of this, of course. I'd already kept them too long, said too much. Someday, though, when Susan was in school, I thought, I'd fight the good fight again. But I was a practical person, too, and when I thought of Clyde losing his job, our sole paycheck, when I thought of the baby in my arms who was completely dependent on that paycheck . . ."

"What was the one more thing?" asked Brenda.

"That's what the FBI wanted to know. 'Ma'am? One other thing, you said?'

"'Please,' I said. 'I beg you. *Please* don't tell my husband I was ever involved in anything political. If he knew, he would kill me!'"

"Smart," my father said.

Brenda laughed. "Don't throw me in the briar patch," she said.

"Exactly," said my mother. "I don't know how I thought of it on the spot. But it worked. An ingratiating smile bloomed on that guy's face. 'Oh, honey, is that what you're worried about? Your husband finding out? Put it out of your mind, sweetheart. Your secret is safe with us.'

"'Thank you,' I said. 'I'm so relieved. Because I'm serious, my husband would kill me.'

"They left, got into their shiny, black car and drove away. 'I saved your Daddy's ass,' I whispered into Susan's tiny ear. 'And you, my darling baby, you saved mine.'

"Clyde was coming up the street and I knew he hadn't seen the men, because he was singing in his raspy voice as he turned into our front walk, 'Oh What a Beautiful Morning!'

"'Get anything for me?' I asked, as I always did when he came home from the library.

"'You're trembling, Evie,' Clyde said. 'What's the matter?'

"'Here, take Susan. Come inside. I'll tell you inside. Did you get anything for me?' I asked again, to steady my voice.

"'*Désirée*,' Clyde said. 'Just came out. Should be good, my darling.'

"Clyde reached for the baby and I took the library books and I led my family inside, locking the door behind us, and they followed me up to our apartment at the top of the stairs. I was pleased with myself. I felt smart and powerful for a while. But as the weeks passed, and the months and years, the feeling faded. The last laugh was on me. Shortly after that day, I agreed to move out of the city and into the suburbs, to this house. The ruse about Clyde being ignorant of my politics was a clever trick and I'm still proud of it. It worked. No one bothered Clyde or me after that. But the act I put on at the end, the little woman terrified of her husband and no longer with a political thought in her head—that wasn't really an act, was it? It was true. I was merely a wife and mother. That's all I had become, no threat to anyone, no power in the world."

My mother stood up and gathered her bag and keys from the buffet. "But no, Brenda, since you asked, I didn't hate it here," she said. "Sure, I have plenty of regrets, but this was my home. This is where I raised my family."

"Don't go, Evie," my father said.

"It's late," my mother said. She let herself out through the kitchen door.

CHAPTER 12

Tuckahoe

I met Evie in 1942. It was very romantic with the war on. I left the HNOH at seventeen, and I'd been on the outside for a while already—four years living with my mother in the Bronx and four years on my own—when I went down to Baltimore for radio school. I was hoping a radio technician's degree would get me into the Army Signal Corps, so I headed south and rented a room in one of those Baltimore row houses with the marble steps. My landlords, the Bravermans, were Yiddish-speaking shopkeepers who took in boarders to help put their son through medical school.

The first few days were terribly lonely. I was no longer a little boy in a row of iron cots, but I felt the same heartache. I had lived by myself off and on and that was swell, but this was different. I was among strangers. At breakfast the first morning, I met the son, Nat, who barely looked up from his newspaper. I cleared my throat. "I'm sure glad this coffee's strong, because I'm gonna need it. Today is my first day of school." I spoke with childish enthusiasm, an attempt at humor. "At 25 years old, I should be out of school by now," I said.

Nat put down the newspaper. "What school?" he said.

"Radio technician's school. They hold their classes over at Boy's Tech."

"No kidding? Boy's Tech?" Nat said. "I'm at Johns Hopkins."

Heat spread up my neck the second the little shit opened his mouth. "Very nice," I said.

"I study a lot," said Nat. "So I ask boarders to keep noise to a minimum." He wiped his mouth and got up to leave the table. "Good luck at radio school."

Right away, I started sleeping with the daughter. Shirley was about as sharp as a marble, but fairly companionable. Mr. and Mrs. Braverman seemed oblivious, but I liked pissing off their son the doctor. Then I met the little sister, who'd been away at the shore. I had just heard the news about the Nazis goose-stepping into the Nile Delta, and my thoughts had been somber riding the streetcar back to the Bravermans. As soon as I let myself in the front door, wild shrieks and bursts of laughter rang out, shattering the normally quiet household. Footsteps pounded overhead. A door slammed. I joined Shirley in the living room. She said her sister was back. The radio was on, an Emerson in a walnut cabinet I admired.

"How many tubes does this thing have?" I asked.

"How would I know?" said Shirley. Her lousy mood had nothing to do with the Nazis. It was the secretarial-pool supervisor who chewed her out for being five minutes late. The stairs creaked and I glanced up to see a girl coming down in a skirt and blouse, bobby sox and saddle shoes, chestnut hair tumbling over her shoulders.

"This is my sister, Evie," Shirley said.

The sister swayed to the swing orchestra on the radio, then caught herself when she saw me, and laughed. It was hard to tell her age. She had the bright eyes and glowing skin of a child, while nicely filling out her blouse. "So you're the new boarder. Do you like candy?" she said.

"What are you, crazy?" I said. "Who doesn't like candy?"

"Wait here." She bounded up the stairs, and then clomped down again holding a small white box. "Salt water taffy? St. James. From the boardwalk in Atlantic City."

"Why, thank you, Evy." I picked strawberry and put it in my jacket pocket for later.

"Not *Evy*." She scowled. "My name is not short for Evelyn. It's pronounced Ee-vie with a long "e." Evie is the diminutive of Eve."

"Ah. The diminutive of Eve. So where have you been, Eevie?"

"Atlantic City, where do you think?"

"Right," I said. "Hence, the salt water taffy."

"Are you British?"

"I hail from New York City. The Bronx."

"I think you use British expressions to hide your Bronx accent," she said.

"Really? Is that so?" I couldn't believe how frank this smart-aleck girl was. "Who are you, Sigmund Freud?"

"Leave her alone," said Shirley. "She's just a kid."

"I'm not a kid, Shirley. I'm sixteen."

"Sixteen. Very grown up," I said. "I like your bobby sox."

Evie looked down at her white socks and then up at me. Her cheeks flushed. "They're not bobby sox," she said quietly. "They're anklets."

Ordinarily, Shirley was an indoor type, but egged on by Evie she agreed to a double date biking in Druid Hill Park. Evie's date Bernard was home for the weekend, from Princeton, no less. We cycled along the winding lanes toward the botanical gardens and parked our bicycles under a tree. I watched Evie run ahead in white shorts, her long legs making great strides as she led us to the conservatory. Shirley plodded heavily up the hill, while I fought the urge to leave her behind, and Bernard, too. "When I'm old enough," Evie said when we caught up, "if the war's still on, which I hope it won't be of course, I'm joining the WACs."

"You're kidding," Shirley said.

"I'm not kidding. I want to see the world, fight the fascists. Why should I be left out because I'm a girl? I would have gone to Spain with the Lincoln Brigade if I'd been older."

"I wanted to go to Spain, too," I said.

"Why didn't you?" said Shirley.

"Yeah, you're the right age and you're male," said Evie. "What was your excuse?"

"Christ, you're so direct," I said. Her words stung, but I tried not to be thin-skinned. "My excuse?" I said calmly. "I'd just left the orphanage, come home to live with my mother and support my family." I noticed they weren't criticizing Bernard for his college deferment.

"I'm sorry," said Evie. "That's a valid reason."

"Thanks for the reprieve," I said. "It's a valid reason, but hardly romantic."

"Romantic? You Clyde? I thought you were the big realist," said Shirley.

"You're a realist? You don't say," said Bernard.

"I'm a realist about men and women," I said. "The romance of politics is another story."

"Clyde doesn't believe in love," said Shirley.

"I couldn't agree more," said Evie.

"She gets that from her Communist club," Shirley said.

"What, Evie? You don't believe in love and romance?" said Bernard.

"The girls at school make me sick with their swooning and childish fantasies," Evie said. She kicked a pile of leaves into the air. "I've read Karl Marx. A wife is property. When a woman marries she's sold into slavery."

"Evie, relax," said Bernard.

"I don't want to relax," she said.

I continued my affair with Shirley, but when I was done with class in the afternoons, I entered the house with only Evie on my mind. My body thrummed but I kept the volume low so I could hear Evie's voice in the kitchen or on the second floor by the radio or the third floor where, due to unbelievable luck or possibly divine intervention, both Evie and I had our sleeping quarters. If I didn't hear her when I came in, I went straight up to my room, stretched out on my bed, and waited for the door to open, the house filling with Evie's warmth and laughter, her step on the stairs. Sometimes she'd knock and come into my room with a question about homework. Was Walt Whitman a transcendentalist? Could I help her locate Singapore on the map?"

"Singapore? You bet." I leapt to her side.

"Thanks," she said, holding open an atlas, offering the world.

My cheek grazed the top of her head and I inhaled her perfumed hair and tried to peer down her blouse, but she had it buttoned to a triangle of porcelain skin. Still I throbbed. I pointed to the Malay Peninsula. "I had a lady teacher who also didn't know where Singapore was," I said.

"You must think women are really dumb." She clapped the atlas shut.

I withdrew a finger. "Au contraire," I said, cradling my wounded hand. "I adore women. I worship them."

"We don't want to be worshipped."

"No? What do you want?"

She tilted her head and her eyelids fluttered. I imagined her looking inward. Seconds passed. "I want to be known," she said. "And understood."

I let seconds pass on my side. "Don't we all," I said.

At first I didn't give great importance to what was happening. It was a game, a fantasy. The usual lust for a young girl. But then I started to notice when Evie wasn't home I was truly miserable, and when she was there I was happy. I continued my affair with her older sister, uncertain of whether I was a louse for doing so, or a prince for sparing Shirley's feelings.

It was easy enough to find ways of being with Evie that would not arouse Shirley's suspicion. I had only to suggest a number of activities in earshot of both girls to have the right girl volunteer, since Shirley was a killjoy and Evie was up for almost anything—walking for hours in the cold, running races, friendly wagers, silly songs. She told jokes in Yiddish and that colorful language coming out of her angelic mouth had me in stitches.

"You boost my spirits," I said.

"They need boosting?" said Evie.

"Of course. I'm a stranger in your house. An outsider."

"*Der zaytiker*. I hadn't thought of it that way," she said.

"Of course not. You're not a snob."

"Well, gee. Who am I to act superior? We take in boarders to make ends meet."

"Who are you? You, my dear, are the daughter of a property owner."

"Clyde, you should join the Party. You're one of us and you know it."

"I am. But I don't want to be told what to do or what to think," I said. Although, I thought, at that particular moment standing on the corner of North Avenue and Monroe Street in the frosty night watching the red bloom on her cheeks and the tip of her nose, she could have persuaded me to cut off my right arm.

The next night when I came back into my room after brushing my teeth and taking a piss, she was sitting on my bed. She put a finger to her lips, got up and closed the door, then leaned against it and pulled me to her. I kissed her but she had her lips pursed, teeth clenched. I laughed. "You kiss like a little girl."

Her eyes flashed. "Then teach me to kiss like a woman," she said.

Reader, I did. And then skillfully unbuttoned her blouse and kissed her innocent breasts.

She was too young, and Shirley's feelings had to be considered, of course. But it was the brother, Nat, savior of the family, who was starting to get suspicious, so I tried to make friends. I lent him a book of short stories by Chekhov that I thought he'd appreciate as a fellow physician, and I invited him to the opening of *Casablanca* at the Hippodrome along with Shirley, Evie, Evie's friend Shana, and my friend Chick Scheiner. The movie was so romantic and couldn't have been more current. Roosevelt and Churchill were meeting in Casablanca the very same moment we were taking our seats in the theater. I had Evie on my left and Shirley on my right. Near the end of the picture when Laszlo says to Rick, "Welcome back to the fight, this time I know our side will win," and the camera lingers on Ingrid Bergman's face, I looked down at Evie and saw tears glittering on her cheeks. I wanted to pull her close and kiss the tears away, but I couldn't, and I thought how being forced to hide our feelings from the others created a powerful kinship between us and the tortured lovers on the screen. I was moved by their sacrifice, and as I furtively held Evie's hand in the darkened theater, it became clear that we were doomed. Evie was a child. I had to go away.

The radio course ended, I got my certificate, and I enlisted. After all my trouble, I wasn't chosen for the Signal Corps. They put me with the Engineers.

Somewhere In England
3 April 1943

Dear Evie,

After several anxious weeks waiting to ship out to an unknown destination—in the army it's always SNAFU, that is, Situation Normal All Fucked Up—and then two really trying weeks on a troop ship zigzagging across the Atlantic, we arrived safely. It's really hitting me hard. I won't see you again until the war is over. I believe in love now, because now I know for certain that I love you, and you love me, and to hell with the age difference, or whatever it is your small-minded family objects to about me.

I can't tell you where we are—practically every-thing we do is a military secret. The other night I walked into the nearby town, and you can plainly see how low the standard of living is here. It's an Army rule never to accept food when invited to a home, you may use up their entire week's allowance.

A very rickety portable Victrola in the "Y" hut grinds out "As Time Goes By" on a well-worn record for me several times a day. I think of you constantly. Well, so long, darling. Regards to the family, and tell Shana to write.

All my love,
Clyde

CHAPTER 13

Susan and my mother didn't want me encroaching on Brenda's territory, so I asked my stepmother deferentially, did she mind if I called their doctor to discuss my father's condition? "Knock yourself out," Brenda said. Cromwell answered the phone himself, as if he expected my call. "Your dad asked me to put him in the hospital," he said. "I told him that was ridiculous. I said I'd come over and hold his hand if he wanted." Cromwell laughed and my body went cold with dread. He was the first of many doctors who would make me feel like Mia Farrow in *Rosemary's Baby*: completely alone, everyone you ever trusted conspiring against you. Cromwell used to get a kick out of my father's shtick over the years. But the headache was not an act. The doctor should have known the difference. I said my father had been called a lot of names before but never a hypochondriac. The doctor chuckled. "Look, honey, we've done every test. Ask Brenda. I sent him to a neurologist. An ENT specialist. He even had that little surgery for the deviated septum."

I was naïve. I thought sickness didn't have anything to do with me. Now all of a sudden, there was nothing else. "Listen, Cromwell," I said, stepping up my game. "My father is no faker. We're getting a second opinion." Maybe I didn't call him Cromwell. But I did say we'd get a second opinion, the only threat I could think of. I was screwed. I hadn't expected to get involved, not like this. I was there to do dishes, nothing more. It was Wednesday. My return flight was booked for the following Tuesday. I'd try to make it. First I'd call my mother's friend Shana Bloom—her son Mike was a doctor. My mother's brother, Uncle Nat, was a respected physician, but I wasn't about to call him. The pompous ass hated my father. They hadn't spoken in years. So I'd call Mike

Bloom, and take his referral, and the new neurologist would find out what was wrong, and very quickly my father would have surgery to correct the problem, or drugs to cure it. I'd make sure Brenda was on board with the treatment, and I'd go back to my life.

"Do what you want," said Cromwell. "But the fact is, Clyde just needs to be a big boy."

I hung up the wall phone in the kitchen next to the tacked-up shopping list. The sun was winking through the trees on the backyard hill. Shadows fell across the sink and striped the metal cabinets. I wanted to sit at the table, the old one with the red Formica surface and black-iron legs, and have my mother serve me a grilled cheese sandwich and a glass of chocolate milk. I wanted to be from a family where the parents were still married to each other and the mother took care of dire situations like this one.

"He wants to wear that dreadful hat," Brenda said, on the morning of the second opinion. "Don't let him." She had her coat on. She was off to work. My father liked wearing his green beanie all the time now, he even slept in it. The knit hat made him feel better. "It's hideous," Brenda said. She reached over and plucked it off his head. He whimpered like a dog. I watched her put the hat on the shelf in the closet. "I gave him his pain pills but he won't swallow them," she said. "You deal with it. Have fun with your new doctor."

We listened to her car warming up in the driveway and then the Mazda's engine getting fainter as she rounded the corner. "Do you want your hat back?" I said. My father nodded and I brought it to him. "What was that about?"

"She thinks I look like a dirty hippie." He shrugged. "What's the name of this guy again?"

"Dr. Heidenheimer. Hard name to forget."

"Don't be a wise guy," he said. "I have to wear the sweater I got at Bloomie's."

I knew why he wanted that one. I went through his dresser drawers, scraping them open and clapping them shut until I found the sweater he'd bought shopping with Darleen. He was always telling me what a great sense of style Darleen had. My mother and Susan couldn't stand Darleen because my father praised her so much. She was his own Eliza Doolittle; she used to say "don't" for "doesn't" when she first took his class, so now he went wild about her accomplishments—her "gourmet" pot roast, the great birthday presents she gave him. I liked Darleen, though. She got me.

"What time are we supposed to be there?" he said.

"Ten." I left the room while he put on his clothes. Out the picture window slanted needles of rain hit the driveway and the dead lawn. What was wrong with Brenda? His hat made him feel better. Didn't she care that he was in pain? Did she honestly believe he was faking at this point? I went to the stereo cabinet and picked up the photo album she kept on top and sat in the recliner leafing through the pages. Who was Brenda McLean really? She once told me with pride that a professional photographer had taken these pictures when she was seventeen, about to graduate from high school. In most of the photos, she's posed against a broad tree trunk, her strawberry blonde hair in a side ponytail curling down the front of an orange shift. She was slender as a teenager, thin-armed, and her eyes told the camera there had been boys. Boys who no doubt felt the cold center where there should have been heat.

Hoffman jumped up, put his paws on my thighs, and sent the album sliding off my lap onto the carpet. I put my arms around his neck and buried my face in his fur. I was feeling sorry for myself. The rain had turned to sleet. My father would criticize my driving on the icy roads, where I parked, how I held his arm.

"Joanna! Come back. Put on my socks," he called. "Please." I got up reluctantly and Hoffman hopped down. I scooped up

Brenda's album and put it back on top of the stereo. In my father's room, I kneeled at his feet and shimmied a nylon sock over his thick, crumbly toenails.

"Why won't you swallow your pills?" I said.

"Can't."

I helped him walk to the dining room and I sat across the table from him with a pen and note pad to make a list of questions. He handed over a bundled washcloth. "Put this in your pocketbook," he said. I uncurled a terrycloth corner and took a peek—false teeth, uppers and lowers. Choppers. "Hurts," he said, so he'd taken them out. He was lucky—the bushy mustache covered the sunken part of his mouth. You couldn't even tell. I watched him while he gathered his thoughts and I drew his picture on the note pad, a wide cartoon head, squinty eyes, a broad thin line for a smile, short verticals for the mustache, a lion's mane of curly-cues for hair.

"Don't forget the leaf theory," he said. "Tell this Heidenheimer what I told you. I woke up with the headache back in October when I was raking leaves. You know how I grind them up with the lawn mower for my compost heap? Maybe I inhaled something."

"Can't you tell him yourself?"

"Write it down, goddamnit. If they hadn't banned leaf burning this never would have happened."

"Remember those bonfires we made?" I said.

"Write it down," he said. "Maybe I inhaled a small particle of leaf up my nose into my sinus and that's what this whole nightmare's about."

"Leaves! Leaves!" he used to yell to us, his call to action in the autumn. The stately pin oaks that saved our neighborhood from suburban blandness left a deep blanket of colorful leaves. "Who's gonna help me rake these leaves?" Susan never wanted to. "Mom's doing my hair in a pageboy," she'd say. She always had a reason.

"Where's the other one? Get out here, Joanna! Help me rake these leaves. C'mon. What's the matter with you? Step lively." It was a raw day near the end of October. Halloween was always cold, always a coat over my costume. My hands were chapped and the tip of my nose and my cheeks were red. I remembered he asked if I wanted to start a vegetable garden in the spring. "You and me," he said. "Lotsa work, though. Digging, sowing, weeding. You up for it, kid?"

"A time to reap, a time to sow," I said.

"You're quoting the Bible." He handed me a rake.

"I'm quoting the Byrds." I was twelve.

"Oh yeah, smartie. Where do you think the Byrds got it?"

His sarcasm stung, although it turned out we were both wrong. The Byrds got it from Pete Seeger (who got it from the Bible). My father was so afraid of being left behind, he could never let me get ahead of him in any way. He had to be up on whatever was young and new and next. We gathered the leaves we raked into our arms and heaped them onto a fallow flowerbed and set fire to the heap and threw in potatoes wrapped in foil. He called them mickeys, unbothered by the slur. We went up the hill and raked more leaves while the potatoes roasted. The fire snapped and crackled and the burning smell was intoxicating, but its heat didn't reach us. It was the physical exertion that eventually warmed me. The harder I worked, the better I felt. I stopped thinking about how I wished I were smarter, quicker, more like him. I let my body fill with a quieter feeling, a feeling of strength and peace. We paused, each resting on a rake. It seemed as if we could see the whole world from our backyard. From the top of the gentle slope behind the house and over the rooftops to the houses rising on the hill across the creek. The pin oaks ringed the horizon, their bare branches like etchings against the autumn sky. "Do you really not believe in God?" I said. The potatoes were ready, and we left our rakes on the ground and went down to the fire. I grabbed the weeder pole leaning against the fence and stabbed a mickey with the weeder's forked metal tip lifting the potato out of the fire. I broke open the charred jacket with a stick and steam billowed out. It was too hot to eat.

"I know you say you don't believe in God, but then what do you believe in?"

"What are you talking about, kid?"

"What's the meaning of life, I guess that's what I'm talking about." I wiped my nose on the sleeve of my pea coat.

"There is no meaning," my father said. He grabbed the weeder pole.

"OK, then what do people live for?" I had broken the spell of peace and strength. I knew it, but I couldn't stop myself.

"I'm an existentialist," he said, without looking at me. He kept poking at the fire with the pole. "We pretend there's meaning. You know you're gonna die someday, right?" He turned and glanced at me for a second. "But you don't dwell on it." My potato had cooled off so I bit into it. "Gimme some of yours," he said. He came closer, and we touched shoulders. "You pretend it isn't all going to shit, so while you're alive, you do the right thing."

I wondered why I had heard people say that existentialism was cynical and hopeless. It seemed almost childishly optimistic the way he explained it. I didn't know how to ask about the discrepancy though.

"OK. You're an existentialist," I said. "So how come you send us to Baltimore Hebrew for Sunday school?"

"Because I can do it for free. That's the only reason I teach Jewish literature there. The free tuition for you kids."

"That doesn't make any sense," I said.

"Look kid, you're Jewish. I'm not finishing the job for Hitler."

We discarded the tinfoil remains, then went up the hill again and heaped more leaves into a trashcan. He paused for a second on one knee and caught his breath. Then he lit a cigarette and smoke came out of his nose like tusks. "You know, we used to roast mickeys all the time at the Home," he said. The feeling of peace returned. We worked silently. He held the cigarette tightly between his lips and we stuffed armloads of leaves into the trashcan, then carried the can down to the fire, each holding a handle, and set it down.

"You really don't believe in God," I said. "Not at all?"

"Stop bothering me," he said. He grabbed the weeder pole and stirred the ashes. "Go help your mother. Leave me alone."

Sleet turned back to rain pounding the backyard, the somber sky graying the morning light. I turned on the lamp in the dining room. "Did you mention the leaf theory to Dr. Cromwell?" I said.

"Yeah, yeah I told him." The leaf theory roused my father so much he put on his glasses. "Tell this Heidenheimer I'm always hungry but I can't eat. I eat two bites and it's like I ate a sack of potatoes."

I wrote *sack of potatoes* under *leaf theory*, imagining a dozen whole potatoes sitting in my own stomach.

"It hurts, Joanna," he said. "I want to shoot myself."

"Let's go, let's get out of here. Let's get you some help." I jumped up, slung my bag over my shoulder, and tucked the list inside next to the vial of Tylenol with codeine, a bottle of ginger ale, and his choppers in a washcloth.

"Wait! Write down *relentless*," he said. "Tell him the pain is more intense when I lie on my back. Joanna. . ."

"What?"

"Tell this doctor . . . how I used to be."

Rain pattered on the gravel roof. How he used to be. What popped into my head was his picture in the *Baltimore Sun*. He'd gotten into a shoving match with the mayor, on behalf of the teacher's union. I glanced over his shoulder now at the Jackson Pollock imitation behind him on the wall. I remembered when he laid the big piece of masonite on the picnic table, and poured the red and yellow and black straight from the can, making his own splatter painting. Aronson '64. How was I to describe him to a stranger? Maybe bare-chested, as I saw him in the orphanage Picture Booke, astride his horse Playboy.

He was disappointed when he got a look at Heidenheimer in the doctor's office. The man was bald and pasty-faced. "What did you expect?" I said. "Albert Einstein? Someone like you?"

"That's right," he said.

"Tell me about your headache, Mr. Aronson." The small man sat behind an enormous mahogany desk and we sat in chairs facing him. His office was spacious with an examining table at the far end.

"She'll tell you."

"I want to hear it from you," said Heidenheimer.

"I have a headache," said my father. "Bad, doctor. Get out the list, Joanna."

"How long has your voice been hoarse?" the doctor asked.

"It's always been this way," I said. "His brothers, too." I told Heidenheimer about the leaf theory and how my father had difficulty swallowing anything except very slippery food.

"A sack of potatoes, is that right?" Heidenheimer said.

He led my father to the examining table and left him with his legs dangling. I started for the door. I didn't want to see him undressed, if that was going to happen. I had done enough, the socks, the teeth. He grabbed my arm and pulled me back. "Stay here." Like a magician, Heidenheimer produced a feather from his pocket. He brushed it against my father's cheeks and chin. "Can you feel that? That? That?"

"Yes, no, yes."

"Why aren't your dentures in place?" the doctor said.

"Hurts."

"There's some numbness on the right side," said Heidenheimer. He put the feather in his pocket, held his forefinger up and moved it back and forth slowly. He asked my father to follow with his eyes. I watched with alarm. My father's left eye moved in the direction of Heidenheimer's finger, but the right eye lagged behind. His right eye barely moved at all. The doctor seemed unconcerned.

"Take off your socks," Heidenheimer ordered.

My father summoned me, and I peeled away the nylon. Flakes of dry skin fluttered around his ankles like confetti.

"What's wrong with your feet?" Finally, the doctor was alarmed.

"I'm not here about my feet," my father said.

"You need those nails taken care of. Have your daughter take you to a podiatrist."

"Doctor, I'm in pain! Help me!" my father said.

Dr. Heidenheimer tickled his feet with the feather. My father kicked. He felt that. I put on his socks and shoes.

Back in our chairs, Heideheimer paged through a book. "I don't want you to think I'm belittling your pain, Mr. Aronson. But I believe you may have cluster headaches. See this picture?" He held the book open to a drawing of a man with sweat pouring from his brow and tears streaming down his face. "This man has cluster headaches and he is obviously suffering. I just want you to know, I appreciate how much pain you're in."

I wasn't sure how my father's slow eye fit into the cluster headaches theory, but I liked cluster headaches too much to question it. Cluster headaches was even better than the leaf theory. My father was not faking. He had a very bad headache. But that was all. He'd get well. Earlier, though, making the list, sitting at the table listening to the rain, I had decided no matter what Heidenheimer said, we weren't leaving his office with a prescription on a lousy square of paper. We weren't leaving until my father was put in the hospital.

"I think he has cluster headaches," Heidenheimer said. "But I agree. Let's get him over to Admissions."

By the time Brenda got to Sinai Hospital with his overnight bag, he was sitting up in bed in Room 605 with a loopy grin on his face. The shot of Demerol he'd gotten seconds ago was already working! I wanted to shout with joy. This was the first time since I'd arrived four days ago, except for the moments when my mother reminisced about the war and the FBI, that I'd seen him happy. I felt like I'd been shot in the ass with Demerol myself. I laughed at nothing. I wanted to hug everyone. He clutched the TV remote and flipped past *Wheel of Fortune*, and then President Reagan denying he knew about the Iran-Contra deal, and settled on the music channel.

"In case you're interested, Dr. Cromwell doesn't have privileges at Sinai," Brenda said, smiling thinly. At the time, I didn't understand how important this was, or how troubling for her.

"If we listened to Cromwell," I said, "my father wouldn't be in any hospital."

"What's so great about being in the hospital?" Brenda said.

"Look at him," I said. He was merrily conducting the Muzak version of "Penny Lane."

"He's drugged up like a junkie," said Brenda. "Big deal."

My father dropped his arms into his lap. "I told you she said terrible things."

Apparently, my plan wasn't working. Brenda wasn't getting on board. She was neither curious about what was wrong with him, nor happy to see him feeling better. I had actually thought I would be on a plane on Tuesday, heading west. Who was I kidding? I'd have to cancel my flight. I'd have to stay and see this thing through. I'd have to quit my job.

"Pfft. Here. I brought your pajamas," Brenda said, "I'm going home." She kissed my father and left.

CHAPTER 14

He stayed in Sinai for ten days. No matter how early I got there, he was watching the clock.

"Where were you?"

"What are you talking about? It's nine in the morning," I said.

"They came and took me down, and you weren't here."

"Who came?"

"They came and took me downstairs for a bone scan and a CAT scan," he said. "It was awful."

"A scan doesn't hurt—does it?"

"It was fucking unbelievable! They had me down there for two hours and no one was there to give me my shot when I needed it and I had to lie on this table, and you know, Joanna, how much it hurts me to lie down completely flat. They gave me a bone scan. That wasn't a problem. But then they wheel me into another room for the CAT scan, and you're not gonna believe this, but I'm lying on a table and they're running this gigantic million-dollar machine and this guy, some kid with pimples, he says, 'We ran out of paper.' Fucking unbelievable! Million-dollar machine and it breaks down like the Xerox at the library. Some kind of printout comes out and they ran out of paper so I have to lie there for hours. They're talking like I'm not there. I say, 'You ran out of paper? What do you need paper for?' And they're ignoring me. I'm the one on the table. I'm the one this is about." He shook his head in frustration. I put the milkshake I brought on the windowsill along with my bag and coat and pulled the blue chair up to the bed. He watched as I moved around the room and I noticed his right eye had gotten even more sluggish, lagging considerably behind his left eye. I handed over the milkshake, a real one, not the thick McDonald's kind, but the kind that was easy to drink, made with real ice cream and milk. He sucked on the straw for a second and passed it back with a frown. He couldn't even swallow a milkshake. I lit a cigarette and he took a drag. Implausibly, he got away with smoking in the hospital. In those days, it was easier. Everyone smelled of smoke, if not firsthand, then secondhand. The food service lady rolled in her cart with Salisbury steak. I grabbed the cigarette and hid it behind my back. "He can't eat that," I said. "Doesn't he get a liquid lunch?"

"I don't see anything on his chart," she said. "Why can't he eat?"

"Nobody knows."

Eventually someone went out and bought paper for the Xerox and he had the CAT scan and we waited for the radiologists to give us results. If this wasn't a case of cluster headaches—if this was a tumor growing in his head—why didn't I witness the slightest sense of urgency from the medical staff? Meanwhile, no matter how many times I told the nurses, the food service people, or any doctor who momentarily stuck his head in the door, that my father couldn't eat, they kept bringing him roast chicken and hamburgers.

Brenda came to the hospital almost every night after work, but never stayed long—she had to go home to feed the dog. Shep came, and Susan, of course, and Uncle Harry flew in twice during those ten days at Sinai. Darleen showed up a few times, and Liz Stone came mainly to see me. I complained my mother didn't visit often enough. "I'm here now," she said. "What do you want from me?" He sat up, squared his shoulders. "Evie!" he called out happily, Demerol fresh in his veins.

"How's the patient?" my mother said, laughing. His illness was funny. It was ridiculous. It wasn't Clyde. Everyone had reasons for not taking the illness seriously. I pulled my mother aside and told her she better keep after the doctors because clearly, Brenda wasn't going to. "Not me," my mother said.

"I'm not his wife anymore, and I won't be holding a vigil at his bedside."

20 April 1944
Somewhere in England

Dearest darling sweetheart,

I knew the army would solve our dilemma one way or another. It is a strange thing, but by going away I really found you. Keep writing your soulful letters, darling Evie. Some day soon we'll be together again if what's in the works (that I can't talk about) goes well. Wait for me just a little longer, while the whole world waits out this nightmare until the dawn. We soldiers wait as well, not knowing where we'll be sent or when, but wherever it is, it'll make little difference. One adapts a "don't give a goddamn" attitude because it does you little good to worry about anything. Practically everything that happens to a soldier is dependent on forces outside of oneself. Meanwhile, one just "sweats it out," as the army saying goes.

They say man's only way to achieve immortality is through his children. I should have liked to have a child with you. Some day, I hope. And it will be a son. Then I shall hold you in my arms and close my eyes, and think back to this time when I sat in my tent on the cold English moor and spoke to you across the ocean, sharing with you all the things I have in my heart.

Forever,
Clyde

The pace at Sinai was slow, Dr. Heidenheimer said, because it was almost Christmas and the hospital was short on staff. He had stopped by to tell us the bone scan was negative, which was good news, but not a surprise. He ordered the test because back in 1983 my father had prostate cancer (successfully treated, or even cured, with radiation). The negative bone scan confirmed the pain in his head wasn't prostate cancer recurring and spreading, because prostate cancer would show up in his bones first, before traveling anywhere else. That was what prostate cancer did. Besides, no one had heard of prostate cancer ever spreading to the sinus, which was where, as it turned out, the radiologists found a shadow on the CAT scan. Heidenheimer mentioned this casually, as an aside. He seemed fearful of upsetting my father. "It's just a shadow, Mr. Aronson. We don't know what it is yet."

I walked the doctor out into the wide white hallway. "It could be cancer," Heidenheimer said. "There's a possibility it's cancer. We don't know. It could be tuberculosis. A liquid cyst of some kind."

"Tuberculosis. Really? That'd be good," I said. "You can survive TB, right?"

"Yes."

"It's not cluster headaches, though."

"No."

Still, there was hope. TB.

He'd need Magnetic Resonance Imaging next to get a three-dimensional picture. "You should call for the MRI appointment right away," Heidenheimer said. "Try Copeland on Reisterstown Road."

"You want me to call? Isn't that something the hospital does?"

"No. You better do it today. They're usually booked up, especially this time of year." Sinai didn't own an MRI machine. Patients were sent to an outside facility. I figured they must take in-patients to the outside facility in an ambulance.

"No," said Heidenheimer. "Somebody has to drive him there . . . in a car." He glanced down the empty hallway. "You, I would imagine," he said.

The appointment was set for the following week. Meanwhile, my aunt and uncles were coming to visit. Just before they were due to arrive, Brenda hid my father's hat again. His head felt cold on the inside, he said. There was metal jangling in his skull. The green beanie was the only remedy. He pulled it down over his ears. Brenda could not stand the dirty homeless hippie look. That his head was cold on the inside and metal clanged in his ears she could stand. I went down the hall and recruited his favorite nurse Debbie to intervene. Debbie came and held out a hand. Brenda opened her purse grudgingly and gave the hat back. He put it on just in time. His brothers and sister busted onto the sixth floor ignoring the level of quiet in the hall. We could hear Uncle Harry and Uncle Alvin roaring out room numbers as they searched for 605, while Aunt Vivian explained hospital etiquette in her New York squawk to her ignorant brothers. And then Uncle Alvin's wife Aunt Gladys was yelling, "Where you running? Wait for me!" in a Queens accent so thick it sounded like a parody. They swarmed around my father's bed. He winced. I thought it was less about the headache than the humiliation. He was their big brother, "the professor," they called him. But the professor was weak, and not how he used to be.

"Clyde," said Uncle Harry. "Brudder."

My father smiled. "Brudder," he said.

"Guess who I talked to on the phone today?" Uncle Harry said. He was wearing a driving cap and a gray tweed overcoat that smelled of wind and cold. "Manny Bergman."

"No shit," my father said.

"You remember Bergman, don't you Brudder?"

"His feet, I remember, more than the rest of him," my father said. "Sticking out from under a car."

Uncle Harry laughed. "Manny taught me how to rebuild an engine." Harry turned to the rest of us. "We had all kinds of mentors at the H. Older guys, teachers. There was always an older brother around to teach you something."

"Day and night," my father said.

Debbie came in and asked us to go out for a few minutes while she changed the sheets, which she knew how to do without my father even getting up, so we left him and walked to the end of the corridor where a window overlooked Pimlico Racetrack. We could see everything from the sixth floor—the infield, the muddy track, the grandstand, and the clubhouse. Tears were rolling down Uncle Harry's cheeks.

"You know what Clyde said to me?" he asked.

"What?" I said.

"Be a man."

Uncle Alvin was staring out at the track. He looked up. "What's that, Harry?"

"Not now. Clyde didn't say it in the room," said Uncle Harry. "Back then he said it. The day Mama left us at the Home. 'Be a man,' Clyde says. I was five years old." Uncle Harry took a handkerchief out of his pocket and blew his nose.

"We just need to get him something to eat," said Uncle Alvin. "You see how thin he is?"

Uncle Harry looked at me accusingly. "Did you give him those Pecan Sandies I sent?"

"Yeah, I gave him the Pecan Sandies." My father could just as soon eat a box of nails, but I didn't say so. I was careful with my aunt and uncles. Any one of them could go off at any time. Harry was so easily slighted, and while Alvin was fun and upbeat, that lasted only until you needed something from him. I liked Aunt Vivian—I liked all three of them some of the time—but Aunt Vivian made up stuff for no apparent reason and couldn't be trusted. And yet, she was often brutally honest, telling the truth when no one else would. She was a nurse in the army during World War II, and then a civilian nurse until she began writing prescriptions for herself and lost her license. The four of us were silent for a few moments watching a woman carrying a balloon bouquet into another patient's room, the balloons going bap, bap hitting against each other.

"My big brother, Clyde," said Harry. "He was always looking out for me at the Home. But guess what? Clyde was scared to death, too. He was so scared he shat his pants."

"Wait a minute," I said. "My father told us you were the one who shat your pants."

"No," said Uncle Harry. "Not me. Him."

"They probably both shat their pants," said Aunt Vivian.

CHAPTER 15

Tuckahoe

"Company E! Up! Upstairs! Bedtime! Upstairs! Companies E, D & C!" Hordes stampeded the grand central staircase, the kitchen stairs, the back library stairs. They poured through all doors into the dormitories in the east and west wings on the third floor. Line up in your underwear, wait your turn behind thirty strange kids, pee, wash hands and face, brush teeth, stand at attention by your footboard, watch for the Colonel's signal, slice of the cane, put on pajamas, everyone all at once. Slice of the cane, climb into bed.

One night as we all stood at attention, this kid Irving Weiss came sauntering in humming to himself, lost in thought. Shorty blew his whistle, then yelled at the top of his lungs: "Wrecking crew! Wrecking crew!"

The kid looked up and the guys swarmed. "Get him! Get Irving!" They came from all sides, tall and short, bruisers and weaklings, piling on, a tangle of legs and windmilling arms. Isn't somebody going to help him? I thought. Whoever's in charge? I stood by my bed and scanned the room for Beiderman, Miss Beaufort, somebody, anybody. Then I saw Colonel Anderson by the door observing. After a while the Colonel gave the nod to Shorty. "OK, all off," Shorty said. Irving's pants were missing. He sat dazed on the floor in his skivvies. Lights out until morning.

Up! Up! March! March!

I kept moving toward every other Sunday, holding the pure inviolable image of my mother in my heart. I would pass through each day of the week and then pass through them again, and she would come to me, and this time she would take me home.

After school I waited and waited on the baseball field, but no one picked me for his team. No one even knew me, what position I was good at, or that I was clever, and yet I felt like everyone was looking at me. Shame spread up my neck like a rash. I had to get away, so I ran off the field and kept going, my long legs taking me far. I ran up the road past the auto shed. I ran past the chicken coops and the potato fields. I ran until my chest hurt and my lungs were about to explode and I had to stop. When I caught my breath, I entered the cool dark of the barn.

Inside the quiet cathedral, I calmed down. I liked the smell of horseshit and hay, the animal sweat. I touched one of the worn leather harnesses and tried to figure out the purpose for each of the iron tools hanging on the rough wall. I felt better in the barn. A dray horse nickered and tossed his mane. It was Playboy. I went to his stall halfway down the muddy alley. His nostrils were huge up close. I reached up and stroked his silky hide. He was warm. I dragged my fingers through his mane. Playboy looked at me with one eye and I looked back. I felt like he knew me. I could have curled up on the straw next to the gentle animal and drifted off to sleep. I stroked his neck instead and held onto the peaceful feeling until a twig snapped down the alley and Playboy stomped his hoof. A high-pitched laugh ricocheted off the rafters and I froze. Shorty Lapidus. I knew it. Then a smaller boy's squeaky voice: "A dime! You promised!" I ducked into the empty stall next to Playboy's and hid behind a bale of hay. "A nickel. That's it," said Shorty. "I'm not doin' it," said the small voice. "You're doin' it, alright." A thud. The clank of a belt buckle. "Ow!" Grunting and crying. I covered my ears but the sound came through my fingers. "Shut up." A strange feeling in my dick. "Almost," said Shorty in a strangled voice. Thrashing, clanking, a slapping sound. A flash of bare ass. Drawn-out groans, and then silence. "Pull your pants up, homo. Pansy! Fairy. Faggot," Shorty said.

"Gimme my nickel," the squeaky voice said.

"When I'm good and ready."

"You swore!"

"You rat me out," said Shorty, "you know where I'm gonna stick your frickin' nickel?"

They walked out of the barn like it was nothing. I was trembling and my face burned with shame once again. Why? I hadn't done anything. It wasn't me. I didn't want to be seen, not by them or near them. I counted to sixty. One-twenty. One-eighty. Two-forty. Three hundred and I slipped out like a burglar, ducked behind a stand of trees, made a looping detour through the chicken coops, and finally, because I had nowhere else to go, I trudged up the steps of the big brick building smack into a fat white stomach in a stiff shirt.

"Son, why aren't you upstairs?" Without the megaphone, Piggy Rosenthal's voice was kind and gentle. I told him I was new and I'd gotten lost. I didn't mention the barn. He said he'd heard I was new and he patted my hair and asked if I understood what happened to boys who were tardy. No, I said, I didn't know what happened. He nodded in sympathy and then slapped me across the face. I was so shocked, I didn't cry. "Next time I'll do it with my fist," he said.

Upstairs, Shorty was already in the center aisle of Company E blowing on his whistle. Had he seen me at all? I was no snitch. I wouldn't rat out the creep. I stood in line and took a pee and washed up and brushed my teeth. Then I walked the plank floor back to my bed.

"Wrecking crew! Wrecking crew!" Not again. Get him! Who? Aronson! Get Clyde Aronson! *Do you know what happens to boys who are tardy?* Had Shorty seen see me in the barn? *You know where I'm gonna stick your frickin nickel?* "Wrecking crew!" Don't break my glasses. Not my glasses! I threw up an elbow and blocked my face.

Harry ran toward me yelling, "Brudder! Brudder!"

"Stay back, Harry," I warned.

I woke up smelling my mother's cold cream. Nurse Flanagan leaning in with an ice pack. Soft bosom in white cotton.

"The 'H' ain't so terrible," Jesse Hoffman said.

"Where am I? Why are *you* here?" I said.

"Who do you think hauled you in?"

I smiled. Jesse handed over my wire-rimmed spectacles. They'd survived in one piece.

"Look, I made it through this shithole so far," Hoffman said. "You will too. I'm leaving, though."

"You're leaving?" I immediately regretted the plaintive tone in my voice.

"It's my birthday next month," Jesse said.

"So?" I said angrily. I felt the loss too keenly.

"Tell him, Flanny. See, all boys turning nine in 1924 leave Company E and move up to Company D on the first day of 1925."

"That's right," said Nurse Flanagan. "That's how it works."

So Jesse was only going to the other wing, moving to another dormitory and not really leaving at all, just as I must have known I wasn't leaving anytime soon. I bit the corners of my mouth to try to keep from smiling too much. A million beatings were nothing compared to the possibility of friendship.

CHAPTER 16

The four of us huddled at the end of the hospital corridor staring out the window at the cars glinting in the parking lot and then beyond to the racetrack and grandstand, waiting for Nurse Debbie to finish changing the sheets. "You're probably right," I said. "They probably both shat their pants."

"Of course I'm right," said Aunt Vivian. "My mother used to tell me things."

"Like what?" I said.

"What some of those boys did to each other."

"Never mind that," said Uncle Harry. "My sister doesn't know what she's talking about."

Uncle Alvin continued to stare out the window. "I hate hospitals," he said. "Let's get out of here."

"Yeah, I'm hungry," said Aunt Gladys.

Aunt Vivian looked down at the purse hanging from the crook of her arm and gaping open. She snapped it shut. "You know, I hate to tell you this," she said.

"What? What is it you hate to tell us?" said Uncle Alvin, scorn raking his voice.

"I hate to tell you," Aunt Vivian said, "but Clyde looks like a man who's dying of cancer."

Uncle Harry reached out and steadied himself against the wall. I felt like I'd been hit with a plank and clutched my stomach. *No, no, it's TB!* But I knew my aunt, like most pathological liars, was brutally honest. Uncle Harry's face reddened with rage. "You don't know!" he said. "All these fancy doctors can't figure out what he's got! But my sister, Vivian, she knows."

"I was a nurse for twenty years," Aunt Vivian said. "I know what a cancer patient looks like."

"C'mon. Let's go eat," said Uncle Alvin.

They invited me to dinner. "You go," I said. "I'm fine here." I watched them walk out through the lobby doors, shoulders hunched in their winter coats. It was dark already. A blast of cold air and then the doors sealed shut. I thought when the time came, I would find Ye Olde Picture Booke and give it to Uncle Harry. I went back upstairs.

"I'm glad they're gone," my father said. "Too much. You know what I mean?"

"I'll go too if you want—you can sleep."

"You? You're a saint. You stay."

"I'm not a saint," I said.

"Yes," he said. "You are."

I made the blue chair recline and I stretched out and we both closed our eyes. I was thinking about the mentors Uncle Harry said they had at the Home. My father was always saying he didn't believe in coddling. He didn't have a father to help him, so why should he help me? But the truth was, as Harry described it, my father had lots of help. Day and night, my father admitted. Teachers, big brothers. He felt like he was alone, though. He thought his shitty father was what he needed, and no one else would do.

In high school, I made friends with a girl named Eloise Sandler, who asked my father for help with an English paper. I was surprised he agreed so eagerly since he wasn't available to me. If I didn't grasp a concept or had difficulty with a book I was dismissed with such dispatch. "You're a phony," he'd say, meaning not as serious a student as I pretended to be. Would I have been more serious if he had tutored me in writing or gone over my book reports? If he had shared his own writing? Even sharing his lesson plans for classes at City would have been interesting. He must have been afraid I'd reveal my utter stupidity, or possibly that he would fall short in some way. I could see Eloise and my father at the table across the hall from where I sat waiting in the big gold armchair in the living room. They leaned over Eloise's typewritten pages tête à tête, concentrating on her words. When Eloise finally went home, I asked why he didn't help with my English assignments. You never asked, he said. Now I wondered if it had something to do with Lake George. If the camping trip hadn't happened would we have talked about poetry? Would we have trusted one another? Maybe, but probably not. Boys are smarter. There are no great women chess players. Susan was lucky. She wasn't interested in chess. She wasn't a phony, according to him. She was proud to be a girl.

Now though, he wanted only me and I was elated. I came to the hospital early and stayed until eight or nine at night, as if it were my job. He had visitors, but for hours every day it was just the two of us. I began to think of my other job—the one at the newspaper—as pointless. Certainly not a matter of life or death. When I got to Sinai in the morning he was usually in pain, his face gray, the Demerol worn off, his green hat limp on the pillow. I suffered with him. It didn't seem like a choice.

"My father needs a shot!" I demanded at the nurse's station. "Room 605!"

A woman in a white Nurse Ratched hat, not Debbie, raised her eyebrows and continued shuffling papers behind the high counter. "We'll get to him," she said.

"But you waited too long. He's in pain again."

"Miss, we have other patients besides your father."

I went back to his room.

"Where'd you go just now?" he said. "Where were you?"

"I went to find a nurse to get you a shot."

"You looking out for me, baby?"

"Yeah."

People gave me advice. Take a break, call a friend, go shopping, buy yourself something. No one seemed to understand I was exactly where I wanted to be. I had my father's undivided attention. In the quiet of the white room, he was all mine. I thought of bringing up the camping trip. We might speak about it as adults, wade into the lake water always lapping at the edge of consciousness. But during the long quiet days, I didn't bring up any of that. Not Lake George or Nola Swenson. If only he would go on living, so that I might talk to him when I was ready.

How strange looking back, that he spent so much time in the hospital with no treatment, just waiting for scans. He could have gone home, but he stayed for the Demerol. They let you do that sort of thing then. He slept and I finished *Time and Again*. The descriptions of old New York were beautiful, but the dreamlike pace made me sleepy and I was glad to start *Jane Eyre*. Charlotte Bronte's writing was so matter of fact. Right away, the novel spoke to me, an orphan's tale told by a bold girl. I thought it was unfortunate I hadn't read it in childhood. He woke in pain and I closed the book and again went chasing down nurses for a shot. He slept some more and I was restless, so I took the elevator to the fourth floor and visited the newborns in the maternity ward. I wanted a baby, but I wanted to be something first. I went down to the lobby and called Fred. I felt better talking to him until I heard the clackety clack of his keyboard. We hung up and I went to the cafeteria and ate a vanilla Dixie cup with a wooden spoon. Ice cream was the only hospital food I could stand. No boiled cabbage smell. Cold, frozen.

Most nights I spent at my mother's. She made dinner, or we went out. These interludes in the real world were supposed to renew my spirits, but I had no appetite and only wanted to go to bed so I could wake up in the morning and rush back to my charge. My mother was worried I wasn't eating and dragged me out to a favorite Chinese place.

"Brenda's been harassing him about his will," my mother said as soon as we ordered. "She wants more money."

"When did he say this?" I said.

"The other day when you went out to get cigarettes. He was upset. 'Brenda said terrible things to me. Terrible!' he cries to me."

"He said that to me, too. She calls him a junkie."

"Yeah, not that. This time it sounded more like she threatened him."

"Threatened to do what?"

"He wouldn't say. Maybe she threatened to kill herself again. I don't know. Maybe she threatened to kill *him*. Give him an overdose. Who knows?"

"It's strange," I said. "I mean, how much could a high school teacher have in his will?"

"Not much," my mother said. "The house is the big thing. She's getting that. But she wants more."

"Is there more?"

The waiter brought the won ton soup and the broth was soothing and I got my appetite back. I slurped up a dumpling and bit into the little pouch of ground pork and I felt good for a few minutes.

"There's the credit union account we started in 1953," my mother said. "You know I didn't take my half when I left. I should have, but I didn't, I guess because we never touched that money. I figured it would sit there and he'd keep my name as beneficiary."

"Oh. So you think Brenda's bugging him about that?" I said.

"Yeah. You know, when they were first married and he told us he wanted to leave her the house, I was furious. I don't know if you remember that. We had a fight about it. I said he should leave the house to his children. He got mad and we didn't talk for a while so I wrote him a letter. I told him I didn't want to be unkind. It was just that we spent thirty years together, and bought the house on Cedar Drive new and we had children together and raised them there. I must have made ten thousand meals in that kitchen and cleaned up twenty thousand more, and it was hard for me to see my house go to a stranger."

"Did he write back?"

"He called me at work. He said my letter made him cry. Then he says, what do you think the kids would do with the house? I said, they'd sell it, but so would Brenda."

"He should have taken your advice," I said.

"The thing is, I started to agree with him," my mother said. "Brenda's entitled not to be kicked out of her home. And I'm entitled to the money we saved together."

He was waiting for me in the morning, sitting up in bed with his hat at a jaunty angle. I lowered the safety rail and he grabbed onto my arm with all his weight, which wasn't much at that point, and swung his flannel-covered legs over the side and I put on his slippers and helped him walk to the blue recliner chair. He smelled smoky in a good way, like caramelized sugar. I pulled the small chair close to him and sat down and gave him the milkshake I'd made in the cafeteria by violently mashing the contents of two chocolate Dixie cups in a glass of chocolate milk. But like the milkshakes I got at the deli, he couldn't drink it. He tried. He took a wincing sip and passed it back.

"How has Brenda been treating you?" I said.

"She says terrible things to me," my father said.

"Like what?"

"Terrible things. Never mind what."

I could not get him to talk. Nurse Debbie came in, gave him a shot and tidied up, and while she was there, I felt comforted and supported in a way I wasn't used to. I thought maybe I'd like to live in the hospital too, high on Demerol with Debbie taking care of me. She seemed to sense what I was feeling and lingered in the room, filled the water pitcher, threw away some paper cups. Just as she was about to roll her cart out the door, she stopped and asked if my father and I had always been close. I stammered. "Yes . . . no . . . I'm not sure. Sort of." I felt embarrassed not knowing.

He was certainly around all the time when I was growing up. He was in the kitchen making supper. He was in the tent by the lake. I saw him every day, but like I said, he didn't see me. Now, at Sinai, I basked in the sweet burn of his attention, an intense feeling that I remembered having one other time, in 1969, the summer I turned fourteen. It was after the camping trip and the moment was brief, the length of a car ride from the swimming club to Cedar Drive. It was the end of summer. School was going to start soon. I hadn't said a word to my father in two weeks. He begged me to speak to him. We were at the pool. "Will you ever forgive me?" he said. I ran out the gate in the chain-link fence and down the street. He came looking for me in his car. "I'm sorry," he said. He gave me a striped beach towel. "Will you ever speak to me again?"

I took the towel and wrapped myself in it and sat beside him on the front seat. We drove over the railroad tracks and he cleared his throat and blinked several times behind his glasses.

"It's hard having a father," I said.

"Yeah, I guess it must be," he said.

"I mean, it's hard having you for a father."

"It's funny," he said. "I always knew it was hard *not* having a father. But I never thought about how it might be hard *having* a father." He was staring out the windshield. He wasn't the kind of person who kept looking at you when he was driving. He drove fast but always with his eyes on the road. Only at the red light, then he turned and faced me, and what I saw was that no one else had it as bad as he did. But at least he was looking at me, he was listening to me. I felt the burn in my chest, the ache. There I was. Someone who had a difficult father. The car bumped over the railroad tracks, we passed the billy goat tied to a post out in front of the little train store, we drove down the road, we raked leaves in autumn, he unzipped Nola's sleeping bag, we shoveled snow in winter, planted flowers in spring, didn't speak, picked beans in summer in clover among the bees.

Now we sat knee to knee, the colorless day stretched before us, listening to nothing but the muffled footsteps of nurses coming down the hall and the faint pong of the elevator bell.

CHAPTER 17

The day finally came for the MRI. I thought it was preposterous, having to drag my father out of a warm hospital
bed and into his cold Camaro to drive all the way out Reisterstown Road. But Heidenheimer didn't think me having to
drive him was such a big deal. "Mr. Aronson isn't hooked up
to anything," the doctor said. I was still anxious about taking
him. No one seemed to understand how serious his situation
was. If anything, he should have been choppered in the way
they do it in the movies, greeted by a team of experts ducking
from the wash of the helicopter blades.

My father felt the way I did—it was preposterous. The day
of the appointment, he refused to change out of his pajamas.
He wanted to keep the flannel comfort layer next to his skin,
so he put his jeans on over the red-and-white pajama bottoms
with the peppermint stripes sticking out of his pant legs. Then
the red tartan bathrobe Susan bought him, which hung down
past the hem of his overcoat. Topped off with the green knit
hat. We thought the whole trip was crazy. He wasn't supposed
to leave the hospital until they fixed what was wrong with
him.

It was raining, as it was so often that December. I brought
the car around while he waited in the lobby in a wheelchair.
He knew he looked pathetic, especially in that loony outfit, so
whenever someone in a white coat walked by, he mugged and
called out "Help me! Help me, doctor!"

"I'm sure they didn't think that was funny," I said when my
father recounted this in the car. "I wasn't kidding," he said. I
drove us west on Northern Parkway, a wide road with white
pavement that turned a melancholy cola color in the rain, and
then north on the potholed blacktop of Reisterstown Road.
The radio played to the beat of the windshield wipers. *I am a*

poor boy too pa rum pa pum pum. I turned up the volume a little bit. Both of us were suckers for Christmas songs. We passed the old Ameche's Drive-in, the bowling alley, Sol Levinson & Sons Funeral Home, and the Plaza. Cars hissed by in the opposite direction, tires spraying. Miller's Delicatessen, Amy Joy Donuts, the Howard Johnson's where Susan and I had been waitresses. *People passing, children laughing,* over the beltway, and left into a mini mall in a wooded lot. He stayed in the car while I checked in at Copeland Imaging.

"It's outside," the receptionist said.

"What is?"

"The MRI." She spoke with a thick Baltimore accent. M-R-Ah.

"But it's raining," I said.

She laughed in a good-natured way. "It's in the trailer."

Oh. The thing I saw in the parking lot and thought was a bookmobile.

He struggled getting out of the Camaro's bucket seat, grabbing onto my shoulders. "That's how new the MRI is," he said, as we linked arms and slowly made our way to the trailer, dirty puddle water splattering our legs. "So cutting edge the machine isn't even unpacked. Still in the box."

I was grateful for his positive spin on the crappy situation. It was 1986 and we thought the technology was awesome. I gave him the umbrella to hold and I went up three portable stairs. A technician opened the trailer door a crack. She didn't have to come out from behind her desk to do this. She said to wait in the parking lot. Was everyone nuts? Couldn't she see his pajamas sticking out of his pant legs and mopping up the puddles? She shut the door on me and I backed down the steps. I took the umbrella and held it over us until it was my father's turn to go in. When they were finished with him, we drove back to the hospital and he changed out of his wet clothes and got back into bed.

That was the point at which I started to take what I needed. Not from him, but from the nurses. I pushed through staff-only doors and carried off supplies – extra blankets, gowns, stacks of foil-covered juice cups, a shower chair, a foam egg crate for the bed, towels, washcloths, body lotion. We were stocking up to wait some more, this time for the results. Then it would be the next test, and the next. I lingered in the hall until the nurse's station was unmanned and slipped behind the high counter to search for my father's loose-leaf binder. Every patient got a shiny blue one like a seventh grader. I found his, flipped it open and read the notes. *White disheveled male, 69, headache of unknown etiology.*

CHAPTER 18

Tuckahoe

I was pretty sure David Copperfield, and even Oliver Twist, did not suffer the torture we Homeboys did. They never had to march along the perimeter of the gym in silence behind Al Shack, around and around. My legs ached. Knees high, everybody! But my legs ached! Hour after hour. I would have preferred a beating from the wrecking crew, no bull. Forced marching in endless circles was a far worse discipline than it appeared to the outside world, and therefore regularly employed by the Hebrew National Orphan Home staff. Some evenings, though, for no apparent reason, instead of a forced march we got to roller skate around the same gym. The first time, confused by the abrupt change in policy, I hesitated before the mad dash to grab a pair of skates, but not for long. The speed was exhilarating, the freedom, the chaos and shrieks of joy were only intensified by the capriciousness of the supervisors' decree. Afterward, Chick and Jesse and a few others from Company E went out onto the library steps to cool off, so I followed and Harry followed me. Shorty Lapidus perched on the metal banister. He hung around the younger kids even when he wasn't on monitor duty, unlike the other seniors.

"Got candy on you, shit for brains?" Shorty said. "Sunday loot of any kind?"

I shook my head no. Pussy Alice the barn cat rubbed against my leg. I turned my back on Shorty and thought of something to say to Jesse. "Say, why aren't you ever down on the lawn having a picnic?"

"On Visiting Day?" Jesse said.

"Yeah."

"I'm a full orphan."

"So then you're not destitute and neglected?"

"Guess not," said Jesse. "No one to neglect me."

I knelt down and stroked the cat.

"Hoffman was born at the Foundling Hospital," Chick said.

"Hey asshole," said Shorty. "Don't feed Pussy Alice. She's a mouser."

"I'm not feeding her."

"Why else would she hang around a crumb like you? Even your ma don't want you." Shorty took a piece of gravel out of his pocket and turned it over in his hand.

"Don't talk about my mother like that," I said. I discovered I wasn't afraid of Shorty anymore. Without his wrecking crew, he was a coward.

"I've heard of fathers leaving their kids here, but not mothers," he said.

This stopped me. I was pretty sure he was wrong, but a worm of doubt crept into my head. Maybe Harry and I were the only ones with a healthy, living mother who left them here. "So what?" I said.

"So I'm getting out of this shithole, that's what," said Shorty, fingering the gravel.

"Yeah?"

"Soon as my father finds a wife." He leaned back, flicked his wrist and sent the stone spinning toward the playground. "Pop can't stay home taking care of kids like a woman."

"Where's your mother?" I said.

"She's dead, moron. I wouldn't be here if she wasn't."

"Oh."

"Your pa dead?" said Shorty.

"No," I said, not quick enough to lie. "He disappeared."

"That's some trick," Shorty said. "Houdini, is he?" He laughed his old geezer cackle. "Left your ma high and dry."

"Yeah? Well, guess what?" said Harry. "Our mother gets a discount at Kohl's."

Shorty cackled long and hard. "Did you fellas hear the pissant?" He slapped his knee. Then he cornered Harry on the porch. "She get a discount on her army boots, too?"

I put myself between them and stomped on Shorty's foot with all my weight. I might have heard a bone crack. He started hollering and lunged at me, but the other fellas held him off, and Shorty limped whimpering to Nurse Flanagan. That was the beginning of my true friendship with Jesse and Chick—the kind without pity.

Every other day there was another initiation to endure, some cockamamie way I'd have to prove myself. Beiderman insisted the new kids go on a tour of the building—it was more important than a bar mitzvah, he said. We told him we'd already seen every corner of the shithole by now and Beiderman said, "Oh yeah? I think not." He sent five of us rookies into the cobwebbed basement and corralled us into a dark room under the stairs already crowded with junk. Harry tripped over me and I landed on my ass on top of a piece of furniture. Beiderman switched on the light and there I was perched on a coffin. The room was crammed with them. Stacks of coffins. "In case you little shits don't follow the rules," Beiderman said.

Later, back in Company E, Jesse said Beiderman was full of it. The coffins weren't for us, they were left over from those German Oddfellows. They needed a shitload because the old folks usually moved out of the Oddfellows Home feet first. Not only that, the place was sold to us, Jesse said, because a German Oddfellow supervisor and a couple of Oddfellow porters went to jail for murdering inmates. The old people were causing a nuisance, shitting themselves and refusing to die. That's why the supervisor did it, according to a porter interviewed by the *New York Times*. It was all in the paper, except for the shitting part. Jesse embellished that. He found the clipping in the *Oracle* newspaper office. "Chloroformed," Jesse said, "Eight of 'em in their beds."

"Holy cow," I said. "Murdered somewhere in this building."

"Did they kill the little kids, too?" Harry asked. "Or just the old people?"

"Hard to say," said Jesse. "Nobody notices when an orphan goes missing."

"Guess not," said Harry. "Not full orphans anyway."

I'd notice if Jesse went missing, I thought.

Next day, chicken soup for lunch and Company E ordered NOT to go outside afterward like usual. The supervisors instructed boys five to nine years old to go downstairs to the gym. "Roller skating!" Harry called out. He started running toward the equipment table. Jesse grabbed him by the shirttail and pulled him back. No skaters careened around poles. Instead, a single line of boys snaked from the gym entrance where we were standing, clear across to the far end where a gymnastics pommel horse was set up against the back wall, and next to that a music stand, and next to that Colonel Anderson. We waited our turn.

"Irving's the cause of this," Chick said.

"Irving?"

"Irving Weiss. The tardy kid," Jesse said.

"See, if a moax don't follow the rules, then we all get demerits," Chick said. "That's why the Homeboys called out the wrecking crew. Revenge on Weiss."

"I was tardy, too."

"No, you weren't," Jesse said. "We hadn't even finished washing up when Shorty called the wrecking crew on you. He must of had his own reasons. Know why?"

"Dunno," I said. "What's demerits?"

Jesse reached the front of the line. "Drop your trousers, boy," said the Colonel. "Drawers, too. Bend over."

Hoffman unbuttoned his pants and pulled down his drawers. He looked over his shoulder before grabbing hold of the pommels. "This here," he said, "is demerits." The cane whipped through the air with a hissing sound and whacked against his bare butt cheeks. Hiss and whack, red welts rising on Jesse Hoffman's flesh. Hiss and whack. I could see his balls trembling. A boy with more dignity than anyone I would ever meet. Streaks on his face. Hot burning tears of pride.

"Pull up your pants, Hoffman. What are you waiting for? Next!"

The cold air lapped at my ass.

Where's Harry? I can't find Harry. I ran to the barn. I ran to the auto shed. I ran to the ball field. To the main building flying down the stairs to the gym. No Harry. Upstairs, casing the freshman dorm and the freshman washroom, the junior dorm and the junior washroom and the showers and toilet stalls, up and down looking for feet. I found feet, only how the hell did I know who was in there taking a crap, reading a comic book or God knows what, when we all had the same shoes, but I didn't stop to think, I had a hunch. I backed up, hauled off and kicked open the stall door. Both of them were facing me—Shorty Lapidus on the can with his drawers around his ankles, my brother sitting on Shorty's disgusting lap.

Shorty was wrong, of course. Other healthy mothers dropped their kids at the HNOH, and other guys had disappeared fathers, too, fathers whose pictures also appeared in the Gallery of Missing Husbands, or a father in prison, or even a set of living parents too poor to feed their children, or maybe some kid had a mother who jumped in front of a subway train like Shorty's mother did.

Before the movie in the gym Wednesday, new inmates were sent to the barbershop on the ground floor. It was odd having everything under one roof, never going outside the gates and into the world. I wondered what Vivian and Alvin were doing. Was Gertie talking yet? I hadn't known I cared about my hair until the barber buzzed it off. He said it was for health reasons, which I knew meant lice, which I told him I didn't have and he said don't worry, my hair would grow back. Harry seemed to take it better. Neither one of us could stop rubbing his head against the grain to feel the prickly stubble. When we entered the gym there was a chorus of "Baldies! Baldies!" along with whistles and whoops.

"Baldyhead!" Chick continued to taunt. "Baldyhead!"

"You have the same haircut as I have," I said, noting his red bristles.

"Yeah, no kidding," said Chick. "Welcome to the 'H.'"

"You wanna know something, Harry?" I said.

"Yeah, what?"

"Everybody else in here, Harry, and I mean everybody, has something to be ashamed of, not just us."

"What have we got to be ashamed of?" Harry said.

Just before Christmas it snowed. The timing meant nothing, because Christmas itself meant nothing to a Hebrew Homeboy. Nothing except a more colorful version of the warmth and bounty we were excluded from every other day of the year. Only now it was visible, glittering beyond our gates. Nevertheless, it so happened on Christmas Eve morning we woke to a snowdrift piled in the corner of Company E, the snowflakes sifted through a crack in the window blown in all night by a shrieking wind. In joyful pandemonium we built an indoor snowman and had a rousing snowball fight before the monitors broke it up. Harry and I doubled up for a few weeks, and so did most of the others, or we would have frozen to death. No doubt some of the doubling up was not by mutual consent, but warmth was warmth. We survived and first chance we got went scavenging the barn, the woods, the basement, the boiler room, the boiler yard, and the kitchen yard for barrel staves and lumber scraps and metal trays—whatever we could find and use for sleds. Boys of all ages belly-whomped down twenty acres of hills and dales, Chick and I piled on one barrel stave, and just before the big oak tree swerved to the left, or else we would have crashed.

CHAPTER 19

I nstead of waiting around for Dr. Heidenheimer to give us the MRI results, I took the elevator down to nuclear medicine in the basement to find out for myself. The radiologist on duty must have been bored, because he agreed to show me the MRI film that Copeland Imaging had sent to Sinai Hospital. When I returned to the sixth floor, I saw Heidenheimer leaning on the high counter at the nurses' station going through a blue binder. He looked up. "We got the report," he said. I pretended I didn't know. I let Heidenheimer tell me about the mass they found. He used the same wording as the radiologist had downstairs. "There's a mass between the cheekbone and the maxillary sinus." Heidenheimer seemed less concerned, though, than the radiologist who had stroked the coarse hairs on his chin repeatedly as he spoke to me, as if to soothe himself and ward off my grief and terror. There was no need. I was calm. Relieved, in a way. It turned out my father wasn't a crybaby. It wasn't nothing. At last, he would get treatment. Finally, the time had come to cut out the massive headache and give it a name.

As I pretended to hear the news for the first time, I noted that Heidenheimer didn't mention the second shadow the radiologist had pointed to on the light box and identified as a brain lesion (assuring me brain abnormalities resulted from many conditions, including meningitis, a complication of TB). I thought it was odd that Heidenheimer omitted the brain lesion, so I had to tell him about it myself and reveal that I'd gone around him and had already been down to see the radiologist.

"No, they're wrong," Heidenheimer said. "What they think is a brain lesion is just a reflection from the other mass, like a double image." He grabbed a fountain pen and sketched a few blobs on a scrap of paper and showed it to me. A blob with a mirror-image blob. Doctors, in my limited experience, assumed non-doctors were idiots who needed stick figure drawings to understand basic concepts. I believed Heidenheimer at first—I didn't need his crude illustration. I may not have wanted the pain to be a phantom, but I certainly didn't want my father to have a lesion on his brain. The thing between his cheekbone and maxillary sinus was enough.

"I'll give your dad the results on evening rounds," the doctor said.

"It could still be tuberculosis, though, right?" I said.

"Yes," Heidenheimer said. "TB is still a possibility."

"That's good," I said, a little surprised both Heidenheimer and the radiologist were keen on the TB theory. I bit my lip to keep from smiling. I didn't want him to see how encouraged I was, afraid he might take it back. "So when do you go in there and do the biopsy?"

"Hold, on," Heidenheimer said. "Not so fast. First, I want a consultation with an Ear, Nose and Throat man." He scratched his head, then brought his hand down to scratch his wrist and slide his watch higher to peek at the time.

A chill prickled my neck and I shuddered. He was entitled to check his watch. He had other cases to see to. But I detected something more, a subtle shift in his attitude. The realization blew through me like a ghostly draft. I hugged my cardigan tighter. Dr. Heidenheimer didn't want a patient like my father. He was trying to get rid of him. That was why he lied about the double image. Surely, radiologists knew how to read MRIs better than anyone else. They dealt with blobs and mirror images on film day after day. But Heidenheimer disregarded the radiologists' report about the brain lesion because Heidenheimer was a neurologist—a brain man. If the brain were involved, Heidenheimer would have to take care of my father, a disheveled and difficult man who looked like he was dying of cancer. If just the sinus were involved, Heidenheimer could pass off the patient to an ENT doctor. I was starting to see what was going on. He was not going to help us. No one, not Dr. Cromwell or Dr. Heidenheimer, not Brenda, not my mother or sister, wanted to open the door even a crack and have to deal with the giant insect on his back.

CHAPTER 20

L iz Stone met me in the hospital cafeteria. Seeing her was like taking the cure at Baden-Baden or getting a blood transfusion or something. I was so grateful she came, and then absurdly happy when she wanted to have the same thing I was having—my usual lunch of coffee and a vanilla Dixie cup.

"I didn't expect you to be doing this," Liz said. "I thought it'd be Susan."

"Doing what?" I said. "Oh. At the hospital every day."

"I'm just surprised you're this devoted to him considering how shitty he was to you," Liz said. She was direct. We had that in common.

"It doesn't make sense, does it?" I said.

Liz laughed. She expected me to be defensive. "So why then?"

"Stockholm syndrome, I guess," I said. "I don't know. I mean, you know! I don't have to explain myself to you of all people."

"It seems like Susan's never around for the bad stuff," Liz said.

"He loves that about her," I said. "No darkness between them."

"Yeah, but I still thought she'd be here, not you."

"She has kids, I don't. That's the reality. Anyway, I forgave him and c'mon, you forgave him, too. Eventually. And you didn't have to! You didn't have to speak to him ever again after the camping trip, or hang out at my house, and you did."

"True," Liz said. She took a mouthful of ice cream and sucked on the wooden spoon before stabbing it back into the cup. "Whenever I'd come over, he'd pull me aside and ask me about something I was doing, like those speaker cabinets I built, remember those? And he wanted to know the details, how many nails I used. He showed me his tomato plants, and he'd put his arm around me, not in a lecherous way, not usually, it was more conspiratorial. He'd tell me some insight he had, like some key to happiness he just thought up, and he'd make it seem like I was the only one he was telling this stuff to. Like everyone else was stupid. Just him and me, we were the only ones in on the secret."

"He does that, doesn't he?" I said. I asked Liz not to come up to the room with me, though. He wasn't in the mood to see anyone. Talking hurt his head. Besides, Liz giving all her time to me was good for everyone. It was amazing what seeing a friend for a couple of hours could do when you were in some kind of nightmare.

CHAPTER 21

At fourteen, I was a moody teenager—self-serious, more introspective than Susan—and it was at this tender threshold, just at the moment in my development when I could have begun to know my father and let him know me, that he put up a barrier. He might not have realized his bad behavior created an obstacle between us, not consciously, as I didn't then either. But it was as if he raised the drawbridge and slammed shut the castle gate. He could have been the ideal father, a teacher and protector. Instead he fell in love (that was how he described it) with someone Susan's age. Susan had nothing to do with it, but I did. The girl was Liz Stone's cousin.

My mother let it happen. This was the sixties, free love and everything. She didn't put up a fight. She didn't get involved. She was her usual laissez-faire self. It bothered her, but she was quietly plotting her escape.

That summer I decided not to go to sleep-away camp. My father grumbled about how I was moping around doing nothing. Why didn't I learn to play tennis, he said, or volunteer, find something useful to do? I didn't know where to sign up. I didn't own a tennis racket. Most of my friends were away at camp or on family vacations. My mother was working at Beautiful Kitchens and taking community-college classes at night. Susan had a job at a clothing store called The Crotch. In those days, in the late sixties, it was very exciting to have a store nearby with a dirty name like that. I was bored. I got up late every day. That summer was especially hot. The cicadas surged. Not the seventeen-year locusts, but the cicadas we had every summer, and the sound, surging high up in the tree-tops and dying down and surging again, always made me feel I was being called outside from miles away and drawn into the woods. I put on shorts and found a sleeveless top that wasn't too rumpled and I slipped on my Keds with the backs flattened and I went outside. If Liz were home I would have answered the call and hiked with her into the woods behind her house. But Liz was away at Green Mountain, a horseback riding camp. I kicked at stones in the gutter for a while, and then sat on the curb under the maple tree and peeled the bark off a stick. The faint dinga linga ling of the Good Humor truck rose in the air like vapor over a distant street. I hoped Tom from next door wouldn't see me on the curb. I'd grown out of Tom. After a while, I went inside and lay on my bed and read *The Good Earth*, my mother's recommendation, and at some point when my mind was free of everything except the world of the novel, my father's voice and Johnny Dolan's in the kitchen broke into my thoughts. Johnny Dolan had just joined the English department at City, and he was my father's new best friend. "You got anything good in here?" Johnny said. He must have been leaning into the fridge. My father offered him the flank steak leftover from last night. "Here, I'll make you a sandwich," my father said. Johnny was a lot younger—even younger than Shep Levine. He could have been my father's son. When Johnny finished eating the steak sandwich, he wandered into the back of the house and knocked on my door and came into my room. I turned *The Good Earth* face down on the blue bedspread so I wouldn't lose my place. He was wearing cutoffs and no shirt. He was sweaty and smelled of cut grass. Johnny didn't like teaching summer school, so he made money in the summer mowing lawns, riding around in his red Triumph Spitfire with the top down and the lawnmower sticking up in the back seat. He asked what I was doing and I said I was reading. Then he left and went outside to help my father dig up a tree stump in the yard.

Finally, weeks later, Liz came home from camp and redeemed herself for abandoning me by inviting me on a road trip. In the space of a few seconds I went from bored and restless to wildly happy at the prospect of Liz's older sister Mandy and their cousin Nola driving us up to Canada in the Stone family's big old Pontiac Bonneville, camping out the whole way. Canada! The birthplace of Leonard Cohen and Joni Mitchell! We were going to cross the border into another country and drive all the way to Quebec City where I could practice my eighth-grade French. It was insane to let four teenaged girls camp on the side of the road hundreds of miles away from home. Fortunately for us, our parents were oblivious.

Not every young person was a hippie then, although most pretended they had been in retrospect. But the four of us were. We didn't use that word often though—hippie. We called ourselves freaks. We were outsiders—shy kids, artists, sensitive types, poor kids. Our lives were saved by the counter-culture, goofy girls like Liz and me, girls who didn't know how to be girls, only now we could wear blue jeans and secondhand clothes and be cool, so we wore thrift-shop dresses and jeans and painter's pants, and then there were girls like Mandy and Nola, older girls who did know how to dress and apply makeup and would have been popular in any group, but rebelled anyway and called themselves freaks. Even in old, torn clothes, Nola looked fresh and clean, with her flaxen hair and white teeth, like an Ivory soap girl. When I said Nola was beautiful, Liz got annoyed. "You're beautiful, too," Liz said. "You're beautiful, too," I said.

I went with Liz to Nola's once. She lived in an apartment with her mother. She'd never even met her father. There was nothing to eat. No knickknacks or junk either, no trace of family life, just pastel-colored furniture and two gray cats. There was a high partition between the kitchen and living room, and the slinky cats walked along the top of it like runway models.

Liz brought Mandy and Nola over to my house to look at my father's maps. Among my friends, I had the only father who talked to us. He was curious about what young people thought. If those other fathers ever said anything it was mumbled in tight voices in the backs of their throats. My friends called my father Clyde—even to me, they usually referred to him as Clyde and not "your father." He liked kids. Not me, but other kids. With me, it was as if I were his hired hand. You don't think about liking your hand. My friends could come to our house and get help with their papers like Eloise did and talk about anything. They couldn't shock Clyde. He liked to shock them, though. I was proud of having the coolest father. But something changed that day when Liz and Mandy came over with their cousin Nola. He took off his glasses to read the small print on the map spread on the dining-room table and started pronouncing the Canadian towns with an exaggerated French accent and pursed lips. Trois Rivieres. Notre-Dame-de-Montauban, L'Ancienne-Lorette. There was something creepy about his wet lips shaped in an "o." He sat in front of the map, and we gathered around him. I had a turn tracing the highway route with my finger, and I was upset. I whispered in Liz's ear that it looked like I would get my period on the trip, probably around Montreal, maybe sooner. I got it bad. Every month for four or five torturous hours I wanted to die. I imagined myself in agony tossed around in the car and trying to sleep on the stony ground. I left the four of them studying the map and I flopped onto the sofa. After a while, Liz came over and sat by me. "Bummer about your period," she said. "So, we were thinking . . ."

"What? No, no, don't switch anything on my account. I'll be fine."

"The thing is, Mandy's worried about money. The Bonneville's a gas guzzler."

"We're all chipping in," I said.

"Yeah, I know, but she didn't realize how far it is to the Canadian border. And then Quebec, that's really far. And Mandy and Nola are the only drivers."

I sat up in alarm. "We can't cancel it! We'll go somewhere closer. Maine. Cape Cod. What about Cape Cod?"

"Mandy's dead set on Canada," Liz said. "It's an obsession or something." She took a big breath, held it for a second and let it out. "Listen, Joanna, there's still a way we can go." She paused. "Clyde said he'd drive," she said. "We'll take his car and he'll pay for gas. We'll be able to do a lot more."

"My father? You invited my father on the trip?"

"He offered and Mandy said yes."

I fell back onto the sofa.

"Don't look at me like that," Liz said.

I felt the blood draining out of my face.

"Stop staring at me," Liz said. "You're freaking me out. It's the only solution." Liz was half-sitting on a throw pillow and I yanked it out from under her and covered my face with it.

My father came in. "What's wrong with Joanna?" he said.

Couldn't he see I was dead? He went outside without waiting for an answer. The screen door banged.

"What's wrong with Joanna?" my mother said.

"She's bummed because she's going to get her period during the trip," Liz said.

"Poor girl," my mother said. "She gets it bad." My mother leaned over and tried to take the pillow away from my face, but I held onto it. Liz got up and my mother sat in her place. "You're upset because Daddy's going on the trip, aren't you?"

I spoke through the velveteen. "How did you know?"

"Just a lucky guess."

"Where is he?" I asked.

"Outside with Liz's cousin."

I slid the pillow away and held it against my chest. "Why does he have to take over everything? This was MY trip, with MY friends!"

"Is it that bad?" my mother said.

"This is my territory," I said.

My mother brushed a strand of hair off my forehead and looked at me with her soft brown eyes. "You'll have plenty of trips in your life without him," she said. "And didn't you have fun when we went cross-country, and in Ireland? Daddy's fun to travel with. It's better than not going to Canada at all, isn't it?"

"No," I said.

"Look, Jo," my mother said. "It's not safe, the four of you girls traveling on your own. This way you still get to go."

Liz came over and swiped the pillow. "Don't hate me," she said. "Hate Mandy."

I wondered if my mother minded being left behind. Over the next few days, I watched her watching us drape the big tent over the hedge to air it out in the sun, and later, folding up the tent and packing our bags, loading our gear into my father's green Ford Torino GT. I didn't detect envy or concern. My mother seemed happy to get rid of us.

CHAPTER 22

I walked Liz from the Sinai cafeteria to the parking lot. I was freezing without a coat. We hugged before she got into her car. I didn't want to let go. "The sun's going down so early," I said, and both of us realized at once it was the shortest day of the year, December 21st. When Liz and I were twelve, my father enlisted us to help him make a papier mâché sun to celebrate the Winter Solstice. We papered over a supersized balloon, attached cones of newspaper for rays, painted the whole thing orange and yellow, slathered it in shellac, and hung it from the rafters in the living room over the objection of my mother who felt it clashed with the room's décor. Eventually, she relented and allowed the sun to stay until the spring equinox. This was in 1967, and my father hung it up every year thereafter until he married Brenda, because at that point he could justify having the real thing, the originally coveted, enticingly taboo thing, which was a Christmas tree. Until then we stacked our Hanukkah presents under the sun. I finally let go of Liz and she got into her car and drove away.

My father's room was dark. He was sleeping, covered in two white cotton blankets. I didn't want to disturb him. I figured we could talk about the MRI results in the morning. But he liked to know when I was leaving for the day, so I reached over and touched his hand curled by his cheek on the pillow.

"Brenda?" he said.

"Joanna."

"You're still here?" He turned onto his back and felt for the button to raise the bed. Only his left eye was open. His right eye had stopped moving completely. His eyelid was shut and bulging like a frog's.

"Yeah, I'm still here. But I'm about to go. I'm sleeping over at Mom's tonight."

"Brenda gets lonely, too, you know."

"It doesn't seem like it."

"Well, she does. You could sleep there once in a while."

"Guess what? Today's Winter Solstice."

"I know, kiddo. I know. Happier times."

I kept the overhead light off and opened the curtains. The street lamps in the parking lot splashed silvery rectangles over his covers like moonlight.

"Don't go," he said.

I sat on the windowsill. "I'm not going. Not yet."

"That Heidenheimer was in here."

"Yeah. I spoke to him, too." I swung my legs and kicked at the heating vent with my boot heels.

"So you heard. They found something."

"Yeah, but they don't know what it is," I said. "Could be TB or something else benign."

"Joanna, listen. Come closer. Don't sit way over there. Pull up the blue chair."

I hopped off the windowsill and pushed the recliner across the floor and right up to his bed. I sat down and reached across the covers to hold his hand.

"Listen, I've got to ask you something." He gently squeezed my fingers. From somewhere far away a female voice repeated a doctor's name, and we both looked up at the ceiling and listened. She spoke so softly over the intercom she could have been whispering to her lover. Then it was completely quiet. He let go of my hand and met my eyes with his one eye. "Tell me something, Joanna," he said. "Seriously. Am I going to come out on the other end of this thing well—or am I going to die?"

A cart rolled by, wheels clicking. My heart thumped.

"You're the only one I can ask," he said. "You're the only one I trust."

On the camping trip the woods and lake were dark, water lapping at the shore. In the morning Nola was wearing his jacket with floppy sleeves too long for her. "I can't trust Joanna," he had said to my mother when we got home. "I'll never be able to trust her again." I was stunned. It was the opposite. How could he lie like that? I was shocked. And yet, he wasn't entirely wrong. You couldn't trust someone if you knew she couldn't trust you.

"Me?" I said in the silvery light of his hospital room. "I'm the one you trust?"

"Yeah, you. Who else?"

I sat there and blinked the way he blinked when he was thinking. Again, he wasn't wrong. For whatever messed up reason, or perfectly good reason, no one was more loyal to him, not even Harry.

CHAPTER 23

Tuckahoe

We were permitted to go back to the Bronx for the eight days of Passover—but no longer. If your family could afford to keep you more than eight days, they could afford to keep you forever. So said Miss Claire Beaufort, the social worker. I was nervous. I didn't know what to expect. Would my mother change her mind and decide to keep us forever? She came to Yonkers to pick us up and clung to us but we pulled away. We stood on the trolley, and wouldn't sit on her lap on the bus or train either. On the walk from the subway station, I noticed girls everywhere. Girls on the Grand Concourse and across 166th Street, on Sherman Avenue and Morris Avenue. I didn't often see girls. Vivian on Visiting Day didn't count. Then before I knew it, we were on College Avenue, my own block where I used to play stoopball and ringolevio, yet I felt awkward. Was the Bronx home or was The Home home? After a couple of days, I figured it out. I decided the city was like a big noisy family at the poker table having an argument, and the country (when the supervisors left us alone) was like hanging out with your friends not needing to talk, just kicking stones. I wondered where I would live when I grew up, how would I choose, city or country, and if I would always have a divided heart.

"Everything they have there at the HNOH," said Mama at the seder table. "Horses, they ride. Like a boarding school."

"Is that right?" said Aunt Adele. She was Rich Uncle Seymour's gentile wife. I liked her. She knew games and rhymes.

"We don't ride them," I said. "They're dray horses. They pull the plow."

"I want to live at the HNOH," said Alvin. Everyone laughed.

Gertie was talking. "Kwai! Kwai!" she called, reaching her arms out. She couldn't pronounce the "l" or "d" in Clyde. Vivian dragged Gertie around like a doll but Gertie wanted me. "Kwai, hold you," she said, mixing up her pronouns.

My mother told me to go help Aunt Sadie and Grandma, so I gave Gertie back to Vivian and went into the kitchen.

"You always defend Ruth," Aunt Sadie was saying to Grandma Cohen.

Ruth was my mother. I didn't like Aunt Sadie talking behind Mama's back.

"I don't take sides," said Grandma Cohen. "Have some pity for your sister."

"Pity? She has two boys stuck in an orphanage, while she's riding around in taxi cabs like Lady Astor!"

"Sha. The children," said Grandma Cohen.

"Who does that? I ask you?" Aunt Sadie said.

Aunt Adele cleared the soup plates and carried them in. "Does what?" she said.

"She always defends Ruth," said Aunt Sadie.

"Ruth is my daughter," said Grandma Cohen. "Hand me the seltzer in the icebox."

"I'm your daughter, too," Aunt Sadie said.

"So I defend you, too," said Grandma Cohen.

Aunt Sadie found the seltzer bottle and rattled the icebox shut. "New hats she buys," Aunt Sadie said. The kitchen was small and wherever I turned perfumed bosoms cushioned me in flowery prints.

"It wouldn't hurt *you* should buy something new," said Grandma. "Maybe a man should look at you."

"Here, Clyde, take the seltzer, put it on the table."

When we visited the Aronson side of the family, my father wasn't even mentioned. I'd been thinking lately how I used to put the things I did with my father in the category of last year. Last summer, my father and I built a balsa wood model of a Curtis Jenny biplane, or last summer he was supposed to take me swimming, or last Christmas, my father came home with a box of Christmas-tree lollipops given out by the Metropolitan Life Insurance Company and my mother laughed about bringing *treyf* into the house, but she let us eat them. This year, though, when I thought about what happened last year, I realized none of it had anything to do with my father. Most of it didn't even happen in the Bronx, or with my mother, either. Last year happened on Tuckahoe Road. Last year I was already in the orphanage. My father *had* disappeared. I couldn't pretend anymore. He wasn't coming back. This would keep getting more and more true.

For eight days, my mother tucked us into bed and kissed us good night. She smelled like Nurse Flanagan. At the end of the week, Harry and I were returned to the orphanage.

CHAPTER 24

"Is it true Daddy didn't speak to you for two weeks after I was born?"

"Who told you that?" My mother was sitting on her navy-blue velvet sofa having a cup of coffee. I'd just come in after being at the hospital all day.

"Aunt Vivian," I said. "She said it last week when she came to Sinai. And the time I saw her before that. She always says it." I threw my bag onto a chair and took off my coat.

"Aunt Vivian exaggerates," my mother said.

"Is it true?" I said.

"Your father had a habit of not talking to me when he got mad," she said. "He still does. Hang up your coat."

I glanced down at her manicured toes squishing luxuriously in the shag carpeting. My commie mother fled the suburbs for a less bourgeois life downtown, but then she went and got pedicures and decorated her pad like a mafia wife—mirrors behind the velvet sofa, lime-green shag, chandeliers. "So then it's true," I said.

"Why bring up that old history? Tell me about the x-rays."

"An MRI is not an x-ray," I said. "And I told you the results on the phone. I'm bringing it up because I saw Liz and I was telling her how Da went bat-shit crazy because I wasn't a boy."

"Your father certainly doesn't feel that way anymore."

"The damage is done," I said. I put my coat on a hanger and forced it into her packed closet. Her boyfriend Marty was keeping some of his jackets in there. I was grateful to Marty for staying away when I slept over. It was bad enough I had to deal with Brenda.

"What damage?" my mother said. "You look perfectly fine to me."

"I can't believe you're a therapist," I said.

"Now you're going to insult me?"

"God, Ma. Can we stick to the subject of me for at least ten seconds?"

My mother and I could gossip together for hours—not really gossip, just laugh about the weird things other people did, hoping to make sense of it, knowing we were inclined to agree—and neither of us could do this with Susan. My sister wasn't going to waste time on annoying people. So parsing personalities along with stories about the past was an important bond between my mother and me. But when we landed on the emotional landscape of my childhood, my mother shut down.

"You were an infant when Daddy went on that jag. You had no idea what was going on."

I glared at her, not sure I wanted to get into an argument over infant cognitive development, a concept she didn't believe in, apparently. I was always left feeling foolish for bringing up slights from the past and so I didn't do it very often. My grievances were childish, both my parents said so. But they couldn't keep the images from flitting through my mind: Susan's fair curls in a velvet bow, her poufy party dress filling the frame and blocking me out, flashes of color, the smell of fresh paint, the woods, the lake, the blonde curtain of Nola's hair blocking me out. After hours in the hospital at my father's side, naturally my head filled with scenes from the past. "Why did you save Susan's school projects and not mine?" I asked.

My mother tried to suppress a laugh, not expecting such a small complaint. "What, you mean the stuff from Ireland?"

She didn't appreciate how much that year meant to me. I'd been a mere child, she said enough times. It was her adventure, her creation. She was the one who urged my father to apply for a Fulbright. But Ireland was significant for me in a different way. Being a mere child, it was the year I discovered the world. In America, I had known only the sleepy house and the windy yard. My mother would go back to bed after she got Susan off to school and I waited hours, it seemed, for her to wake up. Only then in the sunlit day she put a ruffled apron over her shirtwaist dress and ran into the street to stop the Rice's Bakery truck calling "Wait a minute! Wait a minute!" We sat at the red kitchen table with the wrought-iron legs dreamily eating white powdered donuts from the Rice's man, watching the silky line of smoke snaking up from her cigarette in the ashtray. Then poof, without much notice, I was launched down the gangplank and into the rough, raw streets of Belfast under a coal-blackened sky to play among ragamuffin children with dirty knees, castles, and a queen. Ireland was a transitional place, both real and made-up. I was born yearning for the past and then I got on a ship and time-traveled to it.

"You're talking about the stuff from primary school?" my mother said.

"Yes." For other families—wealthier, well-connected families—living abroad for a year didn't amount to much, but for us, it was a big deal, and everyone else on dinky Cedar Drive thought it was a big deal, too.

"Susan was older," my mother said. "Her schoolwork was more interesting. You were only in first grade. Sit down. You want some coffee?"

"Coffee? Who drinks coffee this late? I should go to bed." I doubted Susan ever looked at the workbooks they saved, or read the letters her classmates wrote and presented to her as a farewell gift. For Susan, Ireland was a nightmare best forgotten.

"I've got herbal tea," my mother said.

"No thanks," I said. She was wrong. My Nature Studies would have been interesting, even thrilling for me to look at. The children in the first grade at Orangefield Primary School gathered twigs, leaves, berries, and feathers from the boggy park to bring to class for Nature. We pasted the treasures into booklets and labeled the pages. I drew my T's curled up at the bottom like the other children in Northern Ireland, and "to-day" with a hyphen, as I first learned to read and write there. We slithered on our bellies in the loamy bog on the wooded edge of the park and reached our jars into the cold pond water to scoop up jelly eggs from the muddy bottom, then watched the eggs grow into frogs in the back of the classroom. "There was plenty that was interesting," I said. "Sums. Spelling. Religion."

"Religion, yeah. We tried to get you excused from that but they wouldn't have it. Look, Joanna, I had a lot on my mind over there. Things were going on you didn't know about."

I got a 92 in religion for correctly naming scenes depicting the life of Jesus painted on giant cards. "I was looking at the letters you wrote to Shana," I said, "and you hardly mentioned me or Susan, as if we weren't even conscious, when we were the ones who came home with Irish accents, not you. We were the ones who absorbed everything like a sponge, force-fed gruel, and hit with a ruler."

My mother got up and brought her dishes to the sink. She let out an exasperated sigh. "What was I supposed to write? You were little kids. And you're correct, you weren't conscious. Children don't come into consciousness until what? Nine or ten. I remember when you turned eleven, you started to be more interesting. You were funny, too."

She waited for my reaction to her flattery and when I didn't warm to it, she ran the water in the sink, rinsed the dishes, and put them in the dishwasher seemingly lost in thought. After she finished wiping off the counter with a sponge and washed and dried her hands, she came back to the sofa where I had stretched out. She lifted my legs and sat down with my stocking feet in her lap. "I'll admit a lot of it was my fault," she said. She sighed, sadly this time, and closed her eyes. I perked up. Did she just say a lot was her fault? Was my mother suddenly taking responsibility for her neglect? I was deluded for a second, soothed by her warm hand holding onto my foot. But she wasn't referring to anything having to do with me, as I should have known. She and my father spoke about their lives in such epic terms, and

I took this so much to heart, there seemed to be no way my own life could be as important as theirs. They lived through the romance of world war and radical politics. Their great love was forever entwined with history. My mother wasn't thinking about me, she was thinking about her marriage. She meant Caitlyn Callaghan was her fault, and the affairs that followed. I had to admit, my mother's story was a good one, and while I doubted she'd ever admit it, in some ways, it was my story too.

Caitlyn was her fault because my mother was the one who wanted to experiment. She was the one who wanted to live abroad. She wanted to lead an exciting life. She craved experience. She wanted Clyde and Evie Aronson to be like Jean-Paul Sartre and Simone de Beauvoir, sitting in cafes all night discussing philosophy and literature, and most importantly, having an open relationship. It was my mother's idea, one of her utopian schemes, and with it came the slow, steady demise of our family.

"You know, Joanna, I've told you this, but after you were born, I was sure my life would never be anything more than washing diapers, ironing Susan's dresses, and oh my God, listening to the two of you fight. So I lobbied for going overseas. I got Daddy to apply for the Fulbright. He never would have done it on his own. I was adamant—we were going to live in swinging London for a year. It would be an adventure, and I figured in a far-away location I could apply my Marxist ideals, if not to society at large, then to my own marriage. Can you blame me? I was a virgin on my wedding day! I saved myself for your father, God knows why, but I was chaste for the three years he was away in the war."

"Chaste? No other boys from the time you were sixteen?"

"Well, not exactly. I told you. I went to dances at the YCL, the AYD, the USO. I kissed boys. We fondled each other. But nothing more. And then as soon as Clyde comes home from the war, we get married, have children, I give up my political life, move to the suburbs, and Joanna, time was passing me by. I wanted to be a part of the world. I wanted the freedom men had. I thought if we lived abroad away from my judgmental family and our nosy neighbors, we could have affairs without the usual gossip. Unfortunately, there was only one option on the Fulbright application for exchange teachers requesting placement in London. What a joke. I brought your father a No. 2 pencil and I stood over him and watched as he filled in the bubble next to Great Britain. We waited weeks and weeks, and the letter finally came and he was accepted! It was very exciting getting that letter. But we were not sent to swinging London. Oh no, we're sent to Belfast, a city celebrated for its shipbuilding."

"I know. I was there."

"You were six years old. You knew bubkas. Anyway, I figured even in uptight Belfast, after a year I would come home to the US with some experience, having changed in some way. But then—and isn't it always this way for women? All I can manage is a one-night stand with that taciturn friend of Nora Trimble's in the backseat of an Austin Seven. I can barely remember his name. Well, that's not true. Jim Harkins. But I hardly even remember what he looked like. Whereas your father—what does he do? Your father goes and falls in love. Do you know how small the backseat of an Austin Seven is?"

My mother documented the year in letters, posting one to Shana Bloom in Baltimore every week. "We set sail on August 17, 1961," my mother penned in her forward-leaning hand-writing, the pages of which Shana typed up and inserted into a binder. "The passengers flung colored streamers off the SS *United States* into the milky green water of New York harbor and the band played and the foghorns blew and the people on deck were laughing and waving to the people on shore who were getting smaller and smaller until we couldn't see them anymore and our attention turned to the Statue of Liberty."

Occasionally my mother mentioned the kids in her letters to Shana, as in "we went to a cocktail party for the Lord Mayor of Belfast and found someone to stay with the kids," but in over fifty-two letters, the name Jo or Joanna came up a total of three times. Fortunately, I kept my own travel diary in my mere child's head. I remembered well how I stood on deck with my father after dinner that first day at sea, as we glided through the black waves of the North Atlantic.

"This is the fastest ship in the world," my father said. "And the safest. You don't have to worry about fire."

I wasn't worried about fire.

"You see," he said, "there's nothing on board made of wood. Except for two things that absolutely must be made out of wood. Can you guess what they are?"

I couldn't guess. I hadn't even started school.

"The piano and the chef's chopping block," he said. He tried to light a cigarette but the wind kept putting out the flame. "The chef insisted. Everything else that looks like wood, like the railings lining the corridors, that's all made of a new substance called Neotex."

"You mean the ballet bars?"

"Yeah, the ballet bars," my father said.

The ship's prow cut through the waves at record speed. I held my father's hand, smooth and dry as always. "The stars go all the way to the edge," I said.

"The horizon," said my father.

Our house in Belfast was at No. 19 Orangefield Gardens and our school was called Orangefield Primary School. I thought the name had to do with orchards and sunshine, but I never saw an orchard and there was no sunshine. Everything was orange for William of Orange, the king who staked claim to the North for the Protestants way back in 1690 during the Battle of the Boyne. In 1961, the northern province of Ulster was mostly quiet, except for kids throwing rocks, and a bomb in a van parked at the border. At Belfast Technical College, my father was assigned a student teacher called Caitlyn. A boy hit her with a rock because she was Catholic, my father said, and she had to get stitches. But the Troubles wouldn't fully begin again for almost a decade, with the Battle of Bogside in 1969.

Orangefield, where we lived, was on the rich, Protestant side of Belfast, but it didn't seem rich to Susan and me. No trees grew on our block and we were the only ones with a car or a refrigerator and nobody, including us, had central heating. All warmth came from the fireplace in the sitting room. My mother didn't take her coat off for a year. In the morning, Susan and I put on our red or black Danskin tights under the covers. Susan was eight, so it was her job to go outside to the coal bin in the morning and fill the coal scuttle. I sat halfway down the chilly stairs on the cabbage-rose carpet, pleasantly half-awake, waiting for my sister to restart the fire while our parents slept. On the way to school, boys taunted us because we wore exotic colored tights instead of white socks like Irish girls. "Licorice legs! Licorice legs!" they hollered every day as we hurried down the lane.

At primary school, the teachers hit us for missing sums or spelling. I didn't mind. The system was fair. Whoever got one sum wrong was called to the front and we held our hands out and Mrs. Graham went down the line and slapped each open palm once with a ruler. Two wrong came up together and got two slaps, and three and so on. Same for spelling. She whacked us hard and it stung, it really did, but you knew what you were getting and why. I minded very much though, when she whacked our knuckles, arms, and legs for misbehaving, because that was like getting hit just for being a child, and what else could you be? None of the beatings, though, compared to the torture of lunch for Susan and me. The other children were grateful for the midday meal, but Susan and I lived in mortal fear of it. The teachers ordered us to eat every gristly scrap of funky mutton and lard-reeking lump of congealed mash, to swallow every spoonful of watery pudding from seemingly bottomless bowls. You weren't allowed to bring a bag lunch from home.

"In America," I said to the kids in the food line, "you get fried chicken for lunch at school."

"Nay," they said.

"Aye," I said. "My sister told me so." The line moved inside and I spotted Susan at the third-graders' table. Her face was grim. She held an oversized spoon to her mouth and barely opened her lips. I tried to get her attention, but she wouldn't look at me. If our eyes had met she might have cried. And she couldn't cry, not in front of the thick-skinned Ulster kids.

I had only one friend, Hazel, who wore shabby jumpers and smelled like milk. "Hazel has no teeth," I told my mother.

"Her baby teeth fell out?" my mother said.

"Her wee teeth, and the big ones, too. She hasn't any teeth at all," I said.

"She must be from a poor family," said my mother. "Possibly Hazel ate too much candy and never went to a dentist."

"It's sweets, not candy," I said.

"Sweets, then," my mother said.

I didn't want a poor friend with old clothes and no teeth. But no one else would play with me in the cement yard because I was a foreigner. Even though the primary school was built on the edge of the park with woods and a pond, and a little bridge over the Knock River, our playground was a prison yard out of Dickens. My mother said it was the Scotch Presbyterian influence and that was why at the park they tied up the swings on Sundays. I wanted to be friends with a girl called Polly Williams, who had teeth and wore bright clothes, especially a dress I liked made of dotted Swiss.

I thought about Polly Williams every night in bed and every day at my desk with its inkwell from another time. At last, I found my opportunity. Polly was absent from school and Mrs. Graham asked if there was anyone who lived near her who might give her the work she missed. She lived on Orange

Avenue, Mrs. Graham said. My hand shot up. Orange Avenue had to be near Orangefield Gardens. The teacher handed over the workbook to take to Polly. On the way home from school, I had to beg Susan to search the street signs with me to find Orange Avenue. We passed Orangefield Green, Orange Grove, Orangefield Lane, and Orange Parade. When we got home, my mother said she wasn't sure where the girl Polly's street was with everything Orange this and Orange that.

"But I have to go there," I said. "You have to find it."

"Wait until Daddy comes home," my mother said. She had been downtown all day with Nora Trimble and let the fire die and now she was sitting in the kitchen in her yellow leather car coat with the electric oven turned on and the oven door wide open. "You're bugging me," she said.

"In America, Daddy came home early," Susan said.

I waited for my father and Susan was angry because I had held her up searching for the street and now Pamela next door had gone to the shops without her. Children in Belfast roamed the city freely. We rode the red double-decker buses, ran errands, and went to the baths (an indoor swimming pool with a balcony) unaccompanied. Susan slapped me and I hit her back. "Stop it! Stop it!" my mother screamed. When my father got home, he said he had a meeting and he had to go out again.

"Please," I said. "I have to give Polly Williams the homework. I promised the teacher. Can you take me? Please. I'll get in trouble. She'll beat me with a cane."

"The Colonel used a cane," my mother said. "In the orphanage. Right, Clyde?"

"Never mind that," my father said. "I survived. They'll survive, too."

I followed my father into the parlor. "I've got something for you two. You're gonna love it," he said. He took a record out of his briefcase and put it on the record player. "All the kids in America are listening to this."

"C'mon, let's twist again, like we did last summer," Chubby Checker sang.

Susan started swiveling around to the music. "I know how to twist," she said.

"Me too," my mother said. "C'mon Joanna. Pretend you're drying yourself with a towel and stamping out a cigarette with your foot at the same time." My mother held out her arms and moved her hips and put out the imaginary cigarette with her square-toed high-heeled shoe, and I imitated her.

"You're doing it wrong," Susan said.

I stopped dancing and leaned back against the windowsill. "Daddy, please," I said. "Let's go. You have to take me. I'll get in trouble. I swear, they'll beat me with a ruler. Get out your map."

"Who is Polly, anyway?" said Susan.

"The pretty girl in my class," I said. "I told you. The one with the white dress and the wee red velvet dots."

"All right, I'll take you after dinner," my father said.

I thought the meal would never end. My father smoked a cigarette with his coffee. I watched the ash getting longer and longer. It was late. "Pep your cigarette," I said. He flicked the ash into the ashtray, took a last drag, then squashed the cigarette in the ashtray and lit another one. Polly would never get the homework and it would be my fault. My mother told my father a joke in Yiddish and he laughed his almost noiseless laugh, his shoulders moving up and down. He stubbed out the second cigarette and stood up. "Let's go," he said. "C'mon. What are you waiting for?"

We got into our little Renault that we pronounced with the "l" and the "t." It turned out Orange Avenue was far away, over on the other side of the school. We drove silently through the night.

I stood at the door. Polly didn't even come downstairs to see me. Her mother took the homework absentmindedly, staring out at my father in the idling car.

"So, you delivered the homework?" my father said.

"Aye."

He saw that Polly had no use for me. I had caused trouble for him, and for Susan, for nothing. My father swung the car around and down a hill. He had an errand, too, he said. We parked on a street with trees and he took me up to Caitlyn's flat, his student teacher. She stooped down in front of me like my mother when she tied the strings on my parka.

"Aren't you a bonny wee one?" Caitlyn said. She had pale skin and a brown bouffant hairdo. I wondered if she would give me chocolate. The Irish were keen on chocolate. "What solemn eyes," said Caitlyn.

"You should see the older one," my father said. "A *shayna maidel*. That's Yiddish. You wanna know something? I'll tell you something. Yiddish is a lot like Gaelic." He laughed and so did Caitlyn. "Go ahead. Say something in Gaelic," my father said.

"*Tha gràdh agad orm*," said Caitlyn.

"What does that mean?" I said.

"You love me," she said. "In Irish."

"I love you?" I said.

Caitlyn clapped her hands and laughed. "No. *You* love me," she said.

"Lost tribe of Israel," my father said. "The Irish."

She didn't offer chocolate and then we left.

"Porcelain, her skin. Did you see that?" my father said in the car.

"What's porcelain?"

"You know what porcelain is. Sinks are made of porcelain, and toilets."

"She has skin like a toilet?"

"Not like a toilet, stupid. White, smooth, flawless."

We drove down the Grand Parade past the butcher, the baker, and the sweets shop. I had trouble getting to sleep that night. I thought of Polly upstairs in her dotted Swiss dress knowing I was there and not coming down to see me. The bed creaked in the next room. I could hear them talking through the wall.

"You started it with that Jim what's his name," my father said.

"That was nothing," my mother said.

"You were the one who wanted this," my father said.

My mother sighed. "You weren't supposed to fall in love," she said.

He stayed late at Belfast Tech two nights a week and on those nights I lay awake next to Susan with our wardrobe looming in the darkness until I heard the Renault chugging around the bend toward No. 19.

My sister was unhappy. She missed the USA. My mother didn't know what to do. I didn't want to hear the screaming, so I went outside and kicked a wiffle ball around the front garden.

"I can't believe you let them hit me! What kind of mother are you?" Susan cried. Flashes of color moved behind the window glass.

"We went to the headmaster. What more can we do?"

Susan wailed. "I wanna go home!"

"Stop it!" my mother shouted.

"Please, take me home! Please!"

Tommy from up the street stopped his bike in front of our house. "Get your cheeky sister out here," Tommy said.

"What would I be wanting that for?" I said.

"Go back to America, you raving lunatics," he said. His clothes were gray like Hazel's.

"Why is your sister crying?" said Roberta from across the street.

"Susan doesn't like Belfast," I said. I threw the wiffle ball in the air and caught it.

"Why not?" said Tommy.

"She hates pudding," I said.

"Hates pudding? You're daft." Tommy rode off. He skidded to a halt in front of Martin, who was kicking stones in the street.

"Martin, Yank says her sister hates pudding."

"We'll have to put an end to that," said Martin.

"What do you mean?" I said. I moved inside our gate.

Roberta skipped off to the shops with a string bag. Martin bent down, gathered the stones he was kicking and stuffed them into his pocket. I ran into the house. "The kids can hear you crying!"

"Shut your gob, you little brat. Do you think I care?" my sister said. She brushed her tears away.

"They're throwing rocks," I said.

"They are not," said Susan.

Clank.

"Oh shit," my mother said.

Stones clattered against the windowpane.

"You dare-tee Jews!"

My sister gasped.

"How do they know we're Jewish?" I said.

My mother gave me an impatient look. "Where the hell is your father when we need him?"

I raced to the kitchen. A crowd had gathered mugging at the side window. Martin made a hocking noise. A glob of phlegm hit the pane, then slid down to the sill.

"Dare-tee Jews! Dare-tee Jews!" the crowd chanted.

"That does it! Now we *have* to go home!" Susan said.

I was afraid. Not of the rowdy children, but afraid that Susan would have us sent back to America and spoil our adventure. My mother had a brilliant solution. She went outside holding her yellow car coat closed around her hand-knit jumper, and invited the neighbor kids to lunch on Saturday for American hamburgers.

"I don't want those disgusting tinkers in here!" Susan said. "They spit on our window! They're anti-Semitic."

"What's that?" I said.

"They hate Jews," said Susan.

"And Catholics," I said.

"*Everyone* loves hamburgers," my mother said.

Everyone did love the hamburgers. On Saturday, we had seven kids squeezed around our kitchen table. My mother was pleased with her diplomacy.

"There's a place in America called Burger Chef," I said. "Sorry, Ma, but their hamburgers are even better than yours."

"Don't be disrespecting your mam," said Tommy.

"Aye," said Martin. "There are no better hamburgers than these here."

As luck would have it, our adventure was not cut short. We stayed as planned until the end of June. In the weeks leading up to our departure, I lay in bed listening for my father's car and I tried to picture home. Our bedspreads were blue in America and the walls of our room were pink. Girls wore cotton shorts and sleeveless blouses.

"What are you going to do?" my mother asked. "Stay here?"

Did my parents think Susan and I couldn't hear them? That we were always asleep? Did they really believe we weren't conscious yet, not thinking human beings? We were upstairs and they were downstairs, but the walls were thin and their voices carried. I sat up in bed.

"Stay here? In Belfast?" my father said. "I'm not staying here!"

"You don't want to leave Caitlyn. What then?"

"I'm not staying here. It's not for me. Anyway, everyone's trying to get out. Both sides."

He meant the Catholics and the Protestants.

"So you're coming home with us?" my mother said.

"That's right," said my father. The poker clanked and scraped the hearth. My father stirring the coals. "But I want to bring her back."

"Bring her back?" my mother said. Her voice rose. "What does that mean, bring her back?"

"To Baltimore," he said.

"What? Are you crazy?"

"Susan," I whispered to the next bed.

"Put the pillow over your head," Susan said.

"Do you know what they're talking about?"

"Go to sleep. They'll be fine in the morning."

There was another clank and rattle, the poker returning to its place. "It doesn't matter," he said. "She won't do it."

"Bring her back like a souvenir?" my mother said, not hearing him.

"Bitch."

That word was just for girls, meant to cut them. The t-part in the middle stabbed my heart. The ch-part froze it. I looked over at Susan. She was sleeping.

"Bitch? Me?" my mother said. "The open-minded idiot who started this whole thing?"

"That's right!" my father shouted. "*You* started it. You don't care about me. You're not even sad. You don't love me."

"I love you so much look at what I accept! But it's never enough!"

They didn't speak for a while after that but I couldn't sleep. I was scared of the wardrobe in our room. My mother said I should remember it was just a place where we kept our clothes, but it loomed in the darkness. My father started talking again, but quieter: "She broke it off with me," he said.

"Caitlyn?" my mother said.

"Who else?" he said angrily. The poker clanked again. I strained to hear. There was a loud crash and I jumped out of bed in fright, but a dull thud stopped me in my tracks. I listened. The sofa creaked and groaned under a shifting weight. I heard a gasp, and a strangled breath and a cry, and I ran down the stairs. I did not think about what I would do when I got to the sitting room. I wasn't concerned with how I would stop a fight between two adults twice my size, one wielding a poker, or that I might be punished for getting out of bed. I was frightened, something bad was happening, that was all I knew, and so I ran to offer comfort to the people who were supposed to comfort me. I stopped short at the doorway not sure at first what I was seeing on the sofa—whose body was whose, what was happening, who had cried out and why. Coals glowed red in the fireplace. The telly was tuned to a news program with the sound off. My father was partly on top of my mother with one leg draped around the bottom part of her body possessively. Above the waist, though, she was in possession, cradling him in her arms. Her lips were pressed to his forehead tenderly. His glasses were off, he lay with his cheek against her breast. He was the one who was crying.

"Caitlyn doesn't want to see me anymore," he said.

My mother held him and kissed his tears away. "Poor boy," she said. "Poor boy."

CHAPTER 25

Tuckahoe

"The Colonel hits us," said Harry. "With his cane."

Mama cut a piece of halvah for me. It was Sunday and Jesse Hoffman was sharing our picnic. Jesse mugged and Gertie giggled.

"Clyde, is this true? They use a cane?"

"Not all the time," I said.

My mother laughed.

I stared at her in disbelief and glanced nervously at Jesse. Maybe it was better having no family at all, no one to laugh at you at the oddest times, no one to disgrace you. I had to lash my right arm to my side to keep from striking her. "Why are you laughing?" I asked coldly.

"It's you, Clyde," my mother said. "You've been like this since the day you were born."

"Like what?"

"They hit you, but not all the time. *Aynzen gut.* You find the good in anything. You'd drop your frankfurter and tell me it tasted better with a little dirt."

"Don't laugh at me," I said.

"It's a good character trait," my mother said.

My blood cooled a little as I watched Jesse roll down the grassy hill with Gertie. Hoffman had nobody. Nobody. I shrugged. "Isn't everyone like that?" I said. I assumed all people found the good in things so they could tolerate the way life was.

"Oh, no," said my mother. "If only."

Jesse held Gertie's hand as she toddled back to the blanket.

"It's not just the Colonel," said Harry. "The seniors hit us, too. The monitors."

"Clyde? Jesse? Is this true?"

"Will you take us home if it's true?" I said.

"I'll speak to Miss Beaufort, that's what I'll do." My mother stood up suddenly and brushed off her dress. She kept batting at the pleats.

"Please don't," I said. "Don't say anything." I glanced at Jesse, but I couldn't read his face. He merely looked thoughtful.

"Harry, shut up, awright?" I said. "You don't wanna be a stoolie."

"I ain't no stoolie," Harry said.

"It'll be worse for us if you complain," I said.

My mother sank back onto the blanket. "So many boys they have to keep in line," she said, mainly to herself.

As time went on, and it became more and more evident that Harry and I were not going home, at least not anytime soon, I haltingly adjusted my view of the future. One day, Jesse and I were sitting on overturned buckets in the boiler-room yard flicking chickens when he suggested I join the marching band. First we held the birds by their hideous pipe-cleaner feet and dunked them into a pot of scalding water so the feathers came off easy.

"Don't we do enough marching around here already?" I said.

"This is different. The music carries you along." Jesse rapped on his thighs with his palms. "You can be a drummer like me."

"I don't know." Joining the band seemed like a real commitment. Something for the full orphans, not for somebody who might conceivably leave at any moment.

"The band gets to travel," said Jesse.

"Where to?"

"All over. Mount Vernon, Valhalla, Hartsdale, Scarsdale, White Plains, Hastings on Hudson, Croton on Hudson. The Yonkers Fireman's Parade. We get food. Sometimes ham sandwiches from the yokels who don't know any better."

"They give Hebrew orphans ham sandwiches in White Plains?" I said. I threw down my bird and wiped the feathers off my hands and onto my trousers.

"You bet. Beer, too."

I hadn't been outside the gates since Passover. I wanted to see the world again. Maybe if I went traveling with the band, I'd have a better chance of finding my father. He might be in the crowd on the sidelines at the Yonkers Fireman's Parade. He might see me marching along beating a drum.

I picked up my chicken and resumed flicking. "All right," I said, trying not to sound grateful. "I'll join the band."

Since the HNOH was founded on the Lower East Side, its grammar school, PS 403, continued to be part of the New York City school system even after the H moved to Westchester County beyond the city limits. Except for the fact that PS 403 was located inside an orphanage, it was strictly a public school, not parochial. Hebrew classes were taught separately in the shul by the Home rabbis. I preferred regular school. I liked all of the subjects—English, arithmetic, history, geography—and I greatly appreciated the safety and sanctity of the PS 403 classrooms where the teachers ruled, and not the Colonel. After lunch, we played baseball. The guys knew me now. They knew I could run the bases, and I wasn't a terrible hitter. One afternoon I was daydreaming in the outfield, inhaling the heady smell of burning leaves when a formation of honking geese came flying so low I could see their mouths moving. I gazed up in astonishment only vaguely conscious that a ball might sail my way, when Harry appeared and brought me out of the trance.

"What are you, crazy?" I yelled. "Get out of here. There's a game going on."

"C'mon to the fence," Harry said. "Slow Uncle Archie's got Walnettos."

I threw down my glove. The boys hollered at me but I followed Harry away from the ball field past the cottages and toward the line of golden maples bordering the western edge of the Home's twenty acres. It was a strange sight, my uncle in an ill-fitting suit on the other side of the orphanage fence, his long arms stretched through the pickets, flailing around reaching for me.

"Get over here Clyde my boy. Give your uncle a hug."

Harry's face was scrunched up chewing on a nutty caramel Walnetto. Drool slobbered down his chin. Paper wrappers were strewn on the ground.

"Careful, Harry," I said. "You'll take out a tooth."

"Hey, Clyde, what time is it when you go to the dentist?" said Uncle Archie.

"I don't know," I said, annoyed. Sometimes I thought I was the grown-up and my uncle was the child, I really did.

"Two-thirty," said Uncle Archie. "Get it, Clyde? Tooth hurty."

I came closer and let Slow Uncle Archie grab me by the shirt. We hugged with the iron fence between us. I wanted to save the Walnetto and savor it in private, but I was afraid some hooligan might swipe it meantime, so I unwrapped the candy and bit into the caramel and nuts. Sugary saliva pooled in my mouth and waves of pleasure turned my body slack. I leaned on the fence for support.

"I miss you kids," Uncle Archie said. He paced on his side of the grass. "You know, if it was up to me . . ."

"I love Walnettos," said Harry.

"Me, too," I said.

Whoever came or didn't come on the official designated Visiting Day, the farther away in the week we got from it the better we felt. Most relatives followed the every-other-week rule, and I found that I liked certain things about the weeks when my mother wasn't coming, and neither of my two grandmothers. I could relax, not have to hope for anything. I used to feel sorry for the full orphans who had nobody, but

Visiting Day was the worst for kids with relatives who said they'd come and never did. We had plenty of kids like that, not just Shmecky. I came to the conclusion Hoffman's power had something to do with his not having to wait for anybody to show up. Ever. That was freedom. Jesse was left once, when he was too young to remember it. Whereas guys like me were left every other Sunday.

Weeks passed and leaves fell, allowing us to see more of the world through the bare tree limbs. I thought the winter landscape on Tuckahoe Road was beautiful, a picture by Currier & Ives, unlike winter in the Bronx with frozen dog turds on the sidewalk. But the country was brutal in its own way. The cold was colder. Winter descended on us with a chill I couldn't get rid of. That cold, cold smell of the dark night David Copperfield talked about—that was the smell of an institution not getting the proper amount of coal. Frosty mornings rung out of bed. That was us. Shmecky was right. Dickens sure knew the H. There were holes in the roof of the big building and warped sashes on those cracked dormitory windows. In the mornings, condensation dripped into puddles on the windowsill and sometimes great hunks of ice formed on our bed frames and the supervisors came with pickaxes to chop it from our beds before we could even begin to make hospital corners. I heard more keenly than I did in the city. The north wind blasted down from the Adirondacks across the plains of Westchester whistling through the trees. Branches creaked, hickory nuts hit the roof, coyotes howled at the moon, and little boys cried out after wetting the bed. I felt everything harder and more deeply, because there was more space to feel it. Not just more space in the landscape, but more space inside myself, which was loneliness, but also freedom.

Pussy Alice had another litter of kittens and not enough teats. Carl Grimm, the second chef, who did not seem like a hobo or an ex-con but more like a teacher or a scientist, brought a glass of milk from the kitchen and an eyedropper from Nurse Flanagan and sat on the ground in his white chef's uniform. He held the runt, a gray fluff ball, in the crook of his arm and fed her milk with the eyedropper. Then Mr. Grimm let me try. The little puss was so sweet. She sucked the milk from the eyedropper with kissing sounds.

"Is it wrong to feed her if she was supposed to die?" I said. I'd read about natural selection.

"Maybe I'm a softie," said Mr. Grimm. "But I believe in helping those who need a hand and I believe Mr. Darwin does, too. What about you, Clyde? What do you think?"

"Me, too," I said.

Mr. Grimm had to go back to work. He stood and collected the empty milk glass and the eyedropper. He was covered in straw and animal hair. He brushed himself off but the sticks and fur clung to him. "Let's hope there's not a scold around to notice," Mr. Grimm said. He smiled like we were in on it together. I liked that about Mr. Grimm. He slipped a white chef's hat from his pocket and put it on his head at a jaunty angle. He wasn't one of them. He was one of us.

Jesse Hoffman and a few others packed their bags and moved up to Company D. They were juniors now. I missed having Hoffman in the dorm, but I still had Chick Scheiner. At least Chick was easygoing, whereas Jesse was a smart aleck. He couldn't help it—Jesse was ahead of everyone, clever, inventive, hilarious. In fact, I thought, Jesse was a lot like me. Chick was the opposite, even-tempered, never conceited. He had a great laugh. He'd throw back his red head and roar, and sometimes he slapped his knee like a country bumpkin, and when Chick laughed like that at one of my jokes I felt like a million bucks.

Chick, Jesse, Harry, Manny Bergman, and I sat on the library stoop carving our names into the soapstone. It was Friday and we were shooting the shit while the staff bustled around the kitchen yard getting ready for the Sabbath. Some seniors, whose names were already carved into the steps and indelibly inked with years of dirt, loitered around the porch giving instructions on how to hold a penknife, and other sage advice.

"Just wait until tomorrow," said Young Connie. "You're going to be so sorry the Colonel retired the pommel horse."

"Wasn't the Colonel who did away with it," said Jesse. "It was Mr. Laudenbacher. The Superintendant."

"All the same," said Young Connie. "You'll be beggin' for the pommel horse."

"Baloney," said Harry.

"You don't know what you're in for," said Young Connie. He ran a finger over the letters cut into the fourth riser: Young Connie Schreiber, 1922. "Frickin' detention," he said.

"So tell us."

"Try standing still for one, maybe two hours," said Jesse solemnly. He'd had detention once since he moved up.

"Big deal. I can stand still," I said.

"With your arms out?" said Jesse.

"I can do that," said Chick.

"Oh, yeah, smartie? How about holding a pillow?" Young Connie said.

"A pillow? Geez, that's nuttin'," said Manny Bergman.

"A pilla's a bag a' feathers is all," Chick said.

"Weighs nuttin," said Harry.

"Light as a feather," I said.

"Yeah? How about a shoe?" Young Connie said.

"A shoe? I don't know about a shoe."

The Sabbath, Shabbos, the day of rest, the holy day, was for some cockeyed reason considered the correct day to mete out punishments based on demerits collected over the week. Company E had accumulated a fair amount for talking at meals, tardiness, marching out of step, and fighting. Instead of going downstairs to the gym to drop our trousers after shul as usual, we were told to go to our dorm and line up in a column down the center aisle.

Superintendant Laudenbacher was a good man, but misguided. Standing for two hours without moving a muscle was the worst torture of all. I'd have given my right arm to march in a circle, not to mention submit to the wrecking crew. I'd have gladly bent over the pommel horse if it meant I could shift my weight. When Manny thought nobody was looking he scratched his head and Beiderman socked him in the mouth so hard he went down. Two seniors carted Bergman off to Nurse Flanagan. Then the Colonel ordered us to hold our arms out. Boom, another kid down without even being punched—he fainted—which was lucky for him because he was carried off to Flanny as well. I wondered why everyone didn't fake fainting, but there must have been a reason. I didn't think I'd be able to hold my arms up any longer when the monitors grabbed the pillows off our beds and placed them onto our outstretched hands. For ten seconds my pillow was a marshmallow. On the eleventh second, a sack of potatoes. Get this thing off me, I screamed in my head. I cried but my eyes were dry. I pretended I was a rock. A rock can't move. The tears flowed backward into my skull.

People on the outside, they didn't know about standing detention. On Saturday afternoons in spring and summer after several hours of shul and punishment, we marched two miles into Bronxville where we were treated to first-run movies at the Palace Theater. Townspeople on the street stopped in their tracks and shopkeepers in their aprons came outside to marvel at the parallel lines of well-behaved Hebrew orphans in knickerbockers and newsboy caps marching in lockstep.

Around Christmas, Harry grew sullen. He was angry. For days he didn't speak to me. I had turned nine back in April and there was nothing I could do about it. I couldn't not turn nine. I waited for months and now January 1st was fast approaching, time to advance to the junior dorm. Harry had friends but he was attached to me. He didn't want to be left behind. There would be no more doubling up in bed once I moved into Company D.

On New Year's Eve we pinched ourselves to stay awake. Cheesie was lookout. He had a sixth sense and got his name from calling "Cheese it!" whenever he spotted coppers. We scrambled back under the covers and faked sleeping when the Colonel made his rounds. Then just before midnight, a crowd of freshmen sneaked around the corner to the east wing into the junior dorm where many of us (me included) would move the next day. The seniors came down from the fourth floor with pots and pans and soup kettles, spoons, ladles, and spatulas pilfered from either the meat kitchen or the milk kitchen. Pious Pussy Friedman would have squealed if we used both. At the stroke of twelve we threw open the windows and leaned into the bitter night glittering with stars and banged our kettles, clanged our frying pans. Jesse produced a rousing drum roll, a paradiddle, and a ratatatat—boom, crack, clickety boom—and the rest of us rattled and clinked and cheered. Three hundred and eighty-one orphans hanging out the windows shouting with glee: Happy New Year! Happy 1926!

CHAPTER 26

My mother and I had our squabbles, but spending short periods of time with her during the winter of my father's illness was mostly therapeutic. It was liberating to get away from Brenda, and my mother's place on Charles Street was so clean and free of clutter I felt a kind of lightness there, the way I felt in hotel rooms. Her apartment was so unlike the house on Cedar Drive where even the dust accumulated meaning. I'd look under the bed and swear those were the same dust balls I saw in 1959 when my mother lifted the hem of the quilt to show Susan that our missing grandfather wasn't hiding there. "See? Nothing!" my mother said, calming Susan's fears. In her uncluttered apartment, we could look back more objectively. Not much, but a little more.

"It was my fault," my mother said with a faraway look in her eyes. "What we started in Ireland."

I encouraged her to talk about herself. I wanted to know her, but I was searching for myself between the lines. "Did you come home a changed woman?" I asked. "That's what you wanted, right?"

"Did it change me? I suppose, in a way."

I thought it was sad how Susan and I lost our accents in a matter of months, carelessly discarding the Irish inflection like a sweater on a hot day. No one thought to record our voices.

"Your father and I were closer when we got back," my mother said. "We'd been through a lot together. We had experiences no one else had. So things were better, at least for a while."

I remembered family coziness when we returned—unexpected after the Caitlyn drama. Laughter, joking all the time, half the jokes in Yiddish, summer thunderstorms, rain pattering on the gravel roof, winters sledding down the backyard hill, even my mother occasionally belly-whomping on our Flexible Flyer. Dinner at 6 o'clock on the dot, my father was adamant. I liked the forced togetherness of those dinners at home in America—at least when I was little, not so much when I was older—but in elementary school the feeling I got with the four of us squeezed around the kitchen table in the yellow light was better than sleep or food or a movie.

The room was so small we didn't have to stand up to get pickles or ice. My father tipped his chair back and swung the refrigerator door open from his seat. He had a sweet tooth so we drank orange soda or grape soda or Coke. If there was none, he put pineapple jelly in a glass of seltzer. "This is the way we made soda at the Home," he said, and stirred up the mixture, furiously beating the spoon against the glass. After a few seconds the jelly settled at the bottom in a glob.

We told stories and whenever one of us tried to locate an event from the past, we asked the others was it "before Ireland or after Ireland?" I thought we would always divide time that way, but the "after" part kept growing and the "before" part stayed the same, until Ireland was no longer a useful marker.

But stirring the jelly soda around the table we were still tethered to that time and to each other and my father stirred and stirred but he couldn't get the jelly to dissolve. He drank it anyway. "Delicious," he said. My mother took a sip. "Delicious." "You making fun of me?" he said.

They shared a private smile, and she stretched out of her chair to get her cigarettes on the counter. She wore a tight sweater and a slim wool skirt with two kick pleats in the back. My father put his hand on her rear end. "She's making fun of me," he said. She seemed to like his hand there, pushing back into his palm rather than moving away from him. "Not me. I'm not doing anything," she said. She finally turned her body out of his grasp, settled into her chair, lit a cigarette, and inhaled.

"Kid. You," my father said, pointing at Susan. "You ever go to bed hungry?"

My mother lifted her chin and blew smoke at the yellow walls.

Susan smiled at him adoringly. "No, Daddy."

"No is right. I didn't have a daddy to bring me bubblegum. Steak, shrimp these kids eat."

"Tell us the rest of the Shmecky story," Susan said. "Tell us. We're old enough."

"Shmuel was his real name, though. Shmecky was a nickname. . . ."

"We know! We know!"

"All right, I'll tell you the rest of the story. You listening to your daddy? So Shmuel, or Shmecky if you want, waits for his mama every Sunday rain or shine. And she never comes, right? Until one day she *does* come. She shows up at the H—the H was short for the Home."

"We know!"

"You know? OK, so Shmecky's mother shows up at the H and she takes him back to Brooklyn with her. Nice story, right? But that isn't the end of it. Two weeks go by, and then, lo and behold, who's back at the Hebrew National Orphan Home but Shmuel Hefter. 'What's the matter, Shmecky?' we said. 'What're you doing back in this shithole?' Which it wasn't, by the way. But that's how we talked. And Shmecky says, 'I forgot my Yiddish while I was at the H. And my mama doesn't speak English.' Poor Shmecky, for two weeks he and his mother sat across the kitchen table in Flatbush with nothing to say. He managed, though, with the few Yiddish words he remembered, to beg her to take him back to the orphanage. And so she did."

"That's sad," Susan said.

"Sad? Yeah," my father said. "But you know what? He survived. Kids get over all kinds of shit. Look at me, for instance."

My mother laughed on cue and I glanced up. White dotted lines were darting past the window above the sink. "Look!" I said. "It's snowing!"

My father shouted like a little kid. "It's snowing! It's snowing!"

We both jumped up and got our coats and clambered into the carport, Susan and my mother close behind. The four of us stood at the top of the driveway, an entirely white Cedar Drive spread before us. "It's a veritable winter wonderland," he said. We all laughed. He said it every time it snowed, clapping his hands together in delight, a sound that echoed in the cold. We listened to the shush of tires over on Patterson Avenue and after that nothing but the kind of quiet you feel after someone has read a poem.

"It was my fault. But he wasn't blameless," my mother said. "Your father wanted his freedom, too. He was confused, though. He was jealous of my affairs, and complained because I wasn't jealous enough of his! I quoted his precious Sartre—'jealousy, like all passions, is an enemy of freedom.' But he saw it as proof I didn't love him. He couldn't deny, though, that I knew him better than anyone. I knew him and accepted him as he was. How's that for true love? Of course, with him it was never enough. And then the sixties exploded and he went wild."

He grew a mustache and bushy ringlets. This isn't my era, my mother conceded, and continued to get her hair teased and sprayed at the beauty parlor. She had done it all before, the rallies and protests and passionate intensity, and what had it got her? My father was surrounded by students, infected by their youth. It went to his head. He wanted to be one of them. I took her place, marching at his side to end the war in Vietnam.

For my fourteenth birthday, my parents gave me "The Sixties Songbook for Keyboard," and our friend Johnny Dolan gave me a purple bikini. I learned "Golden Slumbers." My father stood behind me at the piano while I played and we sang together: *Once there was a way to get back homeward.* My voice was high and thin. *Once there was a way to get back home.* His voice was so deep the walls trembled.

CHAPTER 27

Tuckahoe

Rain pattered steadily on the slate roof of a Saturday afternoon as I made my way down the shadowy corridor to the library to sit at a wooden table and read in the lamplight, a pleasure we were allowed on inclement weekends. Jesse caught up with me. "You're gonna be approached," he said. "I just got word. You'll be asked to do something, some feat of bravery. Whatever it is, do it. After that, you'll be left alone. But if you chicken out, they'll make your life hell. Got it?"

"What is it? What do I have to do?"

"I don't know. But whatever it is, Clyde, you've got to have chutzpah. You're a junior now. You gotta have balls."

I scowled at my friend. "I will. I do," I said. He disappeared into the shadows again.

That night I lay awake mulling it over. My white-iron headboard was up against the wall under a drafty window and another bed was up against my footboard with Skelly Schwartz in it, two rows deep on either side of the center aisle. Manny Bergman on my right, Chick in front of me to the left of Skelly. A lot more snoring and plenty of farting in the junior dorm. A hundred-and-thirty boys, some whose balls hadn't even dropped, others with great hairy balls and putrid body odor and feet that stank like Limberger cheese. I mulled it over. A feat of bravery. They might dare me to swim across the B. A. Creek. The guys knew I didn't know how to swim. I might have to shimmy up the flagpole or sleep in a coffin in the basement. A rite of passage, Jesse said. Shit. Shorty Lapidus in the barn. Shit, piss, and corruption. The clank of his belt buckle rang in my ears like he was standing right next to me. His cackle sent a shiver down my spine. I felt a hand on my shoulder. Or was I just imagining it? Shit. "Shove over, Aronson."

CHAPTER 28

At the Hot Shoppes on the New York State Thruway, Nola ordered tea. She fished out the Lipton's teabag and wrapped the string around the bowl of the teaspoon squeezing the teabag like a tourniquet, dribbling the soaked-up liquid back into her cup.

"Hey, that's very clever," my father said. "I'll have to try that."

Liz and I exchanged a look. Not daring to roll our eyes, we barely fluttered our eyelids. Under the table she nudged my knee with hers. Nola bit her lip with her two big childish front teeth and watched the drips falling from the teabag. I tried to unravel the puzzle of her good looks. Everyone had eyes, a nose and mouth. Why couldn't I stop staring at Nola? Was it her high forehead? No, because sometimes that was ugly. It was everything combined, the sheen on her silky blonde hair curving to the shape of her skull, deep-set eyes, cornflower blue, that were not too close together or too far apart. It was the high cheekbones, although not the blueblood kind, hers were high and broad like a farm girl's, and the summer tan on skin that appeared to have no pores, those dazzling teeth and a smile like a branding iron.

We pulled into the Lake George campground at dusk. My father blamed Liz's sister for the descending darkness, for driving like a snail when it was Mandy's turn at the wheel. "I drove over the speed limit!" Mandy yelled back. "You said we could get to Lake George before dark and you were wrong!" Now a storm was gathering. We tried to jam the tent poles into the lakeshore but they wouldn't stay upright in the sand, so we had to throw our stuff back into the car and trudge into the woods until we found a spot where the ground was firm and level among a few scrubby pine trees. Nola brought the car around to our new site. My father yelled instructions for putting up the tent over the roar of the wind and I wished I were brave enough to talk back to him like Mandy. I'd tell him he was a stupid, stupid man. If I had been the one who mapped out the itinerary and we ended up trying to pitch a tent in the dark, boy, would I have been told off. You stupid, stupid girl.

"Pretty fucking stupid," I muttered under my breath.

"What did you say, kid?"

We were at the trunk unloading supplies when it started to rain, fat drops plunking on our heads slowly at first, and then faster. I grabbed the Coleman lantern from Liz, while she carried a sleeping bag under each arm, and we ran for cover. The five of us crammed into the tent (made to sleep four) just as the drops merged into sheets of rain lashing the canvas. We laughed with relief.

"Are we lucky?" my father said. "Is that great planning or what?"

"Yeah, great planning," I said. I turned to show Liz my smirk.

"Are you two conspiring against me?" my father said.

"They're just counting their blessings, Clyde," Mandy said.

My father slept against one side of the tent, then came Nola, then me, Liz, and Mandy against the other side. The tent reeked of mildew even after being draped over our bushes in the sun, and pebbles poked through the canvas floor and into my back. I shifted and squirmed until I found a smooth patch of ground and fell asleep for a while, but I woke to a rustling sound. The rain had stopped. It was dead quiet for a few seconds and then the rustling picked up again. Fuck. Black bears lived in the Adirondacks. I was scared and moved closer to Liz, but I was not as scared as I might have been or should have been because I figured even if it was a bear my father would know what to do. He wasn't afraid of anything. It probably wasn't a bear, though. All kinds of smaller critters lived in these woods, I told myself—raccoons, badgers. I put the folded up T-shirt I

was using for a pillow over my head, and tried to go back to sleep, but the rustling intensified, and I was losing my nerve. I was about to wake up my father when I realized with a jolt that the rustling was coming from *inside* the tent—the shrill rubbing of nylon against nylon. Then a girl's giggle and my father's hoarse whisper. The growl of a sleeping-bag zipper.

Oh, please God, no. Not this. I moved away from them like an inchworm in my mummy bag pressing against Liz, hiding my face in her Herbal Essence hair. Liz didn't wake up, nor did I try to wake her up. I pretended I was asleep too. More rustling and the tent zipper, zhrip, zhrip, and my father and Nola climbing out. Zhrip, zhrip closing us up again. Branches snapped under their feet. The car door croaked open. They would do it in the Torino. At least not in here. Liz and Mandy slept. Still, I didn't wake them. I wanted Johnny. I wanted Johnny to hold me.

In the morning, I expected my father to expend a lot of effort in my direction, making nice and sweet-talking to me, but I was mistaken. He despised my stricken face, my rubbery arms and legs, my bloody heart wrapped in rags.

"Don't just stand there. Help out. You think you're here to get waited on?"

I kneeled on the dew-soaked ground to gather the felled tent poles and slid them clanging like bells into their nylon bag. Then I started stuffing my sleeping bag into its own bag, punching the fiber-filled nylon to the bottom. I positioned the sack between my knees and punched and punched. The sun was out but the morning air was chilly. Nola wore my father's tweed jacket with elbow patches and laughed when the too-long sleeves flopped around.

We drove into town and I was bleeding, doubled over in pain. "I got my period," I whispered to Liz. She fished a Darvon out of her purse and I went to the public ladies' room with the pill and a tampon in my back pocket. I gulped the Darvon with water cupped in my hands at the filthy sink and walked back to the car. They were waiting for me. They wanted to stroll around the town.

"I'll stay here," I said. "I can lie on the backseat."

"You be OK, baby?" my father said.

I looked away. "Yes, go."

The Darvon was useless. I lay with my knees drawn up and rocked in agony. Nothing helped, not lying on my side or on my back with the soles of my feet against the window, not on my stomach with one arm raking the dirty floor, nothing, until I pushed open the door, lurched into a patch of weeds and threw up. I felt only halfway better after that, but enough to fall into a fitful sleep with my cheek pressed to the cigarette-stinking vinyl seat.

For nine days and nights we pretended it wasn't happening. I didn't say a word to Liz or Mandy until the last rest stop on I-95 before the Baltimore beltway. Nola went out to wait in the car and we were left in the ladies' room. Of course Liz and Mandy knew. We'd all known since the first night. My own silence for all that time mystified me.

"What happened on the trip? Why are you so upset?" my mother asked.

"He was mean to me, yelling at me the whole way."

My father came into the kitchen.

"Why were you picking on Joanna?" my mother asked.

"Obnoxious teenager," my father said. "Snotty kid. I can't trust her. That Liz Stone, too. Disrespectful. They were terrible, terrible. I was stuck with them for ten days."

I was stunned by his brazen lies. I didn't expect or even want him to confess to my mother. I wanted to protect both of them, as always. But I couldn't understand what he gained by turning on me.

Johnny came over the night after we got back and I asked him to go for a walk. I was relieved to get out of the house. We went slowly around the block twice and on the second loop stopped at the corner three houses before mine to sit on the curb side by side. I cried into his V-neck sweater. He agreed I should say nothing to my mother. She would find out on her own, he said. He held me against his chest stroking my hair, my cheek, smoothing the nap of my eyebrow. "He didn't think you knew," Johnny said.

"I'm not stupid," I said through my tears. Johnny kissed them away. He slipped his hand under my blouse and I closed my eyes. I felt his fingertips brushing my nipple, touching the shape of one breast, the budding warmth, then shivers. I didn't wear a bra. He liked to come into my room when I was doing my homework. He kissed me. Johnny complicated everything. His tongue was hot and gentle, and I felt better.

CHAPTER 29

Tuckahoe

A week passed with no one asking me to shimmy up the flagpole or sleep in a coffin. Nothing happening except me looking over my shoulder every time I lined up to piss and brush my teeth or marched to class, or trudged up to the farm to muck out the stalls, until finally I was approached, just like Jesse said.

"Hey, Aronson." A column of sunlight slanted into the barn between the slatted timbers. Stanley Hirsh stood at the entrance illuminated, his meaty fists on his hips.

"What?"

"I got a proposition for you and Chick Scheiner. A way for you saps to make some dough."

I dropped my shovel and stepped out of the stall. This was it. "Yeah?" I said.

"Charlie the porter. He has a job."

"A feat of bravery?"

"Huh?" said Hirsh. "Listen, Aronson, you up for it?"

"What is it?"

"Whatever it is?"

"Sure," I said. "Whatever."

"Go see Charlie when you're done here."

My heart raced. I prayed the swimming hole was frozen, and I prayed for Shorty's death. I saw Chick. "Wait up." We headed down to the cottage that Charlie the porter shared with Carl Grimm and Hymie the handyman.

"Aronson. Scheiner. Been waitin' on youse." Charlie handed each of us a gunnysack. "Go to the barn. Collect as many kittens as fit. Bring 'em back to me."

Kittens? I looked past Charlie to see if Mr. Grimm was inside the house. I wondered what he would think. Whatever it is, Jesse had said.

On the way up to the barn we passed Harry and Pinky coming from the opposite direction.

"Hey small fry, where you headed?" said Chick.

"Candy store," said Harry.

"Oh shit," I said. "Where'd you get that nickel?"

"I found it."

"Better not be from Shorty Lapidus."

"I told you," said Harry. "I found it."

"You better have found it. Now scram, the both of youse. Go get your candy."

We had a job to do. Here kitty, kitty. Alice's new litter, and others. Her grandchildren. Great grandchildren. She'd been around a while. I plucked a kitten clinging to Chick's pant leg and dropped the cat into my sack. Big old Pussy Alice lay on her side and licked her paws. A gray fuzz ball slept next to her. The runt. Whatever it is, do it. I peered into my bag. I had four or five already. Chick had the same. It was enough. I let the fuzz ball sleep.

Charlie the porter tied the sacks shut with twine. "Take the path down to the creek over toward the aqueduct side. You know what I'm talking about?"

"Yeah, we know." We stood in the driveway.

"You put the sack in the water, you hold it under."

"What?"

"It ain't frozen over. I seen it."

"But the kittens . . . They'll drown," said Chick.

"That's the idea."

Chick and I kicked at the gravel. We were only nine, going on ten.

"We got too many on the grounds here. It's a threat to the public health."

We shrugged and stared at our feet.

"Far worse starving to death," said Charlie.

"All right," I said. "We'll take care of it."

"Then go. Get on with it."

We passed through the orchard where each tree was just a bundle of dead sticks that implausibly would bloom into thousands of sweet-smelling white blossoms in a month or two and we clambered down to the gully, half-muddy, half-frozen and reached the gurgling, babbling, splish-splashing creek. A pink nose pressed against the opening of the burlap neck I held in my fist. I hardened my heart and plunged my sack into the icy water. Chick did the same. We held them under, felt their fragile shoulders under our thumbs, a haunch, an ear, forced down to the bottom. Our hands turned blue. The whitewater noise of the Sprain Brook drowned out the mewling cries.

In the spring, a team of us rebuilt the dam and reinstated the Bare Ass Swimming Hole, a task I relished and that did not require knowing how to swim. We had to engineer the whole thing on the sly, of course, since we were trespassing and the Grassy Sprain golf club members complained we were trampling on their turf. On top of that, we were forbidden to work on Saturdays. Beating children on the Sabbath was fine, apparently, but building our own Garden of Eden offended God. Supervisors and monitors occasionally traipsed through the woods to catch us in the act, so we had Cheesie as lookout. The job required days of labor. We hiked to the spot after synagogue and after classes. A bucket brigade formed for dredging mud. Slimy rocks were dug up from along the stream bed and passed from man to man until the dam wall was neatly assembled by seniors waist deep and then chest high in the cold creek creating a mighty wall of stones, logs, twigs, and mud trapping the water to a depth of five feet so we could jump in, maybe even dive. Well, so they could dive. I could wade up to my neck and I loved making things and listened closely to the older guys as they discussed the mechanics of dam building. During the week we talked of nothing else. At night, surrounded by the sighing inhale and exhale of sleeping friends, I lay in bed thinking about the task ahead, each step in the process, and what a paradise the place would be when we were done. These thoughts while lying awake were some of the most peaceful in my life. We cheered when the water rose. I spent many summer afternoons lazing on Bare Beach under the weeping willows.

Chick and I joined the farm gang because we both liked animals, especially horses. The barn didn't interest Harry or Jesse. Most kids hated the farm detail when it came up in chore rotation. They preferred peeling potatoes, scrubbing enormous soup kettles or even scrubbing the washroom floor. Harry couldn't believe I chose weeding in the hot sun, much less shoveling horseshit. His horse was strictly an iron charger. He hung around the auto shed watching older inmates build a motorcycle engine from scratch, learning from their grease-monkey talk. To each his own. Weeding allowed time to think with no one interrupting my thoughts. No one bothered us on the farm. The supervisors hardly ever came up there. Chick and I brushed down Joe, Playboy, and Sally the mare, then watched how the older guys harnessed the horses and hitched up the plow. Each of us learned what we wanted from the older guys. Not just dirty jokes. I admired the seniors most of all when they fearlessly, it seemed to me, left the grounds of the Home and our exclusive (orphans only) public school, and went off to Roosevelt High where they were supposed to blend in with the normal kids who wore sporty clothes and glowed with good health. But we didn't blend in. Kids from the Home were easy to spot, the smell of poverty and death clung stubbornly to our faded hand-me-downs.

High school was a few years away for me. I tried not to worry about it. Chick and I filled the water buckets and feed buckets. I felt at ease in the barn and outside in the fields. It was a chance to be away from the regimentation, away from the Colonel, the cane, the rabbi, the pommel horse, the supervisor, the monitor. Farm work was hard, but a chance to be free.

Sometimes I talked to Playboy when I was alone. I told him about the Colonel and we shook our heads and snorted about human nature. Who was Tom Anderson? Where did he come from? Was he ever a little boy? The other supervisors I understood, but the Colonel had a blank stare. No matter how often he struck, either spontaneously, or after much planning and marking off on rosters, I was taken by surprise. Even in his military uniform, even with his weapon at the ready posing as a crutch, still, I never expected swift action from the Colonel because he appeared indifferent. Even when his eyes popped like boiled raisins he seemed vague and distracted, which I learned was a particular kind of evil.

The wind blew cold, leaves rattled and fell. We raked them into piles and climbed into the trees and jumped onto the crispy heaps, then lit a bonfire in the fallow field and threw mickeys into the flames. Those who had gloves pulled the hot potatoes out when they were done, and we tossed them from hand to hand, poked the jackets open with a stick and let the steam pour out. Always too hungry to wait, we burned our mouths.

I couldn't picture my father's face anymore, but I could smell him, the toasty aroma of his ironed shirts like a mickey plucked from the flames. Up the hill on the farm, we could see down to Tuckahoe Road, and sometimes we stopped what we were doing to stare as roadsters sped around the curves to the Grassy Sprain Golf and Country Club. Why did I imagine my father there, hopping out of a Packard or a Marmon Speedster? He wouldn't have been allowed in. He was a Jew like me. We tossed our mickeys from hand to hand.

He was somewhere, though, out in the world with the twenties roaring, flappers flapping, and swells flashing their C-notes, all while the roof leaked on the Oddfellows Orphan Home, and the wind shrieked through the cracks in the windowpanes, and the cold seeped into our bones and stayed there until April.

CHAPTER 30

"It's in a difficult place," said Dr. Heidenheimer. "For a biopsy, you'd have to go up through a nostril, or in through the soft palate." No one at Sinai was skilled enough to get to it. Maybe there was somebody at Johns Hopkins, he said. He wanted my father gone from his hospital altogether, it seemed. I told the doctor I was surprised that just a biopsy could be so complicated. Meanwhile, I wondered to myself if I had said the right thing the other night when my father asked if he was going to die. In the silvery light of his room with the blue recliner pushed up to his bed, I sat and considered the two issues he had brought up. Not life and death, but trust and truth. He said he trusted me, of all people. He was depending on me, yet as a child, I could hardly trust or depend on him. Unfair as it was, though, I accepted the responsibility. Why such devotion, Liz wanted to know, and she wasn't the only one. Maybe it was just that in other ways, he and I were alike.

He said he wanted the truth. He could handle it. Clyde Aronson wouldn't be played for a fool. He was a thinker and a poet, or at least a poetry teacher, and poetry was obsessed with death. He wasn't afraid of the subject. He kept a copy of Philip Larkin's poem "Next, Please," taped to the inside of the Camaro's trunk lid, a reminder that a ship with a black sail was coming for him, a ship with no bounty, only a huge and birdless silence in its wake, and he had better hurry up and live. I thought about answering his question by boldly telling him Aunt Vivian said he looked like a man who was dying of cancer. Or I could describe the evasive, guilty look on Heidenheimer's face. Or I could tell the honest truth, which was "I don't know." But I didn't think the truth my father wanted was a cold assessment of his situation, despite the bleak poetry. If he wanted something cold, he could ask Brenda.

"You're going to get well," I said. I would fight for him and he would live, at least for a few years. We'd find out what this was and zap it, or cut it out, or both. "You're going to get better." He blinked his one eye, concentrating on my words. "I'm going to make sure of it," I said. I wasn't shining him on. I sensed he was asking for more than a medical opinion. He was asking that the wolf be kept from the door long enough to make this into something we did and not something that was done to us.

CHAPTER 31

Baltimore was a small city. You could be in a high-rise overlooking the harbor and fifteen minutes later, deep in the countryside. Sidewalks in every direction ended at the woods. I was searching for a pharmacy that carried controlled substances. I parked in front of a drugstore on the edge of a dead cornfield bordered by bare-limbed oaks and scruffy loblolly pines. I need methadone, I told the pharmacist. He went to get it, and left me alone with the Dobermann snarling behind the counter.

My father was about to be sent home from Sinai, to wait for an appointment with a Johns Hopkins surgeon. First, though, he had to be weaned off Demerol injections and onto the tiny methadone tablets used to detox heroin addicts. The process would take days. I brought the pills back to the hospital and Nurse Debbie coaxed my father. "Come on, Mr. Aronson. Be a good boy and swallow." Christmas came and went, and finally, he was discharged. He was happy about it, but I wasn't. I didn't want to go home to a place with no Debbie and no Demerol, where the sheets weren't changed every day, where Hoffman, who missed his master as he used to be, whined and swished his hairy tail. Home to dirty dishes in the sink. Home to Brenda.

Brenda wasn't happy to see either one of us and went around muttering curses under her breath. *Goddamn Aronsons. Son of a bitch. Goddamn junkie.* I couldn't bear the weekends when Brenda was in the house all day long.

To be fair, this was not how Brenda had imagined married life. She was forty on her wedding day and my father was sixty-five—but he was a young sixty-five. He had a string of ex-girlfriends and adoring students, drove a muscle car, kneaded his own pasta dough, and mowed his own lawn. She fed off his vitality.

"You look like an old man in a nursing home slumped in that chair," Brenda said.

He begged her to rent a hospital bed since it hurt to lie down flat, but she refused to have the ugly contraption in her house. She complained that his three humidifiers were ruining the furniture. *Goddamn humidifiers.* His mouth was dry. He couldn't swallow. She shut off the steam when he wasn't looking. He resorted to sucking on Wintergreen Tic Tacs and spit the bleached nubs into crumpled tissues he left in his pockets.

I didn't know what I was supposed to do about Brenda. We were obviously at cross-purposes. I was obsessed with saving my father's life. She wanted to get rid of her houseguests (mainly me) and have her life back to normal. I understood wanting that. But she wasn't facing reality. She may have thought I was a weakling, but she wasn't as strong as she pretended. She lacked the moral fortitude required for extreme circumstances. Even Nurse Debbie had asked, as she phrased it, why on God's green earth did your father marry Brenda?

People were always asking me that question. Relatives, friends. They were all mystified. The first I heard of the marriage proposal, I couldn't believe it either. Fred and I were living in New York and my parents stopped to see us on their way to a wedding in Connecticut. When he sprung it on us, I thought he was joking. My parents had been divorced very recently after years of separation, but they were both going to this wedding so it made sense to drive up together. My father came into our apartment yelling, "Where's my pastrami?"

He was nicer once he'd had a few bites of his sandwich. We sat at the table by the open windows just below the sidewalk and watched the bottom half of people walking by. A balmy April breeze drifted in. "Ah, New York," my father said. "My town."

"No place like it," my mother said.

"You wanna know something, Joanna?" my father said.

"Yeah, sure I wanna know something."

"You make good coffee."

I beamed in the glow of his approval. "I make it strong. That's the secret."

"Tell your mother. Hers is lousy."

"I beg your pardon," my mother said, trying to make a joke of being offended. But I could see the insult stung.

"Be nice," I said. "Her coffee isn't lousy." I chafed when he played us against each other.

"Why do you think I left him?" my mother said. "He's never satisfied."

"There! She admitted it. You heard her, Fred. She's the one who left me. I never left anybody."

"You didn't have to," my mother said. "You made it impossible to stay."

"Bullshit. If I'm so impossible why are women waiting in line for me? And they want marriage." He conducted an invisible orchestra drawing the syllable beats in the air. "Mahr-eee-ahge."

"I believe it," my mother said. "I see the women down at the club. They don't know what they're in for, though."

"You're kidding," Fred said. "You two belong to the same singles club?"

"I see her down there, across the room, dancing with those salesmen," my father said. He and my mother traded smiles.

"By the way, are you still going out with what's-her-name?" my mother said.

"Who?" said my father. He took a bite of a prune Danish.

"You know. What's her name?"

He kept eating without saying anything. He sipped some coffee. Finally he said, "You mean Brenda McLean?"

"Yeah, Brenda. Who did you think I meant?"

He brushed the crumbs from his mustache. "We broke up," he said.

"Really?" my mother said. "I didn't know you were going steady."

"You guys think it's funny. It's not. That Brenda kept giving me ultimatums."

"What kind of ultimatums?" my mother asked.

"If I don't marry her, she won't see me anymore. Stuff like that."

"So that's why she broke up with you? Because you wouldn't marry her?" I said.

"Yeah, but it's complicated," my father said.

"Well, I'm glad you told Brenda no," I said.

"Yeah, but that Brenda, she's keeping at it with the ultimatums," my father said.

"I don't get it," my mother said. "How can Brenda be giving ultimatums if you already broke up? In that case, she gave her ultimatum and it backfired. Am I right?"

"Yeah, yeah. You're right," my father said. "But it's not that simple. She's all fucked up. She gave me a different ultimatum this time. This time, if I don't marry her, she'll kill herself."

"Oh, no. You're not going to fall for that, Clyde?"

"I don't know. She loves me. She'd rather die than live without me. But you wouldn't understand that, Evie."

"Oh, I understand it. It's called emotional blackmail." My mother got up and went over to the sofa. She took one of my father's cigarettes from the pack on the coffee table and lit it. "That's not love," she said. "Jesus, Clyde."

"I don't know what to do," my father said. He reached over and ate the last piece of my mother's pastry.

"Hey, that was mine!" she said, and came back to the table.

"But I didn't get any cherry!" he said. "What's the matter? Am I an orphan or something?"

My mother laughed. They never ceased laughing at each other's tired jokes.

Now Brenda was striding into the living room on Cedar Drive, cranking the drapes open with the pulley making a familiar sound: *reek-shh, reek-shh.*

"Hey!" my father yelped from his chair. "The light hurts my eyes."

"It's depressing in here," Brenda said. "I hate having the curtains drawn in broad daylight, it's so goddamned depressing." *Reek-shh. Reek-shh.* She opened the drapes wider and wider.

I stayed out of it. It *was* depressing. But for fuck's sake, the light hurt his eyes. What was so hard to understand? I folded my sheets and blankets without looking at my father or Brenda, and went to take a shower. As soon as the hot spray hit my back, I was lulled into a trance. I wanted to stay in my private watery chamber forever, the door locked against my father and Brenda, but we only had one bathroom and I was, as always, condemned to be considerate of others. While getting dressed, I noticed a vial on the sink next to the shaving cream. I picked it up and read the label without even thinking about Brenda's need for privacy. I was no saint, in spite of what my father said. I probably wasn't even all that considerate, in ways I couldn't see. It was Lithium. So she was manic-depressive or bipolar, or whatever they were calling extreme mood swings these days. I'd heard about her weekends under the covers, but I hadn't heard anything about the manic part. I should have felt more sympathy for Brenda after the discovery, but I didn't. I hesitated leaving the steamy bathroom and entering the dry hallway, the stale Benson & Hedges air. In the living room, the drapes were now three-quarters of the way closed, a compromise. Brenda was leaning over my father. She kissed him.

"I'm taking Hoffman to Sudbrook for a run," she said.

My father reached out from his chair and grabbed Brenda around the hips. She held her arms airplane-style to keep her balance. She was laughing. I wondered how they came to the compromise on the curtains. She slipped from my father's grasp and opened the closet to get her coat. Hoffman went so wild with excitement she had trouble fastening his leash. Sudbrook was my old junior high. I would have liked to take the dog there and run around. But I was planning to sleep at my mother's and I'd have a break then. The door clapped shut and the glass storm door clattered behind it. I turned the humidifiers on when I heard Brenda's Mazda chug away.

"My head hurts," my father said.

The methadone wasn't working at 5 milligrams, so I called Heidenheimer's office, but it was Saturday and the answering service took a message. I doubled his dose anyway, and brought him the extra pill with an inch of Coke in a paper cup. He napped intermittently in his chair while I read *Jane Eyre*. The refrigerator hummed and shuddered and then went off. It was quiet now, except for the soft gurgling of the humidifiers. I was getting close to the end of the book. Jane's awful, pious cousin wants to marry her, but Jane doesn't want to because then, she says, "I would be forced to keep the fire of my nature continually low." I underlined the phrase and thought about how often I turned down the fire of my nature so as not to disturb Fred. I felt a pang of guilt for marking up the book and dog-earing the page, but not enough to go looking for a bookmark. For once, the fire of my nature said to fuck it and stop worrying about everything.

"Will you be OK here with Brenda tonight?" I said when my father opened his eye. It was Saturday. I was desperate to get away. Brenda would be home all day on Sunday, so I wouldn't be needed. If I went to my mother's, I could sleep as late as I wanted. "She takes good care of you, doesn't she? She rubs Lanacane on your forehead, right?"

"She's OK, but she's a *shiksa*."

I laughed. "That's the problem? You're kidding. That isn't fair."

"Not fair to Brenda?" he said.

"Not fair to *shiksas*."

"It's fair," my father said. "They don't know how to take care of someone the way a Jewish wife would."

"Oh, c'mon Daddy. You mean a Jewish wife like Mom? The least doting mother in the neighborhood?"

"Some other Jewish wife then," he said.

He was trying to be funny. The hippie teacher taking the old-country view. He wanted to provoke, but the effect was sometimes just shutting down the conversation. I wanted to talk to him seriously about Brenda's motivation. I wanted to talk to him about bigger things, too. Jewishness and prejudices. He was more open and expansive when he was young, judging from his letters to my mother. I wished I had known him then. He said in his letters to her that he was a hardened realist, but more often, it seemed to me, he was passionate and earnest.

Somewhere in England
30 May 1945

Dearest Evie,

How are you, darling? I'm sorry I spoiled your happiness over VE Day. I'm also sorry you called me cynical and other unkind words. I hate it when we quarrel. That is why I wanted to tell you about a more optimistic feeling I just had about the world and our future together. I was thinking back to a Home reunion I went to in 1938 and how I stood up and made a resolution protesting some action of the Hitler state, and the religious elements in our alumni group fought against my resolution because they said it wasn't good for the Jews to call too much attention to their plight. Spain was going down into the mud of fascism in those days.

And then, just now, seven years later, I looked through the window of my hut, out across the rows of buildings, the machine shops and the bomb dumps and the petrol tanks and all the tremendous installation of this great airfield to the landing field to the rows of giant bombers and I thought well, once we Jews were alone, but look what has been arrayed against our enemy and what has beaten him into the ground as we were once beaten. The American war machine is a great and mighty thing and for whatever mixed reasons, it lined up alongside the revolutionaries. And that is no mean accomplishment for some people who were once trampled by policemen's horses, run down by New York City's finest, just so the German-American Bund could hold their meeting in Madison Square Garden. You know what I'm talking about, darling.

Well, I am going to quit now and light a stinking cigar and lie on my cot and think about the beautiful spirit-satisfying world of you. Write to me, darling Evie. Tell me you love me.

Yours forever,
Clyde

CHAPTER 32

By Tuesday, in time for Susan's visit, he was feeling better. She was flying down from New Jersey and would spend New Year's with us, and then come to the appointment at Hopkins. All morning I tidied up, emptying the dishwasher, dumping out ashtrays heaped with butts, rinsing the three humidifiers and refilling them, adding salt to the two that required salt, throwing away the paper cups scattered around the house each with an inch of barely touched Carnation Instant Breakfast. "Survival" my father called it, but he couldn't drink it. Brenda had been grocery shopping the night before and bought fresh flowers. All because Susan was coming. I was glad. I needed my sister's support.

My father came into the kitchen. "I'm making chicken soup," he announced.

I couldn't believe it. He was up, walking around like a normal person. I laughed with joy. "Look at you!" He was already chopping parsley, working the cleaver vigorously with a seesaw motion. I was so excited I called my mother. "He's making chicken soup!" I exclaimed.

"You're kidding?" She laughed with joy, too. He must be getting better. She had to hang up though, off to meet Susan's plane from Newark. I could hardly wait for them to come. I hadn't realized how lonely I was. They were taking forever. I leaned with my palms on the windowsill and watched the pink sky darken and finally my mother's car pulling up to the curb. Susan was somber coming across the lawn. In the dusky light I could see her holding back as if the house had a magnetic field around it repelling her. But then she came in through the kitchen and I went in. My father dropped the big spoon he was using to taste the soup and spun around.

"My Susan!" He grabbed her and they hugged.

Her face was transformed, no longer a trace of holding back. They pulled apart so they could look at each other and she was smiling her wide movie-star smile and laughing like ice clinking, saying his name in the clear, certain voice of an eight-year-old. "Daddy! Daddy! How are you?" Susan filled the shadowy kitchen with sunlight.

"I'm not so good, baby. You heard? But today I'm good. You brought me luck."

I thought my sister would spell me for a while and I'd get some extra nights at my mother's. But when Susan saw me gathering my things to leave, a scowl furrowed her brow. "What? You're not staying here? C'mon, Joanna. You're kidding. Aren't you?" I was surprised by the fear in her voice. "I mean . . . I just . . . I feel funny around Brenda," she said. I put down my bag. I knew how much someone's mere presence (or absence) could mean. "All right. I'll stay." Susan was relieved. I was annoyed, but secretly relieved, too. If I stayed away too long, I might risk my claim to sainthood.

Since there was only the sofa, no longer a bed in the spare room, just Brenda's sewing machine, the two of us slept in the living room head to foot. In the morning my legs hurt from being bent against Susan's ass and the backs of her knees.

"She hides his cigarettes," I said. I was sitting at the kitchen table while Susan cleaned up the breakfast dishes. "She gives him Benson & Hedges Lights and then he cries about it. He can't stand Lights. They're sick, both of them. Her more. Sick in the head."

"Well, he shouldn't be smoking, should he?" said Susan. She gave me a look before scraping a few bread crusts into the garbage. It was pleasant watching someone else do the cleaning up for a change.

"She's mean," I said. "She humiliates him. She puts a pee pad on his chair. He's not incontinent! He thinks it's all because she's a *shiksa*."

"Ha!" said Susan. "As if Mom's all touchy feely."

"That's exactly what I said."

"At least we had one parent who was warm and loving when we were growing up," Susan said. She glided a dish towel down one curved side of a metal bowl and up the other side. I wasn't sure who she was talking about at first. "I always knew Daddy loved me just for being me," she said.

I was quiet, tracing circles on the table with my finger.

"What?" Susan said. She finished drying a ladle and a whisk and clanked them into a drawer.

"Nothing," I said. I was thinking, did my father love me for being myself? I didn't remember feeling unloved. But I didn't remember the warm and caring father Susan described either.

She reached up to put away a stack of plates. "Mom can be so judgmental. Whereas Daddy . . ." she said, coming down on her heels, "Daddy thinks whatever I do, I'm the cat's meow."

The cat's meow. How strange that her experience was so alien to mine. Even stranger, I hadn't known it until then. I'd never thought about how my father made my sister feel. I knew her relationship with him was less complicated than mine, but I hadn't realized it was distinctly better. If I ever felt loved just for being myself, it was by my mother, although in her offhand manner. The love I got from my father was about him—I made you, you belong to me. I certainly didn't feel that he loved me for being myself.

"It's different for me," I said. "He was weird with me. He wanted me to be a boy. He used to hit me."

"He hit me too."

"Not as much as he hit me."

"You just don't remember when it was me," Susan said.

"Remember when we were little and he took off his belt?" I said.

"Yeah, as a joke, though," said Susan.

If we kept talking after our mother kissed us goodnight and turned out the lights, he'd storm down the hall, his terrifying voice booming: "If you don't close your eyes and go to sleep, I'm getting out the strap!" Naturally, we erupted in fearful whispers and excited giggles, so as promised, he unbuckled his belt and pulled the leather strap through the loops with a flourish, while we shrieked in not quite fake terror. What would it feel like to be beaten with a leather belt? I shuddered on my bed hugging my pillow and squeezed my eyes shut waiting for the blows to strike. Was I strong enough to withstand it? I thought I was. Would he hold the belt by the buckle, or would he dangle the buckle and strike with its metal edge? I braced for the first blow, but it never came. He didn't mete out punishment. He struck only in the heat of passion, usually when he thought I was mocking him, and then only with his hand.

"Look," Susan said, eager to get back to practical matters. "All I'm saying is, let Brenda do what she's supposed to do. She's his wife. Then you can go home to Fred where you belong."

"Don't worry about Fred. He looks out for himself very nicely," I said.

"Really? Larry can't stand it when I go away even for two days."

"Fred wouldn't shorten one of his trips for me, why should I go rushing back to him?"

"Whoa, that's harsh," Susan said.

"Fred's not the sweetheart everyone thinks he is. Anyway, Daddy's the one who needs me."

"Like Daddy's a sweetheart to you?"

"Listen, Susan, you remember the thing Uncle Harry said? You know, put Brenda's suitcase in the driveway, change the locks on the doors?"

"Yeah. I was there when Uncle Harry said it. Daddy didn't have the heart to do it, though."

"I know, but maybe it's not such a bad idea. Maybe it's exactly what we should do. What do you think?"

"What do I think?" Susan said. "I think Uncle Harry is nuts and so are you. Lock Brenda out and there won't be anybody to take care of Daddy."

"He's going to get better, Susan. And when he does, I don't want her here to spoil it."

On New Year's Eve, Brenda made crab cakes and I made a cheese soufflé we hoped would slide down my father's throat now that he was feeling better thanks to Susan, his good luck charm. But he couldn't swallow any of it. He was exhausted from making the soup the day before. His luck seemed to be petering out. He claimed he liked watching us eat, though.

"Too bad Clyde can't enjoy these delicious crab cakes," Brenda said. It was always unsettling to see Brenda in my mother's seat, stiffly presiding over the table, with my father's wild splatter painting on the wall behind her. "He probably won't touch the soufflé Joanna worked so hard on either. All he eats are soft boiled eggs that look like snot."

Susan shot me a sympathetic look. Finally.

"Brenda," I said. "Please."

"If eggs are the only food he can eat," Susan said, "why would you want to make them sound disgusting?"

Brenda sniffed. "He's the one who wants them cooked that way."

I couldn't tell if my father was listening. He had his head in his hands, a cigarette poking out between his fingers. He cleared his throat, pushed his chair back and got up, shuffled into the living room and slunk into his recliner.

"Daddy? You OK?" I asked.

He shooed me away. "Eat your crab cakes. Enjoy your dinner."

We did as he said and finished the meal. Brenda finished the wine, and Susan and I did the dishes and then got into our nightgowns and sat with my father in the living room. We turned on the TV so we could watch everybody in Times Square. I knew it was corny, but I loved New Year's Eve— the nostalgia, the sentimentality—and I didn't want to be left out of it. The year was turning for me, too, even if I didn't have much to celebrate. The dressed-up smiling people inside the Waldorf Astoria looked the same as always, although it was Dick Clark hosting and no longer Guy Lombardo. Outside in Times Square the people were rosy-cheeked, an excited mob, girls sitting on guys' shoulders, everybody grinning in ski hats and mufflers, the way it was every year.

My father seemed almost comfortable stretched out in the recliner. We turned down the TV so we could talk and he lay with his eyes closed and then surprised us by joining in the conversation now and then.

"Supposed to be a big storm tomorrow night," he said. "You'll be OK, Susan. Be cleared away by the day you leave. Very high tides, too. Because the moon is passing almost directly between the sun and the earth. Makes a gravitational tug like they've never seen before. A rare alignment, they say. Very rare. Syzygy, it's called."

"Yeah. It was in the *New York Times*," I said.

"I could read yesterday," he said. "Today, no."

"Just what we need on top of everything else," Susan said. "Snow."

"Hey, remember that winter we were snowed in?" my father said.

"Yeah," said Susan. "And you and Leon Greene had to walk to Woodmoor?"

"Leon and I, and two other fathers on the block, Lefty and Abe Lubin next door."

"Not Lefty," I said. "Lucky. You always call him Lefty."

"Lucky, is it? OK, Lucky. A band of us went to get supplies. No one could get his car out, and Mary needed formula for the third kid, what was her name?"

"Amy Beth," said Susan. "See, Joanna. You say I don't remember anything. But I remember that kid's name and I remember that snowstorm. You were too little."

"Those were happy years," my father said. "My happiest."

"Really?" Susan said. "Of all the things you did in your life?"

"By far. Are you kidding? The years you two were in elementary school, sure." He looked at us candidly with his wide-open eye and smiled to himself. "You came home with all kinds of things you made. Drawings, projects. You would sing and dance for us, put on shows."

"But you did so many more exciting things," I said. "What about the army?"

"The army? Are you crazy?"

"What about teaching at City?" I said.

"City, yeah. That was going on at the same time, all good. But watching you grow up on Cedar Drive? The most important experience in life. Right, Susan? Tell her. Just wait until you and Fred get married and have kids."

"You know what? I do remember that snowstorm," I said. "I wasn't too young. I remember Daddy pulling us down the middle of the street on the sled. And Tom's father pulling him."

"Yeah, Abe. Nice guy. It was '58," my father said. "The great blizzard of 1958."

"I used to love this book they had in the Campfield school library. *Snowbound with Betsy*," I said. "I can still smell the pages, that library smell. Betsy's friends were forced to sleep over because of a storm and they made popcorn and the grownups had to be nice about it because they were stuck. Like we're stuck here, in our pajamas together. We wouldn't be all cozy like this if you weren't sick."

"I'd be in New York at a party," said Susan with a laugh.

"You'd be at your New Year's parties, I'd be at mine," said my father. "The orphanage was like that. Snowbound on Tuck-ahoe Road, like your book," he said.

Brenda appeared in a new red bathrobe she'd gotten for Christmas, a gold zipper up the front with a gold ring. She was glowing. She bent down and kissed my father. Then she climbed onto his outstretched body in the recliner, and lay face down on him. Any other time Susan and I might have cringed, but this time we were thrilled. If they were affectionate with each other, we could relax about leaving him alone with her. This was the way a wife should be to her sick husband. Brenda's face was turned away from us. My father rested his chin on the top of her head.

"Nice," Susan said. She gave him the OK sign. I gave him thumbs up. My father pointed down at Brenda's prone body. "Drunk," he said.

Around midnight, we turned up the TV. "The mayor has cued the Big Apple," Dick Clark announced. It was the first year they were going to drop a lit-up apple instead of a ball. "In a few moments, three-thousand pounds of confetti will descend upon us." He counted down. The apple plunged. "It's 1987!" Dick Clark shouted. "Hooray!" the crowd cheered. They rattled their noisemakers. Dancing couples sang with the band. "Should auld acquaintance be forgot," their voices rose, "and never brought to mind . . . "

I opened the heavy front door, held the glass storm door ajar and leaned into the cold midnight. Firecrackers whined and popped, and horns honked in the distance. I feared the coming year.

CHAPTER 33

He said those were happy times, so it must have been true, the years I was in elementary school, the years before the summer of love, before Nola Swenson. I remembered happiness, the feeling I had walking home from school on a windy day in March, coming around the corner holding onto a crayon drawing that was fluttering in the breeze. Were we ever a normal family, though? Dinner on the table at six o'clock. That was normal. He was a hardworking man, a homeowner, patriotic, a veteran, a breadwinner who wanted most of all to be able to support his family. He didn't want to be like his father. He would not abandon his children. He gave up his dreams in exchange for a schoolteacher's paycheck. It was only in Belfast that he ever felt like a real success. There he was not just a breadwinner, but a Fulbright winner. Imagine, Clyde and Evie Aronson invited to ship launchings, the Queen Mother's garden party! He was interviewed on ITV and gave a lecture at Queens College on the Beat Poets.

Susan and I thought he was God. When we returned to the US, he continued his subscription to the *London Observer* to keep up with the news overseas. One day when the lilacs were blooming against the shingled house, he called us to the dining room table. "Susan! Joanna! Get over here!" I was drawn to the window, distracted by the pale purple flowers and the birds twittering in the bushes. "Pay attention!" he said. He flipped open the *Observer* magazine to the centerfold with a photo spread of four musicians from Liverpool, a place I was familiar with because the ferry from Belfast to England docked there. "You see these guys?" my father said. "You're going to be screaming for them in a few months." It was 1963, a year before the Beatles appeared on the *Ed Sullivan Show*. We looked at my father like he was daft. He was God, but we didn't actually believe he could see into the future. "No, we won't! You don't know that about us." We smirked and walked away. But my father could see into the future.

Big changes were coming. We learned for ourselves in 1965 when we drove to California to visit Uncle Harry, singing in the car the whole way: "See the USA, in your Chevrolet, America's the greatest land of all!" In LA, girls wore bell-bottom pants like sailors, a fashion that wouldn't reach Baltimore for two more years. Uncle Harry flashed hundred-dollar bills, paid for my mother to get her hair done like a Hollywood starlet, and treated us to prime rib and lobster. He'd been out of prison only a year, after being sent away for embezzlement. The word was dazzling and I thought his crime must have something to do with jewels.

Back at home we started the school year and my father, not flashy like his brothers, remained an earnest, dedicated teacher. Unlike Harry and Alvin, he paid his taxes. But he was no patsy, no rube. He became a leader in the teacher's union, a position my mother surely envied. It was important work. There was a movement going on in the schools to abolish the college prep program at City College High School. The A-Course, as it was called, attracted bright boys, my father said, and gave the high school its prestige.

I noted that, as usual, boys got the best of everything. The words "bright" and "girls" were never even paired together. Before *Brown v. the Board of Education*, the bright boys at City were white boys only. Even after the landmark case, progress was slow. My father believed the A-Course program would light the way, encouraging integration by casting a wide geographical net, since City offered more than a standard neighborhood school. Most teachers were as desperate to save the program as he was, and this pitted them against some of the black leaders in the community who believed the A-Course was elitist and designed to exclude minorities. My father acknowledged that he'd never know what it was like to be black, but he chafed at being called elitist. "You don't know hungry like I know hungry," he'd tell his students.

When he practiced the speech he was to give to the school board commission, tears came to his eyes. He loved his school and he was certain his was the enlightened view. He stood before us in the living room. "Ladies and Gentlemen, I implore you. Keep the A-Course for the aspiring young boys of the poor families of this generation. Give them the opportunities that City College High School was able to offer the disadvantaged minorities of the past."

"Hear, hear," my mother said.

"Don't reduce City College to the status of a neighborhood school, which given the present pattern of racial residence, must in a few short years become once again a segregated high school, completing the cycle begun in 1954 and thus effectively repealing the decision of the Supreme Court. Ladies and Gentleman, I urge you with all my heart to act now, to prevent a catastrophe that we will live to regret."

My mother and Susan applauded. I cheered and whistled.

But the board said no. The A-course was racist, they said. The program was scrapped. A year later, in 1967, the membership of the teachers' union went on strike demanding a voice in policy-making, as well as higher salaries. My father led his students singing City's fight song, conducting with his cigarette baton from the back of a paddy wagon just before it carried him and Shep Levine, Bob Moskowitz, and several others to the city jail for picketing the school. They were defying a court injunction forbidding a strike. By 1968, barely two years after the A-Course program was scrapped, City was a segregated school again—all black instead of all white, but segregated just as my father predicted. With the A-Course gone, the eighteen rules of grammar went out the window. It was considered elitist. Shakespeare, too. The dedicated faculty was demoralized.

My father became irritable and moody. He grew cynical. He was easily enraged. He didn't like it when I had supper at a friend's house. He wanted me home. What's wrong with our house? My cooking isn't good enough? This was before Johnny, before Nola. I stayed home and he got angry when I wouldn't eat the mashed potatoes my mother had plopped onto my plate. I was turned off by the lumps. He slammed his open hand on the table. "Eat those potatoes, goddamnit!" I took a forkful. "Don't look at me like that, you snotty kid." I gagged, then opened my mouth and let the lumpy blob fall onto the plate. He jumped up knocking his chair over. I jumped up and made a run for it, but he chased me down the hall whacking my back and shoulders hard before I got to my room and was able to close the door against him. My mother told me later she threw a shoe at him and hit him on the leg. After a few minutes, there was a knock at my door. My shoulder was throbbing. He stuck his head in. "I'm sorry," he said.

CHAPTER 34

"**S**usan! Joanna!" We shot up from the sofa like soldiers at reveille. "It hurts. Get in here." He was sitting on the edge of the bed smoking. "I can't sleep," he said. The light blazed in his room. "I've been looking at these magazines." He pointed to a stack at his feet. "So I was reading this magazine and I had a revelation."

"It's good you were able to read," Susan said.

"Sometimes I can do a page. So I'm reading *New York* and John Simon writes these nasty things about Barbra Streisand and I have this revelation. You wanna hear it?"

"Sure," we said.

"Everything is both true and not true."

Susan and I exchanged a look. He woke us up for this?

"Listen, I have to ask you girls a question, a favor. This is important." He patted the bed and we sat down, the three of us in a row facing his dresser against the wall, above it the only photo of him as a small child, fists balled, in his sailor suit. Aunt Adele had sent the photograph years ago, in a fancy frame wrapped as a gift. "I want to know if both of you will give your inheritance to your mother," he said. "You know, if I leave you money in my will, you'll give it over to her."

I glanced across the hall at Brenda's closed door. Was she listening? Would she be angry knowing the concern he had for our mother? I desperately wanted to go back to sleep. "What are you talking about?" I said. "You're going to get better."

"Yeah, I know," he said. "But I want to know if you'll give up your inheritance."

The whole thing was strange, waking us in the middle of the night to tell us what? That we were being disinherited. Why did he have to put it that way, "give up our inheritance," as if he were cutting us off and casting us out, rejecting us for some trespass or disloyalty? "Yes, of course," I said. I should have said no, I should have realized his request was anguished, that he really wanted to leave money directly to my mother so that he did not have to ask this of us, but he was afraid of Brenda. We should have realized his choice of words was a clue, a warning. He was provoking us, trying to get us to object and stake our claim the way Brenda so confidently staked her claim.

CHAPTER 35

Tuckahoe

Why didn't we object? Why didn't we rise up and challenge the authorities? I couldn't understand it. Why didn't we band together against the supervisors? "We'd get kicked out," said Chick. "And then where would we go?" "Maybe one day," Jesse said.

I was waiting for it. I felt it coming, all the while my hatred of authority, of monitors and supervisors, of rules and regimentation, infiltrated every atom of my flesh and blood and spirit. These were the circumstances that organized my world-view.

Things were different for Harry. The longer Harry stayed at the H, the more chaotic he became. He no longer complained about beatings to Mama, but he was often caught fighting with other kids. He talked back to teachers, goofed off in class, and sometimes went AWOL. Bull Pushkin, the juniors' supervisor, offered to train Harry to box, to give him an outlet. Bull's nickname fit him well. He was stocky and muscular with an aggressive style. Bull hated nothing more than stopping a fight. He loved sports of all kinds and coached kids at baseball, basketball, wrestling, and boxing. He liked to be thought of as a pal. Which was a bunch of bull, if you asked me. He'd egg Harry on, be his booster, and then match Harry with bigger kids and watch those kids beat the crap out of my brother. I despised the man, but he was the one supervisor Harry trusted, for a time. Harry craved attention and Bull gave it to him.

In the spring we built the Bare Ass dam as usual, with many close calls but luckily no prisoners taken during construction. One summer's day, our paradise complete, a bunch of

Homeboys were splashing around, cannonballing from a rocky precipice. I chose to lounge on the bank just upstream, fishing with a rod I fashioned from a green branch. All of a sudden Cheesie called out "Cheese it!" and everybody scrambled out of the water, except for Harry. He'd taught himself to swim just as he had taught himself to roller skate and ride a bike, but now he'd caught his foot between two stones and was wedged in tight. He grabbed onto a clump of swamp grass and called, "Brudder, help me, Clyde, don't leave me here!" And I was thinking, shit, what if I fall in, I'm the one who can't swim and the water's high, but I braced myself on the bank and reached in for Harry to grab hold of my fishing rod, which snapped in half, so I waded in just a few inches and grabbed a hold of Harry's hand, coaching him to gently turn his foot and meanwhile, I hear "Cheese it! Cheese it!" and the sound of keys jangling— Piggy Rosenthal, it sounded like. The leaves started trembling like there was a rhino thundering through the trees just as Harry's foot came loose and he stumbled onto the bank and we ran for it. I hauled ass being lean and lanky, whereas Harry had a pugilist's body, solid and muscular, handsome and strong but not fleet, which may have been why Harry loved wheels, roller skates, cars, motorcycles. Had to have wheels, he loved wheels and he loved boxing, and the jailor's keys jangled louder scaring the shit out of the birds and rabbits, and out of the woods came not Piggy, but Bull Pushkin. I figured when Bull saw his little protégé he'd calm down. But no, he started yelling. I couldn't leave Harry there. I hid behind a bush to make sure the motherfucker didn't kill my brother. I was wearing pants but Harry was bare-assed, trembling, his trousers still in a ball under his arm, and I heard a crack! It was Bull Pushkin's fist connecting with Harry's skull. Harry fell back onto his ass crying, and Bull pulled him up and started screaming into Harry's poor hurt ear about insubordination and Harry, holding his head, said, "But Bull, I was only swimming, is that a crime?" and Bull said, "Mr. Pushkin to you, boy.

Put your clothes on, boy, don't just stand there." I ducked in and out of the shadows behind Harry following Bull down the path and back over the aqueduct, and I saw Harry put his hand to the side of his head and then look at his hand, and there was blood on it. Bull had ruptured Harry's eardrum. He was deaf in that ear from then on. It would keep him out of the service in the world war we didn't know was coming. Harry never, ever told the story the way it happened. When asked about his hearing over the years, he always said he ruptured his eardrum straining too hard on the toilet.

Lying awake at night during that time, in the early 1930s, when I wasn't imagining building the dam, or going over in my mind the next steps for whatever I was making in wood shop, or plans for an editorial or the landscape I was painting in art class, I thought about how was I going to get back at the Colonel and that fat-fuck Piggy, and that two-faced son-of-a-bitch Bull Pushkin. There had to be a way. There were more of us than there were of them. If we sat on our asses, nothing would change. We had to take action. Action was everything. I went to sleep thinking about it.

CHAPTER 36

M y mother called in sick and went with us to the Hopkins appointment. Brenda opted out, she had to be at work, so it was the four of us like old times, an American family off to see the USA in our Chevrolet, only we were going to see Samuel Geest, the renowned Johns Hopkins head and neck surgeon. I had a canvas bag packed with methadone, a bottle of Dr. Brown's Cel-Ray Tonic to wash down the tablets, the CAT scan and MRI film, hospital records, and a plastic urinal Brenda insisted he bring along.

Susan drove us down the Jones Falls, gliding around the banked curves on the expressway past church spires on hilltops, past the Beaux-Arts Belvedere Hotel and the Maryland National Bank building with its copper mansard roof. Our spirits were high. A lot of it was gallows humor, but we were hopeful about our pilgrimage to Baltimore's own temple of scientific achievement. My father was having another good day, my mother was glad to be with her girls, and Susan didn't seem preoccupied with thoughts of Larry and their kids. For once, Susan seemed to recognize the value of her original family. It was the last time the four of us would be together.

"I want the main entrance," my father said. "The cobblestone drive in front of the old dome building. You know what I'm talking about?"

"Don't worry, you're getting the main entrance," Susan said. "Would I take my father to any lousy side entrance?"

"If you have to come to Johns Hopkins, you may as well do it right," said my father.

"Only the finest entrances for the Aronsons," my mother said. "I think they have a policy, people carrying urinals come in through the front door!" My mother laughed heartily and we all joined her. We went over the Orleans Street bridge and down into the urban landscape. Leaning in from the backseat, I could see a tear shining in the corner of Susan's eye.

"I'm weak," my father said. "You're making fun of a sick person."

The brick Victorian hospital pavilion with its pitched slate roofs, spires, and a majestic dome, was the main building when it was built in 1889, but it was now the administration building and not even close to the main entrance. We went inside anyway, into the rotunda where a ten-foot Jesus in flowing marble robes greeted us with outstretched arms. My father was pleased. "Look at this!" he said. "Better than Sinai. Here you get all the trappings."

I tried to see Jesus as a bonus as my father did, but I thought the words carved into the base of the statue were pathetic. "Come unto me all ye that are weary and heavy laden and I will give you rest." I didn't want to be coaxed into submission. Did he?

In the waiting room he asked for a pen and paper, apparently inspired by the words of Christ. He scribbled a poem on the back of an envelope my mother extracted from her purse.

> They gave me CAT scans,
> MRIs in the rain,
> But all I want is
> Out of pain.

"Very good, Clyde," my mother said.

He beamed in his wheelchair like a toddler in a stroller. She had a faraway look in her eyes.

> Somewhere in England
> 10 Oct 1944
>
> Darling,
>
> I want an end to this aching loneliness. It reminds me of the orphanage. Always in the midst of our jokes

and horseplay, each soldier has his mind and heart thousands of miles away. We need the warmth and love of a woman to shield us and comfort us. It's silly of a practical guy like me to make a frail 115-pound girl the repository of all my hopes. But that's how it is. See how much I need you?

All my love forever,
Clyde

His name was called and I wheeled him in. Susan and my mother stayed behind, their choice. Dr. Geest had a strangely familiar cleft in his chin, gentle eyes, and sandy-colored hair that curled over the collar of his lab coat. "The mass is in a difficult spot," he said. He helped my father from the wheelchair into the examining chair and felt his neck, observed his bulging eye. "How long has your voice been hoarse?" Dr. Geest asked softly.

My father frowned. "Look, I'm not here about my voice. Can you help me, doctor?"

"I may have to go in through the soft palate," the doctor said with whispery urgency. "Or the nostril or through the ear." He scheduled a biopsy for the following week.

"It's an amazing coincidence, isn't it?"

"What?" my father said.

"Geest looks so much like Johnny Dolan. The cleft in his chin. His eyes. The long, wavy hair. Even the hypnotic voice."

"You've got something there."

The resemblance irrationally gave me hope. If Dr. Geest were anything like Johnny, he would know us and care whether we lived or died.

"I still miss that boy," my father said. "That Johnny."

CHAPTER 37

My father and Johnny Dolan became close friends in such a short period of time they reminded me of my own friends then—thirteen-year-old girls—always whispering together, sharing private jokes and secrets. I'd watch them standing at the bottom of the driveway, my father with an arm draped around his buddy, his wrist a fulcrum on Johnny's shoulder, his other hand busy with all kinds of gestures and punctuation. Both smoking, laughing at intervals. My father couldn't be like that with Shep Levine. Shep was too tall, for one thing, and too good a person. Johnny was damaged. He ran away from home when he was sixteen after his alcoholic father beat him up for the last time. They were lost boys, Johnny and my father, robbed of childhood. In time, they would rob me of mine.

Johnny was twenty-seven when he and his wife Linda first came to Cedar Drive, a tantalizing age in those days. Young enough to trust and old enough for experience. He took Susan out to practice driving. When my mother was washing dishes, he came up behind her and kissed her neck. I was the only one who told him to get lost. I said I wasn't going to be his pretend little girlfriend like Susan. In the beginning, I told him to take his hands off me. We were on the sofa. Linda was helping my mother in the kitchen. I slapped him and twisted out of his grasp. Johnny was patient and things were changing so fast. He was interested in what I thought about everything. At my parents' cocktail parties he was at my side, choosing my company over the adults. What was my favorite flavor of ice cream, had I read *Narcissus and Goldmund*, why did I prefer the woods to the beach? No one had ever asked me questions like that. I complained about family life and he wanted to know every detail. I told him I was tired of sharing. I couldn't take the last slice of cantaloupe because God forbid somebody else might want some. I didn't have my own bicycle. It belonged to Susan, although I rode it so much, the bike was like an extension of my body. It would be a waste of money to buy another bicycle since Susan never used hers. The next day, Johnny came to the house with a cantaloupe. We hid it in the milk box in the carport, and when he left and I was alone, I took the melon down to the curb with a knife and sat there and ate the whole thing, minus the rind, of course. I punctured the globe with the point of the knife and sat there hacking off pieces, gobbling up the sweet orange flesh, juice running down my hands, my arms, dripping from my elbows into the gutter.

The world was black and white, and then the sixties happened, the Beatles arrived, the world exploded into living color, and Johnny pulled up to the curb in his red Triumph. He entered the house and all four of us came alive.

For two weeks after the camping trip, I didn't speak to my father. Two weeks—nothing in a lifetime—but try it for a while, not speaking. I still emptied his ashtrays when I came home from school—the ashtray on the end table next to the sofa, the ashtray on the elephant leg table from Delhi, the one on his night stand, on the dining room table, the kitchen table, all heaped with disgusting butts. I scraped the yellow crust of sunny-side-up egg from his breakfast plate and loaded his dishes into the dishwasher. When necessary to avoid confrontation, I grunted yes or no to a question, but nothing more. It wasn't long before my mother knew about Nola, just as Johnny predicted. It was hard not to know. My father was in love. He could barely keep from grinning when he wasn't storming the house in a fury. My mother approached me cautiously. She touched my shoulder. When I didn't flinch, she put her arms around me. "That was a difficult trip for you," she said.

I nodded in the warm curve of her neck. She pulled away to look at me.

"Do you want to talk about it?" she said.

"No," I whispered, and she left me alone. That was all.

"What happened?" Susan said, but she didn't stop walking down the hall.

"Ask him," I snapped.

All week he raged. "Why isn't the kitchen cleaned up? What's that bag doing on the table? Get that shrieking off the stereo!" He was in love and the rest of the world could go to hell. He went to see her on the weekend.

"Where are you going?" my mother asked.

"Out," he said. He didn't come back until Monday.

I despised the sight of the green Torino nosing into the driveway after an absence. My sister was angry, but not at him. She was mad at my mother—why had she let her man get away? Why didn't she do something? Scream, cry, bake his favorite cake? I couldn't accept my mother's role in this even a little, and I gave Susan no credit for understanding some things better than I did. She was Daddy's girl, though. All I had was my mother.

On Labor Day, the last day of the season at the swimming club, my father approached me. He loved the club, though he didn't swim. He'd sit on a chaise and trade recipes with the women. When it was really hot, he'd dunk himself up to his shoulders in the five feet end. He shuffled over to where I was sitting. I kept my eyes down and stared at his untied desert boots. Eventually, I lifted my gaze to his wrinkled swimming trunks, his round but strangely hard belly, his ridiculous straw gondolier's hat. I was eating a chocolate snowball. I drew the cold paper cup to my chest. He wasn't getting even a chip of ice. The red ribbon on the gondolier's hat was feminine, but he was able to carry it off, he said, because like a real gondolier, he had machismo. At that moment, though, the limp ribbon was pathetically girlish.

He stuck out his lower lip in a pout. "Are you ever going to talk to me again?" he asked.

I didn't want to say yes and I didn't want to say no, so I got up, left the cup with the melting snowball on the chaise, and walked past the folding table where a kid sat and punched membership cards. My father followed, but the metal gate clanked shut against him. Outside of the chain-link fence, I broke into a run. I was wearing the purple bikini Johnny had given me for my birthday. Inside the gate with everyone else wearing skimpy bathing suits I was fine, but now outside the gate, I felt undressed. The swimming club was on the border between county and city, and as I ran through the neighborhood, split-levels gave way to narrow row houses from another era, left standing like Roman ruins. I saw a man in a suit getting into a car. My chest was bouncing and so I did not run as fast as my legs could take me. I was ashamed of my body, and I was also ashamed of not running faster and I didn't know what to do, where to hide, whether to go fast or slow. A woman in a party dress corralled her children inside, holding her hand over her little boy's eyes. I wasn't naked, but I felt naked. The woman acted like I was naked. I ducked behind a hydrangea bush on her next-door neighbor's lawn just as the Torino came cruising down the block. He saw me and stopped the car. I stepped out covering the tops of my breasts with one arm, and the tops of my thighs with the other arm, trying to hide the pubic hair curling out of my bikini bottoms. He leaned across the seat to open the passenger door and handed me a striped beach towel. I wrapped myself in it and sat beside him. He made a U-turn and we drove down Milford Mill Road and over the railroad tracks. I felt better wrapped in the towel. I had been thinking, if having a father was so important to him that the fact that he didn't have a father defined his whole life, then why wasn't his being a father to me just as important? But I couldn't organize my thoughts to form a spoken question. Other people my age had it all figured out. They seemed to know who to hate and why, how to rebel, but I remained stuck in my father's story. He drove past the clearing in the woods I liked where the county kept yellow school buses crammed together in a little dell and he cleared his throat and blinked several times behind his glasses.

"I'm sorry," he said. That was all he could think of.

"It's hard having a father," I said.

Possibly, I forgave him too soon. One evening, he insisted I come home from Liz's house because he was making a special dinner. When I got back I saw that we were having spaghetti. I mocked him for calling it special. No one liked being mocked, but for him, it was intolerable. He turned into Bluto from a Popeye cartoon. Steam came out of his ears. He chased me down the hall and caught up to me and whacked my back with the flat of his hand making a hollow sound— clop, clop, clop. "I work hard to put food on the table, you snotty kid." Clop, whack. I landed in my room, slammed the door and locked it. A few minutes later there was a knock. He was sorry again. Would I forgive him?

He decided to make it up to me by inviting Johnny over for dinner the following night. He and my mother were going out, Susan had a date, and I was going to be home alone. Johnny would keep me company, and we would eat the left-over spaghetti. I liked spaghetti reheated in a frying pan with bits of sauce clinging to the strands and the bottom burned until it was crispy. When we finished dinner, it was still light out. Johnny told me to lie on the sofa. The drapes were open. Kids were playing in the street. I knew them. I could have been outside kicking a ball around with those kids. I lay down and he kneeled on the floor beside the sofa and kissed random places—my ears, my neck, my hair. He took off my glasses and laid them on the coffee table and he kissed my cheek-bones and forehead and my mouth. Children called to each other between spurts of breathless laughter. I worried about the drapes being open, and then I stopped thinking about it. I was wearing red flowered shorts I had sewn in Home Ec. The shorts had an elastic waistband—we hadn't learned zippers yet—and Johnny looped a finger inside the elastic and took the shorts down over my tanned legs. He did the same with my pink and white striped bikini underpants, and then he moved my tanned knees apart and kissed the top of each thigh. He came in closer and kissed me where I peed. It felt good, very good, but not as good as it would feel every time from then on, because the night of the spaghetti dinner I was astonished it was happening at all.

CHAPTER 38

After the Geest appointment at Hopkins, we returned my father to Brenda and went out to eat. Susan and I told my mother about how he'd woken us up in the middle of the night and asked us to promise that we'd give up our inheritance and turn the money over to her. We told her we promised, and we expected her to be pleased. But my mother was not pleased. She was upset. "He should be able to leave money to his children AND leave me the money I deserve."

"What money do you deserve?" Susan said.

"How many times do I have to tell you? The money from the credit union!"

In retrospect, it's hard to believe Susan and I didn't see that Brenda was strong-arming my father to exclude my mother from his will. But my father's will wasn't real to us at the time, because his death was an impossibility.

In the same way, I thought, my mother did not believe in their divorce. Having been with my father since childhood, the idea of either one of them going ahead in life without the other was impossible. They were separated for seven years before my mother filed for divorce, and she did so then only because her friends pressured her and she relented, not thinking it would really change anything in the end. My parents did not get along, but there was never any question they belonged together.

I never felt more certain of this than the day my parents drove up to New York and had pastrami sandwiches at my brownstone apartment. Although my father told us that day about Brenda's ultimatum, and said outright he was considering marrying her, I figured it was more of a threat than anything else. He wanted to see if he could still hurt my mother. He wanted to see if she still loved him. When we finished off the pastrami and the last of the pastry and my fabulous coffee, my father asked Fred to tune the radio to WNEW. He wanted to practice dancing before the wedding they were going to in Connecticut, and he wanted something by Sinatra. "I've Got You Under My Skin" was playing. My father took my mother by the hand and they waltzed around the living room staring wistfully into each other's eyes.

That was April. In June, I got a frantic phone call from my mother. I'd never heard her so upset. My mother was the calmest person I knew. She liked to bicker about trivial things, but about big things she was usually unruffled to a fault, but now her voice was trembling. She'd spoken to my father. He decided to go for it. He and Brenda were getting married. My mother begged me to come down to Baltimore. "I can't talk to my friends," she said. I took the train from Penn Station. She paced her apartment. She was smoking again for real, not just bumming random cigarettes. She talked in a nonstop stream rehashing arguments, second-guessing herself. I'd seen friends in this state—unhinged by a man's rejection. I'd been in a similar state myself. But this was not the mother I knew.

"Don't you understand, Joanna? Don't you see? This is big. Marrying Brenda changes everything. She'll have rights."

"You were the one who wanted the divorce, remember?" I said, unhelpfully.

"I wanted the separation. I did not want the divorce."

"But you were the one who asked for it."

"Right, right! You're right! I'm the idiot who finally filed for divorce, it was me, I was the one! But I didn't really want it. You know your father's impossible to live with. And Jesus Christ, I gave him slack, but he went too far. With Nola he went too far. He was indiscreet. Everyone and his uncle knew what he was up to. It was cruel. Look at how he treated you. With Nola, he crossed a line. So yes, I wanted the separation. But not the divorce. I only asked for a divorce because of my stupid friends. Because *I* was stupid and listened to my friends! I resisted their advice for a long time. Seven years we were separated, and I was doing just fine. Never listen to your friends, Joanna. Seriously. Don't ever take advice from friends. You have to move on, they kept saying. "You have to get on with your life. It's been *seven* years." But I was happy separated. I had my own apartment, I was going out with guys, your father was seeing Darleen, but we were still connected. Clyde is my family. I don't want that to change. He'll always be my family. But my friends thought our relationship was sick. I was stuck in a rut, they said. I wasn't married, but I wasn't divorced. It bothered them. Why did it bother them so much? I was happy, so what was the problem? But then I started to think there had to be something wrong with me. My life wasn't progressing, whatever that means. I should have realized, what it means, to them anyway, is that marriage is everything. They thought my attitude would change once I was divorced. I'd be more open to other men. I wasn't giving these other guys a chance since Daddy and I still saw each other, we went to the movies, had dinner, saw our kids together, and somehow this wasn't normal, since I was sleeping with these other guys. Maybe my friends were jealous, I don't know. Maybe they didn't like that I had it both ways. Men get to have it both ways if they want. Men get away with it all the time, they have their cake and eat it too. But God forbid a woman has some fun. So I listened to my friends and I filed for divorce and now look what happened. I mean, look who's getting married now?"

"I hate your friends."

"No. Don't hate them." She stopped pacing and sat at the table with me and stubbed out her cigarette in the ashtray. "They thought they were doing the right thing. Maybe it *was* the right thing." She folded her arms on the table and lay her head down on them.

"So if Daddy doesn't get married, are you saying you'll go back to him?"

"Maybe. I don't know." She brought her head up. "Maybe. I could definitely see living next door to him."

"I always liked that idea," I said. "But seriously, can you imagine being a couple again?"

"I think I can. Now that I'm seeing my reaction to Brenda, it's stirring up a lot of feelings." My mother was quiet. Her eyes darted back and forth. "Yes," she said. "I want to get back together. I do. I don't want to lose Clyde. He's the love of my life. Do you realize how long we've been together? I was sixteen when he walked into my mother's house and rented a room."

I hesitated leaving her so upset, but she asked that I act as a go-between and I agreed. So I packed an overnight bag and left her apartment to spend the night at my father's. He met me at the kitchen door with his arms open, in his usual way. We hugged and then sat in the living room and he gave me some of the jelly beans he liked to eat at night, and we chatted about my latest underachieving job as a proofreader and Fred's latest published story and whether we had gotten around to painting the ceiling in our apartment to lighten up the place, which of course, we hadn't. My father asked questions, but he controlled the flow of conversation. Otherwise, he wasn't easy to talk to. He could be dismissive, that hadn't changed much. Less than an hour had passed when he told me to go to bed, he wanted to read.

In the morning after a breakfast of bacon and eggs, we went out back to his garden to harvest string beans. I admired his rows of tomato plants tied like marionettes to a wooden contraption he built. Then I got down to business on my knees in the grass, plucking beans while he sat in a lawn chair gripping his weeder pole like a staff. It was the middle of July, hot and humid. The cicadas droned and surged and the sun beat down on us. He was shirtless, with beads of sweat glistening in his graying chest hairs.

"Why are you sweating?" I said. "I'm the one doing the labor." I snapped off a bean to prove my point, and tossed it into the basket beside me.

"You think giving orders is easy?" he said. "Here, borrow my hat." The girlish ribbon fluttered.

"No thanks."

"This isn't some crap you buy at a souvenir stand, you know. I order them from the place where the real gondoliers get theirs." He took a sip from the coffee cup he had balanced on the fence post. "You wanna take a break, you poor girl?"

"Let me finish this row." I thrust my hands under the scratchy plant leaves feeling around for the beans that dangled like earrings.

"Hard work is good for you. Nothing better. So what do you think of Brenda?"

"She's OK, I guess."

"She's just like your mother."

I sat back on my heels. "Brenda? You're kidding. She's nothing like Mom.

"Yeah, she is. I always go for the same type of woman. Brenda's a downer. Evie's a downer. They're down and I'm up."

"Wait. That's not fair. I mean, I agree Mom can be passive— or passive-aggressive is more like it—but she's not a downer." I stopped what I was doing and pushed my damp bangs out of my eyes. "C'mon. Mom's always up for fun. She loves to tell jokes. She's lively. She laughs all the time. Brenda's so reserved. I have no idea what Brenda thinks."

"That's not what I'm talking about."

"How can you say Mom's a downer? She doesn't get depressed, she has tons of friends. You told me Brenda doesn't have any friends."

"Why are you bad-mouthing Brenda?" My father pulled up the weeder pole and speared it back into the ground again.

"You asked what I thought."

"Look, you think I don't know Brenda's a downer? She's down and I'm up, just like it was with your mother."

"Stop saying that!" I stood up and brushed the dirt off my knees. "There is no comparison!"

"Brenda's a strange lady, I'll give you that," my father said thoughtfully. He reached for the cup of cold coffee on the fence post and sipped it. "Ah," he said, with satisfaction. He put the cup back on the post. "She's strange, all right. I'm going to marry her, though. You wanna know why? I'll tell you why. Her *persistence* is greater than my *resistance*. How do you like that?"

"Everything isn't a joke."

"Look, kiddo, I'm here by myself. You have Fred. What about me? You want me to be alone?"

I didn't want my father to be lonely, but what he said made me think of myself, how fear of being alone kept me with Fred. Fear cemented the relationship. Fear that I would have no clout in the world without a man. The opposite was true, too, though. I would never be anybody if Fred was my proxy.

"So? So?" my father said. "You want me to be alone?"

"You could get back together with Mom," I said.

"No," he said. A shadow passed over his face. "No. Can't get back with your mother. It's too late. Too much baggage."

There was the dismissive tone I dreaded. The conversation shut down. What did he mean by baggage? That things were said that couldn't be taken back? That my mother had seen him at his most vile, and he couldn't live with that? Once when I was little, he slapped her across the face and made her lip bleed. For days there was a dark red scab. He threw a plastic cereal bowl in a rage. She ducked and it hit the wall. He was violent, but she provoked him.

I remembered we were having pancakes. I must have been eight or nine. My father asked if my grandmother had been invited for Sunday dinner. My mother said no, she didn't want her

mother to come. He said, "Evie, you have no compassion, you have no heart." My mother was hurt and angry. "Goddamnit, don't tell me how to act with my own family," she said.

"I don't understand you," he said. "If *my* mother were alive, she would live with us!"

"Your mother? Live with us?" She laughed sarcastically. "Over my dead body."

I was stunned by her cruelty. Her mother-in-law was long gone. It would have cost my mother nothing to agree with him.

"You know, Clyde," she said, "if your mother were still alive, you probably wouldn't think she was so great." She pulled out the last cigarette and crumpled up the pack.

"My mother was a saint," he said.

"Oh yeah," my mother said. "A saint." She struck a match, drew in on the cigarette and exhaled. Her voice was tired now. "Right," she said. "The saint who dropped you off at the orphanage."

I put the basket of string beans on the picnic table and sat down on the bench facing his lawn chair with my back against the table. I stared at him, forcing him to look me in the eye. "All right. Fine," I said. "So you have a girlfriend, a significant other. You don't have to marry her."

"Joanna, listen to me." My father's eyes were provocative slits behind his glasses. "Brenda loves me like you wouldn't believe. This is no bullshit. She said she would kill herself if I didn't marry her. Did you ever receive such a declaration of love?"

"No, thank God. C'mon! Threatening suicide? That's manipulative. Mom's right. That's emotional blackmail." I let that sink in and flicked off an ant that was crawling into my sneaker.

"She agreed to separate bedrooms. She doesn't like it, but she agreed."

"I don't want you to be lonely," I said. "You know I want you to be happy."

"Who said anything about happy?" His crusty voice was edged with derision. Then he softened. "In my day, we didn't know from happy. Either you had enough to eat, or you didn't."

"That's bullshit and you know it," I said. I laughed. I hoped he knew I wasn't mocking him, just telling the truth. "You've spent your whole life talking about how to be happy."

My father smiled. "You know when I'm happy? When I'm alone at night with my books, a hunk of candy, a smoke, thinking about what I'm going to have for breakfast."

"Exactly. Didn't you tell me you can't wait until Brenda goes home and you have the house to yourself?"

"You hungry? I'll make us something to eat," he said. He pressed the sharp fangs of the weeder pole deeper into the ground next to him and leaned on it to help himself out of the lawn chair. "Listen, kid, your mother had plenty of chances. That wedding we went to up in Connecticut, for instance."

"When you danced in my living room."

"We had a chance then," he said. I followed him across the soft grass and over the cinderblock path I helped him build years ago. "At that hotel up there. How about some tomatoes right off the vine, a little olive oil, the finest extra virgin? A nice piece of bread." I followed him into the kitchen. "You know your mother was the great love of my life. She always will be."

Somewhere in England
28 Dec 1944

Darling Evie,

I just finished *A Tree Grows in Brooklyn*, the full book, not the abridged version the army had at first. It was great. Would you call it a proletarian novel? I'll tell you why I'm in doubt. Most books about the poor are somber, almost morbid, and leave you feeling badly. Maybe that's what they're meant to do. But this one was different. I never laughed so much, especially about Flittman and his feud with the horse, and Sissy and her lovers. The characters were so real, they made me feel alive too. A lot of the novel was parallel to my own experience. You said you felt that way as well. Francie was so precious, I fell in love with her, and she became you, so I didn't leave her when I finished the book. Because you were Francie, and you are all the girls in all the books I ever read.

All my love,
Clyde

My mother was distraught, frantic, miserable. "What did he say?"

"He said it was too late."

"He's going to marry her," she said. "Goddamnit! I never thought he'd do it." She opened up the linen closet where she kept a few bottles of liquor on a shelf among the neatly folded sheets and towels, and she brought out a jug of Gallo burgundy and poured us each a glass. "You know, we missed a chance to get back together," she said. "I was ready. I might have done it."

"He told me."

"Told you what?"

"About Connecticut."

"We stayed in that little hotel together. It was a little white hotel with black shutters."

"Yeah. In the same room, he said."

"I guess we were trying to save money. There were two beds. He was in his and I was in mine and he said, 'get in here and show me how much you still love me.'"

"What did you do?"

"I didn't do anything. I didn't see why I should have to go to him. I lay there waiting." My mother toyed with the stem of her wine glass. "I wanted him to come over to me." She looked up. "Why? What did he say?"

"He said he wanted you to come over to him."

CHAPTER 39

Tuckahoe

"Slow Uncle Archie's here? On Saturday? Why didn't you say so?"

"I'm saying so," said Harry.

We ran holding onto our caps toward our uncle behind the fence, his suit pockets bulging with Walnettos.

"I came to tell you, your mama can't visit tomorrow," Uncle Archie said.

Oh, no, I thought. Here it comes. The beginning of the end. I'd heard the stories. Like a clock, my mother said. First, it's every week, then every other week. Then they come once a month. Then it's once in a while. We'd all seen the kids waiting for relatives who promised they'd be there on Visiting Day and never showed up. Always something getting in the way. Work, maybe, Sunday inventory, or no carfare, or any kind of excuse they can make up because who wants to schlep all the way up to Yonkers and back. Why did they put us away in the first place? To make their lives easier. I'd heard Miss Beaufort's smug reproach when she left her office door open: "If it's so hard to leave your boy here, Mrs. Levy, Mr. Chaim Pipik, Mrs. Rosenbaum, Mr. Shlongstein, then why don't you just keep 'em at home with you? Huh?" The supervisors hated Visiting Day. They discouraged visitors. They didn't want us complaining to outsiders. They didn't want us getting used to mollycoddling, coming back inside on Sunday nights all soft. Like a clock, my mother said. Every other Sunday. Rain or shine. What was her excuse now?

"She's sitting shiva," said Uncle Archie.

"What?" I said.

"The baby died."

"What baby?"

"Your little sister."

"Gertie's not a baby anymore." Archie was so dumb.

"Who died?" said Harry.

"A baby," I said.

"What baby?" said Harry.

"Gertie," said Uncle Archie.

"What are you talking about? Speak English! Gertie's two and a half," I said. "She walks, she talks. She comes here and we roll down the hill together. Right, Harry? This hill we're standing on."

Uncle Archie started bawling. Even a child knew more than he did. "Gertie," Uncle Archie cried. "Poor little kid. She caught a cold at the nursery and died."

I reached between the iron pickets and grabbed the lapels of his cheap suit and shook him. *What are you talking about Archibald? Are you fucking crazy? Sitting shiva for who, you numskull?* I let him go, and I darted away. He'd probably get us in trouble for coming up here on the Sabbath. His arms flailed between the fence posts trying to grab me. It was so easy to dodge him, I had to laugh. He looked ridiculous. His pants rode too high on his waist and a teardrop was caught on the mole on his cheek and wouldn't fall off. Fall off, you stupid freaking teardrop! I sneered at Uncle Archie, but he didn't change his story. I came close, taunting him. Why were his lips always wet? I came dangerously close, until he grabbed me and pulled me against the wrought iron with one arm, grabbing Harry with his other arm. With my face pressed against his jacket I could smell the lavender water Grandma Cohen sprinkled on the handkerchief she placed in the pocket over Slow Uncle Archie's heart. "No," I said. I sobbed and he held me tighter until the iron bars were digging into my ribs. "Poor little kid," he said. "Caught a cold."

CHAPTER 40

We were delusional, out of our minds with excitement because of a biopsy. Hooray. Diagnostic surgery. You would have thought we were going to Disneyland. It was action, though. Something, finally. We were all dying for something. Brenda was encouraged by how well the operation went, and Dr. Geest peered into my father's mouth and admired his stitches, such delicate handiwork. "He'll have a nosebleed, that'll be the worst of it," the doctor said. I asked, absurdly in retrospect, if it looked like tuberculosis.

Even in his compromised state my father dictated the mood, propped on an elbow on the gurney ride from recovery back to his room singing loud enough to draw attention: "Que sera, sera! Whatever will be will be!"

"Is it TB?"

"We can't tell anything so far," Dr. Geest said. "The cells we got in the frozen section are undifferentiated."

"Meaning?"

"Meaning we can't tell what they are."

The final pathology report from the lab would take a few days, or even a week. They had to fix the tissue in paraffin, slice it up and put the paraffin slices on slides, stain the tissue molecules with dye, search for tumor markers and so on.

"You'll help me, won't you Dr. Geest?" my father said.

He said yes, nothing more, but he didn't leave. Dr. Geest stayed in the room in his green scrubs that were too big for him. He floated inside them like a boy dressed in his father's clothes. He looked lost. He looked like Johnny Dolan come back in a dream.

The next morning when I got to the Meyer building, my father's room was empty. His bed was made so taut you could bounce a nickel on it. The ninth floor was deserted. I searched the halls, glancing into doorways at horizontal legs and feet, until I found two nurses behind a desk, a young one eating a bagel, and an older one with a koala bear clamped onto her stethoscope.

"Do you know where Mr. Aronson is? Room 949?"

"He's down in Oncology," the young one said, peering at me over the top of her bagel.

"Oncology?" I said. "You mean the tumor was malignant? You mean he has cancer?"

The nurse shrugged. Her mouth was full.

I was trembling. The older nurse gave me an odd look. How could they be so insensitive? He was alone—he was hearing the news alone. I sped to the elevator, jabbed at the down button, stamped my feet in the plunging car, sprang out when the doors opened on the ground floor. I rushed through the carpeted corridors into the glass breezeway, past the cafeteria and the odor of burnt pizza, into the main hall, past the busy glass doors, the mauve blur of Admissions and the burst of color at the flower shop to another bank of elevators and down again, below deck.

No one in Radiation Oncology knew where he was. I drummed my fingers on the information counter and waited, idly flipping open one of the blue vinyl binders laying there, surprised to see a brightly colored Polaroid fastened to the first page. It was a photograph of a starvation victim with a chicken neck, the head too wide for the skeletal body. The patient had one bloody nostril and just below it, the thick hairs of his mustache were sticky with bright red blood. *He'll have a nosebleed, that'll be the worst of it.* I held the photograph up to the light and stared in horror and disbelief at the starving man who appeared to have lost a fistfight. I was confused. It didn't make sense. Who took this picture? When? What were the circumstances? I shut the binder and continued my search down a narrow hall and around a corner where my path was blocked by an abandoned wheelchair. It turned out the wheelchair wasn't empty and I knew immediately—by the way the man was slumped in it, and his hat was perched and his bathrobe tied—the Polaroid had been taken only minutes ago. The hallway had banisters like a ship's corridor and I grabbed onto one and clung to it. The nurses upstairs weren't being cruel. They had no idea someone could be so delusional they could look at my father and not know he had cancer.

He was assigned an oncologist, Anton Jelinek, who didn't know for sure without the final pathology report, but said that Mr. Aronson most likely had a primary head-and-neck tumor—a nasopharyngeal carcinoma that was probably squamous cell cancer, and the result of smoking. Jelinek was not absolutely certain, however, because the cells were undifferentiated, which he explained when I asked, simply meant that the cells were difficult to tell apart and identify. My father was having so much pain and had lost his appetite because the head-and-neck tumor was pressing on his cranial nerves. The third cranial nerve caused the headache, the sixth cranial nerve affected his eye, and the ninth cranial nerve would give him gum and jaw pain as the tumor grew. This kind of cancer was treated with surgery and radiation, but Jelinek warned that the surgery was often disfiguring. I'd seen a woman in the Meyer day room. Half her face was scooped out and she had a Frankenstein scar, but she was alive. I said if the tumor was growing wouldn't it be a good idea to zap it with radiation while we waited for a surgery date, and Jelinek said the tissue couldn't be radiated until after surgery and Geest would not go ahead with surgery until the final pathology report. In other words, still no treatment. My father was discharged. I took him home with his pajamas in a paper bag.

Such scraps we ended up accepting with gratitude. They gave us a name. It was something. With a name, we were a little less helpless. Now instead of "goddamn Aronsons," Brenda went around the house muttering "nasopharyngeal carcinoma," and I muttered along with her. We listed the cranial nerves together and recited which parts of the face were affected—like a catechism for her, an incantation for me. Brenda and I got along fairly well during that time, and my father no longer bullied me as he had back in December. Now I knew how to make his tea. He did snap sometimes. I asked if he remembered those Christmases before Uncle Seymour died when we drove up to Scarsdale and he growled: "Whaddaya think I do all day?" But he only meant—yes, of course I do, what else is there, the past is all there is—and he softened, and we talked about how great it was that Aunt Adele was gentile and provided us with a Christmas tree and presents for a few years when I was little, the whole schmear, except we had pastrami around the poker table instead of ham.

"They're rich," my father would say.

"Do they live in a mansion?" Susan would say.

"Yes," my father said.

We came out of the Lincoln Tunnel to horns honking. My father rolled down his window. "This is my town!" he called to passersby, absurdly considering we were hicks with Maryland license plates. We laughed merrily at his antics. To us, New York and my father were synonymous. We could have gotten off the turnpike at the George Washington Bridge, but he had to drive through the city. "MY town!" he said. By the time we got to Westchester, night would have fallen, and windows blazed like fire through the winter trees.

"There," my father said. "Up ahead. If you go down that road, you get to the orphanage."

"Where? Where?"

"There." A dark and winding road, a vanishing point. Deep in the woods, Christmas lights glowed.

"Can we go there?" I said.

"Torn down," my father said. It wasn't long before we pulled into Uncle Seymour's driveway.

"If this is a mansion, why aren't there pillars?" Susan said.

"They're rich, I tell you, rich," my father said.

My mother dealt the cards around the table. "Seven card stud. Deuces wild."

"How much you get paid at that grammar school in Baldymore?" said Uncle Seymour.

"Never mind," my father said. "You see me asking for handouts?"

"Ooh," said Uncle Alvin. "The professor has a conscience."

"Pair of eights bets," said my father's cousin, Fat Ellis.

"What're you crazy?" said Aunt Sadie. "Pair of kings! Mitzi's got a deuce showing."

"I see you don't mind eating my pastrami," said Uncle Seymour.

"My brother Harry never comes, never brings his kids here," Aunt Vivian whispered to my mother, "because he's still mad at Seymour and Adele for not taking in the two little boys."

"What little boys?" my mother said.

"Harry and Clyde! My brothers! Who do you think?" said Aunt Vivian.

"Harry's at sleep-away, that's why he's not here," my mother said. She took a bite of her corned beef sandwich.

"Yeah, Harry took money from his partner," said Aunt Vivian. "But even when he's not in jail, he never comes. Did you know the Home wouldn't let them out for Gertie's funeral? But Alvin and I went to the cemetery with Mama, the three of us in a taxi, Mama with the coffin on her lap."

"What's past is past," said Uncle Alvin. "You talking or you playing?"

For a whole week the adults played and the children played until one night we drove home, our presents locked in the trunk, my mother asleep in the front seat, Susan curled next to me. My father kept his eyes on the road and

I looked out at passing towns and lights in distant houses. I was glad he and I were the only ones awake, although he seemed unaware of me behind him in the dark quiet of the moving car.

We were realists who knew in order to survive we had to be fabulists, so we lived on hope and imagination. Days passed. It was frustrating to wait so long for the final pathology report, but we were confident when the report came in, the thing squatting between his cheekbone and maxillary sinus would be removed at last, and with it his pain and misery. I decided this was a good time to take a break, before the big surgery. I would be needed more during what was bound to be a grueling recovery. So I flew back to LA to rest up. How could I have left him? I did, though.

While I was away, Brenda was asked if she wanted the oncologist, Dr. Jelinek, to manage my father's case, or would she prefer their family doctor? Brenda chose the latter. That was Cromwell, the sarcastic hand-holder who was incurious about my father's symptoms and unmoved by his suffering. I was angry. My mother appealed to me to be more sympathetic to Brenda. Brenda had a relationship with Dr. Cromwell. She could reach him on the phone easily and he knew my father's history. I wished I could have supported Brenda's decision, I really did. But on top of everything I loathed about Cromwell, he didn't have privileges at Johns Hopkins.

"What's so great about Hopkins?" Brenda said. "A lot of good they've done."

I reminded her Hopkins was where my father's tissue now sat in a lab under a microscope, and where his surgeon practiced. What I thought didn't matter, though. The doctors wanted to deal with one family member only, whoever was next of kin. That was Brenda. I was thousands of miles away. She was in charge again.

At first I couldn't get used to being away, not knowing what was going on minute to minute. I wasn't sure I would last for two long weeks in LA. Then I got I got used to the freedom. I rode my bike down to Hermosa Beach to visit a friend a couple of times, and I started writing again. I was sitting at the desk in the bedroom noodling with a short story about a freaky Greyhound bus trip to nowhere, when I got a call from an old boss in New York. She had started working at GQ magazine and wanted me to do a story on the differences between dating in LA and dating in New York. Fred pointed out the obvious—that I wasn't dating, so how would I know? Well, gee, I could interview single friends. And right away I had some ideas. Like how at parties in LA people asked, "What do you drive?" Fred said everyone had heard that before, and maybe the assignment was a lot to take on while caring for my father, so I called the editor and said I would pass. I trusted Fred so much then. "You're better off working on your short story," he said.

"Do you really think the Greyhound story is good?" I said. We were in the den, Fred's office. I struggled to pull out his rolling desk chair—it was difficult with him still in it—but I moved it far enough so I had room to climb onto his lap. He put his arms around me. I was relieved. GQ was intimidating. The assignment came at the wrong time.

I finished the Greyhound story and started a new one, a story I had been thinking about writing for a long time, about Johnny. But I was struggling. I couldn't even think of a fictional name for him. Bobby wasn't right. Tom was close, but I didn't want to give him my childhood friend's name. Not finding a name for him felt like a sign. Don't go there, everything about Johnny is too weird.

With nothing to work on, I got agitated. I called Cedar Drive every day, always with the same two questions: How is my father and have you heard from pathology? He's fine and I haven't heard anything, Brenda always said. After a week of this, I suggested instead of waiting, she ought to call pathology herself.

"I'm sure they'll call when they have anything to report," said Brenda.

Take care of yourself during the break, my mother said. Be good to yourself. Get a massage or something, Susan said. So I got a haircut, and decided to go really short. It was a reckless decision. My small face looked smaller and my nose looked bigger with no hair to hide behind, but I tried to embrace it. I did feel lighter. That was good. I felt I could levitate if I wanted. I was a warrior, ready for battle, at least on behalf of my father, if not for *GQ*. To further my self-care, I went to see my gynecologist for a checkup and we chatted. She said, "Undifferentiated cells? That's bad. I'm sorry." I was shocked. I shouldn't have been, but I was. Why hadn't *his* doctors told me undifferentiated cells meant a poor prognosis? I'd done my own research, but the books about cancer I'd taken out of the library used the same language as the doctors, in the same way, talking about the cells as if they weren't attached to people, telling me nothing, allowing my massive denial. I cried to Fred, and he cried, too. After a while, I squirmed out of his arms and I went and watered the flowers on the patio and deadheaded the wilted blossoms and sprayed the lemon tree with biodegradable soap and that calmed me down. I saw a few movies with Fred during that week and I had lunch with friends, but I wasn't really present. What could the holdup possibly be about? I figured if I wanted to find out I'd have to call pathology myself. I was put through without delay. No one asked what kind of kin I was, and I was told immediately they had results. I felt regret and shame for not calling sooner and fury at Brenda for not calling at all. Our détente had come to an end.

The final results were a surprise, not at all expected. He did not have nasopharyngeal carcinoma. The undifferentiated cells were adenocarcinoma, not squamous cells. Primary

head-and-neck cancers were not adenocarcinomas. The name they gave us was the wrong name. The mass pressing on his cranial nerves was a metastasis. It had traveled from a distant site. But what distant site? The doctors scratched their heads. They were clueless. All they had to go on was his history of prostate cancer. Prostate cancer was an adenocarcinoma.

I expected Brenda to be angry I went over her head, but she didn't seem to mind. She called Dr. Cromwell with the news and he spoke to Dr. Jelinek and they agreed to give him DES, the notorious drug prescribed to prevent miscarriages that was found to cause cancer in the children born to mothers who used it. DES was banned for women, but still used to curb testosterone in men with prostate cancer. I couldn't believe we were taking this giant step backward. Hadn't we been told months ago prostate cancer traveled to the bones first and foremost? And my father's bones were fine. Hadn't we been told prostate cancer was not known to travel to the sinus? Like, never. I called Jelinek's office and shared my concern. "That's all true," Jelinek said. "But he had prostate cancer once, so we're going with that."

CHAPTER 41

Had Brenda always lacked compassion? I couldn't say, since I had childishly ignored her for so many years. Had she always possessed such steely self-interest? That was even harder to figure out, since to my mind, she had no self to be interested in. She was a zero, a cipher. Ignoring her had always been so easy. I thought of the time a couple of years ago when my mother, Susan and I were at the house, and my father, perhaps meanly, brought out the slides from Ireland and set up the projector using the living room wall for a screen. Brenda dragged in a dining-room chair and placed it in a corner slightly behind the four of us crowded onto the sofa, and she sat with her hands folded in her lap, the way she must have sat for the nuns at school, while we excitedly called out the names of towns and castles our younger selves were posed in front of. I had the usual smug sympathy for Brenda then. But we were the dupes, not her. She was the winner, lawfully wed. The second my father got sick, she came out of the shadows to claim her rightful place and it was jolting, as if she had flipped on the lights during our slide show and turned our Kodachrome memories back into a blank living-room wall.

My break came to an end and I flew to Baltimore. My mother and Marty picked me up at the airport. I dumped my bag into the trunk and slid into the back seat. My mother swiveled around so she could look at me. "Your father is not the man you left two weeks ago," she said. "I'm warning you. Be prepared."

"So Brenda did nothing the whole time I was gone?" I said.

"Nothing," my mother said miserably.

I stared out at the woods along the parkway. The pavement hummed as we drove over the Patapsco River, and then we were flanked by woods again. A white-tailed deer darted between the trees as we flashed by.

"Whatever you may think of me and my faults," my mother said, "the way Brenda's treated him since he's been sick is appalling. We've got to get some food into him. We've got to get him into the hospital again. Somehow, some way, they've got to feed him. Stick an IV in his arm, whatever they do."

"Big snowstorm on the way," said Marty.

"Shana says they don't admit people for malnutrition," my mother said. She turned to Marty. "Shana Bloom's son's a doctor. You met Mike. He says we should say Clyde's having a heart attack."

I was pleased my mother was getting involved. I needed her help, and I welcomed Shana's advice, too, and Mike's, of course. I leaned forward to see Marty's reaction, but his face was blank. He thought my mother was too involved to begin with.

"We were in Washington yesterday," my mother said, "and I bought your father some Senate bean soup."

"What's that?"

"You never heard of Senate Bean Soup? It's great. He'll be able to eat soup. It'll slide right down."

"Thick, sticky bean soup?" I said. I was already losing confidence in her. "He can't even swallow Jello."

"He'll like this. It's famous."

My mother said she would stay only a minute. Marty waited in the car. They had to beat the snowstorm home, but she wanted to give my father the soup. Brenda opened the kitchen door. I had forgotten the dry smell of smoke, of nothing bubbling on the stove. My mother grabbed my arm to slow me down, to remind me with the pressure of her hand about what she had said. He is not the man you left two weeks ago. I slid my palm along the wall from yellow to white—the demarcation where the kitchen ended and the hall began. I went slowly and stopped at the opening to the living room.

"Oh, Daddy." I put my hand to my mouth. He was thin when I left but this was different. His cheeks were hollow. Parchment skin hung on his bones. His once straight, fleshy nose was a bony hook. The concentration-camp victim comparison was inevitable. I dropped my bag on a chair and went to him and put my arms around his bony shoulders and my face in his scrawny neck. How could Brenda have let this happen? How could anyone? "I'm back," I whispered into the fabric of the chair.

"My Joanna came back," he said quietly.

"Senate Bean soup," my mother said. She held the can up to show him. "Joanna can heat it up. It's gourmet, you'll love it. You've heard of it, haven't you, Clyde? Look," she said, bringing the can closer.

"Shut up, Ma," I whispered into his ear.

"Yeah, Evie," he said. "Shut up."

My mother put the can on top of the television set. "Well, if that's the way you feel about it," she said.

I straightened up. "I told you he couldn't eat that stuff."

"He could give it a try."

I crossed over to the TV and picked up the can. There was a picture of the U.S. Capitol on the label. "Oh," I said. "Senate Bean Soup."

"Well, what did you think I was saying?" My mother made a sputtering exasperated noise.

"They serve it in the Capitol cafeteria," Brenda said.

"There you go," said my mother. "At least somebody appreciates what I'm talking about." She buttoned her fuzzy purple coat, and patted my father on the hand. "Anyway, I brought your daughter, Clyde."

"A saint," said my father.

My mother hurried outside under the heavy sky and drove off with Marty. I was left with my starving father and Brenda who wasn't showing the mildest concern. I understood that she wasn't me, that I was as abnormally devoted as she was abnormally repressed, but I was unprepared for the bizarre turn things were about to take.

"We have to get my father admitted to a hospital."

"Oh, really?" said Brenda. A small smile of superiority lit her face and for the first time I saw that while I pitied Brenda, she pitied me. The overwrought care, the pointless racing around hospital hallways, it was pathetic to her. "What's all the who-struck-John?" she said, one of her favorite expressions. "He's been in and out of the hospital and it hasn't helped one bit."

"He's going to die of hunger."

"Don't blame me. You know he won't eat," Brenda said. She raked her fingers through Hoffman's fur, and fed him a Snausage-in-a-Blanket from the box on top of the fridge.

"Have you spoken to anyone about how much weight he's lost—Jelinek or Geest?" I said.

"I spoke to Dr. Cromwell."

I tried not to react negatively, to stay focused on my goal. "OK. That's good. Let's call Dr. Cromwell and tell him we think my father's having some kind of heart trouble," I said, taking my mother's and Shana Bloom's advice.

Brenda eventually turned her attention away from the dog. "I suppose we could say he's having chest pains," she said. "I'll call Dr. Cromwell in the morning."

"Thank you." So she wasn't a complete monster.

Brenda put my father to bed and he went willingly, like a horse led back to the barn, his head down, resigned.

When I woke up the world was white. Snow had tumbled out of the sky while we slept, transforming the lawns and street and sidewalks into massive rolling drifts that reached past our windowsill. Icicles a yard long dripped from the overhang. Trees loaded with snow were not just outlined, but blotted out. Cars were snowdrifts with side-view mirrors peeking out like little ears.

I had never regarded snow from this window with such anxiety. It was always delight, schools closed, the promise of snow forts and sledding. *Marie, Marie, hold on tight.* But now looking out at the veritable winter wonderland, my heart sank. How would we get to the hospital? I went and took a shower, dressed, and dried what was left of my hair. It was early but Brenda was already waiting expectantly in the swivel chair—her chair—when I came out. She was wearing a skirt and blouse, stockings and pumps and seemed ready to go out, but I doubted her office was open with so much snow on the ground.

"Good news," Brenda said cheerfully. "I got your father admitted to the hospital."

"You did?" A big smile spread on my face. I was silly with relief and gratitude, and surprise, too. She let him starve for two weeks, was seemingly incompetent, and now here she was making things happen before I was even out of the shower. She must have gotten some perspective last night. She'd been too close, living with him day to day. But last night, she must have seen my father through my eyes and realized how bad he looked. My impulse was to hug her and I came toward her, but Brenda's rigid posture held me back.

"Did you tell them chest pain?" I asked. We agreed "chest pain" was the best wording.

"No, said Brenda. "I got him in for an orchiectomy." She patted the yellow telephone on the table in between her chair and the recliner. "Surgery tomorrow morning at 7 a.m."

I told her I didn't know what an orchiectomy was, and Brenda seemed pleased that for once, she understood the medical terminology and I didn't. "It's castration," she said. She watched me, an amused smile playing on her lips. "Get him in anyway you can, you said. So there you are, Joanna. You should be happy."

I wasn't happy.

"I believe it's frequently done to men who have prostate cancer," Brenda said. She raised her eyebrows for emphasis.

"But prostate cancer is just a theory," I said. "Because they can't think of anything else."

"Tomorrow morning, 7 a.m., he'll be castrated. Surgery's always bright and early, have you ever noticed that?"

"You're not joking, are you?"

"I got him back into Hopkins," Brenda said. She sat with her hands folded in her lap, a good girl, a pious woman. The bright white landscape out the window was like a wintry scene in a fairytale. "That's what you wanted," she said. "It had to be Hopkins. And let me tell you it wasn't easy setting this up. Dr. Cromwell doesn't have admitting privileges there, but his friend does."

"We were going to say chest pains," I said. I was paralyzed, glued to the spot where I was standing when I decided not to hug her. "Don't look so scared," she said. "I already told your daddy about the operation, if that's what you're worried about."

I shut my mouth, which had been hanging open. Was this some sick joke? Was Brenda not a cipher but a psychopath? I understood she was following their doctor's advice, and at least from one vantage point, there was some logic in choosing this surgery as the way to get admitted to the hospital. But the idea was to find a vague, non-invasive reason. To run some tests! Not to admit him for a major unnecessary surgery, much less one weighted with meaning and reeking of vengeance. And really, if anyone were entitled to seek this sort of revenge, it would be me, and I wasn't interested. I always suspected one of the reasons he married Brenda was to punish us. I hadn't thought that it might be to punish himself, a little boy so bad his mother sent him away.

I called my mother, and then Mike Bloom, and then the one doctor friend I had in New York. It was too early to wake up anyone in LA. I was advised to go along with Brenda and Dr. Cromwell and their demonic scheme simply in order to get my father into the hospital. He was supposed to check in today, so he could be prepped for the surgery tomorrow. The plan was, once checked in, I would question the wisdom of actually going forward with the procedure. When I got off the phone after the last call, I went down the hall. "We're going to the hospital today," I said. "You heard?"

My father was sitting up in bed. "I heard," he said.

I put my coat and boots on and went out to the carport. The air was so cold it froze the inside of my nose. I pulled my gloves on and took the snow shovel from the utility room. The shovel scraped the bare concrete in the carport and then glided silently over a powdery drift. I trudged to the end of the driveway sinking up to my knees in snow, and looked down the street, squinting in the brightness. I began shoveling. The physical work was gratifying, the effort, the weight of the snow on my shovel, the satisfying loft and release, and after a while, the tan concrete showing through, the clank and scrape and loft again. Meanwhile, across the street, neighbors in long quilted coats worked on their sidewalk.

Everyone on our block now was black, except my father, and Zucker who lived on the corner, and Lucky and his wife down the street. When the suburban neighborhoods of Baltimore were new, white people lived in the houses, and when the trees matured, the white people moved away and black people from the city moved in. During a brief period in the seventies, our neighborhood was integrated, but it didn't last long. Fear-mongering prevailed. Children lived and breathed fear growing up off Liberty Road in Baltimore, not fed to me by my lefty parents, for the most part, but by many around us. The local real-estate industry fostered much of it, hoping to cash in on white flight, redlining, flipping houses, creating new markets. So whites and blacks never even got the chance to try out living with each other. It seemed that white people like me unconsciously put the blame for our lost childhoods, our lost innocence, on the darker-skinned people who replaced us. When my mother used to drive us downtown into the past to show us where she grew up, we felt like outsiders, and now

I was starting to feel like an outsider on Cedar Drive. I doubted the feeling even approached how black people must have felt, brutally treated as outsiders in most places from the start. As a result, everyone in Baltimore, black and white, seemed to have a chip on their shoulder. We drove over abandoned streetcar tracks looking for the entrance to the woods, to the candy store. This was our home, and yet we didn't belong.

Next door on the north side, Mr. and Mrs. Rollins came out with snow shovels and started clearing their driveway. They waved to me. In summer, my father gave them zucchinis from his garden. He believed in neighbors. The superficial talk over the back fence was an enjoyable necessity, exchanging news of a shared world down to the grass and ants. They looked out for each other, if it only meant noticing a rubber-banded *Morning Sun* that hadn't been picked up.

I wondered if Mrs. Rollins—Lydia was her first name— imagined me as a small girl playing under the apple tree where the wild violets grew between our houses. I wondered if she knew I had been inside her house many times when my friend Tom lived there. (Had she put carpet over the linoleum? Tom's mother never had.) More likely, she saw me only as grown, a vague blur of a person coming in from some other city, with little connection to Cedar Drive. Now she came toward me sinking into her white lawn. "How's your father?" she asked.

"We're going to the hospital today," I said.

Mrs. Rollins called to her husband, and he called to the neighbors across the street. One of the men shielded his forehead with the edge of his hand and looked across at me in the brightness. Then he and his wife lifted their shovels and the man next door to them lifted his shovel, and they climbed up over a snow bank and crossed soundlessly to my side of the street and began shoveling our driveway. "Thank you," I said. My eyes teared, and the tears froze on my face, and my cloudy breath blew toward the creek. I wanted to tell Mrs. Rollins everything—about my father pulling us on the sled, and the

Good Humor truck in summer, and walking home from school with my crayon drawing fluttering in the breeze.

"Your dad was friendly to us when others weren't," Mrs. Rollins said. "Go on in the house now and help him get ready. We'll finish up."

I didn't want to go. I wanted to stay outside in the snow with her people. But my time on this lawn and these sidewalks, in the grass and the snow, was over. Anyone could see that.

CHAPTER 42

Meanwhile at Johns Hopkins, the surgeon sharpened his knife, nurses got on the phone and rearranged their schedules, and interns scrubbed their grubby little hands. We were caught in the machinery. A theory had been proffered and rationalized. It was business as usual. If we didn't do anything to stop the gears from turning, my father would be castrated in the morning.

Brenda helped him through the admissions process, while I hurried off to sound the alarm, explaining the situation to Dr. Jelinek, expecting him to slam on the brakes. The surgery was absurd, it made no sense. Right away, Jelinek reached into his pocket for a pen and drew two big circles on the tissue paper covering his examining table. He labeled the circles "testicles" and sketched three arrows coming out of each ball. Over the arrows he wrote the letters DES. Then he underlined the letters. "Your father is taking the drug DES to inhibit testosterone production," he said, clicking his pen. "Testosterone is produced by the testicles. So you see, removing his testicles altogether would more effectively stop the production of testosterone." He clicked his pen again, released the point, and underlined the balls.

I went back upstairs. The surgeon was just coming into my father's room leading a crowd of five interns, the requisite visit before an early morning procedure. I followed behind the last intern. Brenda looked up from the roast chicken she was picking at on my father's dinner tray. The surgeon introduced himself as Ved Ramanujam, chief of urology. He looked like a movie star from the 1930s—black pompadour, a lab coat draped over his suit like a cape. He stood back with one hand in his jacket pocket and let the lead intern speak.

"Say, Mr. Aronson, how're doing? Gee, your eye doesn't look so good. Has that been bothering you much?"

"Are you some kind of a wise guy?" my father said. "What's your name?"

"Macomber."

"Macomber," he said. "'The Short Happy Life of Francis Macomber.'"

The intern gave him a blank stare. He hadn't expected words to come out of the skeleton with the bushy mustache and bulging eye.

"Hemingway. Don't they teach you boys anything?"

No one laughed.

"My father was an English professor," I said. His brothers always called him professor. And then when he left City to teach community college he officially earned the title.

"Ah," Ramanujam said. "*Professor* Aronson." His accent was lilting and dignified. "So, I understand, Professor, you are here at the Johns Hopkins Hospital prepared to have surgery tomorrow morning. Macomber, perhaps you can give Professor Aronson an idea of how the procedure will go."

"Wait a second," I said.

"What is it, ma'am?"

"Go ahead, Joanna," my father said.

"This operation doesn't make any sense. We don't even know if he has prostate cancer."

"Is that right, Mr. Aronson?" Ramanujam said.

"That's right, doctor. Listen to my daughter. Joanna, go on. Tell them my story."

I hesitated, not sure what story my father wanted told. He was pointing at me like I was being called on in class and I had better come up with the right answer. I took a moment and then I began to describe the morning three months ago when my father woke up with the mother of all headaches and I explained how that headache had never gone away and life was never the same again. I told them about the sack of

potatoes and how he could hardly swallow tea. I told them about the terrible pain, and how no one believed him and Dr. Cromwell suggested he hold my father's hand and how Heidenheimer said he might have cluster headaches, and then his right eye stopped moving. I told them about the nasopharyngeal carcinoma diagnosis and the adenocarcinoma cells and that yes, it was true, he'd had prostate cancer, but he'd been cured four years ago, in 1983, with radiation, and the cancer had never shown up again on any bone scan or blood test. Finally, I told them that the surgery they were planning for tomorrow morning had been scheduled without my father being examined by a single urologist, and so going forward with this "procedure" would be a terrible mistake. I glanced over at Brenda. Her face was stony. Finally, I said how desperately we had wanted my father admitted to the hospital, but only because he was starving to death.

Dr. Ramanujam came closer to the bed and peered down at his patient. Then he backed away again. He took his hand out of his jacket pocket and with one long crooked finger scratched around the roots beneath his pompadour. He turned to face the interns. "Macomber, cancel the surgery," he said.

"Cancel it?" said Macomber. He sounded disappointed.

"You heard the man's daughter, didn't you? You heard the story. Nobody's even examined Mr. Aronson. It's possible this man doesn't even have prostate cancer." The doctor spoke angrily, with compassion. "So no, we are not going to cut off his testicles. If that's all right with you, Macomber?"

"You're my Emile Zola," my father said to me. I had defended his honor. He threw off his blankets and swung his legs over the edge of the bed. "If you don't mind, gentlemen," he said, "I'm going to dance a little jig." His slippers were waiting and he slid his feet into them and did a quick shuffle, then slipped them off and got back under the covers. Even Brenda laughed. She took her heart out of the freezer and left the frozen glob melting on the counter for a few seconds.

"By the way," said Macomber, "why can't he eat?"

"We don't know," I said. "And so far, nobody's been all that interested in finding out."

A full body scan was ordered and carried out. I'd never heard of a body scan. I didn't know you could look at all the body parts at once. But surely Cromwell knew such a diagnostic tool existed, even in 1986. Surely Heidenheimer knew about body scans, and Jelinek knew, and all the other experts who'd examined my father and drew pictures and shook their heads all knew there was such a test. But no one thought to order it. He'd had so many doctors I kept a list, and now there was a new one to add, a gastroenterologist named Nick Morales, who had dimples and a cowlick, and was probably as young as I was. He bantered pleasantly with us at bedside. My father was in a chatty mood, eager to talk about his hobbies—gardening and cooking, and the painting class he was taking. "Well, not now," he clarified. "I'm not doing so well now."

Morales said that made perfect sense considering the body scan showed a fifteen-centimeter tumor on my father's esophagus. While we tried to absorb this news, the doctor took out a fountain pen and doodled on the top sheet of paper fastened to his clipboard. He drew a long tube with a pendulous blob attached to one side. He colored in the blob and held it up. My father blinked. Finally, the artwork matched the truth of his experience.

"I recommend you eat only slippery foods—Jello, soup, that sort of thing," the doctor said.

"Thanks for the advice," my father said.

Morales noted the sarcasm and said he was surprised the tumor wasn't discovered sooner. Had my father mentioned his trouble swallowing to anyone? I wondered then if my father's shtick was the problem. The "help me doctor" stuff. The hat, the mustache, the Hemingway, the cigarettes, the tap dancing. Everything for comic effect. The play-acting about how he couldn't speak for himself, ask my daughter, she'll tell you.

Everything was ironic, meant to show he was no sucker, no patsy, no victim. He thought he'd gain respect that way, calling attention to himself in the bargain, and ultimately get better care. But the result was denying his real need.

It was a lot to take in, what Morales said. I tried to feel some satisfaction at being right. My father did not have prostate cancer. He had a primary esophageal tumor that metastasized to his sinus. Morales scheduled an endoscopy. He'd look through the endoscope to see what was there and cut off a small piece of the tumor to biopsy. At the same time, through the scope he would insert a gastronomy tube—a feeding tube—so my father could get nourishment directly into his stomach. No need to swallow.

"We'll figure out how to treat the cancer and give you a prognosis once we get the biopsy results," said Morales. "But it'll be a squamous cell cancer."

"No," I said. "It'll be an adenocarcinoma."

"No," said Morales. "It's in the middle of the esophagus, not the lower portion. It'll be squamous cell, probably from smoking."

When the doctor left, my father said, "Sleep here tonight, Joanna."

"I'll stay late if you want."

"Not good enough. Tell them to put another bed in here. They'll do it. Ask them."

I hesitated.

"Please."

I went looking for a cot. "Don't do it," the nurse said. "I can get you a cot, I guess. But honey, really. Look how tired you are. You need a break. Just because your father asked doesn't mean you have to do it."

"I guess you're right," I said, and I turned and went back to his room.

Shep Levine was waiting outside my father's door. "You know the poem 'Thanatopsis'?" he asked.

"No."

"No?" Shep said. "C'mon. You should have learned it in high school. William Cullen Bryant. ʻ. . .The gay will laugh/When thou art gone, the solemn brood of care/Plod on . . . ʼ"

"My father wants me to sleep in the room with him but the nurse told me not to."

"Why not?"

"She says I need a break."

"What does she know about what you need?" Shep said.

I had a cot put in the room.

All night my father moaned. The sinus tumor had started pressing on the ninth cranial nerve. "Ah, ah. My gums. Shooting pains. Stop the world, I want to get off." We held hands from bed to cot. In the morning, Morales ordered morphine and over the next two days the tenor of my father's existence changed. He was groggy but pain free. He rarely moved from the bed to the chair. He woke with a loopy grin. His voice weakened until it was barely audible. Orderlies came and rolled him away for the endoscopy and he came out of recovery with a hole in his stomach like a bullet hole in a cartoon man. Miraculously, the hole didn't bleed and the contents of his stomach didn't tumble out. The G-tube protruding from the hole was attached to more tubing that was attached to a pump and a bag of chocolate Enrich hanging on an IV pole, and that was eating.

Now that I was sleeping over, I never left the hospital. There was no reason for it. To my diet of coffee and ice cream, I added little pop-top cans of Beefaroni that came out of the vending machines already hot. The doctors arrived on their morning rounds waking us at dawn, smelling of aftershave and coffee while I still lay on my cot like a child on a sleepover, snowbound with Betsy.

I remembered one Winter Solstice there was an ice storm that ended with a sleepover. "A veritable winter wonderland!" we all shouted at the crystal world from the carport. The other guests had gone home, only Johnny was left. The roads were treacherous and he had to stay the night. I waited in my bed in the dark until I could hear everyone's sleeping breath, the three of theirs, anyway, and tiptoed down the hall to Johnny lying awake on the sofa.

"I can't believe you came out here for me," he whispered. "It's so risky."

I straddled his stomach. He propped himself up on an elbow and we parted the curtains and looked out at the moonlit snow encased in a shell of ice. "I wanna go out there and smash up that crust," I said. "And eat it like the burnt sugar on créme brûlée."

"You have a good imagination," Johnny said.

"No, I don't."

"Imagine that you can make yourself tiny, and then tell me what you would do if you were inside my body."

I believed every question adults asked was a test and most of their questions were probably trick questions as well, so I was thoughtful about my answer. "I would slide down your dick like it was a sliding board."

Johnny laughed and put his finger to his lips to quiet us. "That's great," he whispered. "I love that. What a perfect answer." Then he told me to go back to bed.

I parted the curtain to see the snow piled on the lintels of the Johns Hopkins Public Health building across the street, but it was dark already and our windows were mirrors. I asked my reflection why? Why did I love these flawed men, these hurt men who chose to hurt me? Johnny was right. I had a good imagination. I imagined they were my protectors.

The doctors appeared for evening rounds, their street clothes bristling beneath their white coats, impatient to leave for the restaurants where they would choose wines and clink glasses, cut into veal chops and duck breasts, leaving us behind to face the night. Sometimes I felt as if I were high on morphine, too, everything was surreal, riding my cot like a magic carpet alongside my father and past the Milky Way. I was glad I didn't take the nurse's advice, and listened to Shep Levine instead. My father would die. He would not come out of this thing well as I had promised those long weeks ago. But I would take the journey with him. For as long as possible, he wouldn't be alone.

CHAPTER 43

Tuckahoe

With all the fresh eggs and chickens from our coops, fruit from our orchard and vegetables from the farm, one might assume the boys of the HNOH did not go hungry. But there were so many of us to feed, the chicken coops provided chicken only once a week, and then, with the Great Depression, chicken even for Shabbos dinner was no longer a certainty. The Home had always sold poultry and eggs to the outside. It was more economical since a wagon full of chickens bought a hell of a lot of flour, oatmeal, powdered milk, and powdered eggs. But now with even harder times, the drifters and ex-cons on the kitchen staff, and the shadier porters, handymen, watchmen, and supervisors, which meant practically everyone, started stealing extra and selling on the black market. We orphans continued to receive handouts from the ladies' auxiliaries and other benefactors, but suddenly there was competition. Suddenly everybody was destitute. For years, Colgate donated toothpaste to the Home, hundreds of tubes, supposedly a lifetime's supply for every boy, until abruptly in November of 1929, the last glob splurted out of the last tube and that was it. Toothpaste dried up. Colgate couldn't afford the largesse any longer. It was fortunate, in a way, because we had taken to eating the stuff. Boy, did we have bellyaches in those days. Whatever we could find we ate. Unripe apples the size of walnuts stolen from Kessman's orchard after our own orchard was picked clean, and toothpaste. We were that hungry. From 1929 on, we brushed our teeth with Arm and Hammer baking soda, which wasn't so bad, cheap as dirt and tasted like salt.

Life went on. Even in those tough circumstances time didn't stand still, the world didn't end. I was twelve and studying for my bar mitzvah. It was a group affair, of course, and a truly gala event, a fundraiser for the Home held at the fancy Hotel Astor in Times Square. Dignitaries, luminaries, and benefactors—at least those who hadn't entirely lost their fortunes when the stock market crashed—were in attendance. Three boys were chosen to make speeches—one speech written and delivered in Hebrew, one in Yiddish, and one in English—to a crowd that included our patron saint Justice Aaron J. Levy, Mayor Jimmy Walker, Sophie Tucker, Eddie Cantor, and my mother. Franklin Roosevelt, the Governor of New York, sent a personal note regretting that he was unable to attend. I felt certain I would be picked to give the English speech. My English teacher thought that while I was a wise guy, I was a pretty good writer. In the end, my essay wasn't chosen, she said, because it wasn't pious. I couldn't argue with that. My mother was proud anyway. Who among her acquaintances had Sophie Tucker sing at her son's bar mitzvah?

The culmination of the whole shebang and the ultimate prize for bar mitzvah boys was the privilege of keeping and performing all the laws and customs of the Jewish religion including the privilege of rising before daybreak to lay tefillen. So it was for the Hebrew National Orphan Home confirmation class of 1930.

We anointed ones got down to the synagogue before the younger kids and wrapped leather straps around our arms and heads positioning the little leather boxes with prayers inside on our foreheads and on our hands every single dawning day except Saturday. The ritual was a little easier for the farm gang. We were used to getting up early. We prayed in Hebrew and sometimes in English:

> These words, which I command thee this day, shall be upon thy heart; and thou shalt teach them diligently unto thy children. And thou shalt bind them for a sign upon thy hand, and they shall be for frontlets between thine eyes.

I did it for years. For the rest of our lives it was supposed to be, like the toothpaste, and for orthodox boys who lived with their orthodox mamas and papas, that was probably the case. In the case of most of us institutionalized boys, the "privilege" was indulged only until we got the hell out of there. Meanwhile, I didn't know what I would have done without my buddies in the freezing-ass darkened shul, shivering as we wrapped the leather straps around and around, and placed the phylacteries, careful not to put the head box below the roots of our hair, which, according to some cockamamie holy men, was supposed to upset the order of the universe.

Before shul, I walked up to the farm to help Moti Goldberg and Artie Shack do whatever chores were on the list for the day. I came inside the barn hoping to thaw out and shoot the breeze, but the barn was hardly warmer than the outdoors, and the senior boys had already finished their barn detail, gotten up even earlier than I did that day, and had ridden off in the wagon somewhere. I was left to muck out the stalls, and so I did, and then started to trudge back by myself for shul and breakfast. A thin layer of ice as delicate as lace coated the frozen mud furrows and crunched pleasantly under my feet. I dug my hands into my pockets. I'd lost my gloves a few weeks ago and I couldn't find my hat. The tops of my ears were raw. Across the fields, the Home loomed, its brick edifice dark against the pale blue light of dawn. The institution always looked haunted from a distance. I could imagine an all-American father driving the family Ford around a curve on Tuckahoe Road, the grim building coming into view, and the kids in the backseat shrieking in horror.

I turned my collar up and hunched my shoulders against the cold. The moon was still visible in the pale sky, and next to it, a bright planet. As I made my way across the field, yellow lights flicked on in the building. The kids in Companies D and E were getting up. Soon windows on every floor were ablaze. I stopped in the middle of the field and stared. A confusion of feeling stirred my heart. A few times over the years, I threatened to run away, but I knew there was nowhere to go. I knew deep down that the island I wanted to run away to, the place where I would be accepted, and where I'd have nothing to hide, was here. The Home was the island unto itself where my companions and I ate the fruit off the trees. My eyes stung. I shivered and jammed my fists deeper into my pockets and I walked toward the warmth and light.

Back from the barn and the frozen fields, down in the freezing synagogue we mumbled prayers. We were men now, the rabbis told us bar mitzvah boys. We had responsibilities, said Louis Longbeard, a man who did nothing but pray all day, while we swept the floors he trod and flicked the chickens he ate or sold on the black market, our bellies empty. We hitched up the horses and plowed the fields in summer and the snow from the roads in winter. We shoveled chicken shit from the coops and horseshit from the barn and ashes from the furnace and we didn't mind because it was honest work and not prayer that gave our lives meaning. We drove the horse and wagon to bakeries from Bronxville to Tarrytown picking up three-day-old bread and stale donuts. We mended fences, rebuilt car engines, planted potatoes, peeled potatoes, collected eggs, flicked chickens, did I say flicked chickens already? Well, we flicked a helluva a lot of chickens, drowned cats, repaired radios—we were men all right. And then we were beaten for staring at a supervisor the wrong way. Little kids whacked on the back of the head, carted off to Nurse Flanagan passed out during standing detention, bleeding from their noses, from their ears.

We grumbled all year in the newspaper office, and wrote our editorials, which were censored. We complained to Flanny, to the porters, to Eddie the night watchman, to the kitchen staff. Forget Miss Beaufort, she did nothing for us. Sometimes we complained to visiting dentists when they asked why our

permanent teeth were loose or missing, although we never complained to the Ladies Auxiliary of White Plains; those compassionate women would close down the place, and then, like we always said, where would we go? The talk was big, but the truth was most of us could barely stand to leave the grounds for the ninth grade, so tormented were we by the snobs at Roosevelt High School, we came rushing back each afternoon to the safety of the orphanage.

I grumbled mainly to Carl Grimm. He valued my opinion. Besides being the Home's second chef, Mr. Grimm was a true friend and mentor. He listened to classical music and appreciated abstract art. He was generous, inviting us into the cottage he shared with Charlie the porter and Hymie the handyman, offering snacks, sharing books that were banned, dispensing advice about girls. In the thirties, we destitute and neglected orphans were naturally budding socialists, hungry for news of the world. Mr. Grimm was willing to talk about the food riots, about union men and scabs, the workers storming the Ford plant at River Rouge, and the Harlan County coal strikes.

Later in the newspaper office, Pussy Friedman said, "They're criminals, those coal miners." Pussy was a pious boy. He gave the Hebrew speech at the Hotel Astor.

"You're against the striking miners?" said Skelly Schwartz.

"The miners strike," said Pussy, "and babies freeze to death."

"Nobody's freezing to death," said Skelly. "It's summer."

"They wait until winter to strike! They plan it that way. It's criminal," said Pussy.

"Tell it to the bosses, for God's sake," Moti Goldberg said.

A lot of the guys were stirred up, and most everyone who worked on the *Oracle* newspaper had an opinion.

"Shee-at, I just got an idea," said Oscar Finerman.

"Uh-oh. Finerman has an idea," said Pussy.

"No, this one is good," Oscar said.

Finerman pitched for the varsity baseball team at Roosevelt, which as I said, was outside of the orphanage gates
and a regular Yonkers public high school, but instead of the
Roosevelt uniform, Finerman always wore his Home jersey
with the Star of David emblazoned on the front and "Hebrew
National Orphan Home" stitched on the back. He was proud of
it. Meanwhile, it turned out Oscar, along with being a natural
athlete, was a natural-born leader. He called a meeting in the
barn.

"It's like this," said Oscar. "You juniors are always saying,
if the seniors are such hot shit why do we let the supervisors
push us around."

"Well, why do you?" said Chick.

"Never mind. It's time to put up or shut up."

"Hear, hear!"

"That's right! Put up or shut up!"

"What the hell does that mean?" said Harry. He was
the last to climb the ladder through the hatch and into the
hayloft.

"What's the squirt doing here?" said Moti.

"He's a fighter," I said. "You want him on your team."

"All right," said Oscar. "Lookit. We have a plan, me and
Moti."

Moti Goldberg played in the outfield for Saunders Technical High.

"Yeah, yeah. So what's the plan?"

"We can't tell you," said Moti.

"Stick it up your ass," said Stanley Hirsch.

"Fellas, fellas. It's for your own protection," Oscar said. "I
can't sniff out all the rats. Just show up here tomorrow after
lunch."

When the meeting ended, Oscar stopped some of the older
juniors at the barn door, including Chick, Jesse, and me, and
whispered our orders. Then we wandered over to the cottages
on our way to B. A. Beach. It was hot and we were dying to

get into the shady woods, wade in the cool brook, but we were riled up and hungry so we knocked on the door.

"Hey, Mr. Grimm," said Chick.

"What's on your mind, boys?"

"Nuttin," said Chick.

"Hungry?"

"Always," I said.

Mr. Grimm rummaged around in his kitchenette and brought out some bread and cheese. I loved the cozy clutter of the cottage.

"Tell us again about the Bolsheviks storming the Winter Palace," said Jesse.

"I got into a little trouble over that, my friends," said Mr. Grimm. "Accused of stirring you fellas up." He removed a newspaper from the couch so we could sit down.

"Comrades, you mean." I said.

Mr. Grimm laughed. "Look, fellas. Comrades. The religious zealots who run this joint won't tolerate a socialist and nonbeliever on the premises."

"Plenty of us Homeboys are non-believers," I said.

"Wait a minute," said Mr. Grimm. "You boys just had your bar mitzvahs." He sliced the bread on a cutting board and brought it over with a slab of smelly cheese and a knife.

"So what?" I said. "It was a nice ritual. But that's all it was." I took a slice of the bread along with a hunk of cheese and so did Chick and Jesse. The bread was soft and fresh. We watched each other eat with pleasure, while making sure no one got more than his share.

"It was real nice," said Chick. "You were there, weren't you, Mr. Grimm? At the Hotel Astor?"

"I couldn't afford it. Fifty dollars a plate."

"Fifty coconuts for a piece of chicken and a baked apple?" Chick said. "Suckers."

"Wasn't a baked apple, Chick," said Mr. Grimm. "I'm told the swells got Baked *Alaska*."

"Look Carl, we want your honest opinion," Jesse said. He reached for another slice of bread then pulled back.

"Go ahead," Mr. Grimm said. "Bread, cheese, and my opinion are always free of charge."

"All right then. What do you think of armed rebellion?" Jesse said.

"Ah, the Bolsheviks again," said Mr. Grimm. "Maybe we should keep the conversation to girls."

"Girls are good, too," I said. The three of us snickered. The last time we were over, Mr. Grimm told us some things we could do with women once we got them. He said it seriously, not like the seniors who bragged and smirked and you couldn't believe a word they said, it was all jokes and lies. Carl told us the truth, but sometimes even Mr. Grimm we didn't believe. He told us our wives might do to us what some of the boys did to each other. Put it in their mouths. We laughed ourselves silly. This was too good to be true. We'd heard it, but we were sure it was only whores. "Sometimes you might do the same for her," Mr. Grimm said. Chick punched him on the arm. "Don't tease us." We snorted with laughter. "If you want to be a good lover," he said. He showed us a book he was reading that he held in his hands like a precious jewel: *Lady Chatterly's Lover* by D. H. Lawrence, banned in America. Mr. Grimm had a bootlegged copy. He read us a passage with the most hilarious sentence: "If a woman shits and pisses, I'm glad. I wouldn't want a woman who couldn't shit or piss." We howled and repeated the line whenever we got the chance. Pity the poor Homeboy who said he had a girlfriend. "And does she shit, this girlfriend of yours? How about pissing? She do that too?" Chick slapped his knee.

"Lookit, we're not here to talk about girls," said Jesse. "You can answer one question, can't you, Carl?"

"Whose armed rebellion are you talking about?" said Mr. Grimm.

"Ours," said Chick. "We can't stand it anymore—the beatings, the cruel punishments for sneezing or laughing. We gotta do something."

"I watch them," I said. I had a wad of bread in my cheek, and some soft cheese was stuck to the roof of my mouth, so I chewed and swallowed before I went on. "I watch the little kids sometimes, and it breaks my heart."

"What little kids?"

"The kids in Company E," I said, and wiped my mouth with a napkin. "The little guys. The freshmen."

"What do you mean you watch them?" said Mr. Grimm.

"I go downstairs and stand in the doorway. I'm not doing anything creepy. I swear. They're so little and cute. I can't believe I was that little when I came here. They need their mamas. But God forbid they don't make their beds just right, if the blanket has a wrinkle . . ."

"Whack! on the back of the head," said Chick, smacking the air in front of him.

"What about you?" Mr. Grimm said. "You get beaten, too."

"It's different for us older kids. We're strong. It's the little ones I'm worried about."

"They're not your problem, Clyde. Worry about yourself. Stick it out. Keep your noses clean. You'll be out of here before you know it."

"Four more years of this?" I said. "Are you kidding me?"

"Can you imagine this place without discipline?" Mr. Grimm said. He balanced his cigarette on the edge of a saucer and went to the icebox to get us some milk. "Complete chaos."

"Standing detention is not discipline," I said. "It's torture."

"You're going to fight back, is that the idea?" he said.

"We want change. We want action." I said.

"Don't tell me anymore," said Mr. Grimm. "I'll be forced to report you."

"Who us?" said Chick. "We didn't say nuttin."

For the next twenty-four hours I thought of nothing but how Chick and I, as ranking members of the farm gang, were supposed to leave lunch early, hitch up the horses and start harvesting the potato field in a hurry. Now that we were older, we had the freedom to come and go as we pleased, more or less. No more marching. We had to be present in class, synagogue, Hebrew school, for chores and at meals, but how we got there was our own business. One of the more annoying monitors stopped us anyway, on the way out of the dining room, and asked where the heck we thought we were going, so we told the truth. Out to the farm to bring in the harvest.

Scores of boys got their orders and trudged up the hill after us. None of this aroused suspicion as it was mid-July and the potato plants were well over two feet tall, their purple and white flowers withering, a sure sign the tubers were ready to be dug up. Chick and I harnessed Playboy and hitched up the potato lifter, a wacky-looking contraption with long spikes that raked through the soil like fingernails and brought the tubers to the surface. All the boys had to do was follow along behind us and fill their gunnysacks with as many potatoes as they could carry, careful not to get their arms lopped off by the rotating prongs. I gave Playboy a pat. "Now you can tell your foals you were at the revolution," I said. After Chick and I were done with our part, we gave a hand to Oscar and Moti, who had a team digging a trench. Most of us were stripped to our waists covered in a slick sheen of sweat. Chick's freckled skin burned, so he kept his shirt on, which by this point was soaked through and plastered to his body. It was satisfying work. Every shovelful of dirt seemed like progress, a way to somewhere we hadn't been able to get to before. Pretty soon we had a fifteen-foot-long trench about three-feet deep on the edge of the potato field bordering the service road. We worked steadily until the sun was low in the sky and the heat let up a little. As the last of the bulging sacks was lowered into the trench, the supper bell rang. Normally when the bell rang, we ran like hell for our supper. Now we strained against the urge.

"STAY PUT!" Oscar commanded. "Do not go down to the dining hall! Man your positions! Jump! Get down in the trench."

We crouched, hidden but still able to see. I kept my eyes on the horizon. The bell rang again and again. I'd never heard that before. The supervisors had to be mystified. Why were so many boys missing from supper? A few more extra clangs, then silence. Nervous laughter down the line. *Shut up! Shut up!*

We stayed in the trench. Nothing. My heart pounded in fear and excitement and then died down from waiting, until three heads bobbed over the crest of the hill about a hundred yards away. They were coming to us, just like Oscar said they would. Gasps up and down the line. My heart started pounding again, but no longer out of fear, only excitement. My hand twitched. Now they were so close we could see who they were. From left to right, muscle-bound Bull Pushkin, the bastard; in the middle, a silhouette of Humpty Dumpty that had to be Piggy Rosenthal, the lying cocksucker; and on the right, the towering shell-shocked Colonel in his ridiculous uniform.

"Come on. Suppertime! Suppertime!!" Piggy shouted. He waved his arms beckoning, calling us in.

"Boys! Boys! Let's go!" called Mr. Pushkin.

But there were no boys, not a soul. The three supervisors slowed and stopped and all three shielded their eyes with their hands and scanned the fields, and then their hands dropped to their sides.

"Where is everybody?" said Bull Pushkin.

Piggy Rosenthal blew his whistle furiously at the empty landscape. I fell on my ass laughing in the muddy trench. We were all cracking up, silently of course, well-practiced at that. What a sight those assholes were, waving their arms, scratching their heads. They were quite possibly shitting their pants. Let it be them this time! I got back on my knees and peered out between blades of grass. The supervisors started walking again, fast approaching. They were about fifteen feet away.

"Ready! Aim! FIRE! Oscar shouted.

A barrage of potatoes flew machine-gun style, rat-a-tat-tat! The supervisors threw up their elbows protectively and backed away, but they were getting hit plenty, some in the head. I threw as hard as I could while still taking aim. One after another, digging into the burlap sack at my feet, leaning back, but not too far, as there wasn't room to stretch, I shifted my weight from my right foot to my left, feeling the easy weight of a potato in my hand and the strength in my arm as I lobbed it. I got Piggy on the thigh. Dipped into the sack and lobbed another and bull's-eye, and another and another. I didn't hear Oscar at first.

"Hold your fire! CEASE FIRE!"

My fingers went limp and I let a potato plop to the bottom of the trench. A fourth figure strode up the hill. There was a collective intake of breath. Superintendent Henry Laudenbacher himself, the big man, boss of the bosses, wielding a megaphone.

"Boys! Boys! Please. Why are you doing this?" His voice echoed.

No one moved or said anything, but we didn't duck like cowards either. Then Oscar climbed out of the trench.

"We're on strike!" he called over no-man's land.

Mr. Laudenbacher lowered the megaphone to his side. "Why?" he called back.

"The supervisors are cruel to us. We're not coming in until our grievances are addressed and our demands met."

"All right," said Laudenbacher. "All right. I'll meet with you. You and I will talk this out. Bring a boy from each company."

How sweet to watch the three supervisors file into the infirmary for ice bags from Flanny. At 8 p.m. as promised, Mr. Laudenbacher met with Oscar and his chosen representatives. A bunch of us were loitering outside the office door trying to eavesdrop when Miss Beaufort came by.

"How are my boys doing?" she asked with a big smile, clapping her hands in fake delight. "Have you said your prayers today?" Apparently she was unaware of the Great Potato Rebellion of 1931.

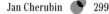

Mr. Laudenbacher's door swung open. "Hello, Claire," he said. "You want to know if your boys prayed today? Why don't you ask your boys if they've *eaten* today?"

Later in the week, Mr. Laudenbacher met with the board, and they fired the head supervisor. We couldn't believe it. The head supervisor was Colonel Tom Anderson. The goddamn Colonel! Axed. A little late, I thought. But still, he packed his bags and he was gone. We kept waiting for the other shoe to drop. It didn't. Instead, things got a little better.

Even Shmuel Hefter was swept up in our good fortune. Some months after the triumph of the Potato Rebellion, a group of inmates watched from the portico as Shmecky clutched his tattered suitcase and walked out the gate with his mother.

At this point I had moved up to the fourth floor in Company B where we had even less supervision than Company C. Chick, Skelly, and I usually woke around four-thirty in the morning, dressed, made our beds, and walked east into the dawn and the pale pink sky at the edge of the world, then up over the aqueduct where our horses were pastured. We stabled Playboy, Joe, and Sally during the day and turned them out overnight in spring and summer. We'd ride them back to the barn, water them, and harness Playboy or Joe for the plow, and hitch Sally to the wagon, then pick up the garbage from the kitchen yard and deliver it to the dump. In winter we'd hitch up the snow-plow to the team, clouds of steam puffing out of their big horse nostrils, plow the roads, then drive around to the boiler room yard and collect the boiler ashes to spread on the service road for traction on the ice. Or if there was no snow, we'd take the ashes to the dump, then pick up a load of coal and deliver it to the cottages. Whatever the season, we'd have to rush back, wash up, lay tefillen, and get down to the shul for morning prayers. I didn't relish getting up early, and barn duty was a lot of extra work, but I took pride in it, and there were rewards. On summer weekends after supper, Chick, Skelly, and I walked up the aqueduct carrying bridles to our horses and raced each other on the trail and around the Grassy Sprain reservoir.

One hot August day after picking pole beans in the blazing sun, when the heat finally broke, I took Playboy out alone as I sometimes liked to, and rode along the trail, galloped into the pasture, then tore around the reservoir and off into the fields. I rode bareback and shirtless and I had such a feeling of freedom. Riding along on my horse with the wind caressing my chest, I started to laugh remembering how my mother bragged about certain equestrian activities at my private boarding school. She wasn't telling tales as it turned out. I coaxed Playboy and we raced toward the woods, and I was laughing at nothing except the wonderfulness of being alive.

CHAPTER 44

More visitors started coming to the hospital. We must have both understood it was to say goodbye, although we didn't speak that way, we didn't speak of death, not since that one night at Sinai. No results were back yet from the esophagus biopsy, but all of us knew, as Aunt Vivian knew months ago, it was over. Shep continued to visit often, my father's most devoted friend. Darleen came to rub Lubriderm on his shoulders. Fred sweetly brought Mozart and Puccini CDs, my father's favorites, and a Walkman, but my father could listen only for seconds. Uncle Alvin and Aunt Gladys dragged bags of deli sandwiches down the antiseptic hallway. Liz Stone came hesitantly at first and then got down on one knee and hugged him in his chair. He asked me to get them each a Coke, not from the machine, from the cafeteria in paper cups with crushed ice. The walk back to the room was slow with the soda crashing in the cups like surf. They looked up when I came in. He was asking about Nola Swenson. She was divorced, Liz said. She had a kid and taught yoga in Boulder. She changed her name to Supritha.

"Was it my fault?" my father said. "Supritha?"

"I don't think so, Clyde," said Liz. "Nola had plenty of other demons."

Back in 1971, he confided in me when Nola broke his heart. How sick was that? But I knew her. If he talked about Nola to me, she came to life.

The big sky was streaked pink on Route 29. I was riding shotgun with my long hair blowing out the window when he said out of the blue, "I loved her, you know."

"Why are you using the past tense?" I said.

He smiled a closed, pained smile. "Some kid who rides a Harley Davidson. She's going away with him."

I was sixteen, almost seventeen by then. If I were younger, I might have been overjoyed at the news. I might have believed Nola Swenson riding away on the back of a chopper meant my parents were going to live happily ever after, and that I would go back to being as confident as I was when I was seven. But I knew better. We would keep moving forward.

"I'm sorry you're sad."

"It's OK," he said. "What is, is. You understand me. You're a chip off the old block."

Susan came to the hospital and once again I was awed by her buoyant presence. She wore her hair in a ponytail, which alone seemed amazing, since I had my hair chopped off like Joan of Arc. The swinging ponytail was full of a girlishness I knew my father would warm to. He'd approve of her painted nails and designer handbag too, signs of a healthy materialism. She was thriving. They spoke brightly about her flight, how he didn't understand people who flew at night, he only traveled in the daytime because you could see the whole country spread out beneath you, and how he remembered when everyone, not just children, would stop in their tracks and crane their necks to look up at an airplane.

Later in the ladies' room, I told Susan she cheered him up and Susan said plainly, seemingly without resentment, "No, I did not. He only wants you now."

Susan was focused on Larry and her kids anyway. "She's rejected her family of origin," my mother-the-therapist said. It was a surprise. They expected me to be the one who bolted. When we were growing up, Susan, being the oldest, was closer to our parents. She and I didn't play together as much as I wanted since she didn't like games or the outdoors. She preferred our parents' company, and was fiercely protective of her superior position in the family. Our friendship was shaky,

never more so than when we were teenagers. I was a freak, she was a sorority girl and not cool in my hippie universe. We clung to each other in small ways, though. When I started high school and Susan was already in twelfth grade, we agreed to share a locker because the school was overcrowded. We were opposites, but we had the same weird family—a father who went "out," a commie mother, and a grandfather who disappeared under the bed. On the metal shelf in the locker, I leaned my algebra book against her Spanish book. She was once the confident big sister who said go back to sleep, everything will be fine in the morning. But in the parking lot at Hopkins, Susan crumpled and I had to hold her up.

The year we shared the locker was the year of Nola. The year of "out" and our parents' separate vacations. They slammed doors, shouted obscenities, and sometimes broke down in giggling fits. On weekends, my father disappeared. For the first half-hour after his car squealed away, I felt the air knocked out of me. Then I'd notice how happy I was with him gone.

One Monday he came home with a big white box that had a hole cut in the top. A pink nose pressed against the opening. He'd brought us a kitten! An adorable gray kitten with white socks. I knew where it came from the second it climbed out of the box, and I was determined not to love it. I did not tell Susan about the gray cats slinking along the partition at Nola's apartment. My father wouldn't let us name the kitten. It was up to him. He called it Larkin for the poet. My father was God and named everything. But he turned out to be the one who didn't love the cat. When Larkin passed him its body slunk to the ground. He refused to have the cat neutered. "He's my only boy," he said. "I'm not cutting off his balls." Larkin prowled the neighborhood until dawn while boys threw pebbles at my window. I kept expecting my father to go "out" and not return. For five years nothing like that happened, and then it was my mother who left.

Somewhere in England
15 April 1944

Dear Evie,

I'm glad you're helping out at these canteens and
dancing with our boys. Sometimes, when you kiss a
lonely boy goodnight, you should think of me, and
that I'm lonely too. Sitting in the movies with my
arm around a girl, my thoughts are always of you. I'm
keeping my hand in at this business of lovemaking so
that when I get back to you I won't be stale at that sort
of thing.

Yours forever and always,
Clyde

Uncle Harry flew in from the West Coast and got a room
at the Sheraton across the street from Hopkins. He brought
twenty-four bags of Pecan Sandies. My father mouthed to me,
"He's a nut." But he and Harry happily planned a trip together
for September, prattling on about driving Uncle Harry's classic
1932 Buick across Australia. Uncle Harry didn't think he could
live without his big brother and scrambled to give my father
reasons to hang on, things to look forward to, and ways to
look back. For the last, he tracked down an old friend from the
Home and got him on the phone.

"Holy shit," my father said. He glanced at Uncle Harry.
"Hoffman, you son of a gun." I perked up. I'd seen photos of
Jesse Hoffman in Ye Olde Picture Booke. The conversation
sounded awkward at first, at least from my father's end. There
was shame in dying, the greatest failure of all. But my father
rallied. "You know what I remember? Well, what else do I have
to do? So I'm lying here remembering how I got up really early
one morning. I'm walking to the farm thinking I'm the only

person alive, feeling pretty fucking pleased about it, and then I hear a racket. Who is it, but Hoffman. You were up even earlier than I was, sitting in the middle of the potato field banging on a drum. . . . I know, man. Only way to practice without waking up the whole damn place."

"Tympanist with the Cleveland Symphony," my father said when he put the phone down. "A big shot. A few years ago I see an interview in the paper, says he learned to play the drums in Yonkers. Doesn't mention the HNOH. Not a word about the orphanage, not a word about being Jewish. Where does he come from, they ask him, and he says he's 'of German extraction.' Homeboy doesn't want to know from his past. Can't blame him, I guess. The kid made something of himself."

CHAPTER 45

Tuckahoe

Even after the Great Potato Rebellion the boys at the H were still beaten for insubordination. We still had detention. But the frequency, the severity, the gross injustice, and a certain relish on the faces of the supervisors disappeared with the Colonel. Meanwhile, we stayed hungry. Hungrier than ever. I was twelve when the stock market crashed, thirteen when the banks closed, fourteen when 20,000 war veterans descended on the US Capitol demanding their bonus pay. The tabloids called them the Veterans' Bonus Army. My mother wrote the American Legion; they suggested she have my father declared dead so she could receive his benefits, should the Veterans' Bonus Army succeed. Unfortunately, Herbert Hoover suggested General MacArthur set fire to the veterans' camp, which MacArthur took literally, burning the place to the ground.

Any hope we Homeboys had that the fortunes of our deserted mothers and widower fathers were going to change for the better turned to Okie dust during the Depression. We read the newspapers with increasing interest and spent a great deal of time hanging out in the *Oracle* offices arguing the nuances of left-wing politics and writing our editorials. Although we were forbidden to attend rallies by the rabbis, we were always on the lookout for action. During a senior outing in Brooklyn, we came upon an anti-communist demonstration in Prospect Park that we razzed considerably.

I read *Das Kapital* and *The Communist Manifesto*, but I had mixed feelings about joining the Party. I wanted to redistribute the wealth into my own pocket for a while. After that, I'd save the rest of the world. At that time, my plan was to finish school, get a job, and join the bourgeoisie. My mother could quit working at Kohl's. I'd come home with a fat paycheck, buy her fancy dresses, diamonds, and furs. I'd take her out for steak. Not once, but regularly, we'd go out for steak dinners.

That was my plan, but I had plenty of time until graduation. I was in no rush. My life had gotten pretty easy on the inside. As a senior inmate, I had no monitors in charge of me any longer. I was managing editor of the paper (Jesse was editor) with my own joint in the suite of *Oracle* offices on the ground floor next to the gym with my own desk and cabinets, my sanctum sanctorum, where I could do whatever I wanted in privacy. That was where I wrote the news stories and editorials for the *Oracle*. But also, Harry and I built a ham radio in there, and on occasion Jesse and I got drunk in my joint on homemade hooch—before Prohibition was repealed, and after. Privately, I scribbled at my desk, mostly poetry, some serious, some doggerel. I'd taken a picture with the newspaper's Brownie camera of Louis Longbeard wagging his finger at us one day after a trip into Manhattan. The photograph inspired some rhyming couplets and that's what got me started on my Picture Booke.

The Sermon At the Gates

Upon his pulpit at the HNOH gates
Louis Longbeard rants and prates
"In hell's hot fires you'll get burned
Yea! All ye prodigals returned.

Back from New York carousing you come
Laughing, gay, and sot with rum.
Fresh out of wicked old New York,
Bellies full of Armour's pork.

A hundred rabbis here have taught you.
A thousand siddurs we have bought you.
With praying bees and fasting bouts
You still remain a bunch of louts.

By this white beard that floats upon the breeze,
If you commit such sins as these
And with the devil cast your lot
A million prayers will help you not."

And ranting thusly onward, Louie
Is greeted with loud cries of Phooey
As off we trot in joyful glee
A score of sinful orphans we.

My buddies liked my verse well enough, so I went into Yonkers and bought a photo album at the Five and Dime, and since the pages were black, a bottle of white ink for the fountain pen the Loving Mothers Auxiliary gave each of us for our bar mitzvah and that, astonishingly, I hadn't yet lost, and I used the white ink for the captions.

I didn't always get the best grades in school—some of the teachers hated me because they thought I thought I was smarter than they were, which I did think, and this led them to predict I would come to no good, joining the prophesies of Louis Longbeard and Miss Claire Beaufort. I was a smart aleck, a wisenheimer. And yet, also thin-skinned. Not a good combination, Hoffman frequently pointed out. I had been known to get into shouting matches with my elders when challenged or mocked.

Hot-headed, yes, but no one could refute my talents after I won a countywide essay contest and got to read my paper over the radio. My essay was all about what the New Deal meant to us destitute and neglected children. I thought it was possible I might receive a letter from my father telling how he'd been listening to WCOH, and just imagine his surprise when my name was announced and he heard my voice and what I'd written, and how proud he was, and how if I'd allow it, he'd like to get to know me. Aw, fuck. What a load of crap. But I did win the contest.

Meanwhile, I'd been hearing from Vivian that it was getting tougher for Mama making ends meet with Alvin growing out of his clothes every other week and hungry all the time and somebody else who preferred to remain nameless coveting dresses and dainty shoes for dance parties if she was to have any chance of hunting down and trapping a Rockefeller. I kept thinking about the months' worth of paychecks I could be earning going down the drain while I sat in a classroom arguing with dim-witted teachers. I made up my mind to quit school, go home to my mother after all these years, and support my family like a man.

"Now class, what scene in the story would you say is the denouement?" asked Miss Campbell, head of the English department at Roosevelt High.

I raised my hand. "It's pronounced day-new-mawh," I said. "I'm pretty sure," I added, although I was positive. "Not dayna-mint."

Miss Campbell curled her lip. "How would you know?" she said. "You're from the Home, aren't you?"

"Lemme see! Lemme see!" The guys couldn't get enough of my Olde Picture Booke. I was leaving the H, and this was their last chance. Al Shack grabbed the album away and they took turns reading the captions, and honestly, I couldn't say I minded. Their laughter was like heroin shot into a vein. Pure bliss. Jesse had the book and he was reading my tribute to Carl Grimm, smiling ear-to-ear and nodding—the response I treasured most from the friend I treasured most: *I get it. I feel the same way.*

Carl Grimm, second chef, bon vivant, and great friend to us.
In the background is his cottage, shared with Charlie and Hymie
Wherein upon a score of joyful occasions
We caroused in rowdy revelry drinking deep and eating full
Until, the dawn approaching,
We'd file back to our beds, the shouted imprecations
Of awakened orphans mingling with our woeful groans
To render horrid welcome to the morning sun.
Mr. Grimm's great generosity in frequent dispensing
Of 'tween meal snacks
From the full larders of the underground storerooms,
His picturesque unfolding to us monastical orphans
Of the joys and glamour of the world awaiting,
His full appreciation of all things creative and artistic,
His sensitive nature that knows not what hate,
Nor animosity means—for all these things,
We will miss him most when we leave. —August, 1934

Jesse liked the one about himself as well:

> *Jesse Hoffman, my boon companion and a partner upon many*
> *an enterprise. He leads a sorry life for he would be a tympanist*
> *and must practice upon drums calling forth the wrath of Louis*
> *of the Long Beard and Eddie the night watchman who would*
> *chop meat and sleep respectively.*

Harry didn't sit with us on the porch, although it was his last day, too. He was nearby, tinkering with the Indian Scout motorcycle he bought for ten bucks. Somehow he managed to scrounge up the dough. As soon as he heard I was dropping out of school, he bailed, too. From the steps I watched as he kept climbing on the bike in the driveway and revving it up whenever he felt he had to divert attention away from me. Chick called him over to look at a snapshot someone had taken of Harry and me that I'd included in the album but Harry declined the invitation, revved his motor and took his iron charger for a spin around the circular drive.

I mixed in a few shots I'd taken one Passover of my sister Vivian posing coyly on the roof at 166th Street that elicited close inspection and some wolf whistles, and a few of my mother in a hat and white gloves. There were snapshots of the B. A. swimming hole, of course. I looked out at Harry in the driveway. We had waited ten years for this moment. We were finally going home, yet here I was dragging my feet, feeling I could linger on this stoop with my friends forever. On the last page of the Picture Booke, I had placed an interior shot of my *Oracle* office with this caption:

> *My joint: the gathering place for the intelligentsia and*
> *social leaders of our time. Thither we cracked jokes, or sat listening*
> *to an opera, or argued the merits of Jean Harlow's figure,*
> *or in hushed whispers planned a raid upon an icebox.*
> *Thither we developed pictures, and thither we made*
> *footlights and radios and spotlights and airplanes.*
> *We repaired us bicycles, we sold candy, we wrote editorials.*
> *Thither in winter we stored us sleds, in summer we loaded*
> *knapsacks.*

Aye verily, a Garden of Eden. I closed the album. It was time to go. The joys and glamour of the wider world awaited.

CHAPTER 46

Mama went ahead and had my father declared dead, so that in 1936 when the Veterans Bonus bill finally passed, she collected $125, a dollar for every day my father served during the Great War. Harry came home from the butcher shop with T-bone steaks and oh boy, did we celebrate. After our steak dinner, we turned on the radio and I pulled my mother out of her chair and waltzed her around the kitchen. Then Alvin tuned in a swing station playing something called "Bugle Call Rag," and he and Vivian started jitterbugging, clattering on the linoleum like they were hopping over hot coals. We hooted and clapped, and then my mother and I started hoofing it up. She was pretty damn good, but seeing each other with limbs all herky-jerky had us laughing our sides off. We were breathless and fanning ourselves so we all went up to the roof to get some air. We could see for miles up there, from the East River to the Harlem River to the Hudson. I had a smoke leaning on my elbows on the ledge and perused the neighborhood, the bushy Bronx treetops black in the night, and farther away, The Daughters of Jacob old age home with its lime-green copper cupola glowing in the moonlight.

"When I was little, I used to pretend that building was a palace," Alvin said.

"Daughters of Jacob?" said Mama. "Such an imagination!"

"The summer residence of the archduke and duchess," I said.

"Of Morrisania," said Vivian.

We laughed, my mother's bright trill the loudest. Her face was rosy from dancing, and her crimped pin curls were coming loose. I thought she looked beautiful with her hair disheveled. The next day, she complained that her cheeks hurt from smiling so much.

The bonus money didn't last long. But we cobbled together a living. I had a stockroom job at Elizabeth Arden on Fifth Avenue, and Harry brought home a dollar every now and then. Still, my mother felt she couldn't afford to quit her job at Kohl's. I figured out (and wished I had realized sooner) my mother preferred working. *Taka*. No kidding. She liked getting dressed and going out into the world. Even combining paychecks, though, sometimes we were short by the end of the month and hid when the landlord came knocking. My mother would not ask Rich Uncle Seymour for handouts, not anymore. The family had been tough on her all those years, and now she could stand up to them. A working woman needed a new hat once in a while. She'd put us in the Home, she had to, but we came out good.

I was seeing a girl from the neighborhood, which cost me plenty, and I stewed about the impossibility of advancing from the stockroom in any way except via the freight elevator. My solution? I started reading Marx and Engels again. More Freud. Oscar Wilde, whose wit I admired as a fellow outcast. Dos Passos and Steinbeck, George Orwell. For a second, I had actually believed I could get ahead because I was willing to work hard at shitty jobs. The rich, it turned out, weren't indifferent to our struggle. They were actively interested in keeping their diamonds and furs from the likes of me. There was no question we poor suckers had to find a way to control the means of production. I switched from strolling up Fifth Avenue yearning for the baubles in the shop windows to marching down Fifth Avenue shouting at the top of my lungs: "Wages up, prices down, make New York a union town!" Demanding that the bastards "Free Tom Mooney and the Scottsboro Boys!" Chick Scheiner, Albert and Artie Shack, and I marched on May Day right alongside Elizabeth Gurley Flynn calling for women's rights. Occasionally Jesse Hoffman joined us with a snare drum hanging around his neck on a leather strap, rat-a-tat-tat, and we'd joke about this penchant we had for marching whenever we got together. But none of us saw much of Jesse anymore. Not since the Ladies Auxiliaries of Yonkers and White Plains raised the funds to send him to Julliard. That was the irony. Guys like Chick and me left school to support our families, whereas full orphans like Jesse had the freedom to go to college.

When autumn came around and Uncle Seymour's carnival was off-season, he folded up his tent and returned to New York to run bingo at the Elks Lodge on the Grand Concourse. He convinced me to quit working for the capitalists like some sap and likewise to quit fighting them, which was just beating my head against a wall, he said. Instead, I should become a capitalist myself. I left Elizabeth Arden and Uncle Seymour put Harry and me to work shilling. We had to memorize the numbers on a particular bingo card given to a little old lady who happened to be on the payroll. To mix it up, sometimes I played the card, or Harry, and one of our cousins would memorize the numbers and call them out. I couldn't stomach the scam, though. Setting up the folding chairs, that was fine. But separating decent people from their last few coins, I wasn't sure about that. The rubes actually believed they had a chance to win, and win big.

"You ain't cheating nobody," Uncle Seymour insisted. "It's the price of a night out."

"Under false pretenses," I said.

He shrugged, called me an idealist.

Harry enjoyed stealing a dollar for a living, but he wasn't reliable. He'd tell us he was going for a spin around the block on his Indian Scout and come back two weeks later. Just like the old man, we all said. It was Alvin who was the perfect shill, with his good looks and easygoing manner, and absent my heavy conscience. That kid was only twelve but already taller than I was, and passed for eighteen, even with his baby face. I got myself some honest work at a brewery in Brooklyn on the assembly line, and caught up on Orwell's *Down and Out in London and Paris* and Freud's *Civilization and Its Discontents* during the long commute. In the evenings, I sat with the family out on the tenement stoop in the warm weather, and around the kitchen table in the winter, talking with my mother, playing poker at one grandma's or another on Friday nights. Harry and I operated our ham radio. I flew kites on the roof with Alvin. It was sweet, after all those years away, but it wasn't much of a life for a young man. I had to admit, wanderlust tugged at my heart. I started hearing about guys going west with Roosevelt's Civilian Conservation Corps—outdoor work, adventure, travel—but I simply wasn't going to leave my mother. Then, thanks again to FDR, I found a gig with the Works Project Administration, and got plenty of fresh air without ever leaving New York—building LaGuardia Airport, a WPA job that utilized the expert ditch digging skills I had acquired during the Great Potato Rebellion.

Prosperity was slow to come back to the Bronx in the thirties, but our domestic troubles were nothing compared with the news from Europe, which was downright terrifying. On Sundays, I started marching on Fifth Avenue with the American League Against War and Fascism. Like most Jewish boys who leaned left, I was itching to go to Spain with the Lincoln Brigade, where, in addition to trench digging, I could use my potato lobbing skills. But again, I stayed close to my mama and supported my family. By the summer of 1938, we were paying our bills on time. In fact, Vivian was so well-fed her head swelled and she skipped a grade in school. A regular genius, said my mother, forgetting that was my domain. Alvin wasn't so crazy about school, but he was making pretty good dough in the afternoons working for Uncle Seymour.

When Vivian got accepted into nursing school, we had another celebratory supper, this time chicken over rice, a recipe I concocted myself. Harry tuned in the same swing station he'd found for our bonus bill party to put us in the mood, and

Alvin and Vivian clattered around the kitchen again. But we couldn't recapture the feeling.

"I don't have the energy I used to," my mother said when I asked her to dance.

She encouraged the four of us to go downstairs to the candy store for malteds, her treat, but I stayed with her, gave her a chair to put her feet on and made coffee.

"If you're so tired, maybe you should take time off work," I said. "Relax, sleep late. Spend all morning reading the paper in bed."

She smiled. "That's what you like," she said. "Not me. I can't lie in bed. But, now that you mention it, I am going to take some time off work."

"No kidding?" I said. I sat down and stirred two sugars into her coffee and two into mine and spooned a little cream off the top of the milk bottle into each cup.

"So listen, Clyde, sweetheart. I've been meaning to tell you. I've got to go into the hospital for some tests, nothing serious."

"What? What tests?" I said.

My mother held up her palms and shrugged comically. "You wanted I should have a rest."

I didn't appreciate the act. "What tests?"

"It's nothing. Female stuff. Did you put sugar?"

"I put sugar. You saw me put sugar. What female stuff?"

"Vivian went with me to the doctor."

"She didn't mention anything," I said.

My mother quietly picked crumbs from the table one by one, and brushed them from her fingertips into the saucer. She looked up at me. "A daughter deals with these things. And Vivian's going to be a nurse. She'll take care of me." Mama leaned forward and swept back a lock of my hair falling into my eyes. "But you, Clyde. I'm counting on you to take care of everyone when I'm gone."

"What are you talking about gone?" I said.

"In the hospital."

"Sure, I'll look after everyone when you're in the hospital."

"Such a mensch, my Clyde. But I wonder who's going to take care of *you?*"

"Don't be silly." I took a good long drag on my cigarette and blew smoke at the familiar black stove on its pudgy legs. "I'm twenty-one. I can take care of myself."

"What I wouldn't give to be able to look after you always," she said, "and make up for the past."

I very gently put out my cigarette so I could light it again later, then took her small hand in mine. My mother's skin was soft somehow, as if she hadn't washed a single dish or scrubbed a diaper in her life. "I never blamed you," I said.

"I know," she said. "You never did."

We were quiet. A chair scraped across the floor above us. A truck rumbled by in the street. I let go of her hand and stirred my coffee. I didn't trust doctors. I figured they were always looking for business.

"You're my first-born. No one can ever take your place in my heart." Her shoulders dropped and she settled deeper into her chair. I sensed her relief at finally having told me about the tests. "Those were happy days," she said.

"When?" I said. "What happy days?"

"When you were a baby. When your father got back from the war. He was doing well as a garment salesman then, before the insurance job. Your father was a good-looking man, you know that, and he liked clothes. That's where a lot of the money went. He always wanted me to dress you in the sailor suit he bought."

"My father bought me a sailor suit?"

"Sure. You remember the picture on the Armory steps." She smiled to herself.

"That picture? I never thought about who bought me those clothes."

"He spoiled you, when he was home."

"Why did he leave us then?"

She drew in a breath. I thought she was bracing herself, preparing to tell me the answer to the big mystery, but she just sighed. "I don't know, Clyde."

At Mount Hebron Cemetery the men said kaddish and my aunts poked around in the weeds with their pointy-toed shoes looking for Gertie's stone. My mother's grave was supposed to be next to the baby's, they said, but we couldn't find the marker. Vivian got on her knees and clawed at the ground. She was crying, her nose was dripping, her fingernails ripping away the trumpet creepers, pulling up clods of clover until she found it: Gertrude Aronson, August 17, 1924–March 19, 1927. And so beside Gertie, my mother, as they say, was laid to rest.

CHAPTER 47

He was stoned. They jacked up the morphine. Uncle Harry, Darleen, Shep, and I were standing around his bed in the darkened hospital room. His voice was so weak he had to scribble notes on a legal pad. He handed the pad to Darleen. "I'm happy," she read, a catch in her voice. "I'm so happy."

"Why are you happy?" I asked.

"Because you're all here," he said.

Just then Dr. Geest and Macomber the intern appeared in the doorway. No official business, they came to hang out.

"Tell them about the trip," my father said.

"When Clyde gets better," said Uncle Harry, "we're driving across Australia—the whole continent—in my 1932 Buick. Original, not restored."

"Now listen," my father said, his voice suddenly strong. "On September 3, 1987, the rest of you will wake up in the morning and you'll open the *New York Times* and there you will see a photograph of the car with my brother Harry and me standing in front of it, and you, Macomber. You'll be there as team doctor. The caption will read: 'Transcontinental Australian Trip.' Come closer. Joanna, make room for them. I'm King Arthur and you doctors are my knights of the round table," he said. I made a space and Geest stood next to me. Surely he and Macomber had better things to do, but they stayed in the trippy room.

"Love is what it's all about," my father said, losing volume again. "I'm experiencing love in inordinate proportions." He had a request. I was summoned. He whispered into my ear. "Hum it. Please, do that for me. All of you."

Any other time, I might have balked. "He wants us to hum 'Chariots of Fire,'" I said, with just a slight wince. I went back to my place next Geest, who put his arm around me and gave my shoulder a little squeeze. I was startled. He let go and I looked up at the surgeon and saw the muscles in his throat moving. He was humming. Uncle Harry and Darleen were humming. Macomber hummed and I hummed, and soon all of us were pounding out the notes to "Chariots of Fire," running on the beach kicking up foam. My father led the choir tracing balletic loops in the air. His face was radiant.

If during the nights he conducted the opera of his deathbed with grace and humor, during the days he was bitter and withdrawn. In the dreamy wee hours it was easy to be King Arthur, to create a world without end. In the harsh light of day, though, the ugly apparatus of defeat was all too visible— the gawky IV pole and plastic tubing, the machinery of the feed pump, the glare of winter through a crack in the curtains.

I requested more morphine for the daytime. Why should he have to suffer, whether it was physical or mental? But he didn't want to be out of it, he said. So the staff experimented with the dosage and found a midpoint where he was alert and relatively pain free, at least for a few hours a day. Then we would talk, or just lie there quietly, each in our beds. I lit a cigarette and he smoked. Amazingly, the staff continued to allow it.

This was my last chance to confront him. I knew one day the surreal hours would end. But I didn't know what to say, or what I'd gain from revisiting the painful past. Would I feel better or worse if he acknowledged his reckless disregard for my well-being? It was all so touchy. Everything came down to sex. I sometimes thought of what happened with Nola and him and Johnny and me as incest by proxy. The notion came into my head unbidden and shocked me. The last taboo, even by proxy, touched a third rail. In the end, though, sex wasn't the point. Sex was just the titillation that obscured the point. The point being I never went to my father for help because, as much as I hated to admit it, I was afraid of him.

Brenda was right. He had me under his thumb. I couldn't stand up to him. For years I thought I was fine, because I didn't cut myself or shoplift or starve myself or get pregnant or shoot up dope or flunk out of school. Everything was OK because I managed on my own. I didn't want to burden my parents, so I didn't ask for anything and I got nothing. After the camping trip, the castle gate slammed shut and that was it for him. My mother was dealing with her own pain and rejection. So I decided what was happening with Johnny was all good, and my father and Nola in the woods was no big deal. No repercussions. Kids get over all kinds of shit. For years I believed that. But I was wrong. I never got over any of it.

I didn't flunk out of school, but I stopped trying. I cared about only one thing. Johnny coming into my room, my body thrumming with excitement. I would never know the eighteen rules of grammar or how to lay out a newspaper. I would never be a chess grandmaster or a great chef. I did not understand what other people seemed to grasp easily. My father had no expectations, except that I find a husband. He thought it was funny to put on the Yiddish accent and tell Susan and me to "find yourselves a guy, you shouldn't be alone." His career advice was "be a teacher like me when you grow up, you get summers off." I figured I'd have to teach the lower grades. I wouldn't be smart enough to teach high school. When I tried to think of what I was good at, all I could come up with was one suspended moment in time when I excelled. It happened at sleep-away camp the summer I was thirteen. The camp put on a cabaret at the end of the season, and since I wasn't good at singing or dancing, I was assigned, along with some other talentless campers, to make the place cards we called Cab cards to go on the banquet table. I got to work drawing a caricature of a every girl in our bunk along with a poem for each card, and the cartoons and words came out of my pen with such ease I felt I had been put under a spell. I was able to capture a likeness with a few strokes, and I instantly made up clever, telling rhymes. The other girls working on the cards abandoned what they were doing and just watched, although I hardly noticed, I was so absorbed. There was no gap that day between what I imagined and what I got down on paper. It was pure joy. Ever since, when considering what I might do with my life, I've thought, well, I can make Cab cards. But of course, it was a joke. No Cab card makers were listed in the help wanted ads. My father must have seen that I was lost, unable to develop, let alone claim a place in the world, but he provided no direction. On the rare occasions when I asked for guidance he offered the usual refrain: "I didn't have a father to help me."

After I finished the cards, a few girls and some of the counselors complimented my work, which felt good, but very quickly camp was over, everyone packed her Cab card (except me, there wasn't anybody to make one for me, of course) and we left. I never did anything as successfully again. When I got home at the end of the summer, Susan couldn't stop talking about this cool new teacher named Johnny Dolan they made friends with while I was away, how good-looking he was, how Johnny took Susan in his sports car for ice cream at Price's Dairy.

I lay on my back with my arms folded behind my head. Next to my cot, my father lay in his bed smoking peacefully.

"You should finish The National Dog," he said after a while.

"The screenplay?"

"Yeah, the screenplay I started about Hoffman," my father said. "You should finish it, Joanna."

"I thought Fred was working on it with you," I said. "He's the screenwriter."

"You always say that. Fred's the writer. What about you? What were you doing at that paper out there?"

"I was a copy editor, that's all. I'm not a writer. No one publishes my short stories."

"You're a throwaway person. That's what you are," he said. His voice was strong. He had these bursts of energy when he seemed almost normal.

"Yeah, I know. I'm a throwaway person. You've said that before." I wasn't sure what a throwaway person was; it might have been something he made up, but I figured he meant that I shrugged off milestones. I remembered he said it when I passed the driving test on the first try and I didn't jump for joy. It was unusual for him to characterize me, so the comment stood out in my memory. Even though it was negative, I still appreciated seeing myself through his eyes. "Have you ever thought about why I might be a throwaway person?" I said. This was a stab at confrontation.

"What? You think it's my fault?"

"You're the one who always told us there're no great women composers, no great women anything. Why would you say that to a daughter?"

"I was trying to get a rise out of you," he said. "Can you give me some of that Anbesol?"

I found the little brown bottle on the window ledge and unscrewed the top. I was thinking I'd like to continue the conversation, but at a more leisurely pace, maybe over the next ten or fifteen years. Oh well. I poured a drop of the caramel-colored liquid onto his finger. He rubbed it on his gums. "Feels good," he said.

"All that negative talk about women had consequences," I said, looking at him through my lashes to see if he could take the criticism in his weakened state. "Sometimes I think those comments hurt me more than anything else."

"C'mon. Don't be so sensitive. You had a nice childhood, didn't you?" he said.

"Yeah, sure. I'm like you. I idealize it. Cedar Drive was the best place on earth."

He smiled. "Yeah, you're like me that way. I was lucky, I really was. I had a Currier & Ives childhood—horses hitched up to a sleigh in the snow, all the kids you wanted to play with. You know, at the orphanage, we were only deprived in conventional ways. Like no mama tucking us in bed. I'll tell you something, though. You wanna know something?"

I was annoyed that he'd switched the subject to himself yet again, but I was also painfully aware I would not be asked that question many more times. I propped my pillow against the wall and lay back on it. "Sure. I wanna know something."

"I'll tell you something," he said. "We escaped the Freudian problem of identifying women with our mothers and then not being able to fuck those women."

I cringed. I hated the word fuck used to mean sex except when you were actually having sex, as in fuck me. In that charged situation, the word was OK. But I hated it casually. The word was also OK as a curse, as in fuck, I forgot my wallet, or I can't get this fucking TV to work. But clearly, he was more comfortable talking about sex than I was. "Yeah, so you escaped Freud's madonna-whore thing. Great," I said. I tried turning the conversation back to me. "You know what? I think I would have been better off growing up in an orphanage. Look at all the mentors you had. Whereas they fuck you up, your mum and dad." That usage was OK, too, especially since it was from a Philip Larkin poem.

"You know Larkin?" he said.

"The cat?" I said, with a smirk.

"Not the goddamn cat."

"Yeah, I know Philip Larkin. You fucked me up, but I'm not completely illiterate."

"OK, so listen. We escaped that problem, the Freudian problem," he said, looking at his cigarette thoughtfully, then taking a drag, exhaling a plume of smoke. "We escaped the madonna-whore problem," he continued, "by not being brought up by a mother. The result is, we fuck anything that moves."

I laughed, but there was that word again, and when he used it that way my stomach tightened. Fuck was pictures of Nola with perky breasts sitting on the piano bench naked, my piano bench, picking out a tune on my piano. A few years after the camping trip, he and I visited colleges just like fathers and daughters across America, and shared a motel room. I remembered standing stiffly between the two beds wearing a childish suit with puffy sleeves and a flared skirt that was all wrong for the interviews. "Don't worry," he said, sensing my anxiety. "I won't touch you."

Now in his hospital room I laughed and he laughed. Not everything was a fucking tragedy. He escaped that Freudian problem. "No mama to tuck you in, though," I said, as I straightened his covers.

"Listen," he said, "kids get over all kinds of shit. Look at me."

"Yeah, look at you." Sometimes I wondered if he had put Johnny up to it himself. Incest by proxy.

"You know that friend of yours, of your family's?" said Donna Landau, this girl I knew.

"Johnny?"

"Yeah. I saw his car up at Milford."

"When?" Milford and my high school were rivals.

"Last week. After school. He was picking up Jody Auslander. She's in 11th grade."

"How do you know he was picking up Jody Auslander?"

"I saw her getting in his car," she said. "He has a red Triumph, right? Besides, that's not the first time he's been up there."

Donna Landau knew nothing. She was nobody. Her big rear end bounced on the springy seat as she rode away on her bike.

"Don't touch me," I said when Johnny came to the house next. I felt ill. I had no control over it. The revulsion was a reflex, coming from a place that was much smarter than I was. He was upset, although he was smiling, acting mock wounded when he was really wounded, the way my mother did some-times. "Don't be hostile," Johnny said. I noticed he was getting a paunch.

He was unhappy. He and Linda were getting divorced and he'd moved into a house with a bunch of people. He was sleeping with a college student living there. They set up a dark room in the garage and he developed pictures he'd taken of me at the swim club in the purple bikini. My father didn't like the girl. She and Johnny drank too much and smoked too much pot.

My father blamed Johnny's death partly on what happened at City, their collegial workplace ruined, the loss of his band of brothers. It wasn't just his violent upbringing, my father said. It wasn't just the new girlfriend, the drink and drugs, or the underage girls. It was work. Johnny had no purpose. "If you have meaningful work you can survive all kinds of other shit," my father said.

The last time Johnny came over to Cedar Drive he got out of the car holding a goblet with a red stain in the bottom.

"I can't talk to you anymore," I said. "It's like you don't know me."

His brow furrowed. He leaned in close, his lips brushing my ear. "When will we be lovers again?" he whispered.

I didn't answer, but when he stretched out on the sofa after dinner, I let him put his head in my lap. He started talking like he was on psychiatrist's couch. "The kids don't listen to me anymore," he said. "It's pathetic. I'm pathetic." It was cold in the house, but Johnny was so drunk he was sweating. "It's not the same as when you were there, Clyde." My father was teaching at the community college now. "The art teacher wears a knife in his sock," Johnny said.

"Johnny, dear, did you call the therapist's number I gave you?" my mother said.

"I will, Evie. I promise. You're not there, Clyde. You don't know how bad it's gotten. Remember how it was, how we were? That's lost."

"It goes back to the great fight," my father said. "They didn't listen to the union leadership. We said keep the A-Course at City. Give these poor black kids a chance."

"It's over," Johnny said. "That's all over."

I was startled by the tap tap of my tears dropping onto the writing paper I held open in the college mailroom. A letter from my father. *Who is left to walk into my house without knocking, and I into his?* Johnny had taken an electric lawnmower cord and hanged himself from the garage rafters. *How could he? This tortured boy, never to see a winter sunset again.* The college girl found him. For weeks he hadn't been able to sleep. He wandered the house all night. *He was a symbol of golden youth to me.* Before he went out to the garage, he baked biscuits and left them cooling on the counter. He was thirty-three. *There were times when I envied him. Life is diminished. When I see you, we'll talk. Love, Daddy.*

I took the train home even though there was no funeral or memorial service. Just a small gathering of shell-shocked friends passing around a joint. At home I sat and watched gold-finches and chickadees flutter around the birdfeeder outside the dining-room window. Susan came in. "What's the matter with her?" she asked.

My father leaned across the table and put his hand over mine. "Joanna feels the way I do," he said. He and I were bound together. He said in his letter we would talk, but my father and I didn't talk. What we had to say was unspeakable.

"Kids survive all kinds of shit," he said, sitting up in bed now under the no smoking sign, but what shit, specifically, did he mean? For instance, why did he have false teeth when he told us volunteer dentists came to the Home twice a year? Was he punched in the mouth by the supervisors?

Did older boys force themselves on him?

During those surreal nights, questions floated on the periphery of my mind, but not in coherent sentences. Maybe if I'd had those extra ten or fifteen years with him, grown older, I'd have known what to ask and how to ask it.

"You said you were just baiting me, you know, with the chess, the no great women chefs bullshit, but you don't realize how your sexist messages affected us."

"You wanted to be a chef?"

"No!" I said. I laughed, but just for a moment. "You know what I'm talking about. Susan claims it didn't bother her, but I felt left out of the world. I still do."

"You feel left out? Try going to high school with rich kids who know you're from the orphanage."

"Yeah, OK. But as a man, a white man, you walk down the street now and nobody knows you came from nothing. A woman can't hide from who she is. A black woman gets a double whammy. We don't have the freedom to reinvent ourselves like a white man does."

"Ah, bullshit. Plenty of women succeed. Look at you, working on newspapers and magazines. Did you ever think you would do that?"

"Not really."

"I always thought it was strange, since you never even tried out for your school paper."

"I was a hippie. I was antiestablishment. And you didn't encourage me one single bit."

"I used to recommend books you never read."

"*Gulliver's Travels* in third grade! I'm not as smart as you."

A nurse came in and took his temperature and wrapped a sleeve around his arm. "Your blood pressure is excellent," she said cheerfully, then wheeled away her equipment.

"I remember you gave a lecture at Baltimore Hebrew College about Saul Bellow and I was curious so you took *The Adventures of Augie March* off a shelf and from the first sentence, that great sentence, what is it? 'I am Chicago born.'"

"I am an American, Chicago born," my father said.

"Yeah, from the first sentence he's puffing up his chest. He's a real American, even though he's a Jew, that's the subtext, right? Well, I read it and I felt excluded. I felt like the world didn't belong to me in the same way. I didn't have the sense of entitlement he had and I was jealous."

"'Chicago that somber city.' You know, there's nobody more patriotic than immigrants and their children."

"He made himself larger than life the way you do."

"Yeah, well, me, not so much . . ." He patted his hat to make sure it was on.

"I'm a girl," I said. "I'd be laughed at if I made myself big."

"What, did I raise some kind of victim?"

"No! You know that's not what I'm saying. I'm saying I felt shut out. I didn't have a lot of confidence. I don't."

"If that's so true how did you have the guts to live in New York and work in journalism?"

"I don't know. It wasn't a plan. I just landed there." I molded my pillow so I could lean back on my cot and see my father at a better angle. He was listening, waiting for what I had to say next. I savored the moment.

"I didn't know what I wanted to do," I said. "I had no particular ambition. But I did start to write stories in college. I can pinpoint the exact moment that happened. Grace Paley came to campus to read and I had this revelation. I think it's common, this revelation about Grace Paley. It sounds familiar, anyway, part of the collective unconscious—for women writers, at least. Like that article in the *Times* about how so many women dream about Woody Allen. Remember that?"

"Do you dream about Woody Allen?"

"I have, a few times. Not lately. So I had this revelation about Grace Paley. I had never heard of her and I'm sitting in a lecture hall in 1974 listening to her read and thinking, wow, you're allowed to write about things like that? I'd read plenty of Philip Roth, and I actually got pretty far into *Augie March* before I gave up, and I'd read Malamud, but it was only when this Jewish woman was standing up there making herself larger than life that I thought writing was something I could do. I left the lecture hall and went back to my room and started my first story.

"So what are you talking about then, not being a writer?"

"You said it yourself. I'm a throwaway person. I'm not ambitious. I don't value my accomplishments."

"Can you gimme more of that Anbesol. Pour some water in my glass first. No, no, not with a straw. I wanna wet my lips. Listen, kiddo, you can sit around blaming other people, your parents, whoever, but the truth is you make your own life."

"Yeah, I know."

"You gotta go out there and do it. And then you get to decide if you're going to be miserable about it or happy about it. It's up to you. It's all attitude."

He might have added, while you're making your own life avoid trampling on anybody else's. Still, I thought his advice was decent. In spite of everything, he had me convinced life was good. You wanted to be around someone like that. You'd put up with a lot for it.

CHAPTER 48

"**D**o you know what I found in your father's esophagus when I went in there with the scope?" Dr. Morales asked like a stern schoolmaster. He had the biopsy results.

Brenda, my mother, and I were squeezed together on a sofa in an alcove next to the nurse's station, the two of them still in their winter coats like armor. "What did you find?" said Brenda.

"Pills of all colors sitting there whole," the doctor said.

Come on, now, swallow. Be a good boy, Mr. Aronson, take your medicine.

I imagined phoning up Dr. Cromwell. Guess he wasn't faking, I'd say. Childish, I knew, but I was a child. Brenda's lip twitched.

"Did you find out what cell the tumor is?" I said.

"You know what it is," said Morales.

"No I don't. No one told me."

"But you already know."

"You mean, it's adeno?" I said.

"Very rare in that part of the esophagus."

"How long does he have?" my mother asked.

Dr. Morales estimated between two weeks and two months. I asked if he could shuffle the numbers when he told my father, because how could a person comprehend having two weeks to live? Two weeks left him hanging from a ledge. It was presumptuous, too. Morales wasn't God. The doctor agreed to an adjustment, waved his wand, and said that instead of two weeks to two months, he would give my father two months to two years.

"I'll tell Clyde if you're scared to tell him, Joanna," Brenda said.

"I think he should hear it from his doctor. Not us," I said.

"I agree," my mother said. "He's not a baby. He doesn't need an interpreter."

"If he's not a baby," said Brenda, "why not tell him two weeks?"

After Morales gave my father the prognosis, the doctor came out, and I went in. He was sitting up with the same hat and curly hair. My father's head hadn't exploded upon hearing the news of his death. "I just want to be able to sit in my garden in the spring," he said. "What do you think?"

A small wish. "I think that can be arranged."

He was sent home with the tube coming out of his stomach. At least he wouldn't go hungry. Morphine was inserted into the tube along with Ensure, no swallowing necessary, no jabs. I was miserable living with Brenda again, but then Fred came to visit and I got two nights at a hotel with him. I expected the time away to be precious and we did have unusually intense sex with death being in the air and everything, getting closer to understanding *Death and Sensuality*. But I was worried about my father alone with Brenda.

My mother made reservations at Zingarro's, a restaurant on the edge of Little Italy, for six-thirty. "You and Fred deserve a nice dinner," she said over the phone. "And Susan too. She came all the way here. It'll be good to get out."

"Why did you make it so early?" I said. "I thought we could spend time with Daddy before dinner. Especially since Susan's staying with you and I'm staying at the hotel tonight. I'm not happy he's going to be alone."

"You spent all day with him," my mother said. "And Brenda is there!"

"You should see her. Cursing under her breath constantly."

"You need to get away, Joanna. Brenda's *his* problem. You don't need to watch over them every second."

Marty drove my mother and Susan downtown, and Fred and I left from our hotel in my father's car. Zingarro's was near the harbor. We found it easily enough but we had to park six blocks away. A bitter wind whipped off the Chesapeake Bay and lashed our faces as we walked to the restaurant. I hoped Brenda let Hoffman in.

"Why didn't my mother tell us there wasn't any parking!" I shouted above the roar. We continued on until our ears ached and our knuckles were raw inside our gloves. The restaurant was warm and pleasantly noisy, flatware and wine glasses tinkling. I blew my nose with a tattered Kleenex and saw my family seated in the balcony, a space up four steps and fenced in by a polished brass railing. There were hanging lamps bathing the diners at each table in a circle of buttery light. I was struck by how pretty Susan looked—her hair freed from its daytime ponytail and falling thickly over her shoulders, blonder than usual in the lamplight. She could be plain and then spectacular in the same day. My mother glowed too, and even Marty looked good. There was a basket of breadsticks on the table and they were munching and talking.

Fred and I went up the steps. I ran my fingers through my hair to fluff it up but it was full of static electricity.

"Why didn't you tell us there was no parking?" I snapped as we approached the table. "That's why we're late. We wouldn't have been late if somebody had told us about the parking."

"I'm sorry," my mother said.

"It's OK," said Susan. "We didn't mind waiting."

"Great. You guys are nice and warm in here, but it's freezing outside and we had to walk ten blocks."

"It wasn't that far," said Fred gently, hoping as the others were, to calm me down.

"Well, I didn't appreciate it."

"Sit," said my mother. "Take off your coat."

"Do you want something to drink?" Marty asked. The menus came. I was sick of pasta. I didn't want a big steaming bowl of library paste plopped in front of me. I ordered chicken piccata, the lemon was appealing.

"There's an antipasto coming," my mother said cheerfully.

Considering my father was dying, I thought it odd how carefree they all seemed. Marty and Susan were across from my mother and me, and Fred was tacked onto the end, his chair in the aisle and his knee pressing against mine. Fred started right in talking about a documentary on stand-up comedians he was working on, but I ignored his attempt to entertain the table.

"So. Do you want to stop at Cedar Drive after dinner?" I said to everyone.

"I don't know, Joanna. Let's eat first, and see how late it gets," my mother said.

"He's up all hours of the night," I said.

Susan ate a piece of roasted pepper, catching its end with her tongue and tried not to look at me.

"You have some crazy ideas about how to take care of somebody," said Marty. "And now you want everyone to be as crazy as you!"

"I'm crazy? Is that really what you think, Marty?" My face burned.

"Wait a second, Marty," my mother said.

"No," Marty said. "It's about time someone spoke up. Look, you can do what you want, Joanna. But your mother shouldn't be expected to go crazy like you. She's not his wife anymore." Marty sat up straighter, emboldened by his argument. "You may wish your parents were still married, but they're not."

"You think I'm crazy?" I said. "I hope you have someone as crazy as I am taking care of you when you're sick."

"Yeah, well. Your mother never even came to see me when I was in the hospital," Marty said.

"That's a lie," said my mother.

"Well, you didn't."

"Why were you in the hospital?" Fred asked politely.

"My leg. I have gout," said Marty. "Me and Henry the VIII." Then he turned to my mother. "You wouldn't drive me home. I wanted you to drive me home."

"Look, I don't want to get into this now," said my mother. "I *did* come to see you, just not as many times as you would have liked."

"And now you're visiting Clyde every day."

"Oh, so that's your problem," my mother said.

"Not every day," I said. "She could do more. And so could you, Susan."

"Me?" said Susan. She had been silent so far.

"You could stay with Daddy overnight," I said. "You could sleep over and give me a break."

"You don't need me," said Susan.

"I do. I do need you. I need all the help I can get."

"Not from Evie!" said Marty. "She's his *ex*-wife."

Fred squeezed my knee under the table. I hadn't been sure until then he was on my side. I squeezed his knee back.

"Look, Joanna," said my mother. "Susan has two children. She can't be as involved as you are. What you're asking is unrealistic."

"One night!" I shouted. "One night is not unrealistic!"

My mother leaned back to give the waiter room to put down her fettuccine and then she turned to Marty. "Clyde is their father and if they need my help I'm going to do what I have to do."

"Good news, though, Marty," I said. "You can thank your lucky stars. Because things won't be this way for long."

"Why?" asked Marty innocently.

"Because he's going to die," I said.

Susan shot me a wounded look. "I'm afraid to stay there overnight. All right? I'm afraid he'll die while I'm there."

The table got quiet.

"I'm afraid, too," I said, finally. "But I stay there anyway. You, you're never there when it counts. When things get rough."

"How can you be so mean?" Susan said.

Maybe I went too far. I didn't want Susan to cry. But I thought it was odd and unfair how sheltered she was from the trouble around her. "Because," I said, searching. "Because it's true. You weren't there for a lot of things. Like you weren't there on the camping trip."

"What's that got to do with it?" Susan said, and the sheen was finally gone. Her face darkened. "I don't even know what you're talking about. I don't even know what happened."

"Because you never asked! You weren't interested!"

"You wouldn't talk to me!"

"You've had plenty of years to ask and you still haven't asked."

"OK. So what happened on the camping trip?"

"He, he fucked Nola, that's what. Under my nose, OK?" I saw my mother's face blanch, and then her shoulders fell in resignation.

"So then why do you want to be his slave now?" Susan said, her eyebrows raised.

"I don't know. I guess Marty's right. I'm crazy. I'm a crazy lady."

"No, seriously, Joanna. You don't have to do this," Susan said.

"You love him too, don't you?" I said. "And he did plenty of things wrong with you. He didn't go to your graduation because he was in Europe with Nola."

"No kidding," said Susan. "Why do you think I didn't go to his wedding? But you went. Why?"

"I don't know. I like him. It's not black and white. He cares what I think. He never cared about how I *felt* before, but he's starting to do that, too, now that I'm looking out for him."

"He should be earning your love, not you earning his," said Susan. She was with me now, at least for the moment. No faraway look.

The others said it was too late but Fred and I stopped off at Cedar Drive. Shep and Darleen were still there. The mood was festive, an extension of the trippy nights in the hospital. Some things were easier at home, like sitting on his bed, which was big and low, and so we crowded on orgy-like and went through a box of pictures. No one wanted to leave when my father was high.

Fred went back to California and Susan stayed for a few more days. My father slept a lot now, so my sister and I had hours alone together. I was tired myself, so tired I wasn't sure if I dreamed this conversation or not, but I think I said to Susan, "You never talk about childhood." And she said, "What about it?"

"I don't know," I said. "Did something happen?"

"What are you talking about?"

"Back then. Daddy. Johnny."

"What?" said Susan.

"Did Johnny, you know, did Johnny Dolan . . . I don't know. Make a pass at you or something?"

Susan laughed. "Well, sure," she said. "Who didn't he make a pass at? But I certainly didn't take him up on it. . . . Why? Did you?"

I opened my mouth and closed it again. "Me? No," I said.

That night, even Susan and my mother piled onto the bed with Darleen, Shep, and Uncle Harry, who had flown in. But Brenda wasn't having it this time. "Everybody out," she hissed. "I have to get up and go to work tomorrow."

My mother was sympathetic and got up, collected her bag and keys, and headed out through the kitchen where she'd cooked a thousand meals. "Well, I'm leaving if that helps."

Susan and I went with her, to a coffee shop where we could talk. We told her about the lineage chart my father had drawn earlier that day in the margins of the newspaper. "You see here," he had said. "I want Brenda to get the house and the cars. And fifty percent of the $47,000 I have goes to her, and twenty-five percent goes to you, Susan, and twenty-five goes to you, Joanna." He wrote fifty percent under one arm of the family tree and twenty-five and twenty-five under two smaller arms. His whole life he saved $47,000. It was a pittance, and yet it was a fortune for a schoolteacher.

"So I was right, dammit. He's not leaving me the credit union money," my mother said. "I'm getting nothing except what he asked you to hand over to me."

"But wait, maybe that sum includes the credit union money," said Susan.

"No," my mother said. "That money wouldn't get divided up."

"He asked if I would help him fill out some forms his lawyer sent over," Susan said.

"The executor?" my mother asked.

"Yeah," Susan said. "Thank God Daddy didn't ask me to be executor of his will."

"She must be pressuring him," my mother said. "Why else call the lawyer?"

"To change things for our benefit because he realizes how horrible Brenda is," I said.

"I hope you're right, Joanna. But I doubt it. So did you fill out the forms?" my mother said.

"I filled in his name and address," Susan said. "His Social Security number. But then I asked for the bank account numbers and beneficiaries, and he said he wanted to take a nap, we'd work on it later, and then he forgot about it."

"Whatever changes he's making must be good for us," I said. "Or he wouldn't have asked Susan to help him with the forms. He would have asked Brenda."

"Not necessarily," my mother said. "Don't be naïve. Something's fishy, I know it."

Susan went home to Larry and the kids and I spent every night at my mother's apartment to get away from Brenda. My father didn't like it when I left in the evening, but I told him I'd be useless if I didn't have nights to myself. As soon as I got to Cedar Drive in the morning, Brenda sped off to her job at Hutzler's. At six, when she returned, I fled to my mother's apartment on Charles Street. At first, the shifts worked well, Brenda and I each with our own domain, but one morning I walked in on a mess, purple morphine stains splattered on the counter and oddly around the burners on the stove, sticky syringes in a jumble on top of crumby plates, pills we would grind up with a mortar and pestle and add to the feeding tube tumbled out of overturned bottles. I wasn't neat about most things but with the meds I was compulsively neat. You had to be. "How's Brenda been?" I asked my father.

"She's no good," he said. "Go get my will." I'd seen it the other day, an extra-long manila envelope swaybacked to fit in the wire basket on the sewing machine cart in the den. Now when I looked, it wasn't there. I rummaged around on the desk, but I was suddenly exhausted. A crushing weight pressed down on me. I came back and collapsed into the swivel chair. "It's not there," I said, "and I'm too tired to look for it."

He reached over and held my hand. "Would you like it if I left you my books and papers?" he asked. I was rattled by the offer. The talk about leaving us money was one thing. But to speak of not needing his books and writing—his mind, his consciousness—that was unbearable.

"Well?"

I felt out of breath as if I'd been climbing stairs, but I managed to say, "Yes, of course." My long-ago wish to walk around in his mind was granted, access to all I had been barred from. Voices came rumbling down the hall, his and Peter Grafton's, when we were children, Marie, Marie, my cousin the arch-duke, the hyacinth girl. I saw the eager boys at his elbow studying headlines, iambic pentameter, Julius Caesar. They were gone now, Peter Grafton descending into schizophrenia. The others went on to live their lives no longer in need of Clyde Aronson's advice.

He said I was a great nurse. I'd make a terrific wife and mother. But Susan was the wife and mother. I was a freak, half-girl half-boy. He called me a saint. I chafed at it. I wanted to be a real person. "You want to get into Harvard, Yale, Princeton? Just do what I tell you," he promised his boys. "I've got recommendation letters in my desk so good they'd get you into a convent." Everyone laughed. Imagine, boys in a convent!

He saw clearly now, though, didn't he? A daughter could share the life of the mind. He could see that now. He would die, but I wouldn't lose him entirely. I would have his poetry. We sat quietly, listening to the wind under the door.

"I'm experiencing such love," he said after a while. "If only I had known, Joanna, I would have been better."

If only he had known what? In what way would he have been better? I almost asked the questions out loud, but stopped myself. Let the possibilities remain limitless. I would add to them as the years went by. He would have been better if only he had known sooner that I was worth knowing.

CHAPTER 49

My mother and Marty were going to New York for the long weekend. Saturday was Valentine's Day and Monday was President's Day. Marty had a convention. "I feel terrible leaving you," my mother said.

"It doesn't matter," I said. "I'm staying overnight with Daddy from now on, so I wouldn't be hanging out with you anyway. I can't leave him alone with Brenda. It's that bad. She stopped washing the syringes. And last night, she made a mistake and he almost overdosed. She started to give him 30 milliliters instead of 30 milligrams of morphine. Thirty milligrams converts to 10 milliliters! That's three times as much! So I'll be here the whole weekend. You might as well have fun in New York."

When I got off the phone he was yelling. "The BED! Joanna, come quick! The BED! The BED! It's on TV. The 800 number. Get a pencil! Hurry!"

By the time I found a pencil, Brenda was in the living room and the commercial was over. "Oh no," she said. "Nothing doing. I told you, mister, I'm not having a hospital bed in this house."

"You don't mean that," I said.

"There's no room for it," Brenda said. "Where would we put it?"

"We'd take out the platform bed. Obviously we can't fit two beds in there. So we'll take apart his bed. I'll do it. I'll get Shep to help me."

"And have the platform bed standing around in the carport? Forget it." Her lip quivered, and for a second I thought she was going to cry. Instead she recovered, put her hands on her hips, and whistled in amazement at how impossible we were.

I waited until she left the room, and whispered in his ear. "Would you be happier without her? If she weren't here, I mean." He had to know what I meant. Just the other day, Uncle Harry mentioned the suitcases in the driveway idea after my father complained about the pee pad. "Would you like it better if she lived somewhere else?" I said.

"Make me a cup of tea."

That night, I tossed on the sofa. As tired as I had been all day, I couldn't sleep. Voices clamored in my head. The will, the will. He was talking to Shep and I overheard him. They're gonna put me in a box, he said. For a second, I didn't know what he meant, and then I shuddered. Sometimes I wished we could talk that way, with brutal honesty, only we each thought the other couldn't handle it. I was all tangled up in the sheet. It was no use, I couldn't get to sleep. I sat up and turned on the light. I didn't know what I was going to do without him. What would life be like? There would be no point to anything if I didn't know what my father thought of it. Who would I be if not Clyde Aronson's daughter? I was a saint. A saint was selfless. Virtually nonexistent. But no matter how small and insignificant I made myself, it still wouldn't keep him alive. And what would be left of me? Nothing. Instead, I had to be larger than life myself. I had to do something big. Drastic measures were called for. I had to get rid of Brenda. Who knew what she'd do next, mixing up milligrams and milliliters, signing him up for castration. The situation was dire. I had to act. The minute she left for work in the morning, I'd jump on the phone and send a locksmith over. Then I'd jam as many of Brenda's belongings as I could fit into her set of sky-blue Samsonite luggage. Of course, I'd be left with no one to help take care of my father. But we'd scrape together the money for round-the-clock nursing. What was the $47,000 for anyway? He might as well spend it on himself. When Brenda got home from work, she'd find the blue suitcases at the bottom of the driveway just like

Uncle Harry said. I'd have to be strong, though. She wouldn't go quietly. No doubt, she'd put up a fight, bang on the doors, rap on the windows, but I wouldn't back down. Just let Brenda tell me I was under his thumb, or her thumb, or anybody's thumb.

I turned out the light, satisfied with my decision, but ashamed of what had become of my family. I could hardly believe we'd fallen so far in just a few months. In September, my father had been full of vitality and happy, for the most part. It was the last time I visited before he got sick, and he was mowing the lawn with his ancient gas mower and hauling forty-pound bags of peat moss from the car. I helped him dig up rocks, for what reason I couldn't remember. He complained about Brenda, but no more than usual. He told me he was busy putting up peppers and beans, taking a watercolor class, absorbed in a book called *Arctic Dreams* by Barry Lopez.

Fred and I were back from a trip to Ireland, and stopped in Baltimore before heading out to LA, excited to show my parents our pictures. After bicycling around the Ring of Kerry, and several days in Dublin, we decided to go to Belfast. We hadn't intended to—it was 1986, still the midst of the Troubles, and the place was bombed every other day—but we were two hours away and I felt I had to see it again. I half-hoped Fred would let me off the hook, say the trip was too dangerous, but Fred was eager to go.

Down the Grand Parade the familiar shops were thrilling and when the taxi driver got lost, I gave him directions from memory, although it had been twenty-five years. Since children roamed freely in Belfast, at least back then, I knew my way. The cab turned onto Orangefield Gardens and dropped us at No. 19. I was dumbstruck standing in the garden where I kicked a ball by the pansy patch those many years ago. What was it about a place where you lived that you hadn't been back to for a long time, not even once, and then you went back to it? It was enchantment.

I'd been told so many times I was too attached to the past. Better to live in the present and plan for the future. The past was for has-beens, it was a rut you got stuck in, the past was dead. But I thought the past wasn't dead since it was always there, whereas the present died the second it happened. I stood in the street in front of No. 19, my mind bending along with space and time, and I stared up at the second floor. As an equal-opportunity time traveler, I dreamed not only of the past, but of the future. I remembered doing so behind the casement windows with the wardrobe looming in 1962, imagining our return to America. Our bedroom walls were pink in the USA. Girls wore cotton shorts and sleeveless blouses. I dreamed of crowds cheering upon our return to the New World. Everyone would be astonished by my transformation.

In a rare happenstance, what I had fantasized behind the casement window about my triumphant return came true. Scores of neighbors from Cedar Drive and most of our Baltimore relatives lined up behind a velvet rope at Friendship Airport and cheered for Susan and me. It was a spectacle in part because we were children traveling alone—our mother and father ditched us for the summer, sent us home to live with our grandmother for eight weeks while they stayed behind to drive around Europe in the Renault and help my father get over Caitlyn Callaghan. In Germany, guards shouted at my parents "*Halt! Kein Ubertreten! Achtung!*" for ignoring the no trespassing signs leading into a Bavarian castle, thus reminding my mother and father of the circumstances under which they fell in love in 1942 and renewing their bond. Susan never forgave them for the eight weeks she suffered separated from her parents by an ocean, or for Belfast in the first place, but I was full of myself, trailing my older cousins on the way to Carvel's during the soft summer nights when we lived at my grandmother's house. From the moment I first came down the steps of the jet plane and crossed the tarmac holding hands with the BOAC captain, I felt full of myself, flushed and feverish, though not in a sick way. The stewardess had given us cherry candies and my lips and fingers were stained red. In photographs taken by a neighbor, I appear lit from the inside, cheeks ablaze, shining eyes, bright lips, and a front tooth missing. I'd just turned seven, and I had so much to tell. When finally I was able to speak over the noise, out came a full-blown Ulster accent, and Tom, who once played with me by the creek, stood back.

My parents pored over our pictures and the street map Fred bought at the same newsagent's where I once paid tuppence for sweets. I didn't expect much of a reaction from my dismissive father who liked to brush you off when you most craved his approval. But I could see it meant something to him that Fred and I went to Belfast. He was emotional in a quiet way. He took off his glasses to study the photos, some from the Falls Road (the other side of town from Protestant Orangefield) where British soldiers pointed their rifles at people on the street and then turned them on our cab. My father asked a lot of questions, and then he was silent, lost in thought.

He might have been thinking had Caitlyn known of the Troubles to come, she might have seized the opportunity my father offered in 1962. She might have seriously considered uprooting her family and moving them from Northern Ireland to live among the Jews of Northwest Baltimore, where they could heat up a *chynik* and have their tea in peace. Eventually Caitlyn and her family did leave Belfast, only much later, after her brother was blinded in an ambush. I found a snapshot among our baby pictures of Caitlyn in a floppy hat meant to protect her porcelain skin from the harsh Australian sun.

He cleared his throat. He blinked. Was it the memory of Caitlyn? Or just the likelihood he would never go back to Ireland as I had?

"You liked it there, did you?" my father asked.

"This time or last time?"

"When you were little," my father said.

"Yes." I watched him watching me. What did he see? That a child other than himself could feel deeply? That adults and their affairs weren't the only worthwhile experiences?

"The year was meaningful?" he said.

"Very."

"I can see that. I know that now."

Fred had meetings in LA, so he left and I spent a few more days in Baltimore. My father suggested a trip to Annapolis with Hoffman. It was probably the best all-around day we ever had together. My father was in an especially good mood. He was glad I liked his dog, but it was more than that. We were comfortable with each other that day. Maybe because I had gone back to Ireland. And maybe because the two years I'd been living in California had given us perspective. He could see from a distance that I was like him. We were interested in the same things. A son might not have been like him.

At the marina in Annapolis, we sat on a bench and ate cheesesteaks and several people stopped to admire Hoffman, and that was when my father got the National Dog idea. Hoffman was a handsome golden mutt and everyone seemed drawn to him. So my father decided he should take Hoffman to Washington and have him declared the National Dog the way Congress had recently passed a bill making the rose the national flower. I pointed out that the rose was a kind of flower, not a single flower, and that almost certainly other dog owners would object, each believing their dog deserved the honor. My father came up with a solution. Instead of actually taking his dog to Congress, he'd write a screenplay about taking his dog to Congress.

When I got back to California, he called every day, which he'd never done before. He'd start out saying "Yeah?" but quickly get to the point. He wanted Fred to help him write a treatment. Fred got on the phone. "We'll all be rich!" my father said, and for weeks Fred and I passing in the hall would repeat the comment and laugh.

Toward the end of October, the calls petered out. Maybe the screenplay was more challenging than my father expected. Maybe it stirred up feelings of regret. I dreaded hearing he had writer's block, and flashed on the day I unearthed Ye Olde Picture Booke when I was twelve and suggested he do something with his talent. Write your own book, he snapped. Now when I remembered wandering the house searching for him, holding the album open in my hands, a line from James Joyce always came to me: *I bore my chalice safely through a throng of foes.*

"I stopped work on the screenplay," my father said. "Can't do it anymore."

I hated hearing this. "Don't give up," I said. It was true his screenplay idea was basically a Disney movie and hardly reflected the lost time he'd captured in his orphanage album, or the political insight he showed in his letters during the war. But I thought the whole wacky National Dog conceit was pretty good, and I was a little embarrassed on his behalf to hear he was thwarted. "I love the National Dog," I said. "Fred does too. Fred says you have a great plot. What's the problem?"

"I have a headache," my father said. "A terrible headache that won't go away."

The sheet bunched up and the nubby sofa fabric chafed my face. I tossed and turned. Drastic measures. Lock Brenda out. The key doesn't fit! I drifted in and out of sleep, grinding metal in my ears, Brenda trying to insert her key again and again, then banging on the door, glass shattering, a suitcase lobbed through the window. Enough. I was overthinking, worrying, and that led to indecision and paralysis. To be or not to be. I was going to do it. I had nothing more to lose. I punched my pillow and sank into a deep sleep.

Dishes were clattering in the kitchen when I woke up. Why hadn't Brenda left for work yet? I had to call the locksmith. I fumbled for my glasses and my watch. It was eight-thirty! She should have left more than an hour ago. Then it struck me. It was Monday. My heart sank. Monday, President's Day! I had completely forgotten Brenda and everyone else in America had a three-day weekend! She wasn't going to leave for work at all. My plan would have to wait. And even worse, I had to spend another whole day with her. I didn't know how I would make it. Saturday and Sunday had been unbearable.

Thank God my mother was coming home from New York. Although I promised my father I would stay with him every night from now on, the long weekend made it too hard. I'd go crazy if I didn't get away and spend the night at my mother's. I had to talk to her, tell her about my plan. I felt a little guilty since I had promised him, but this was the last time he'd ever be alone with Brenda, because the next morning was Tuesday, no holiday I could think of—Brenda had to go to work—and the locksmith would come and Brenda would be out of the picture.

My mother called from New York and I tried to tell her what was going on but she broke in to say Marty had to spend an extra day at the convention and she was unsure whether she was going to stay there with him or come home by herself on the train.

"Please come home," I said.

"I can't decide. It's freezing, but we're still having great fun. Last night, we walked thirty blocks without even realizing it, from Gramercy Park all the way uptown."

"She's impossible," I whispered. "She's gone off the deep end. I'm calling around for nurses. LPNs are cheaper than RNs, but still expensive. Anyway, I can't talk. So come home. I need you." I was unaware I sounded like I'd gone off the deep end myself.

"I'll see," my mother said. "Let me talk to your father."

"Pick up the phone, Da," I said. "It's Mom."

"Evie?"

"Yeah, it's Evie. How're you feeling?"

I stayed on the line, always eager to hear my parents being nice to each other.

"Tell me about New York," my father said.

"Ah. New York. Well, Clyde. You know. It's your town. We had a great dinner with Alvin and Gladys on Friday night. And I can't believe anyone says New Yorkers aren't friendly. We got lost yesterday, so we ask this guy for directions. Not only does he give us directions to the little theater we're going to, but he tells us to eat at this Italian restaurant nearby and we do, and it turns out to be great, of course. You know, checkered tablecloths, Puccini, Chianti. Probably been there since the forties. What specifically do you want to know, Clyde?"

"Tell me everything."

CHAPTER 50

My mother decided to come home. She said she'd catch the next train and we'd meet at her apartment around seven. At five, I opened the front hall closet and got my coat while taking note of his army uniform on a hanger in the back and an old fedora on the top shelf, the crown still dented from the imprint of his grip. I wasn't the only one in the family hanging onto the past.

"Where're you going?" my father said.

"I'm going to stay at Mom's tonight."

"Don't go," he said.

I kneeled by his chair and rested my cheek against the back of his hand. If only he would get better, we would be close from now on. We'd talk about everything. "I have to," I said. "I haven't had a break in days."

"Stay with me. Please." His frog's eye was sealed shut, but his other eye was wide open, imploring.

"It's only for the night," I said. "Tomorrow I'll be here before you even wake up."

"You will?"

I smiled. "Yes, of course. I have to be here early in the morning before Brenda leaves. You know that." I certainly wouldn't want Brenda to be late for work, especially not tomorrow. I wanted no obstacles foiling my plan this time.

"When I open my eyes tomorrow, I'll see you?"

"Yes." I laughed softly at his childlike question. "I'll be the first thing you see."

"You can go, then."

The weather was mild with a drizzle. Toward the horizon storm clouds parted to show a streak of bronze sunlight and two snow-white clouds outlined in gold. It was a beautiful sight. I drove carefully on the shiny black roads. My mother's train wouldn't be in for a couple of hours so I thought I'd cook dinner and stopped at the supermarket. Once at my mother's apartment, I was a little spooked by the empty rooms. She'd been away three days. I looked behind the shower curtain and bolted the door. Then I unpacked the groceries and put the rice on, and I started to feel more at ease, and set the table in the kitchen, and I called Fred. The wall phone in the kitchen had a long cord, so I could talk and pace with the phone wedged between my chin and shoulder while steaming the vegetables. I was making the simplest dinner I could think of—chicken breasts with paprika, the rice and string beans. A few minutes after I hung up with Fred, the phone rang.

"Oh, hi, Brenda. How is he?"

"He's fine, but he wants the *TV Guide*. Do you know what you did with the *TV Guide*? I saw you walking around with it."

"Oh, yeah," I said. "Sorry. I might have left it on a kitchen chair."

"No, I don't see it. That's a bad habit, not putting things back where they belong."

"I know. I'm sorry. But it's there somewhere. I didn't take it out of the house."

"He wants to watch *Dressed to Kill*," Brenda said.

"He loves that movie," I said. I was glad he felt good enough to watch something so intense, or even to want to watch it.

"It's on at eight, but we don't know the channel. Don't have a cow over it, though."

It was a little after seven. My mother would be home any minute. Meanwhile, my father and Brenda had almost an hour to search before the movie started.

"Sorry about the *TV Guide*. I hope you find it." I hung up.

My mother arrived winded and red-cheeked. "I see you turned on every light in the place," she said cheerfully. She was happy to find me waiting for her.

"Oh, man. It's been brutal," I said.

"You made dinner! How lovely!"

"The rice is kind of plain," I called to her as she put her bags in the bedroom. "I added some chicken broth, but that's all I could think of."

"Looks good," my mother said, coming into the kitchen. "Should I turn off the burner under the string beans?"

I ladled out the food, we sat down, and I popped open a Diet Coke. "We're getting rid of Brenda," I said.

"Getting rid of her?" My mother laughed. She thought I was kidding.

"We've got to do what Uncle Harry says. Change the locks. I'm serious." I cut into my chicken with enthusiasm.

"Whoa. Slow down. Wait a minute. I'm not so sure about this, Joanna. You've taken on a lot already."

"That's why I made the calls about nursing. I can't leave him alone with her. Do you understand how bad it's been?"

"Don't you think you should consult somebody first? Like a lawyer or something."

"Shep said he'd talk to this friend of his who just went through a divorce and had to do the same thing."

The phone rang and I stood and answered it, pulling the cord around the corner into the living room. "Hi, Brenda." They probably still hadn't found the *TV Guide*.

"I have some sad news to tell you," Brenda said.

What could be sad compared to our situation? Brenda's perspective was so twisted.

"What?" I said.

"Your daddy just died."

"No," I said. "That's not true."

"Yes, just a little while ago."

"No." People died in bed, in and out of consciousness. They didn't die asking for the *TV Guide*.

"Yes," said Brenda.

She was a liar. It was too soon. He was sitting up. He was talking. He wanted the *TV Guide*! "NO!" I shouted. The phone dropped onto the carpet. "No!" I went down on my knees and I drew a breath in and then I made a croaking sound because I couldn't get enough air. She killed him. She gave him an overdose. That had to be what happened. My mother picked up the receiver and spoke to Brenda and hung up and got down on the floor with me and held me by the shoulders and she was crying, and I was gasping for air, and then she slapped me.

"Do you think she killed him?" I said.

"Sweetheart, he was very, very sick. He was going die, there was no way around it." Tears were streaming down her face.

How could I have been shocked? How could we both have been devastated knowing his disease was terminal? But we were. We got our coats and got into my mother's car like people feverish and weak. The almost full moon was high in the night sky and lit the road with a ghoulish cast. My mother told me the few details Brenda had given her. It happened at about eight-twenty, they found the right channel and he had been watching *Dressed to Kill*. She called the hospice nurse.

"I think I'm going to throw up," I said.

My mother pulled the car to the side of the road, tires crunching. I got out and stared at the gravel shoulder whitened by moonlight. The pebbles were stones in a bowl of milk. I got back in the car. "I don't have to," I said. My mother drove slowly as if we were in a procession. We were keenly aware that something big had happened to us.

"They didn't take him away already, did they?"

"No. Brenda said the nurse told her to wait until we got there before she called anybody."

"You mean Sol Levinson."

"Yeah, Sol Levinson."

There must have been other Jewish undertakers in Baltimore, but I'd never heard of any. We turned at Northern Parkway and drove past Sinai and the turnoff to my grandmother's house, and over the railroad tracks and turned right into Cedar Drive. Just as we passed the willow trees that leaned over the creek where the street curved, a cab passed us. It was rare to see a taxi in our neighborhood. It floated by unnaturally, iridescent yellow with black windows, seemingly driverless. I thought when we pulled up under the maple tree I would have to be dragged out of the car, I'd be too afraid to come inside. But the second my mother shifted into park I jumped out and ran across the lawn as fast as I could, through the carport and into the kitchen. I ran so hard I had to be stopped, and strictly for that purpose it seemed, there was a tremendous woman blocking my path whose body took up the entire width of the passageway between the kitchen and living room. I ran into her and she was soft as a pillow.

"Whoa, whoa. There now, sweetheart, take it easy. I'm Sharon, the hospice nurse, and I want to talk to you before you go in." Her voice was as comforting as hot chocolate. Where have you been? I wanted to say. Where were you all these months when I needed you so badly?

"Is he in the living room?" I said.

"Yes, and he's sitting in a chair," Sharon said. She put her arms around me, pressing me into her big bosom.

I used to forget how tiny the house on Cedar Drive was until I walked in after months away, and saw that it was like a house from Disneyland, three-quarters the size of a real house. Now everything in it was unreal, too. "He's sitting up? He's in his chair? What happened? How did he die?" The nurse held me in her arms.

Brenda emitted a little snort, a kind of half-laugh, and apologized to Sharon. "She's like this," Brenda said. "It's normal for Joanna."

"Tell me what happened," I demanded of Brenda. "Tell me everything."

Sharon nodded to Brenda to go ahead.

"Well, he said he was having trouble breathing and he asked me to open the window," said Brenda, enunciating slowly. "But I couldn't get around the chair so he got up and opened the door."

"The front door?"

"Yes, the front door. But I didn't want him to catch pneumonia, so I closed the door and then he started pulling apart his pajama top, so violently his buttons popped off, and then he sat down in the swivel chair, and he was gasping for breath and pulling at his pajama top and then he sort of put his head down. And I called the number we had on the legal pad, the number for the hospice nurse, and I said, 'I think my husband just passed away.'"

"Was he the one who wanted the *TV Guide*?" I said. "Or was it you?"

"Oh, Joanna, don't be ridiculous. He wasn't angry with you about the *TV Guide*."

"I know he wasn't angry with me. That's not what I meant."

"She wants to know if he asked for the *TV Guide* because she wants to know if he was lucid just before he died," said Sharon.

"That's right, exactly," I said. I looked into Sharon's kind eyes, studied her wide face, her flat bottom lip. How was it this woman I had never met before understood me?

"Yes," Brenda said wearily, as if I were trying her patience. "Clyde was the one who wanted the *TV Guide*."

"Are you ready to go in now?" Sharon asked.

"I think so," I said. I inched my hand along the wall as if I were on a ledge thirty stories high. I'd never seen a dead body, not up close. When the wall ended at the opening to the living room I took one more step and stopped. My father was sitting in the swivel chair in his pajamas and tartan bathrobe from Susan. I hadn't noticed before how Christmasy the bathrobe was. How cheerful. His head was bent and resting on his shoulder as if he had nodded off, and his lips were fat in a pout. He had his green hat on, of course. His hair was the same, his

mustache as bushy as ever. He didn't move. I dropped to my knees at the threshold and sobbed my heart out. "I'm sorry, Daddy," I cried. "I'm so sorry."

My mother stood behind me waiting to slap me if I needed it. When I calmed down I saw that Brenda was carrying a dining room chair and she put it next to him, and sat down in it and kept a frozen smile on her face, as if waiting for her portrait to be taken with her dead husband. It was weird. I didn't know what she was doing there. "It wasn't your fault," Brenda said, still smiling. They were on a stage and my mother and Sharon and I were in the audience. Brenda was glowing, calm and serene. No muttering, no curses. She was much more relaxed with him dead. "Do you think it's your fault?" Brenda said.

I didn't know how to explain, but Sharon, my interpreter, filled in. "Joanna only means she's sorry that he died," Sharon said over a great chasm, speaking across the River Styx to Brenda in the land of the dead. "She's sorry she lost her father."

"Poor Joanna," said Brenda. "This sort of thing is hard for you." She stroked my father's hand.

"You can come closer," Sharon said to me. "You can touch him if you want to."

I came closer and Sharon must have said something to Brenda because Brenda got up and carried her chair with her, and left my mother and me alone with my father. He seemed oddly healthier, his face fleshier, his lips fuller, his belly round. I put my finger on the bare skin peeking out between the buttons that were left on his pajamas and he was warm.

"It's all right. You don't have to be afraid," said Brenda from the hall.

My mother came closer and kissed his cheek. "I love you," she whispered. "I've always loved you."

I stared at her. Had she told him yesterday, last week, twenty years ago?

"He looks exactly the way he used to when he was playing with you and Susan," my mother said. "He would play cowboys and Indians with you, and you girls would shoot him and he'd pretend to be dead."

"We did? He did?"

"Yes, and he would put his chin down on his chest and stick his bottom lip out and pretend. Just like this."

There was a knock at the front door and Brenda opened it. Three tall men entered with faces as white as wall paint and greasy strands of black hair glued to their heads. Sharon whispered to us to go into the back of the house, although I was sure Brenda would have been fine watching the morticians unfold my father's arms and legs and zip him into a body bag.

"Phew!" said Brenda. "I don't envy them that cleanup job."

How could two human beings react so differently to the same circumstances? To me, day by day, my father had become sexless, smooth, soulful, and clean. But to Brenda, he was prosaically dirty, a bum who could use a bath.

They took him away. We called my sister and heard Susan yell to Larry to close the bedroom door so her little girls wouldn't hear her sobbing. Brenda said she was fine, declining my mother's invitation to spend the night with us. When we got back to Charles Street, all the lights in the apartment were still on. Everything there was unreal, too. I was reminded of a dream I had when Fred and I lived in New York. I was awakened by the sound of a party, animated voices, glasses clinking. I got out of bed and went to the top of a sweeping staircase, and down below I saw a replica of myself and Fred eating dinner at a cafe table. This other Fred and I were laughing too loudly with rubbery grins, and the food was too bright. It was a terrifying image.

The dinner we left in my mother's blazing kitchen looked like the dinner in the dream—chicken breasts day-glo orange from the paprika, one perfect bite cut out of each one, mounds of undisturbed yellow rice, neon green beans, a fork balanced on the edge of each plate, chairs pulled out. A garish tableau. What happened here, an archeologist might have asked. Why was this meal interrupted?

CHAPTER 51

B renda leaned over the funeral candle in the tall blue jar decorated with a Star of David and lit her cigarette off the flame. When the smoke cleared, she glanced back at the mourners and smiled wryly. I flew to California with Fred the next day. I'd go through the house and pack up my things some other time. Brenda said fine, whatever, just let her know when I was coming.

My father died in bleak February and I didn't come back to Baltimore to get my stuff until June. It was odd that I stalled since I had been so curious about the treasures buried in his books and papers. I expected to relish the searching, sorting, and curating, but I developed a powerful aversion to the task. Something about dealing with the boxes and jam-packed drawers seemed impossible. It seemed like a test of some kind that I wasn't up to, a sorcerer's apprentice job—endless and confounding, full of riddles and trapdoors. I stalled until Brenda phoned and said you better get back here before I throw your junk in the garbage.

And that was how I ended up dodging the seventeen-year locusts dive-bombing the carport and spending the night with Brenda in the steamy early June of 1987. I ate her cold chicken, and listened to her talk about the guy she was dating, and I tried to bring the ladder inside to go up into the attic, and then I put the ladder back like she asked, and I waited until she was asleep to search the den, and found the suitcase with the yellow handle, brought it to my makeshift bed on the sofa, and began to read the story my father called *Tuckahoe*. In the morning, on my way to loading some things into the trunk of the rental car, Brenda threw her menacing weight between me and the door.

I'd been getting the feeling something serious was up, so I had hastily gathered the framed picture of little Clyde in his sailor suit, put it into the daypack slung on my shoulder, grabbed the suitcase with the yellow handle in one hand, and held aloft the three-legged Indian table in the palm of my other hand like a waiter carrying a tray.

"You're not taking that table," Brenda said.

"Why not?" I said. I put the suitcase on the floor between my legs and clutched the table with both hands. "You don't want it. You told me last night it's a cheap piece of tourist junk." She grabbed one of the elephant-trunk legs. What was she planning to do? Break it off like a breadstick? I tightened my arms around the table, but she was not letting go. We both knew she would win this battle, at least for the moment. It was the judgment of Solomon—she didn't care if the cheap piece of junk broke and I did. I let go, and Brenda pressed the ivory inlay Taj Mahal to her chest, pointing the table legs at me like a lion tamer. Then a corner of the framed photograph in my daypack must have caught her eye, because she dropped the table thoughtlessly, like letting go of a gum wrapper. It hit the floor and rocked on its round top while she lunged for the picture. "Wait a minute," I said. "That's a picture of *my* father." I grabbed onto one end of the boxy frame, and she held fast to the other end. "*My* father." We were only inches apart. Beads of perspiration glistened on her upper lip. "Susan doesn't want it," I said. "I'm taking it."

"You'll do nothing of the kind," Brenda said through her teeth. "You're not getting the table and you're not getting the picture."

"But you don't want any of it. You said so."

"Nevertheless," said Brenda. "My late husband willed the house and its contents to me."

Her late husband. I almost laughed. She used the jargony phrase with such ease, more comfortable as a widow than a wife. "He asked if I wanted his books and papers and I told him yes," I said. I kept possession of the suitcase squeezed between my calves.

Brenda stopped yanking the frame, and I thought she was reconsidering. She looked me gamely in the eye. "I want my money," she said. She pulled harder.

I hung on. "What?" I was sweating now. The sweat was dripping down my back.

"That money was supposed to go to me," said Brenda.

"What money?"

"Don't be coy."

So she knew about the check that landed in my mother's mailbox from the credit union.

"The money my mother got?" I said. "I have nothing to do with that." It dawned on me too late—Brenda planned this tug of war. But I doubted she expected the fury she unleashed in me. This was my childhood house! How could she do this? How could HE have let this happen? I was furious, finally. What was supposed to happen next? Hair pulling? Nails raking bloody tracks? Punching and kicking? She knew she was stronger than I was, I could tell by the smug look on her face. She'd crush me. I didn't want her slimy skin touching me anyway, so once again I let go. She took possession of the picture, then ducked and swiped the suitcase from between my legs. His manuscript, Ye Olde Picture Booke. "You get nothing," she said. "Now get the hell out of my house."

I was shaking, red in the face, crunching cicada shells under my feet as I stormed the driveway to the car. Shells the nymphs shed after living underground for seventeen years. I started the car, threw it into reverse and lurched backward down the driveway clanking into the street. "You won't get away with this!" I yelled through my tears. I slammed the car into drive and called out some other things, too, like "you fucking bitch!" because I was pissed off finally. Now that it was too late, I was shaking with rage at my father, or at least the vile part of him, the part he excised. Not his balls—it turned out his balls weren't the vile part of him. The vile part was Brenda, the part of him that thought he was disposable, not even a mother would keep him, the throwaway part of him that thought he belonged in the garbage.

CHAPTER 52

"So tell me, what shape was the house in?" my mother said. She handed me a Kleenex.

I wiped my tears. "The garden's a mess, overgrown, weeds everywhere," I said.

"Did she rearrange the furniture?" she said.

"Inside it's the same."

I heard a snap, my mother's ankle as she shifted her weight, and the familiar sound was a comfort. She folded her arms and sighed. "We should have realized Brenda knew about the check," she said.

"She's going to throw out all our stuff," I said. I stood in front of the air conditioner with my arms out and let the frigid air cool my hot head and sweaty armpits. "His books and papers, everything." I shivered and went and flopped onto the sofa and my mother came and sat next to me.

"Unless I give her the money," my mother said.

"Yeah. Shit! Ma. The letters! I didn't get to go into the attic." My eyes filled with tears again.

"Don't cry, Joanna. Really. It's OK."

"You took some letters, didn't you? He doesn't, I mean, she doesn't have all of them."

"I still have some in a shoebox." She got up and went to her bedroom, came back and dumped a pile on the coffee table.

Somewhere in England
29 April 1945

Dear Evie,

I haven't had a letter from you in weeks. You are not doing right by your boy. Just when victory is in sight you begin slacking off. From Stalingrad to Kiev to Warsaw, from St. Lo to Cologne to Liepzig you were OK, but now when the boys are in the Berlin subway and Himmler thinks he can decide to whom to surrender, you down tools and go on strike.

Yours,
Clyde

"Were you having second thoughts at this point? Is that why you weren't writing to him?"

"I was scared about him coming home. And I *was* writing, just not as much as he wanted."

"You really don't have any of your letters to him?" I said.

"I told you, he lost them."

"Asshole."

"Oh, so you're finally down on your father?"

"I blame him for this catastrophe. I blame both of you," I said.

"Me? You blame me?"

I couldn't stop crying. The fight with Brenda unleashed a torrent. "Where's the letter that says 'if the greatest catastrophe to befall mankind couldn't keep us apart nothing else could.'"

"I don't know. It's in there somewhere."

"Well, he was wrong," I said. "He forgot about the catastrophe of regular life."

"Yeah, it's a catastrophe all right," my mother said. "But let's not equate it with the Holocaust."

"You guys were much better on paper, that's all."

"It's funny," my mother said, "we were probably never closer, I mean soul-to-soul, than we were during the three years we were apart."

London
1 May 1945

My own darling sweetheart,

I am not overcome with a great feeling of optimism at the outcome of the war. But we shall have accomplished certain things. We shall have turned back the "wave of the future," which almost engulfed us and carried us back to a darker age. The material creations of modern man can indeed become a Frankenstein and destroy its creator. Witness the robot bomb, the rocket shell that rises 60 miles in the air and comes down without being seen or heard to destroy whole communities, or the scientific elimination of peoples by means of the gas chamber and incinerator. Truly we have beaten down a monster, a dark, degenerate foulness which lies buried in all people, in us no less than in those fascist beasts who brought it to the surface in their own people. With passionate emotion I can wish the death of all Germans, but with cold reason I can see that this is not the solution. To simplify it, I should say that when all the world is made to enjoy the 4 freedoms we shall finally be done with war. But the world is not ready to accept world peace.

Meanwhile, darling, my thoughts turn to you and our future together, although I'm beginning to feel like we're Tchaikovsky and Madame Von Meck. They were strictly pen pals, you know, never getting together in the flesh. It was the same for George Bernard Shaw and the actress Ellen Terry, mocked because their affair was all on paper. Until you're in my arms again, I'll think of Shaw's retort: "Only on paper has humanity yet achieved glory, beauty, truth, knowledge and abiding love."

Love always,
Clyde

"Too bad you didn't know your father then, Joanna. He . . ." Her voice trailed off. She was reading to herself.

I would have liked knowing the twenty-something who imagined himself as Tchaikovsky, who wanted to achieve glory, truth, and beauty, who had the potential to be a great father. We failed each other, all of us, me just for being born. Less than a year after he returned from the war my mother left him for eight months. He was devastated. He seemed to have chosen my mother for how easily she was able to hurt him. It was many years later when she left for good, but even then she stayed entangled in his life, much like his own mother who left him not once, and not forever, but again and again.

Among the letters she tossed on the coffee table, a rare artifact—a single sheet from her to him that slipped from the pages of a longer letter and refused to be lost, as all of her other letters were lost. My mother never had a chance to find out who she was. He plucked her at sixteen, before she was fully formed, and she was robbed of childhood, as he was robbed, as I was, each in our own way. Only Susan remained unscathed.

1837 North Avenue
Baltimore, Maryland
November 9, 1945

My darling Clyde,

What do I want now that the war is over? That's quite a question, Aronson. But I'll try to answer it. Besides wanting you, and I suppose children at some point, I want to give something to the world. And for having given, I want to belong to it.

Always and forever,
Evie

"How can you blame me after everything that's happened? Isn't that what I heard?" my mother said. "You blame me for this catastrophe?"

"In part. You always play the innocent."

"That's not true. I take responsibility for a lot."

"You just proved my point."

"Don't take your anger at Brenda out on me," my mother said.

"I'm sorry. You're right, we have to stick together. But when I look back sometimes I can't believe how oblivious you were."

"I'm not oblivious. Don't insult me. You're just upset, so you're giving me a hard time."

"Right. You're not oblivious. So how could you let him do that to me?"

"Let who? What?"

"Johnny. Let Johnny."

"Oh, that."

"God, Ma, I was thirteen, fourteen."

"Jesus, you weren't *that* young."

"Yes I was."

"Out of nowhere, you're bringing this up?"

"Not out of nowhere. Not for me it isn't."

"You really want to talk about this now?"

"How could you?"

"I told you," my mother said. "I didn't know it was happening."

"How could you not know?"

"I just didn't."

Inside the house it was the same. A portrait of the four of us still hanging on the wall. The same sofa by the window where I lay with the curtains open when Johnny delicately took off my glasses and kissed my eyelids, my hair. I could hear the melody of children's voices in the street. He must have heard it, too. I thought I was lucky to be taught so gently by an older man.

I didn't have to deal with pimply boys groping blindly. And I *was* lucky, in that way. I didn't know mine was an old story. I thought lying there with my tanned knees apart granted me access to the world of boys and men, but the opposite was true. I should have been outside playing, laughing and calling to my friends, joining the concord of their voices. I hadn't read Nabokov's *Lolita* yet, but I felt myself slipping under, losing something irrevocable, vaguely conscious that "the hopelessly poignant thing was the absence of my voice from that concord."

My mother folded up the open letters and put them back into their envelopes, and then put them in order according to the postmarked dates. "I'll give Brenda the money if you want me to," she said. "I know how much the stuff in the house means to you."

"No. I don't want you to. That's extortion. I'm not caving in to her blackmail just because he did." My big, important father turned out to be as weak as those pathetic fathers in fairy tales—powerless to protect their children from the wicked stepmother. I was his Emile Zola, he said, his champion, but he was unable to be mine.

"If I keep the money, how will you get his books and papers?" my mother said.

"I don't know. But I'm going to get my stuff somehow, you better believe it."

"You know Joanna, if we don't turn over the check to Brenda, or at least half of it, you'll be breaking the promise you made to your father."

"Don't worry about it. I have no problem breaking the promise," I said. "Just don't think I'm doing it on your behalf. I'm not. I'm going to break the promise I made to my father because he was wrong to ask for it."

CHAPTER 53

There was no point staying in Baltimore. Brenda and I were at a standoff. The executor told both of us his hands were tied. So I went back to California, presumably to look for work since I'd given up the copy editor job to take care of my father. When I got to LA, though, I found out that I didn't know what sort of work I wanted to do anymore. I couldn't concentrate on anything. I kept seeing a garbage truck on a slow rumble down Cedar Drive, Brenda waiting at the curb with an armload of cap guns and Shirley Temple dolls. I was stuck. I couldn't move forward, it seemed, until I got the chance to sort through the past. I tried to think of a way out of my predicament—or really, a way *inside* was what I needed—but I came up with nothing. Instead I started drinking wine out of a beer mug. I paced the patio in frustration wishing I smoked. Then one day while watering the lemon tree, I had a brilliant idea. "Fred!" I called into the den. He was watching a Yankees game. "I'll write her a check," I said.

He put the TV on mute. "You're going to give Brenda the money?"

"I'll go see her and give her the whole $20,000. I'll just hand it over, and she'll hand over my stuff and I'll drive away with everything in the car, straight to the bank, where I'll stop payment on the check."

Fred laughed. "You're a genius, Jo. Ever heard of check fraud? Ask your uncles. I'm sure Harry and Alvin can show you how to kite a check."

"I've heard of it," I said. "But this is the first time I ever realized how handy a thing like that could be."

I crossed fraud off my list, and since I still wasn't giving in to Brenda's blackmail, there was nothing left except to find a good lawyer of my own. I called Anne Brighton, someone I knew from college who practiced law in Maryland. The most obvious action, Anne Brighton said, was to make a claim against the estate, but since my father's will clearly stated Brenda got the house and "all its contents" that path wasn't viable for me. Instead, I could file a replevin suit, which was an action that claimed the right to have personal property returned from the possession of someone with less right to hold it than the plaintiff. It was an old term dating back to the thirteenth century. I liked the sound of it. I'd have the chance to stand up for myself in court. But again, Anne said those suits were hard to win.

"So possession really is nine-tenths of the law? It isn't just a schoolyard taunt?" I said.

"Correct," said Anne. "But even more dicey is the fact that filing a replevin suit is a tip-off. Right now, your stepmother is hanging onto the stuff to use as a bargaining chip. She wants the money, right? As soon as she hears about a viable lawsuit, though, and the possibility of a judge ordering her to hand over certain items with no compensation, there's nothing to keep her from throwing away the things you want."

Brenda would do it, too. The replevin suit could mean losing everything and cutting off all other avenues of recourse. A replevin suit had to be a last resort. I asked Anne if there were other options to try first. She said it depended on what I wanted. "What's your goal?" she asked.

My goal. What did I want? The manuscript, most of all. Ye Olde Picture Booke. His letters, his poetry, my drawings, the rose quartz giraffe from Aunt Adele. And something harder to name—the things I didn't know existed, the things I wasn't even looking for. I wouldn't have said this to literal-minded Anne Brighton, but my goal, when I really thought about it, was to steal back my childhood, so I could have it and then be able to move on. "I have to get into the house," I said.

"OK then. Here's an option where you wouldn't risk losing property," Anne said, "because unlike the replevin suit, this remedy doesn't announce itself. It involves a different kind of risk, though. Rather than risking your belongings, you'd be putting yourself in jeopardy."

I was on the portable phone looking out the window at the solitary mop top of a palm tree way up in the blue, blue Venice sky, listing in the breeze. I'd made a surprising discovery when my father was sick. I'd always thought of myself as fearful, end of story. But I learned I could be brave. A skateboard clacked over the sidewalk joints somewhere down the street. "That's all right, Anne," I said. "I'll put myself in jeopardy. Just tell me what the remedy is."

"I'm talking about self-help," Anne said. "You help yourself to what you want."

"I get it," I said. "I break in." The palm tree swayed, and the skater came into view, his wheels clicking and grinding. It was the kid next door. He balanced his weight on one end of the board and the other end flipped up.

"Break in?" Anne said, all innocence. "Well, no. I wouldn't tell you to break the law. But maybe you know of a time when the maid, I mean, the house cleaner is there?"

"I don't think Brenda has a house cleaner."

"Well then, someone who comes over regularly, who could let you in?"

"I don't know of anyone who comes over regularly. Not anymore."

"There must be someone. Think about it."

I hung up and went to tell Fred.

"Who is she, this Anne Brighton?" he said.

"Friend from college."

"And this friend from college who you've never even mentioned before, she's suggesting you do what?"

"I steal."

For the next several days, I spitballed ways of getting into the house—I'd disguise myself as a Mary Kay lady or a dogwalker or the Fuller Brush man. I tried to think of somebody, anybody, who might visit Brenda and allow me to tag along. Then my mother remembered Darleen's husband Travis did yard work for Brenda. He trimmed the hedges, my mother said, and also did some handyman stuff and so he had access to the inside of the house. "The handyman stuff Daddy used to do," my mother said. We were both quiet for a moment thinking of him.

Travis seemed like a great idea until I considered exactly what I'd be asking. He had an arrangement with Brenda based on trust. I thought it over. I had no problem betraying Brenda. I could even betray my dead father and break the promise I made to him. But I didn't feel right asking Travis to betray Brenda. Shedding my good girl role was a tricky process. There ought to have been a simple con I could live with, but I was stuck. I couldn't come up with a seamless way of getting past Brenda. I kept remembering how she threw herself between me and the door, how undeterred she seemed at the prospect of violence. I was seething over the injustice of it all, my belongings held hostage after everything I'd done for my father. I couldn't let Brenda throw away the manuscript! It was the story of his childhood. I never wanted anything so badly, and yet at every turn I hit a brick wall.

What was my goal? Anne Brighton asked. How much easier that question had to be for her—at the top of her class in law school, hired by a big DC firm, handed a fat paycheck and respect along with it. I bet Anne was motivated in school by something other than sex. From Johnny onward, I cared about nothing else. In high school, college, and later in New York, sex was all I was interested in. I had no ambition because anything I was good at (cartoons and amusing stories) had no value. There were so many guys, I lost count, the only goal to conquer this one or that. I got tired of it, eventually. I got so tired I wanted to go home, but I had no home to go to. My mother's apartment with Marty wandering around in his shorty bathrobe was not home. Cedar Drive with Darleen, and later Brenda, was not home. Then I met Fred, and Fred was home.

What was my goal? Did I have to grow up and move away from home, away from Fred, in order to fulfill my promise? In order to conquer my fears? Fred was so gentle and soft-spoken, I didn't realize how he subverted what little ambition I had. I should have taken the GQ assignment, obviously. How many other opportunities had I missed, trusting Fred's advice over the years? I'd have to figure out my next step. Could I stay with him and still change my life? I'd have to consult with the bold seven-year-old who crossed the tarmac at Friendship Airport with clear eyes, ready to take her place in the world of boys and men, of composers and chess players, of doers, actors, creators. Too bad that seven-year-old girl grew up only to let others steal the spotlight. No more, I thought. I refused to be held back any longer by anyone else's agenda or limitations.

The wind picked up and the skinny palm tree seemed like it might snap in half. Instead, it bowed in a graceful arc, remarkably resilient. I was a throwaway person, my father said. I shrugged off my own importance. A throwaway person who was nevertheless intent on Brenda not throwing anything away.

One day, the brick wall I kept ramming my head against started to buckle. It turned out all I had needed was a deadline. It came in the form of a letter from from the executor warning about the six-month statute of limitations for claims made against the estate of Clyde Aronson. Time was running out. "Please understand that I do not wish to encourage litigation," the executor wrote. "But I wanted you to be aware of this issue of limitations." If I wanted to take legal action against the estate, I should know that August 16, 1987, was the last date I could file. If I tried self-help and failed, I wanted the option of filing a replevin suit. Which meant I had to try and help myself before August 16th. No more Hamlet-like paralysis. I was going to act without worrying about any promises except those I made to myself. I never got the chance to lock Brenda out of the house. Now I sure as hell wasn't going to let her lock *me* out. And since Brenda didn't have a house cleaner I could barge in on, that meant I'd have to break and enter.

The legal deadline was motivation to make a timetable, and the simple act of purchasing a plane ticket set the wheels in motion, turning thought into deed. Fred had a script in production so I had to find some other accomplice, preferably someone bigger and stronger than me, which meant almost anybody. Liz Stone suggested this kid we knew in elementary school, Barry Lerner. I had no idea she was in touch with Barry. "We had a thing a couple of years ago," Liz said. "No big deal. The point is Barry's a drug dealer. He has a gun." Are you nuts? I said. But soon I was taken with the gun idea—as a deterrent, of course. I could see Brenda walking in and physically threatening me. Barry Lerner the drug dealer would point his gun at Brenda and she'd have to back off. It was a sign of how obsessed I was, that I thought a gun was a good idea. Fred said I was out of my mind.

"The only way this is going to get done is if I'm out of my mind," I said.

"Fine, OK, but stay away from this creep Barry Lerner, whoever he is," said Fred.

"Don't worry, I never slept with the guy. Liz did, though."

"No guns, Joanna."

Who was Fred to tell me what to do? But he was right about the gun. So I came up with an alternative. Shep Levine. He'd seen how awful Brenda was firsthand. He was perfect— middle-aged and responsible, but with a sense of adventure. He didn't hesitate. "Just tell me when," said Shep.

I started getting excited. I felt happy for the first time since my father died. I was manic. The more I thought about self-help the more it seemed like the most important thing I would ever do. I was going to break into the house I grew up in and kidnap myself. I was going to break down the castle gate and get back homeward. I sang out: *She came in through the bathroom window, protected by a silver spoon.* Well, no silver spoon for me. And I couldn't count on Brenda leaving the windows unlocked, could I? So I'd have to bring tools. I'd have to get a crowbar somewhere. I could buy one at the hardware store probably, or some place like K-Mart. You didn't need a permit for a crowbar, as far as I knew. I decided not to mention the crowbar to Fred. I lay awake worrying about it. What if I was caught with a crowbar? Or the K-Mart receipt? What if Shep was caught with a crowbar? I decided I would have to call Darleen's husband Travis after all. I wasn't going to ask Travis to take stuff out of the house or to be on the premises when I made the score. But maybe after repairing something for Brenda, he could forget to lock the door behind him.

Darleen answered the phone. She wanted to know how the weather was in California. Warm and sunny. I asked her a bunch of questions about Travis. She said he didn't work for Brenda on a regular basis. He was only over there if Brenda called him with a specific job and there was no way to predict when that would be.

"What's this about?" Darleen said.

"It's complicated," I said.

"Oh," said Darleen. "Because, you know, I have a key."

How stupid of me! Of course Darleen had a key. Darleen and my father stayed close. That didn't change after Brenda, or Travis. The key was big. I thanked Darleen multiple times. But even knowing I had the key waiting for me, I could not dog it. The rest of the heist had to be planned out with precision. Nothing left to chance. My flight east was in five days. I plotted in bed in the dark, with Fred's shoulder listing like a ship in the corner of my eye.

I could not simply arrive in Baltimore one day and waltz over to Cedar Drive assuming Brenda was at work as usual and that she wouldn't be returning until six p.m. I would have to verify that she was actually at Hutzler's department store, at her desk in accounting. Unfortunately, I could not call her there to determine her whereabouts since we weren't on speaking terms. A phone call out of the blue would be suspicious. I'd have to get someone else to call her and act as my virtual lookout. Not my mother or Susan, of course. Brenda would have been suspicious of them, too. And besides, Susan didn't want anything to do with the break-in. Susan could not understand why I would risk so much for his moldy papers. There were other relatives to employ. Uncle Harry hadn't yet decided that I'd broken the promise I made to my father, and he was also still on good terms with Brenda. If he called her it wouldn't smell of anything. He was the kind of guy who'd call someone just to shoot the shit, or maybe he had a reason to call but you could never figure out what that might be. At any rate, Uncle Harry agreed to act as lookout. He had his own stake in the take. He didn't want Brenda throwing away the orphanage photo album.

Uncle Harry still lived out West, but luckily, he was an early riser. The three-hour time difference wouldn't be a problem. He would ring up Brenda at seven a.m. his time, ten a.m. Hutzler's time, on the appointed day. As soon as he confirmed that Brenda was at her desk, he would call to give me the all-clear. But where was he going to call me? Car phones weren't widely in use in those days, and cell phones were unheard of. You couldn't just phone somebody on the road. The good part about those days, though, was when you called someone at work that person was definitely at work.

So far, great. Uncle Harry would ring Brenda and we'd know she was at work. But if Uncle Harry then telephoned my mother's apartment where I'd be staying, in order to give the go-ahead, it would take half an hour for me to get to the house on Cedar Drive. If Brenda ditched work early for some reason, she'd be capable of getting home within that same half-hour and could very well catch me in the act, tiptoeing down the hall like the Pink Panther. It was unlikely Brenda

would randomly go home sick, but I didn't want to chance it. I didn't want to be thinking about her walking in on me. I wanted to pull off the job confident Brenda was far away and preoccupied.

Therefore I had to find a way station close to the house where I could receive the phone call from Uncle Harry. Shana Bloom's was an obvious choice. She lived only five minutes from Cedar Drive. Shana laughed in delight when I asked if we could use her place as a safe house. She loved the scheme. She was an old commie. Shana hung out with my mother at the YCL in the forties, although Shana denied it. Even her kids didn't know. But I knew, and figured she still had some red blood flowing in her veins. "I'll have coffee and cake waiting," Shana said. Those commies knew how to cater a meeting.

Everything was falling into place. I didn't need to case the joint. I knew it like I'd grown up there. I had my crew together. Shep would ride shotgun. He was my bagman. I didn't need a second-story man since it was a ranch house. Shana provided the safe house, and Uncle Harry was lookout.

I was worried about Hoffman, though. Hoffman started getting aggressive after my father died. Sometimes he freaked out around people. He might start barking at Shep Levine. He might even try to attack him. I asked a friend who was a dog groomer about giving Hoffman a dog tranquilizer. "Do I need a prescription?"

She laughed. "It's called a bone," she said.

I told my mother to stop at the butcher's on the night my plane got in.

"Why does the damn dog need a whole leg of lamb?" my mother said.

"Not the whole thing. Just the bone," I said. "I want a big one."

My mother wasn't sure whether to cook the bone and neither was I. She decided to stick it in the oven. We should have left it raw.

I landed at BWI airport and drove a dark blue Ford Taurus out of the Hertz parking lot and went straight to Darleen's. She opened the door of her little A-frame house in Catonsville, and before she said hello, she silently handed over the key, knowing how much I needed the physical fact of it. It was just a key, no key ring. From the door, I could see Travis in the back room leaning over his workbench. I put the key in my pocket. I was itching to be on my way, but once Darleen started talking, she kept going and I sensed she was stalling because, as she told me once, the way I talked with my hands and described stuff reminded her of my father, and she missed him terribly. I was finally able to leave, and I drove over to my mother's apartment. The smell of roasting meat flooded the stairwell. "I got it!" I said, holding up the key. We hugged. My mother wasn't perfect, but we were friends.

"Something smells good," I said.

"Leg of lamb," said my mother.

The next morning, Shep and I met at Shana Bloom's to wait for Uncle Harry's phone call. Shana had a crumb cake waiting as promised, and a pot of coffee on a trivet in the dining room, but I wasn't hungry. I was wired. I had a few green garbage bags—the big kind for leaves—folded up and stuffed in the back pockets of my jeans. The key was in my left front pocket. I kept putting my hand between the layers of denim finding the cool metal, running my fingertips over the grooves. I had the bone in a brown paper bag. I put it on Shana's coffee table. "Don't let me forget that," I said. Shep accepted cake and coffee, cream and sugar. I frowned at him. I didn't want him getting comfortable.

Suddenly Shana's living room darkened. Thunder rumbled and a flash of lightening cracked, then the slap and whoosh of rain hitting the asphalt streets and tiny brick houses. The phone rang and I jumped. Shit, could I really go through with this? Would my legs turn into Jello and my feet turn into lead? Would my hands shake so much I couldn't even try the key? Would I be so afraid that I'd fuck it up? Shana answered the phone. "Hello?" she said, holding back giggles. It was the all-clear from Uncle Harry. Brenda was settled at work, they'd had a nice chat. So Shep and I set out. I was wearing a sweatshirt and I flipped the hood up. Shep held a magazine over his head that he pilfered from Shana's coffee table and we ran to the car and got in. I drove. We left Shep's silver Jaguar XKE parked at Shana's. Way too conspicuous. Besides, the Taurus had a deep trunk.

At the stop sign on Sudbrook Road, I shifted my weight under the steering wheel and slid my hand into my pocket and felt the jagged metal, warm now from the heat of my thigh. I knew the key wasn't a sure thing. If I were Brenda, I would have changed the locks by this point, no doubt. I would have changed them back in February. But there was a chance she hadn't. I drove down Alter Street, the windshield wipers whining and slapping. Shep was quiet. I turned left onto Cedar. Even in the storm, the street had the drowsy feel of morning and stirred my heart. There was a particular texture to the weekday hours before noon on Cedar Drive, a sleepy wonderfulness that was the feeling of waking up when you were so little you weren't even in school. I turned into the driveway and Shep and I got out of the car lashed by the rain once again and slammed the car doors, and ran for the carport. I held the screen door open with my hip and inserted the key. Somehow my hands weren't shaking at all, not even a little bit. The key slipped right in and the doorknob turned and the door opened. I was fine. My heart was beating at a remarkably normal rate, and why not? I was home.

I scratched Hoffman behind the ears and gave him the goddamn bone. I was calmer than I'd been in months. The rain pattered contentedly on the gravel roof, the way rain always did in summer. This was the last time I would hear it.

I was calm, but Shep wasn't calm. As soon as we got inside he put his back flat against the wall, which made me laugh. He wasn't laughing, or even smiling. I couldn't see the dimples that normally made grooves in his cheeks. I had been so worried about involving Darleen's husband, yet I minimized the risk Shep was taking on my behalf. Shep had no trusting relationship with Brenda to breach, which was good, but in that case then, what the hell was he doing in her house? Gee, I don't know, Officer.

"Hurry up!" Shep said.

What was the matter with him? Things were going fine. I was just exactly where I wanted to be, where I had been trying to get to all along. I had no fear at all, strangely. The pictures of me all over the place helped. The goddamn Indian table was still there. She didn't have a clue, that Brenda. I went into his bedroom. The sailor suit photograph was back on its nail. I popped it off and into the leaf bag, then wandered around the house struck with wonder. All the life that went on there. I had to snap out of it, so I focused and went in search of the suitcase with the Bakelite handle. No way she'd put it back in the closet. If she hadn't thrown it out already, and that was a possibility, she would have hidden it somewhere. I looked in the closet anyway, and there it was. Packed and ready to go. Shep went outside and plopped it into the deep Taurus trunk. I continued working on the den, scooping papers and clippings from the bottom desk drawer into the leaf bag. The little pink giraffe gazed down from its perch on the desk blotter. "Don't worry. I won't forget you," I said. I wrapped it in a Kleenex.

"Hurry up!" Shep said again.

Everything was fine. Hoffman was slurping at his bone in the hallway, holding it between his paws licking and clacking the bone against his teeth.

"We have to get out of here," said Shep. "I'm pretty sure the lady next door saw us. She was peeking out of her curtains.

"The slides from Ireland! I forgot about these." Four little orange Kodak slide boxes. "Shep, can you get the ladder from the utility room?"

"You must be kidding," Shep said. He moved sideways down the hallway like a cop in the projects. I tried not to laugh. "Someone saw us next door," he said.

"Mrs. Rollins? On the carport side?" I said. "She knows me. She's nice. She and her husband helped me shovel the walk after the big snowstorm."

"She's Brenda's neighbor, Joanna. I'm not comfortable with this."

"We have to get the ladder. I have to go into the attic."

"It's time to go, Joanna."

Shep carried out my father's Jackson Pollack imitation. It was too big for the trunk so he put it in the backseat. Then he came back in and took me by the shoulders. "I'm sorry," he said, "but this is all you're taking. We have to get out of here. No more time."

Goodbye! Goodbye house. Rain on the gravel roof, the smell of summer through the screen, the neglected garden, my father gone. Shep steered me around Hoffman who ignored us, his world was all bone, through the kitchen door and down the driveway, rain splashing our faces. I forgot something. I ran back and turned the key and I was in before Shep could stop me, scooted inside and grabbed the Indian table with the elephant legs and I ran out again, closed the door tight, down the driveway, lowered the table into the trunk and slammed the trunk shut, got into the driver's seat with Shep already riding shotgun, and I backed out. "All right!" I yelled. I was triumphant, unlike the last time I tried to get my stuff and backed out of the driveway. We didn't get everything, but we had a pretty good haul.

Shep relaxed. "Baby, we did it!" he said. His grin was back, dimples and all. I felt like a million bucks. We talked and laughed the whole way to Shana's where I dropped Shep at his Jag. Euphoric though we were, Shep admitted being relieved to part company with the likes of me. I drove straight to Mailboxes Unlimited, dropped off a shipment, and headed to the airport. For the six-hour flight to LA I stayed put in my seat—no bathroom breaks—my lap weighed down, my arms wrapped around the suitcase with the yellow handle.

CHAPTER 54

At first, Brenda didn't notice anything missing. She didn't even register the blank space outlined by a rectangle of dust where the Pollock imitation had been hanging on the dining room wall. It wasn't absence that tipped off Brenda. It was presence. What was there that shouldn't have been there? The bone. Where on earth did Hoffman get that lamb bone? And who would commit such a hateful act? Everyone knew you didn't give a cooked bone to a dog. Now Brenda had to worry about bone shards perforating Hoffman's colon. She went next door to ask if Mrs. Rollins had seen anything suspicious lately.

In LA, I sifted through the contents of the suitcase cataloguing my trove, and I discovered poor people left quite a paper trail, compelled as they were to seek help from government agencies. The manila envelope I believed was full of boring bureaucratic correspondence turned out to be full of fascinating bureaucratic correspondence. Had my father read this stuff? Among the contents, a social worker's notes describing "domestic disputes" between his mother's family and his father's family, and piles of memoranda from charity workers. My mother said if he'd been through the file, he never spoke of it. Possibly he glanced at it, but didn't read as closely as I did, and did not note as I did, that his father, Isaac Aronson, had done time in New York at a prison on Hart Island, and that even more interestingly, he had quite possibly changed his name to Thomas Marmot, and had likely fled to Chicago. Maybe my father knew but pretended to believe his father simply vanished into thin air. I could understand it. The unknown was infinite and mysterious. The known was just sad.

March 8, 1925
Mr. H.S. Lurie
Jewish Social Services Bureau
1800 Selden St.
Chicago, ILL.

My dear Mr. Lurie:

May we solicit your kind interest in behalf of our client, Mrs. Ruth Aronson of this city, whose husband Isaac Aronson left her and their five infant children on July 18, 1924, since which time he has neither communicated with nor contributed a single penny towards their support, as a result of which the family has fallen a burden upon the local charities and Mrs. Aronson has been compelled to commit her two oldest children to an orphan asylum.

In 1922, Mr. Aronson absconded with $1800 from the Majestic Tailoring Co., by whom he was employed and he was committed to the penitentiary on July 7, 1922. He was released on May 24, 1923, and subsequently lived with his family until the aforementioned date of July 18, 1924.

We have just received word from the United Hebrew Charities that a friend of Mr. Aronson's has reason to believe Mr. Aronson is living in Chicago under the assumed name of a Mr. Thomas Marmot.

I will therefore thank you to follow up on this clue and advise us of your findings. According to our source, "Mr. Marmot" has apparently applied for a position at the Carson Pirie Scott and Company. Isaac Aronson, also known as Thomas Marmot, is 35 years old, 5 feet 11 inches tall, 150 pounds, black hair, black eyes, arrived in this country in 1891 from Russia, and worked as an insurance agent. The family consists of five children, Clyde 7, Harry 5, Vivian 4, Alvin 3, and the infant Gertrude.

Thanking you for your kindness and awaiting your early reply,

Charles Zunser,
National Desertion Bureau, New York

March 16, 1925

Mr. Charles Zunser
National Desertion Bureau
799 Broadway,
New York, N.Y.

My dear Mr. Zunser,
In reply to your letter of March 8th we wish to advise
you that we visited at Carson Pirie Scott and Co. and
were informed that "Thomas Marmot" was in their
employ for one week, upon which time he did not
show up for work again. The address he gave them,
and they provided us, turned out to be erroneous.

If you are able to obtain better information, we shall
be glad to complete the investigation.

Very truly yours,
Henry S. Lurie
District Supervisor
Jewish Social Service Bureau, Chicago

I was so engrossed in reading the file I didn't hear the phone
ring, and the answering machine picked up. Officer Smythe
with a Y from the Baltimore County Police Department asked
that I please call back about a "domestic dispute." Oh, the sins
of the fathers.

Anne Brighton urged me to ignore the message. She
thought I'd be fine, I just had to remember not to answer the
phone, or show my face in Baltimore. "Ever?" I said. Well, at
least for a while. Shep Levine's instincts had been correct.
Mrs. Rollins peeked through the curtains and saw us. "I can't
believe Joanna did this," Brenda confided in Darleen, unaware
Darleen had provided the key. "I'm shocked. I never would

have guessed Joanna, of all people, was capable of taking such a risk." I agreed with Brenda. I, too, hadn't known what I was capable of. "She's damn lucky, too," Brenda added. "Hoffman didn't even get sick. He could have died."

The unveiling was scheduled for October 25th. Would it be safe to come back to Baltimore by then? Everyone I consulted, including Anne Brighton and the executor, believed the cops would not raid a cemetery over a domestic dispute that occurred months ago.

Meanwhile, Brenda was busy making sure the headstone was perfect, going over the brunch menu with Aunt Shirley, and, as it happened, swearing out a well-timed warrant for my arrest. All she needed to trigger an aggressive pursuit by the police was one eyewitness willing to identify the suspect. Fortunately, Mrs. Rollins couldn't identify the tall middle-aged man she saw placing items in a late-model blue car, but she recognized Mr. Aronson's younger daughter carrying out several bulging garbage bags. She remembered me from the snowstorm. Mrs. Rollins was a good neighbor, and naturally wanted to help Brenda, the grieving widow who lived next door, so Mrs. Rollins agreed to sign an affidavit to justify an arrest. I was charged with felony breaking and entering, and grand larceny.

CHAPTER 55

We recited the mourner's kaddish under the chestnut trees, the leaves a riot of color, the ancient syllables like pebbles in our mouths. Shep Levine followed the Hebrew with Yeats's "The Wild Swans at Coole," against a soft blue October sky. How unimaginable not to exist. Never to see a winter sunset, the trees in their autumn beauty, or even conceive of swans. *To awake some day to find they had flown away.* I could hear my father. "Lost tribe of Israel, the Irish," he was saying. Susan and I peeled the veil from the stone. *And now my heart is sore.*

At the brunch, my uncles were furious. "You broke the promise you made to your father!" Uncle Harry yelled. What changed? Uncle Harry had been my lookout. Brenda got to him, that's what changed. She told him she felt violated, which was understandable. I was sorry about that. Brenda also reminded my uncles of the promise they knew damn well I had made to their beloved brother. Loyalty was big in their small-time underworld, although to whom was often up for debate. So they switched to Brenda's side. I was full of righteous indignation. I thought they would appreciate my noble and heroic deeds, saving my father's poetry from the ash heap.

But no, that was wrong. I wanted it both ways—to be a good girl and to be free—and I couldn't have it both ways. What I'd done was not noble. It was exquisite in its selfishness, and that was OK. I was no longer an obedient daughter. I had never been a saint. I was a real person, lit from within, full of myself.

Red lights flashed in front of Aunt Shirley's house. Fred was out in the street demanding to see the warrant and stalling for time. For somber ceremonies like funerals and unveilings, Fred took time away from work. I appreciated him stepping up for me. He was really letting the cops have it. Shep Levine bolted out of the den and grabbed me in a bear hug. No wonder Brenda was missing from the unveiling. She would have been attacked by an angry mob for calling the cops on me. As soon as my uncles saw the police pull up, they switched back to my side. Alvin Aronson was no stoolie. No one ever called Harry Aronson a rat. And Evie Braverman, my revolutionary mother, was no snitch either, with her FBI file as thick as a deli sandwich.

"Joanna Aronson?" Uncle Alvin said to the cop on the front porch. "She was here, but she's gone now."

"My niece Joanna?" said Uncle Harry. "You won't see her no more."

Shep pointed me toward the kitchen door and gave me a push. I burst into the backyard like I was on fire. "Joanna! Come sit with us," Darleen called. She was at the table under the umbrella with Travis, Uncle Lou, Uncle Nat, and Shana Bloom. I kept going. There was no time to explain. When I got to the retaining wall, I hiked up my skirt and hoisted myself onto the ledge ripping my new tights, which bothered me way more than it should have under the circumstances, but they were fresh out of the package. I stood up shakily. My heels kept sinking into the mud when I tried to gain footing on the hillside, so I got on my hands and knees and clawed my way up. I could buy another pair of tights. Men with guns were after me. When I was deep into the neighbor's yard, I looked back. The picnic table mourners had put down their bagels and were staring at me on the hilltop. I continued on, walking quickly around to the front of the strange house on the unfamiliar, deserted street, and stood waiting on the lawn. I half expected my father's Torino to come nosing over the hill. He would hand me a striped towel. We'd bump over the railroad tracks. He'd say he was sorry. But it was Shep's silver Jaguar cresting the hill. He raced toward me and screeched to a stop. I got in and we sped around the winding streets of

Mount Washington, past old houses and old trees and down into a gulley and parked and went into the Mount Washington Tavern where we ordered drinks and waited until the coast was clear.

Brenda couldn't believe I got away. I wasn't sure what she had imagined or hoped for. Money for herself, yes. But prison time for me? Anne Brighton had the warrant quashed and turned into a subpoena and a court date was set for March, which was a few months away, and for which I received a summons in the mail. The whole State of Maryland vs. Joanna Aronson. Brenda did not show up in March on the appointed day and so, lacking any courtroom drama, I was given a kind of probation called a "stet." Cease all burglary for one year and the charge would be expunged from my record. I did not have to return anything I took from the house. It was a relief, but also an anticlimax. After court, my mother and I met Shep back at the Mount Washington Tavern. Shep and I ordered vodka tonics and my mother got her usual champagne cocktail. She told us she heard the house on Cedar Drive was up for sale, which was not a surprise, and that Brenda gave away Hoffman, which I hadn't expected. The National Dog was an orphan. So many losses. Sometimes I thought I'd made the wrong choice. What might I have in my possession now if I had handed Brenda the money she wanted? I never even got a chance to look into the attic. I'd left so much behind, secrets I would never know.

I told my mother I finally felt a kinship with Brenda. Wasn't it ironic, after everything we'd been through? Darleen had been to the house and Brenda proudly showed her a Pendaflex file Brenda had labeled "Warrant." I had the same file, same label. Brenda and I shared an obsession. Brenda, *mon semblable, mon frère*. My mother said I was being ridiculous. Brenda and I were nothing alike. My mother, possibly trying to make up for the past, was sticking up for me, finally, and I was glad. I didn't bother arguing with her about the dark part that exists in all of us.

Shep said he had a present, ordered another drink and went out to his car. He came back with the City College yearbook of 1958, his first year teaching, my father's fifth. Shep said the yearbook was mine to keep if I wanted it. I flipped through the pages until I reached "Clubs and Activities" and found the section on the *Collegian* newspaper. Tears came to my eyes the second I saw the photograph, and then a shiver went down my spine. In the picture, my father stands over a seminar table surrounded by clean-cut boys, raising a cane above their heads. The caption reads: "Efficient work combined with a touch of humor produces an outstanding publication."

It wasn't the familiar face from the past that stirred me most—his black-framed glasses, the private smile—or even the connection I made between the threatening cane my father is wielding in the photograph and the Colonel's punishing cane. What shocked me with recognition was his handwriting on the blackboard behind him.

Who would I be if I'd had a seat at that table? I closed the yearbook and took a long swallow of my drink. I had to step out of my father's shadow, and Fred's shadow too. It was time to start living my life. The joys and glamour of the wider world awaited.

ACKNOWLEDGEMENTS

Many thanks to my editor and publisher, Mike Sager, for being all action. I am grateful for his professionalism and inspiration. Heartfelt appreciation to my early editors and readers: David Hirshey, Daphne Merkin, Susan Squire, Sarah Steinberg, Marilyn Johnson, Lisa Land, E. Jean Carroll, Ellen Hoffs, Naomi Firestone-Teeter, Joy Horowitz, Linda DeCrane, Janne Keyes, Michael Pollan, Thaila Ramanujam, Rachel Brau, Gil Schwartz, Laura Svienty, Carol Patchett, Tom Patchett, Linda Burstyn, Adam Taylor, Annie Stein, Diane Leslie, Ellen Stern, Rina Freedman, and the late Jerry Levin.

For help with research on Jewish orphanages, thank you to Rick Safran and The Hebrew National Orphan Home Alumni Association, as well as the Jewish Child Care Association and the YIVO Institute for Jewish Research. *The Hebrew National Orphan Home, Memories of Orphanage Life*, edited by Ira A. Greenberg with Richard G. Safran and Sam George Arcus, and *Déjà Views of an Aging Orphan* by Sam Arcus, were invaluable resources.

I am indebted to The Virginia Center for the Creative Arts and the Vermont Studio Center for their community and validation, and to Judi Barker, a real patron of the arts, for providing me and other writers and artists studio space at the Santa Monica Air Center.

My love and thanks to my daughter, Chloe Director, for her close reading and constant encouragement. And finally, unending gratitude and love to my partner and consigliere, Roger Director, for taking this long journey with me.

ABOUT THE AUTHOR

Jan Cherubin is the recipient of fellowships from the Virginia Center for the Creative Arts and the Vermont Studio Center. She has an MFA in fiction from Bennington, the college where she first studied writing with Bernard Malamud when she was an undergraduate. Her journalism has appeared in *The Los Angeles Review of Books*, *Los Angeles*, *New York*, *The Forward*, and other publications. Cherubin also does stand-up comedy at clubs in Los Angeles. *The Orphan's Daughter* is her first novel.

ABOUT THE PUBLISHER

The Sager Group was founded in 1984. In 2012, it was chartered as a multimedia content brand, with the intent of empowering those who create art—an umbrella beneath which makers can pursue, and profit from, their craft directly, without gatekeepers. TSG publishes books; ministers to artists and provides modest grants; designs logos, products, and packaging; and produces documentary, feature, and commercial films. By harnessing the means of production, The Sager Group helps artists help themselves. To read more from The Sager Group, visit www.TheSagerGroup.net.

THE SAGER GROUP

Artifex Te Adiuva

CPSIA information can be obtained
at www.ICGtesting.com
Printed in the USA
LVHW031954080321
680887LV00007B/1492